DELLA'S DEED

by *Denis Gray*

iUniverse, Inc.
Bloomington

Della's Deed

iUniverse books may be ordered through booksellers or by contacting:

iUniverse
1663 Liberty Drive
Bloomington, IN 47403
www.iuniverse.com
1-800-Authors (1-800-288-4677)

ISBN: 978-1-4759-0158-0 (sc)
ISBN: 978-1-4759-0157-3 (hc)
ISBN: 978-1-4759-0159-7 (e)

Library of Congress Control Number: 2012905199

Printed in the United States of America

iUniverse rev. date: 5/7/2012

YOU LET ME BREATHE…BARBARA

CHAPTER 1

Della Ballad had beautiful hair.

But today her hair was braided in two long, tightly knotted pigtails that ended at the beginning of each shoulder blade. Ordinarily, Della Ballad's beautiful gray hair would be the talk of most strangers, what would be on the tips of their tongues. But it was best her hair was fixed in a tightly coiled pigtail. It had stayed this way for the past five days of her eight-day stay at St. Bartholomew Hospital because it made for easy maintenance. But Della Ballad's smile still sweetened your day no matter the look of her hair. She was a sixty-eight-year-old woman, a big-bodied, generous black woman who had a bad heart but still had a healthy outlook on living, who was going to fight her heart disease tooth and nail to her grave. She was going to fight as hard as any battle she'd ever fought before, certainly, for as long as there was still fight left in her. And if you asked her, she'd say she had plenty of that.

Della Ballad was looking at ten bottles of pills on a rolling table out of reach to her. Those pills were under the strict supervision of Nurse Susie Myers, her daytime nurse, the only person who could dispense them to her. There was a bottle of pills for this ailment and a bottle of pills for that ailment—the lyric went on and on—and they all looked so significant and proud the way they lined up on the right side of the rolling table, much like a squadron of small plastic soldiers ready to do battle, as if they would save her, would shield her from death no matter the odds stacked against her, as if their reliability, efficacy capabilities should never be challenged or called into question. Della Ballad laughed at their seeming brazenness, but she respected those pills since they were a part of her fight, her daily battle to live.

She'd been afflicted by heart disease for the past seven years of her life. Heart disease was on her mother's side of the family, not her father's. Her mother had died from heart disease, and several aunts and uncles had too. There was a precise pattern here, clear and obvious: her heart disease was hereditary. She'd never considered diet. She loved cooking and cooking in quantity like so many black women of her age and time. She'd never thought about medical science, not any of that stuff—what was there to think about when you have a lifestyle, culturally, that, if changed, wouldn't really be living at all? And she had lived and been productive. Della Ballad had lived a full, active life. There were family and friends and a lot of good times. Of course there were bad times too and things that were more middle-of-the-road.

She survived Frank Ballad. She was a widow. He died five years ago. If he were alive, he'd nurse her back to good health—that she was sure of. She had only loving memories of him. He was the most loving man. The man of her dreams, as they say, and she "nailed him" as she'd often tell others. For with Frank Ballad's name came a medallion with much reputation. In his heyday, he'd broken many a young lady's heart in Myles Day City before courting Della Ballad.

He was a tall, handsome man. Being a barber, a lot of folk in Myles Day City said they never saw a hair on Frank Ballad's head out of place—at least it's what folk in Myles Day City were rumored to say. But it's how he was thought of—straight-backed, decent, kind, dignified, a man who meant a lot to a lot of people who knew him over the years.

Today, in ten minutes' time, Dr. Joseph Ives, Della's doctor, was going to visit her hospital room to talk to her. They were to have a bedside chat—and Dr. Ives was always on time. He was white and tall and handsome but not as tall and handsome as Frank Ballad, although just as good and decent and kind. He'd been Frank Ballad's physician. Dr. Ives meant a lot to the Ballad family. He was a part of the Ballad family's most intimate and personal history. Della Ballad wanted out of St. Bartholomew Hospital in the worst sort of way, and she was hoping today would be the day that Dr. Ives would hand her that wish, her walking papers, free her from St. Bart's.

Della Ballad did not like hospitals, had no liking at all for them.

Well, the news from Dr. Ives was not the news Della Ballad had hoped for: she was doing well, quite well, Dr. Ives said, but not well enough for her to be released from St. Bartholomew, for him to give her a ticket out. In a way, in her heart, she knew this before this morning's consultation. For she was well aware of her physical capacities, and she wasn't there yet. It wasn't there yet. She just hadn't convinced herself enough, for even at her age she could be impatient, impetuous, ambitious—but in her heart, she knew.

She and Dr. Ives had a good lively talk, and they had a lot of laughs (something Della Ballad loved doing). He looked at his watch, being a man married to time, and said, "By the way, Mrs. Ballad, I have a new pill for you this morning to take." And with it came explanation and the pill's function and how often the pill must be taken. And then he left, and she was left with yet another pill to take. Pill number eleven. So Nurse Susie Myers lined the new plastic bottle up with the old bottles on the rolling table for future dispensation.

She'd laughed to herself after Dr. Ives and Nurse Myers left the room, for the new bottle already looked important, had assumed the same proud rigid posture as had all the others. And all Della could do at the time was laugh at the sight of the eleven bottles on top the table and then remind herself that Frank was up to seven bottles of pills before he died.

Della felt her pigtail with her fingers and pulled down on it like a bell ringer and then, with her right hand, did the same with the other knotted pigtail. This made her feel joyful, think of her mother, Blanche Dawson, who'd warn her not to come home from school with one pigtail unbraided, a mess, or else …

Della was thinking a lot of her mother today, a lot about things they did together when she was young. Her mind had been traveling back through a maze of time, way back like it'd memorized every second of it with sharper, heightened recall—could tell you all about it like it'd happened just yesterday. But to ask her what happened two weeks ago would pose her great difficulty. Her mind just couldn't do that. But fifty-five years ago, now that was a horse of a different color—much, much easier for her.

It was near noon, and suddenly, she felt tired. This was how her days went. Every morning she woke at six o'clock, and then she was tired at noon. Her pill-taking had a time schedule to it, of course. Everything was calculated, mapped out. She could doze off now and then during the course of the day, but between eating and pill-taking, she really couldn't tie on a real good nap, so she didn't really try. She'd just close her eyes now and then try to catch herself before her head and her shoulders slumped too much and she swore she heard herself snore, much to her regret and embarrassment.

It wasn't pill-popping time yet. Ummm … she felt relaxed. As idle as the sun, Della thought. Her eyes were shut, and she could count stars if there was a census report due on God's desk, she further thought. *But don't doze off now, Della. Don't doze off. Don't you dare go and embarrass yourself, Della Ballad. You don't want anyone in St. Bartholomew to think you're old! That you fall asleep at the drop of a hat, before the day has had a chance to warm up good.*

Ummm … but I do feel … and I am getting a bit, a little drowsy … I can feel my head swimming … Am I drifting off? It's beginning to feel like I'm drifting off, and I can't do anything, nothing, not anything a-about …

"Aunt Della! Aunt Della! Don't you dare, Aunt Della! Don't you dare!"

"Darlene!"

Darlene Winston charged across the hospital floor as her fingers attacked the leather buttons on her beautifully tailored woolen overcoat.

"Oh, oh no you don't, Aunt Della. No, you don't!" Darlene tossed the coat over an available chair.

"Oh, it's so good to see you, Darlene!"

Now Darlene had literally thrown herself at Della, but ever mindful of Della's delicate condition.

"Like every day, Aunt Della! Like every day I'm here, Aunt Della!"

"Yes, Darlene! Yes. Yes!"

Darlene squeezed Della as tightly as Della's delicate condition allowed, Darlene knowing well her boundaries.

"You feel cold, honey."

"Yes, Aunt Della. It's turning cold outside."

"Your cheeks."

Darlene's hands touched her cheeks. "My cheeks are cold, Aunt Della."

Darlene Winston was a Dawson and, like all Dawson women, was quite attractive. She was tall but slight of frame. Her skin was a cherry brown, not red. If you didn't know how young she was, you'd quickly surmise she was old by her dress standard. She was as neat as a store floor mannequin.

Della's head lay back on the pillow.

"Oh, I was about to cheat, Darlene. Must admit. Doze off. Was. Ain't gonna lie to you about that."

"You were, Aunt Della?"

"Uh-huh. Oh, was I! Had that drowsy feeling. You know. That settle-in-good-get-comfortable feeling. About to get down to business. Tie one on. Was gonna try to catch myself—"

"But if you didn't, Aunt Della …"

"Fine by me, Darlene. Wasn't gonna get in the way of nothing. Ha. Progress."

Darlene sat at the side of the bed, just a foot or two from Della's shoulders. "Aunt Della, Aunt Della, did … did …"

"Yes, honey, Dr. Ives was by. We had that talk of ours. What I told you a—"

"And? And—"

"It's still a no."

"No?"

"Just ain't the time yet, Darlene … Dr. Ives said. Not, it seems I'm not where I should be. Oughta be for now."

"But … but you look so much better, Aunt Della. Now. Then when you got here. First—"

"I do, I do. I know I do, Darlene. But I've got to go on what Dr. Ives tells me. Uh, says I—now don't pout. Push your lips out like that. Ha. Make me … ha … think you're eight, nine years old again. Now."

"I didn't pout when I was ten though."

"Can't remember. But I do remember you pouting at nine. Don't know when you stopped. Was just glad when—"

"But I am disappointed, Aunt Della. I thought you were doing so well."

"Now, now, it doesn't mean I'm not doing well. Dr. Ives didn't say that. Nothing like that—and I certainly don't feel like I'm not. And there's been no setbacks or anything like that. So thank God for those blessings."

"But I … I just knew he was going to say yes. Tell you, you could go home, Aunt Della. I just knew it. I just knew it!"

"Oh, Darlene, Darlene—you're such a good cheerleader, Darlene. Aren't you? Oh … you cheer so hard for me. Same as you did for your uncle Frank when—"

"Uncle Frank wasn't supposed to die, Aunt Della!"

"But we all die, Darlene. All of us, honey."

When Darlene got up out the chair, she walked over to the far edge of Della's bed. Her back was to Della.

"Now, Darlene, it's been five years. Five years. Your uncle Frank." Della's eyes are staring at Darlene's back. "Turn around. Come on, Darlene, now turn around so your aunt Della can see your pretty face." Pause. "And smile."

Darlene does turn around to Della. "I don't want to smile. I don't want to smile, Aunt Della. I don't want to, r-right now."

"No, you don't have to, Darlene. 'Cause I was disappointed too. I was hoping Dr. Ives would say I could go home. Ha. Pack my bags and get the devil out of—"

"Aunt Della, Aunt Della, I—"

Darlene's eyes are looking at the table off by the bed.

"You don't miss anything, do you, honey?"

Darlene's at the rolling table. She's holding the new bottle of pills. "What, what are these for? Are you taking these new pills for, Aunt Della? What's—"

"I don't know anymore, Darlene. Honest, honest, I don't," Della said, shaking her head. "I don't know anymore. Swear to you … I just listen like I do know. Know, but … And just take them, honey. My pills. Do as I'm told. What Dr. Ives prescribes. Goes in one ear and out the other. Take them like a good—"

"No! No! You should know, Aunt Della. You should know. Be aware of … t-this is unacceptable. Not under any circumstance, Aunt Della. I'm … I'm going to—I'll be right back. I'm going to the front desk to page Dr.—"

"No, uh-uh, you stay put, Darlene. Now. Stay right where you are. Now. Don't go anywhere, honey. Whatever it is Dr. Ives's prescribed for me, it's gonna do some, me some good. Make things better for me. For my heart."

Darlene's reading the bottle's label. "I want to know, Aunt Della. I want … but I … I want to know. C-can't I, Aunt Della? Know? Can't I?"

"Of … of course you can, Darlene. May … may. You … you go ahead then, go ahead then. Go outside to the front desk. Out there, uh, page him. D-Dr. Ives. But if you see Susie, Susie Myers—"

"No, I want to talk to Dr. Ives. Deal directly with him, not your nurse, Aunt Della. But directly with Dr. Ives."

"But Susie knows as much as—"

"So you know where I am—either at the front desk waiting for him or I've gone to his office. Either one, Aunt Della. Either condition. But either way, I'll be back, back as soon as we're through talking, Dr. Ives and I, Aunt Della."

"Yes, Darlene. Of course, honey. Of course."

Darlene was feeding Della soup (not that Della couldn't feed herself).

"Lee said he'll call later, Aunt Della."

"He'd better not miss a day!"

"I'm glad I talked to Dr. Ives," Darlene said reflectively. "I told him from now on he must consult with me too as a matter of protocol. W-when it comes to things like this. Changing your regimen, e-et cetera."

Della's eyebrows arched upon hearing Darlene's remarks but said nothing.

"It surprised me, that's all. His disregard for family. He wasn't like that with Uncle Frank ... I ... I ..."

"I ..."

"I can't remember."

"Me, me neither, Darlene. Me neither."

"But that's it. It won't happen again—he assured me."

"He did?"

"Yes," Darlene said, picking the spoon back up, Della blowing on the hot soup, having opened her mouth wide for Darlene and the spoon.

"Do I baby you, Aunt Della?"

"No. No, not at all, Darlene. Not at all."

"I ... I just feel it's my time to do all the things you did for me, Aunt Della. Now that I have the opportunity to."

"And there's no complaint from me. Coming out my mouth. Not a peep. No not from me, honey."

"I love you, Aunt Della."

"How many times do you tell me that a day, Darlene?"

"A lot, a lot, Aunt Della." Darlene laughed.

Darlene glanced at her watch. "Lee said he would call about now. He knows I'm here at the hospital. With you, Aunt Della."

"Now hold your horses," Della said calmly. "Lee's on his job. Ha. Working hard."

"But he should be taking lunch now. R-right now."

"And what kind of sandwich did you fix—pack for Lee today for lunch?"

"Tuna fish."

"Something I know Lee loves. Just loves. 'Cause he loves my tuna fish salad when I make it at the house for him."

"Lee loves everything you make, Aunt Della."

"So …," Della said with a twinkle in her eye, "maybe Lee's enjoying that tuna fish sandwich you made him *so* much he forgot about his aunt Della. Calling me."

"Aunt Della …," Darlene burst out laughing.

"No telling now, honey."

"Let me ring them. Get an orderly in here to get rid of these things for you, Aunt Della," Darlene said, looking at the bowl, plate, glass, tray, and utensils.

"No. No, they'll come, Darlene. Be along. In due time. They won't forget about me."

"No, Aunt Della, you don't have to be surrounded by this mess. In your room."

"Why, why, it's no mess. No mess at all. At home, you know the dishes in the sink aren't always washed as soon as I—"

"But this isn't home, Aunt Della. This is a hospital. And everyone has a responsibility in a hospital. And besides—"

"Then … then you're right. Call them in. Page, uh, get them in here then, Darlene. The orderly in here. Her name is, I—"

Darlene's thumb was pressing the button on the small gadget.

"Now let's see how long it takes them to get here. To clear this mess out your room, Aunt Della."

There's a stretch of silence as Darlene's eyes look intently at the room door. Della sees tenseness in Darlene's neck and a redness.

"I should time them. I should … Really, really should, Aunt Della. See just how efficient they are. Prompt, I mean. I really should time them, Aunt Della."

Darlene's stroking Della's hand, and the orderly has removed the tray and its contents from the room.

"Oh, that feels good, Darlene. So good. Soothing. All right. Puts me right at ease. Right at ease, honey."

"You shouldn't be bothered, aggravated by anything. Worry about anything."

"Especially at my age."

"Sixty-eight isn't—why that's not old, Aunt Della."

"Not until you get there, Darlene. Ha. Then it feels like every muscle and bone you've got has a big surprise for you, and glad about it too. To do you the favor," Della laughed. "Sleep too much on your right side at night and wake the next morning to aches and pains you never had before. You knew of when you were young." Pause.

"And then sleep too much on your left side the next night, you come out with the same bargain. Price for your troubles. Ha. Then say, well … I'll try my back, sleeping on my back tonight. This time. Or sleep on my—"

Ring.

"I have it, Aunt Della. It'd better be—Lee! Oh, it is you. So what took you so long, Lee? To call? Aunt Della and I have been waiting, Lee." Darlene looks at Della. "Haven't we, Aunt Della?"

Della's hand reaches out for the phone. "Now let me talk to my sweet peach, Darlene."

"Uh, just a second, Aunt Della. Lee, there's no excuse for this. None, Lee. None." Della's hand's still outstretched.

"None whatsoever, Lee."

CHAPTER 2

Two weeks later in St. Bartholomew Hospital.

"Why, Margaret, you just missed Darlene."

"D-did I, Momma?"

"She visited me twice today." Pause. "Don't know how that girl finds the time. But she does."

"I'm glad she does, Momma. You need the company."

"Yes, I do. It means so much to me. Having family around me. Come to the hospital."

Margaret Ballad was sitting in a chair by the bed. It was 7:28 p.m. She'd come to St. Bartholomew Hospital from her job at International Retailers Inc., the biggest retailer in Myles Day City. Margaret was a bookkeeper. She was tall like all the Ballads, whether male or female. She had a knockout figure but dressed within a modesty and decorum totally betraying it. She was a beautiful woman with high cheekbones, gorgeous black hair cropped close to her face, who wore makeup like it was invented for anyone but her.

"I think Darlene knows something, Margaret."

"Knows something? What … what do you mean by that, Momma?"

"I don't know. That girl's instincts are so … I don't know the word to use. What I'm looking for … but it's like she's trying to nurse me back to health single-handedly. And I do feel stronger. I do, Margaret. I do. So maybe …"

"Has Dr. Ives said anything more to you, Momma?"

"You know Darlene and him have a good relationship, don't you, Margaret?"

Margaret nodded her head.

"Guess it doesn't hurt to have someone in charge besides myself. Someone like Darlene. She questions everything Dr. Ives does. Every move he makes. That girl."

"Unlike you, Momma."

"Of course. Don't have any reason to question him. Just do what he wants me to do. I'm a good patient. Follow orders like I'm suppose to."

Margaret stands. "I think you'll be coming home soon too, Momma. It's what I think."

"Margaret—"

"It's what you're saying, implying, isn't it, Momma?"

"Uh-huh. It is, Margaret. Right." Pause. "It's just that a few weeks back, didn't make out so hot. Thought I was gonna climb out this bed for good. Ha." Della's hand pats the bed. "Nothing like your own bed to sleep in. At night. No substitute, none, Margaret.

"Could go book me into the Hilton, best suite they've got—and I'd take my bed over theirs any day of the week. Pay top dollar to sleep on!"

"Stop, stop, Momma! Don't go any further, please, please!"

"Yes, sir, that old sagging mattress and bed springs of mine serve me fine, well, Margaret. Wouldn't trade it for anything in the world—not to sleep on!"

Margaret takes to the chair again. "But I do think it's soon too, Momma, that you'll be coming home from the hospital."

"I'm riding high on Darlene's spirit, you know. And I was down for that one day. Spirits got a little low. Messy. But you know, Margaret, honey, I don't let these things get me down too much. Or for too long."

"Not at all, Momma."

Della's eyes brightened.

"Spirit flags, just say to myself: my day will come. I know it will. Didn't even call on God—and you know that's something, really something coming out of me."

"Ha. Yes, it is."

"Don't have to bother him for everything, you know, Margaret. Little thing. Sometimes you've gotta do your own housecleaning. Pull the couch off the wall …ha … to get to the dust. Sweep it out. Keep it from hiding."

"Now you've gone too far, Momma!"

"I know"—Della giggled—"I know. But I ain't apologizing to you or God either!"

"But I am glad you have a good attitude. Always have had one."

"Bring your own set of problems on yourself if you don't. Took time for me to figure that one out."

"You think so, Momma? I don't. I just think it's natural. You have an innate gift, an affinity."

"Call it what you want, honey, but there were times when I would let things grind away in my stomach like glass. Grind it up good inside … Don't let me fool you. Think you develop certain characteristics over time. Keep growing all the time on them.

"Can't let yourself stop. Slow down." Della looks at Margaret, studies her, sighs, and then says, "Royal, we haven't talked about Royal. Not once since you've been here visiting." Pause. "How's my darling Royal doing?"

"Well you know about Royal's job and—"

"School."

"But I'm telling you, Momma, the kitchen table, it's been converted into Royal's desk. Private area … once we eat, have dinner, I clear the kitchen table—it's a mess. A true mess. Nothing but Royal's—"

"Know he's gonna get all As by the time he's through with his courses. Is on the dean's—"

"Technically, he can't … isn't eligible for Haverford University's dean's list, since he's a part-time student. His status, that is. He isn't carrying enough credits to qualify. So he's not thinking like that. Along those lines."

"Not that he would anyway, Margaret. It's just me bragging for him, honey."

"Royal's got an ego, Momma. Don't let him fool you any."

"But it ain't one for bragging. Putting himself first. Out in front of the parade just to impress someone. Make himself look important."

"No, Momma, not—"

"Uh, Margaret—could you adjust the pillow? It feels like it's slipping down somewhat. Thanks. Darlene adjusted it before she left."

After adjusting her mother's pillow, Margaret sits back down in the chair.

"Does that a lot. Soon as it starts to slip, Darlene that girl seems to catch it right away. Right before it slips too far down."

Pause.

"Oh … I'm sorry, honey, it was spontaneous. Spon—what I … I said."

"What, Momma?"

"About—"

"Darlene?"

"Yes, I—"

"By the way, the house looks great."

"I was gonna ask—"

"Practically dustless."

"Oh, ha. Oh, with you and Darlene, you two girls cleaning it, I know it is, Margaret. Does. Does."

"She has her days to clean, and I have mine."

"Uh, uh right, honey. Right. You work on s-separate days. Schedules."

"And separate parts, areas of the house."

"You do the upstairs, and Darlene—"

"The downstairs."

"Division of labor. You two work right down the middle. And speaking for me and the house, we both appreciate it."

"She's—Darlene is a hard worker."

"Can't ever question Darlene's dedication. Determination. Uh-uh … What I was saying about Royal before. Trying to say at least."

"But it's different with Royal, Momma. Much."

"Uh, yes, I know."

"Darlene … Darlene. What can I say about Darlene? What can anybody say about Darlene, Momma?"

"There, uh, there goes that darn pillow again, Margaret. There it goes again, slipping."

"Oh … oh … let me, Momma. Let me."

"And talking about Royal," Della said, taking Margaret's hands before they reached the pillow. "It's time you got home to him, honey. So when he gets in from school you'll …" Pause.

"Still don't know how you two eat dinner so late. Each night." Della sighs. "But you're both young, I guess. Don't have to worry about indigestion. Something I know a little something about."

Margaret laughs.

"Probably don't even know what indigestion is at your age."

"Momma, I am thirty-six, unless you forget. And Royal, thirty-eight. We're not so young anymore by anyone's standards."

"Now don't start making me feel old, because it still feels like you haven't grown a stitch since you were twenty, you or my sweet Darlene for that matter, Margaret."

Margaret was on a bus going home, and she wished she were driving the bus and not looking out its side window but out its front window. She would beat Royal to the house. Yes, they would have dinner close to 8:30 p.m. Yes, this was becoming old hat this routine, this schedule they'd been maintaining for a few months now.

Maybe if she were driving the bus instead of riding the bus, she wouldn't be thinking so much, too much, because she knew she could make mountains out of molehills, let them climb until she'd get frustrated by them, that they were just too tall—high—for her to climb.

Maybe it was punishment for what she'd been, what she'd done—her past life. No, that was a thought she wanted to shake out of her head. Why did it pop up like that? Why did it? Did she let it? She could find the sun and find the clouds, the sunlight and the darkness. But she didn't want to feel the darkness anymore, just the sunlight, but knew that was impossible. So impossible. So convoluted. So opposite the truth. The truth of her life. The truth of her circumstance. The truth of who she was trying to become.

Darlene ... sometimes she wished she were a fly on the proverbial wall, that she could be around, on a wall, when her mother and Darlene were together, just the two of them sitting, talking, alone, sharing their laughter with each other. A fly on the proverbial wall. *Yes, a fly on the wall,* Margaret thought. To hear them. To hear what they said. What they talked of. To hear if her name popped up as often as Darlene's did when she and her mother talked alone, sat, sharing laughter. If Momma brings up her name, refers to her as often as she does Darlene. *My cousin Darlene. My cousin Darlene.*

Margaret wanted her head full of good thoughts since everything was going so well for Royal and her. But here she was, on the bus, looking out the window at Andrew Street in Myles Day City, thinking of Darlene until it made her stomach *grind glass* like her mother said she'd learned to overcome.

But I'm not Momma. I'm not you yet. I haven't matured into that person yet. I'm still too much Margaret Marie Ballad. Those moments I haven't mastered like you, Momma. I can't lose myself to that other person yet, Momma. Who I'm trying to become, Momma. Who you already are. What you've accomplished.

And, yes, her stomach was grinding. It was happening now. On the bus. At this very instant. And the pain … She'd been carrying it for so long but never could get used to it. If only she could rid herself of the pain, or at least be able to tolerate it, or feel there was some way out for her to escape it or crush it—simply crush it, not feel as if it were the only thing for her to always continually feel.

Royal, she didn't share it with him these days. He was on to bigger, better things. She thought, at times, that he'd all but healed, that people could cast stones at him, and his head would be bloodied but unbowed, not in any way fail him.

She was sounding so serious because she meant to. She didn't know how long this was going to last—her and her mother and Darlene. Her mother was fighting for her life; she didn't know how long all of this would last. No one could predict. No one could say. It was the same for her father. It was the same thing then too. No one could predict. No one could say. Not even Dr. Ives. Not even the medicines. There was no magic in anyone's eyes. There was no magic in anyone's medicines. There was just a man, a patient clinging to life before death, before he died.

And now it's Momma. And I'm here for Momma. With Daddy, I lost the opportunity. Darlene was so integral to everything, relevant, instrumental, a part of the whole process, she was dedicated and determined and … and …

She means so much to our family, done so much for our family. Far, far more than I've done. How can I compare myself to her? Compare the two of us? There's no comparison. Absolutely none. It's like comparing a devil to an angel. I have no right to be upset with Darlene. Get upset when Momma refers to her, talks about her the way she does. I have no right. She deserves it. Darlene—and Momma, Momma, she isn't conscious she's doing it. It just happened, came up on the spot in the hospital today—spontaneously, like Momma said. It's how it happened.

No, no, Momma has a right to build monuments for Darlene. Yes, monuments if she wants, to the sky, if she chooses to. Darlene's been there, has always been there for the Ballad family. Not me. Not me. But Darlene. Always Darlene. Always Darlene. Always. Always. Always.

CHAPTER 3

Dr. Ives looked simply impeccable, a fashion plate in whites. His rugged chin looking as reliable as a weather vane twisting in a storm, only not as weather-beaten. He wore the kind of custom-made eyeglasses that magnified his deep sky-blue eyes.

It was Darlene and Margaret and, of course, Della in the hospital room.

"Uh, Susie, take this down: the prescription for good health is surrounding yourself with three beautiful women."

"What about Susie, Joseph?"

"Oh, uh, Mrs. Ballad, uh, sorry, but Susie's heard this line before, I'm afraid."

Everyone laughed.

"Oh …"—Della laughed—"thought so." Della shimmied her rear end in the hospital bed. "But I did put extra rouge on my cheeks today, Joseph, since I knew we were to have this bedside chat this evening."

"So I see, Mrs. Ballad. So I see. You do look lovely. Delightful. Quite." Silence.

"Oh, don't let me stop everyone from talking."

Now there was light laughter, less than before. Dr. Ives seemed to sense his own drama, that anymore jokes, light asides, or intentions to engender humor would fall as flat as a lead balloon with this audience in the room; so he sucked in his trim gut and said, "Mrs. Ballad, you may go home!"

"Home!? Home!"

"Yes, home. Home, Mrs. Ballad, where you belong." Dr. Ives laughed. "Ha. There's nothing more I can do with you. Not here. You've been poked and prodded and pinched and—"

"Oh, so you've noticed."

"And have gotten good, useful rest and food … food—how was the food, by the way, Mrs. Ballad?"

Della glared at Dr. Ives.

"Joseph, why, have you ever had *real* soul food, Joseph?"

"Uh, now, Mrs. Ballad, you know—"

"I can never go back to my old diet, way of eating, Joseph. I know that, but have you ever had you *real* soul food?"

"Well, uh …"

"So don't ask me about the food around here. Hospital food, not until you've had *real* soul food."

"No," Dr. Ives said, coughing as if to stall, "uh, sorry for that, Mrs. Ballad. I should, guess it was a big—"

"Mistake. Just glad you don't err on the side of medicine. Keep that part straight."

Ives laughs. "I've often told you I have a grandmother like you. Grandmother Heidi, who keeps me straight."

"Aunt Della! Aunt Della!" Darlene was hugging Della.

"Thank you, Dr. Ives," Margaret said, shaking Ives's hand.

"Your mother, as we well know, is a, just a wonderful patient. Darling of a patient. Not unlike your father, when he was my patient. We're a good, efficient team that works well together, wouldn't you say, Mrs. Ballad?"

"The best, Joseph! We're the best! Good as they come!"

"So when, Dr. Ives, when? When will my aunt Della be able to come—"

"I was thinking of releasing your aunt Wednesday. Two days from today, Mrs. Winston. Our administrative staff's already been set in motion. Is ready to get started with this. To—"

"What do you mean, Joseph?"

"Home care. A home care a—"

"Home care? Home a—"

"Home attendant. You're, of course, your aunt's going to need a home care a—"

"Not with me around, she won't, Dr. Ives. My aunt Della. Not with me a—"

"Just for a few days, Mrs. Winston. P-possibly a week or—"

"I know how to cook for my aunt Della, feed her, bathe her, take her pulse, what pills she should take. When. Why should my aunt Della need a home attendant when—"

"For, uh, twenty-four hours around the—"

"I knew what you meant, Dr. Ives. Twenty-four hours around the clock. What else? It's what I planned, was planning to do when, already had planned out when—"

"When I released Mrs. Ballad, your aunt from St. Bart's, Mrs. Winston?"

"Yes. Oh yes. Had planned all along. Regardless of anything, whatever circumstances. Yes. Whether my aunt Della would be in need of a home attendant or not. Twenty-four hours around the clock."

"Yes, yes, I understand, Mrs. Winston," Dr. Ives said his eyes focusing in on Margaret and Susie Myers. "You are capable. Quite … and we do work well to—"

"But what about Lee, Darlene? Lee?"

"Lee … Lee … that's all been discussed, Aunt Della," Darlene said dismissively. "Been discussed between Lee and me already," Darlene said, taking in Della's hand, looking into her eyes. "Talked through together."

"Well thank you then, Darlene."

Margaret, who was standing, turned her back to Della and Darlene as Dr. Ives and Nurse Myers began comparing notes.

"Oh, Mrs. Winston, Susie will prepare the schedule for you. Protocol. Yes, you are capable—there' no doubt in my mind about that. And of course the main thing is your aunt will be surrounded by love. It's as good as medicine … as important. And, Margaret …"

"Yes, Dr. Ives …"

"Of course you'll be around your mother too. That Mrs. Winston's plan, I'm sure, includes you. You as well. You're a part of this, this operation too."

Dr. Ives smiled and then began jotting more things down on the short white pad while Nurse Susie Myers nodded and jotted.

*   *   *

The architect knew the house would take two summers and one winter to build. Plywood banged together by hard, steady hammers, long nails, and strong, seasoned hands. It was a house with wide rooms and windows and tall ceilings and an enduring frame and charm. It was a beauty of a house that looked like no other house on the quiet, tree-lined block. A house that had a solid unassuming dignity. A house for anyone to openly admire and render their own personal imagery to.

Lee Winston's car pulled into the house's wide driveway, and Darlene and Margaret and Della were seated in it. Della Ballad was home from St. Bartholomew Hospital. She was in the car's backseat with Darlene. Margaret was in the front seat with Lee.

"We're home, Aunt Della."

"That we are, Darlene. That we are, honey." Pause. "Thank the Lord for that. Feels so good to see the old house again. F-feels good."

Margaret twisted around in the car's front seat to look at Della. Darlene was holding onto Della's hand.

"Park it right here," Lee Winston said. "Right where Uncle Frank parked it. Same spot."

"Every time, Lee. Every time you park the car in the driveway, Lee. Hit the same mark as your uncle Frank would."

"Yes, Aunt Della. Ha. Every time. Just before the oak tree, the beginning of the oak tree. Was how Uncle Frank parked it."

"Was where your uncle Frank would park his car, all right, Lee. Every day of the week."

Lee Winston inched the car forward just so much, until it hit that sweet spot; he braked the car. Inside the car, there was an appreciative sigh of relief.

The car door swung open, and Darlene and Lee and Margaret alighted from the car and helped Della out. Darlene had unfolded the walker for Della, placing it out in front of her. Before Della entered the hospital, she was able to get around without a walker, but not now, after today's release from St. Bart's.

"Oh, this is fine. Fine. Thank you," Della said to one and all. "Thank you."

Della was in her brown overcoat. It was a cold day in Myles Day City. The wind snappy. Della didn't wear gloves—never had. For all the years she'd lived in Myles Day City, its cold, whipsaw winters, she'd never worn gloves.

"You're all right, are—aren't you, Aunt Della?"

Della's head reared back. "It's like I can breathe again," Della said to the three of them. "My oxygen's back. Back in my lungs!"

Lee laughed harder than the three of them.

They'd gotten to the front door of the house, the high oak brown-stained doors, and Darlene's key was drawn, but Della halted her. "Uh, use mine, Darlene. Honey. If … if you don't mind. Use my house key, would you?"

Darlene smiled, taking Della's pocketbook off her arm, opening it.

"I have it, Aunt Della. I have it."

Darlene unlocked the door. Della and her walker walked into 38 Eckert Street in Myles Day City.

"Oh, thank you, God. Thank you." Then Della looked down to her feet. "T-the rugs …"

"Shampooed them, Aunt Della. Tuesday. Yesterday. Aunt Della."

"Oh … they smell it. Smell it, Darlene. They smell fresh, Darlene. Clean."

It's when Della looked straight ahead to the staircase. She's walking toward it, disregarding the huge living room to her right and the huge dining room area to her left and the same big-dimensioned kitchen in front of her, as her walk with her walker across the maroon-dyed rug takes on a stronger resolve, picking up greater steam.

She stared up at the stairs.

"Your coat and hat, Aunt Della. Your coat and hat."

"I'm gonna lick those stairs. I'm going to lick them. Beat them. I—"

"Let me take your coat and hat, Aunt Della. Your coat and hat."

"Uh, yes, yes, my coat and hat," Della said. "Uh, my … my coat and hat, Darlene."

It was a four-poster bed, and Della was lying in it as if she'd never left it. (If she were doing a mattress commercial, you'd buy the mattress plus Della—never mind the price!)

But in Della's heart she couldn't believe she was home, was looking at the unused, unattended fireplace off to the side of the vast room and listening to the heavy-breathing iron radiator, reliable, hearing it release its stream of hot steam as if bragging how warm it maintained the room during the winter, letting you know it wasn't going to let you down, disappoint you, not this winter or any future winter you might imagine. Della delighted in hearing the radiator's vapor of steam hiss, make music to her ears; she could just close her eyes and hear it hiss, maintain its steady, solid presence in the room.

"What a day. What a day. What a day, I'd say, already. Just so happy. Glad to be home. I know St. Bartholomew loves having me as its guest," Della laughed. "But it doesn't mean I'm theirs to keep.

"Oh, the staff is, there, is so wonderful. I feel so blessed, thank God for that. But when Dr. Ives tells me it's time to go ... then it's time to go! He ain't gonna get an argument out of me. Not a one from this old gal!"

"Y-you are comfortable, aren't you, Aunt Della?"

"Why, why—I hope I look it, Darlene. And thank you for the flowers. The lovely flowers you and Lee bought. Put in the room for me. For my coming home."

"Well, why, our pleasure, Aunt Della. Our, uh, you know, Darlene picked them out, but I paid for them."

"Ha ..." Della laughed.

"Aunt Della, we came by this morning, Lee and I. Before we got to St. Bartholomew. I put the flowers in the vase. By your bed, Aunt Della. In fresh water. Thought you might like them there."

"And I do. I do, Darlene. They're just lovely. So lovely." Della leaned over; her nose sniffed the flowers. "Just lovely to look at and smell."

"Momma ..."

"Yes, Margaret? Dear?"

"Royal and I were ... Royal and I were by the house. We ... Tuesday evening, M—"

"To do what, Margaret? What did you and Royal have in your minds to do Tuesday, Margaret?"

Margaret's eyes focused solely on Della.

"I dusted, Momma. On this floor. Swept. And ... and Royal ... Royal vacuumed the rugs."

"Oh, thank you, Margaret. Thank ... And it looks it. My room and the hallway when I, on the way down, I ... it ... and the other rooms too, I'm sure."

"It was Royal's idea, Momma ... so Royal should get, uh, receive full credit for—"

"Too bad Royal's not here—here to see Aunt Della home, come back with us from the hospital." Darlene turned to Lee. "It certainly wasn't easy for Lee to take off, to get a day," Darlene said, turning back to Della.

"Was it Lee? Was it? No, not in the least. Not with Mr. Baker, Aunt Della. Lee's boss, of course, as you know. Mr. Baker's a man who's stingy with—"

"Uh, uh, Darlene, Mr. Baker's not that, all that—"

"Days off. And Lee is his best worker. Best printer. Mr. Baker, even he has to admit that about Lee. Why, Lee's the best typesetter Mr. Baker's got. Tell Aunt Della, baby."

"Uh, well, Aunt Della," Lee said, his finger inching along the top of his shirt collar, "I—"

"Aunt Della, your hair! Your hair! Let me unbraid your hair. I forgot about, all about your hair. Didn't I? I know you're tired, sick and tired of it in those pigtails of yours. How I braided them. That's for the hospital, not home, Aunt Della."

"Yes, my braids, Darlene. I do feel like giving my hair a good scratching through. I do."

"Momma, I ... I was going to do that for—"

"There's no need to, Margaret. None at all. While I'm here. It's why I'm here to do it for—Aunt Della just loves me to unbraid them, her hair. Don't you? Don't you, Aunt Della?"

"Of course, of course, Darlene. Of ... why of course, honey."

"I'll get the brush. Hairbrush."

"Yes, yes—it's in the blue bag."

"Yes, I know. Since I packed it away, put it there, Aunt Della."

"Uh, yes, yes you did, Darlene, you sure—"

"Before you left the hospital today."

"Yes. Uh-huh. You did."

Lee Winston was tall and thin and neat from head to toe. Every day of the week he wore a shirt and tie, no matter the occasion. Like today, he was in a shirt and tie and suit like he'd just stepped out the mayor's office. His shoes were always finely polished, shined even on the coldest days in Myles Day City, days when you'd think the shoe polish just might crack in the cold air. In fact, there was a sweetness in Lee Winston's face, a kindness in it that couldn't go unnoticed, like a pastor (which he wasn't) who'd heeded God's calling as divinely as a saint.

"I'll brush your hair out, all the way out for you, Aunt Della, and comb it and put some grease in your scalp. How's that, how's that, Aunt Della?"

"Oh, I'd love that, Darlene. Even though I'm still gonna scratch it like *crazy*. Dig into my scalp with my fingers, go to town when you're finished greasing it. You know how *crazy* I get with my hair once I get going."

"Lee, Lee, get me the jar of grease, Lee. It's—the jar's in the bathroom. On the bathroom shelf. You'll see it. Even you shouldn't have a problem finding it—I think. Think, Lee."

Lee's out the chair. "Of course, of course, Darlene. I'll … I'll get it out the bathroom. F-for you and Aunt Della, Darlene."

Stiffly. "Thank you. Thank you, Lee."

Della leans forward in the bed. Darlene positions herself behind her. "Comfortable, Aunt Della?"

"Comfortable, Darlene. Oh, just fine. Couldn't be more comfortable, Darlene"

Darlene looks at Della's beautiful gray hair with sudden fire in her eyes. "I can't wait to get started, Aunt Della. To … oh …," Darlene begins unbraiding Della's hair.

"Oh, keep going, Darlene. Keep going. Don't stop. Don't stop."

"How many times have I done this, Aunt Della? For you? How many times over the years? Dare to ask, Aunt Della? Try, try?"

"What, me guess? You're asking me to count, actually count, Darlene?"

"It's out, Aunt Della! Your hair is … and it looks glorious—just glorious. And now for the brush!"

"The brush, Darlene! The brush! The almighty brush!"

"R-Royal wanted to come to the hospital today, Momma, but—"

"Lee! Lee!" Darlene screamed. "What's taking you so long, so long in there, Lee! The bathroom, Lee! I told you. I told you the jar of grease is on the—"

"I'm back, I'm back," Lee said, running back into the room. "I have it. I have it, Darlene."

"I told you where it was. To find it. On the bathroom shelf. Where Aunt Della keeps her personal things, Lee. Anybody who's blind could've seen that!" Pause. "Here, here, let me have it." Darlene snatches the jar of grease out Lee's hand.

Lee smiles at Della.

"Thanks, sweet peach."

"You're welcome, Aunt—"

"Lee, the suitcases, you didn't bring the suitcases, the suitcases in the house. From the car."

`"Right, Darlene. I ... I guess with the excitement and all, making sure Aunt Della was—"

"Would you, then would you get them for me, Lee. Like a sweetheart. A dear. A dear, Lee."

"Yes, Darlene. Yes. Yes, of course, Darlene."

"And my suitcases, oh, I think you know where they're to go uh, you're to put them, Lee. I'm going to stay, sleep in my old bedroom tonight, Aunt Della."

"Yes, oh yes," Della said. "Your old bedroom, Darlene."

"Right next to yours, Aunt Della. Yours, I'll be, I mean I'll be sleeping right next to your room, Aunt Della."

"How I look, am looking forward to it, Darlene. Gonna look—"

"How ... how many days will Momma, is Momma—do you think Momma's going to have, be in your company, Darlene?" Margaret asked.

Darlene doesn't look at Margaret, just at Della.

"Oh, Aunt Della, you know they're talking about a winter storm moving into the city by tomorrow morning, don't you?"

"A ... a winter storm, Darlene? No, I didn't know that. But it ain't gonna change my plans. Ha. Any." Pause. "Well, uh, it certainly is that time of year in Myles Day for one, after all, Darlene. So ... ha ... let it come.

"Let it come. But don't worry any, honey, the pantry's stocked full of food. Canned food. We'll have plenty to eat if we're snowed in tomorrow night. Plenty."

Darlene lifts Della's hand, she kisses it, and then rubs the back of it against her cheek.

"It's something you always taught me, Aunt Della. Always be prepared, Aunt Della, for an emergency. Any kind of emergency."

Della takes Darlene's hand and kisses the back of it.

"And you remember, Darlene?"

"How could I forget, Aunt Della? How? Tell me, Aunt Della."

"Yes, Momma, it is—"

"Aunt Della, I mean—your advice, it's like gold, Aunt Della. P-pure gold to me, it's so precious. There's not a day in this house that I didn't learn something from you. Something of value. Of importance."

Pause.

"It's why I don't know about anybody else who lived in this house ever did when they lived here, but I know I did. I did, certainly did, Aunt Della."

"Momma, your pills. Do you—"

Della looks at the clock on her nightstand.

"My, oh yes, Margaret. Yes. I have to take a pill. Uh, two pills in fact, honey. For this time of day."

"Let me get them then, Momma. For you."

Darlene's upset with herself, that she forgot about her aunt Della's pills. "Right, right. They're in Aunt Della's bag. The plastic bag. All of Aunt Della's pills. I … I put them there for her."

"Momma, I'll put them back. Right back on the tray by the bed for you, Momma." And there was a tray near the bed with a glass and a box of tissues. "Where you kept them before you went into the hospital, Momma."

"Only there're more, Margaret, a whole lot more, as of this morning, before you got to the hospital. Ha. Dr. Ives, my darling Joseph, added more to the arsenal."

Margaret laughed. "Oh, there are, Momma?"

"He saddled me, well … uh … well he prescribed, I'm up to thirteen pills a day now. He put two more on the shopping list just this morning, Margaret."

Margaret counts the bottles while lining them up handsomely on the tray.

"Yes, thirteen, Momma. There're thirteen all—"

"What's taking Lee so long this time?" Darlene asked agitatedly. "You haven't heard him in the house, come in the house, have … have you, Aunt Della? Lee, Aunt Della?"

"You're—why you're asking me, Darlene? With my bad ears? Me hearing, the way I hear things or, should I say, don't hear things these days."

"Only I remember when there was a time, Aunt Della. A time."

"Was there, Darlene. All right. What do they say? *When I could hear a mouse pee on top of cotton in the attic?*"

"Momma!"

"Ha. Now, now, Margaret, you know in this house how I was before my health started failing. That your mother could now, Margaret!" Della laughed like crazy.

"Ha. Maybe, maybe Lee got lost, Darlene. Maybe tomorrow's storm got here already. A day early, honey. Before expected by the weather service. That they ain't always right in predicting you know. No telling. And Lee got caught in it. Ha.

"Oh, it's cold outside for a storm today. But just to hear that old radiator of mine." Della's hand cupped her right ear. "Perking. Steam hissing up a storm—it's, well … well …"

Margaret took the glass off the tray. "Momma, I'll get you your water. Uh, be right back."

"Oh, thank you, Margaret. Dear."

Darlene, for the moment, is greasing Della's scalp. Della's hair's draped across her shoulders full-out. Della's hair looks like it will shimmer like a waterfall, shiny and new once Darlene's through. Darlene looks to be having so much fun though, like a child at play at this point.

"Oh … oh … doesn't, doesn't that feel good, Darlene. Oh …" Della's eyes are shut. "Oh … uh … but, but, Darlene, what a—I forgot to ask you about your work, honey. You staying on with me like you say you are the next few days."

Darlene continues to grease Della's hair. "Oh, that—no need to worry about that, Aunt Della. I'll use your sewing machine to do my work. I brought my work with me. In one of the suitcases Lee's bringing into the house. After all, Aunt Della, it is the sewing machine I learned on. The one you taught me on. The first one I ever used, Aunt Della."

Darlene seems to really be going to town with Della's hair now, really giving Della's hair a good working over. Her fingers creating electricity, like sparks actually flying in the air.

"After all, you taught me everything I know about sewing, Aunt Della. Everything. Pardon me, Aunt Della, but I didn't drop a stitch!"

"Ha. Darlene. Darlene—how clever, Darlene!"

"It's why I'm the best seamstress in Myles Day City, bar none—now that you're retired. Why everybody comes to me with their tailoring needs now. Why I can make a good living from it. A good livelihood, Aunt Della."

"My old Singer sewing machine—"

"Can still work wonders, Aunt Della. Even though I like the new ones, I—"

"Them—with their new gadgets that I can't make heads or tail of," Della said.

"But I prefer yours, Aunt Della. The old Singer sewing machine. There's no better feeling, never feel so good as when I use yours, Aunt Della. Can go back to something I treasure and love, Aunt Della. Learned to sew on when I was eight. Eight. W-when Momma died."

"Yes, uh-huh. You're right, Darlene. Was the same year I taught you to sew, Darlene, when your mother died. Nettie. My sister died. God took her home with him."

"B-but I wanted to learn, Aunt Della. I wanted to learn. So bad. So bad. Not like Margaret. Uh-uh, Aunt Della. Not like—"

"Now, now, Darlene. Margaret's head was into other things at the time. Wasn't into, uh, other—each child's different, ain't the same. Remember that: no two children are alike. Supposed to be—"

"But sewing is what you did, Aunt Della. What you were, a seamstress. I wanted to be like you. Just like—"

"Momma, I'm back with the glass of—"

Margaret hesitated, for she felt tension in the air, but then chose to ignore it.

"Oh, so you are, Margaret. So you are. Umm … let me see then, five minutes after one." Della looked at the thirteen bottles of pills. Her eyes studied them with the intent of a pharmacist with a doctor's written prescription in hand. "The blue bottle. Yes, the blue bottle. And the, yes, the one with the red cap, Margaret."

Margaret handed Della the glass of water. "Right, Momma." Margaret unscrewed each bottles' cap.

"Just one of each, honey," Della laughed. "Doesn't matter in what order."

Margaret laughed. "Yes, right, Momma. Ha. Right."

A pill, a blue one, was transferred from Margaret's hand to Della's. "One a day, it keeps the doctor away." Pause. "My elephant pills, I call them. Even

Dr. … uh, Joseph gets a kick out of it. When I tell him to his face. Call them my elephant pills." Della places one of the pills on top her tongue. Her eyes roll back slightly.

"Well … here goes, here goes, down the h—"

"Oh, there you are, Lee," Darlene said accusingly.

"Back, uh, back," Lee said.

"You did everything? Everything I asked you to do?"

"Uh …"

Della had swallowed the second pill out the red-capped bottle. "Lee, why, we thought you got lost in tomorrow's storm!"

Margaret, Lee, and Della laughed but not Darlene. Darlene's face was still corkscrewed.

"Ha. Might as well've been, Aunt Della. Might as well've been, ma'am."

"Darlene says there's one coming in tomorrow, L—"

Darlene steps away from the bed. "You were smoking, weren't you, Lee? Outside smoking, weren't you, Lee? Weren't you, weren't you!"

Lee didn't respond.

"Uh, sorry, Lee."

"N-no need to be, Aunt Della. I'm used to it by now. Better. I'd better be after all these years coming into the house." Lee looked at Della and then at Margaret. "Why, I remember, recall the first time I walked into the house, in here," Lee's body is no longer slumped. "When Darlene and I first started dating and was about to light up a cigarette, Aunt Della.

"Well … Margaret was the first to give me the eye, old evil eye—remember, Margaret?"

"Do I, Lee. Quite, and quite visibly too. Just like it was yesterday."

"Margaret tried to warn me, but it was you, Aunt Della, you who—"

"Lee, everything's fine. Fine here. Orderly, uh, in order now," Darlene said without any change in disposition. "Your dinner's cooked, cooked at home. You just have to heat it up, up in the oven this evening, Lee. Uh, and I'll call you tonight. Yes, tonight, Lee. Make sure you're … everything at home's all right."

Lee walks toward Darlene, but her eyes seem to repulse him, so he stops. "Uh, sure, Darlene, sure."

"So kiss Aunt—"

"Oh, now, now, you know you don't have to tell Lee that. Do that, Darlene." Della's arms extend out to Lee. "My sweet peach that. No, siree!"

Darlene steps aside, distancing herself from Lee. Lee's unbridled.

Della's arms are outstretched. Della puckers her lips.

Lee kisses Della. "Love you, Aunt Della."

"And love you a million times over, Lee. Honey."

Lee is holding both of Della's hands, extending them out as far as he can. "And we welcome you back, Aunt Della. Back home, Aunt Della."

Della smiles like a ripened peach.

"And I did jump on you real bad that day, Lee. First time I caught you trying to smoke a cigarette in the house, didn't I, Lee? My house. Laid down the law. Right there on the spot."

Lee laughed. "You most certainly did, Aunt Della."

Della's energized—her whole body.

"In the living room. In the living room of all places. My—the nerve. Why—what did I say then, to you back then, Lee? Why—"

"Why—"

"Uh, yes, uh … 'why, there's no smoking in this house, young man!' Uh-uh. Not, not in Della Ballad's house, there isn't. Not in Della Ballad's house. Not under any circumstances. Not ever! Ha!"

Lee looks embarrassed even after all these years. He looks like he's just been chided for a second time, been caught lighting up a cigarette in Della Ballad's house.

"And … and it came through loud and clear, Aunt Della. Made my ears ring, ma'am."

"You scared poor Lee half to death, Momma!"

"And Frank, your uncle Frank, he heard me from upstairs, he said. From the bedroom, he said. What he told me when I got back up. Knew what'd happened. Didn't have to be told. Felt sorry for you, Lee. What your uncle Frank told me that night, in bed."

"So did I, Lee."

Lee walked over to Margaret and kisses her cheek. "See you, Margaret. See you soon. And please say hello to R—"

It's when Darlene quickly closes the gap between her and Lee. "Aren't you, aren't you going to kiss me, Lee?" Her body sidles up to Lee. "Kiss your wife? Give me some sugar, baby?"

It was apparent Lee seemed—suddenly felt special, that he was enjoying this extra attention he was getting from everyone.

"Why, of course, Darlene, of course," Lee said smiling. "Y-you, uh, knew I was gonna do that," Lee said. "Before I left the house. Uh, from out here, Darlene."

Darlene's in Lee's arms as he and Darlene kiss; it's a tender kiss between them.

Pause.

"Uh, so, Darlene," Lee finally said, "you don't know yet when, uh, when you'll be coming h—"

She was out of Lee's arms. "I told you, Lee. I told you I have things to do, Lee. I packed clothes for a few days. That's all I can tell you for now—for the time being, Lee."

"Oh yes, I know. Uh, I know, know you did, Darlene." Lee begins walking toward the door. "I ... I know you did."

"And thanks for the flowers, Lee."

"Y-you're welcome, Aunt Della. Aunt ... Aunt Della. My pleasure. P-pleasure."

Della leans over to sniff the flowers on the nightstand. "Uh, by the way, honey, did you use cash or credit—a credit card for the flowers?"

"Credit card, Aunt Della. American Express. Ha. Strictly credit. Well ... well good, good day, everyone. Like I said. Ha. Good day."

"Darlene, Darlene ...," Della points to her hair.

"Yes, your hair, Aunt Della. Your hair. I have to get back to your hair. M-mustn't forget your hair."

"No, not my hair, Darlene."

Darlene gets back to Della's hair.

A few more minutes pass, when Darlene says, "Aunt Della, finished. Finished, Aunt Della. Done! Your hair's all done!"

Della's face lights up. Then it's like she's savoring the moment; her eyes, cheeks, and spirit don't seem to want any of this to end too soon.

"Well ... Aunt Della ..."

"Yes ... uh... so now, now I can scratch it, Darlene? Right, Darlene? Right?" Della said slowly. "Scratch it, I suppose," Della said, her voice climbing. "Dig into it with my nails? Go *crazy* with it?"

"Yes, scratch away, Aunt Della. Y-you may scratch away. Get as crazy with it as you like!"

And Della began doing that, just that, her fingertips digging into her scalp, Darlene and Margaret, the two laughing hysterically at the sight, not being able to hold back, rein themselves in, Della laughing too as her fingertips fiendishly attack her wild bloom of hair remorselessly, relentlessly.

Minutes later.

"Momma, are you hungry? Have an appetite?"

Darlene has brushed Della's hair. It's neat and luxuriant; she looks the perfect patient.

"You know, Margaret, honey, these new pills of mine ... I do feel hungry, hungrier than usual. At this time of day. Real, real hungry in fact."

"Then, well, then I'll take, I'll just have to do something about that, won't I, Aunt Della? Take care of that problem too, won't I?"

"Darlene, I think I know how to make lunch for Momma. My mother. I think I'm perfectly ca—"

Darlene's off the bed, her arms flailing out in front of her. "No, no, since I'm going to be staying here in the house with Aunt Della for as many, however many days are necessary, needed, I, then I should be the one to prepare all of Aunt Della's meals. All the meals for Aunt Della—no, no one else. It's my responsibility. My job. Yes, yes, no one else's job to do but mine. In the house. In this house."

"But—"

"I'll fix fish sandwiches, a nice, tasty sandwich and soup," Darlene said, cutting Margaret off. "Vegetable soup for you now how's that, Aunt Della? How's that sound, Aunt Della?"

Della looks at Margaret but then back at Darlene.

"Yes, that would be fine. Just fine, honey. Uh, the fish sandwich and soup."

"And I know there're plums in the refrigerator. Two plums, Aunt Della?"

"Two plums. Two plums it is, Darlene. Yes, honey. Mmmm ..."

Elated, Darlene heads toward the door. "And then I'll ... should be right back, Aunt Della. With everything."

"Thank you, honey."

Darlene blows a kiss at Della.

Della laughs. "Got it, Darlene. Got it."

Darlene looks at Margaret. "I suppose you'll still be here when I get back." Darlene's hand grips the doorknob. "Margaret ..."

Margaret does not answer her. Instead, she stands and walks over to the bedroom's far window. Darlene continues staring at Margaret's back and then leaves the bedroom.

Margaret is over at the purple drape in the window. Now her fingers are on the window, its glass. She's playing, with her fingers, what appears to be a silent game. Now, seemingly tired of what she was doing, her attention's turned back to Della.

Della's head's back on her pillow. Her eyes are blank. She's looking up at the ceiling, breathing strong even breaths. She seems content to be in the house, in her bed, out of St. Bartholomew Hospital—among what are old and familiar things she loves.

Margaret, who's angled off to the right of Della, looks at her mother wistfully, as if she's the patient, not Della.

"Momma, how do you feel, really feel, now that you're back from St. Bart's?"

"Why"—Della sighed—"why certainly not my old self, that's for sure. But I'll be up on my feet soon enough. Up and running, that's a fact. You know I'm not gonna let this thing—honey, you know you can't keep a good woman down!"

Margaret's drifted over to her. "You're constantly fighting it, Momma. Fighting this disease, aren't you, Momma? Constantly. Diligently. Persistently."

"It's all I know how to do, Margaret, is fight," Della said gamely. "Don't know if I'm gonna win, but I am gonna fight to the end. The very end." She laughs. "When all your life's been a constant struggle—well, the Lord has his plans, and that's all right. Okay with me too. But I'll keep doing what Dr. Ives asked me to do." Pause.

"I don't know if man's medicine is the answer, those pills of mine on the tray are the cure—but I'll keep taking them and see. They've kept me alive so far. I do thank them for doing that much, Margaret."

Margaret is at the edge of the bed. Della's hand beckons her over. "Come sit. Come and sit next to me, Margaret. Come on, I'll make room for you."

"Momma, you don't have to—"

"See!"

Margaret's sitting next to Della. Della looks up at her. "Oh, let me hold you, honey. Hug you." Della has her arms around Margaret, and Margaret's head falls off to her bosom.

"Oh, I've wanted to do this all day, Margaret. All day long."

"Y-you have, Momma? You have?"

"Ha. All day. All day long, Margaret." They remain like this, Margaret's head on Della's bosom, not until Margaret lifts her head.

"Momma, Royal, Royal was going to come. I mean he wanted to come to the hospital today … but he's, he's so dedicated to—"

"Wait a minute, who's making Such a big fuss out of this anyway? Today, anyway?"

"I … I—"

"Like my coming home from St. Bartholomew today was some kind of homecoming event. Royal didn't have to take off from work. There was enough family, Margaret. To go around, honey. Was no reason for Royal to take a day from the job on account of me.

"And no reason for him to apologize to me either—none whatsoever. And you tell him for me, Margaret. Be sure, honey. That Mother Ballad said so."

"Thank you, Momma. T-thank you."

"Honey, now don't you start overdoing things." Della was serious. "Get into that. This—"

"Overdoing—"

"You know what I mean. Start to get—you and Royal mustn't treat every situation, little thing regarding me like it's a crisis, because it ain't. It ain't. It's … it's just not, honey."

"B-but we owe you so much, Momma. So—"

"Child, you owe me nothing. Nothing, you hear me? Not a thing." Della's head's off the pillow. "I'm your mother. You're my child. What do you owe me but your love and respect?"

"Respect, Momma? S-something I didn't have for myself n-not too long ago. R—"

"But you have it now. It's what counts. Now, now. You went through hell—"

"Yes, hell. Hell, Momma. The same hell I put you and Daddy through, M—"

"You won't let it go, will you, Margaret? You won't let it go. Let it die." Della's up off her back. "Give it a quiet death. Just let it die, honey."

"But I can't, Momma. I can't!"

Margaret runs away from the bed.

She's back at the window. Hearing her mother's breathing, she turns and sees her eyes are trained on her, and then she lies back on the bed, resting her head on the pillow.

"Well, I can."

"I ... I ..." Margaret feels a sharp, cold pain in her chest but now thinks more of her mother than herself. She's at the bed. She touches the top of Della's hand. "How, Momma? How? When it was a part of your struggle. The ... the struggle you ... you now just now admitted your life's been. Something I g-gave you—to you. Was responsible for putting there."

"And what? I'm supposed to cry? Cry over what life might've been without any struggles, Margaret? Is that it? What you're saying? But you see, I don't live in the past, never have, and you know that. I don't ... just don't. Won't let myself. Think about it, the past—but I don't live in it."

"I still do. I still do. Live in the past, Momma."

"And I can't change you. You know that."

"It's only that I wish, Momma. I wish ..."

Della shakes her head with a degree of impatience. "You can't wish it, Margaret. Can't do that. You are who you are. I am who I am. You've always been this way. No different. Since small, little."

"But it's just that you bring so much pain on yourself, honey. Burden. Upon yourself. To your heart. That lovely heart of yours. The world's not in judgment of you every second. Every minute of every day. Everything doesn't have to loom so large. Big for you."

"But, Momma—"

"You just can't be perfect, Margaret. Can't be," Della said forcibly. "And I wish for your sake you'd stop trying."

Margaret fidgets. "It ... it produces the opposite result sometimes doesn't it, Momma? Counter, contrary to ..."

"And so I'll let you answer that one, that question for yourself."

"If ... if I could just learn to forgive myself for what I did to you, Momma."

Margaret seems to be waiting for a reply from Della, but there's none.

She walks over to the window slowly, deliberately taking her time. She pulls back the drapes, and her fingertips are back gliding over the glass, addressing the same game as before.

"Is that part of it? I ... I don't want to feel sorry for myself? Self—"

"Pity?"

"Yes, self—"

"You've still got the best heart and soul of anyone I know."

"Then I must've gotten it from you."

Della's eyes shut. "Don't know. Uh-uh. Won't say I do. Ain't gonna ... ha ... speak for somebody else of a higher, much higher authority than me on that subject. Ha."

It's minutes later when Darlene, with Della's tray full of food, stands at the bedroom door. She's observing things. Margaret's over at the window where she was when she'd left the bedroom; Darlene enjoys seeing this physical gap, the separation between Della and Margaret. She smiles at what she sees.

"Look, look who's back, Aunt Della!"

Della's eyes pop back open. "Oh, so I see you are, Darlene."

Quickly Darlene darts into the room. "With your lunch, Aunt Della. Sorry I took—"

"No. No, now, Darlene, you took no time at all. No time at all." The tray's comfortably set for Della. "Oh, thank you, Darlene."

"Aunt Della, you must be starved by now."

"Close to it. Yes, it's the pills. Those new pills of mine. That Joseph prescribed for me, all right. Added to the list. I guess my system's gonna have to get used to them. What I make of it." Pause.

"S-suppose it takes time. Some time. Something I've got plenty of. On my hands."

"Plenty, Aunt Della. Plenty."

Margaret turns from the window. "Momma, I think I-I'll be leaving. Leaving for home, Momma."

Della's bitten into her fish sandwich; she's caught in an awkward position. "Uh, uh-huh," Della said, nodding her head.

"Let me kiss you."

"Do that, Margaret. Please do that, honey."

Gladly, Darlene steps aside. Margaret bends over to kiss Della, and when she does, Della's arm encircles her waist, drawing Margaret to her and then squeezes her to her. Darlene, seeing this, turns her back.

"As Lee ... like Lee said, Momma, glad to have you back home."

Della gulped down her bite of sandwich.

"Aunt Della, you—"

"Ha. Don't worry, Darlene, don't worry. It went down the proper tube. Ha." Pause. "Home is the only place to be. Not in a hospital bed. No matter how sick you get."

"Yes, Momma. Yes." Margaret looks at Darlene's back. It's as if she wants to say something to her, but it's a struggle. "Darlene, I'll ... I'll—"

"Margaret, you have a nice day." Energetically, Darlene's body brushes past Margaret. "And be sure to say hello to Royal for—oh, Aunt Della, the soup's not too hot for you, is it? I didn't make it too hot, did—"

Della blew on the soup. "Now it ain't."

"Oh, Aunt Della!"

Margaret was at the bedroom door. She looks at Darlene as she kisses the top of Della's oily forehead again. "Oh ... oh, Aunt Della, I forgot to tuck your napkin in your nightgown. How'd I do that? So, so none of the soup will spill, get on your nightgown. We don't—"

"And as careless as I am about eating my food these days. Bad as a two-year-old, honey. How I feel. Eat these days."

Darlene laughed. "Now, Aunt Della, stop exaggerating. Stop exaggerating, Aunt Della."

Margaret looked on as Darlene tucked the linen napkin inside Della's nightgown. Shortly afterward is when she leaves the bedroom, heading down the hallway for the staircase.

"Thank you, Darlene. It's so kind of you. To do that for me. Thanks, honey."

Margaret Ballad and Royal McCloud lived in an apartment in Myles Day City. It's a small apartment, something in keeping with the small brick-built apartment units on the north western strip of Myles Day City. The kitchen Margaret was standing in was small. Margaret's fixed dinner. She's removed her apron. She put the apron on the back of the kitchen chair.

"Be right there, Mag," Royal McCloud yelled from the bathroom. The bathroom's just off the kitchen.

"Why, uh … uh, of course, Royal."

Royal McCloud is washing his hands in the bathroom.

"Take, uh, take your time. There's plenty of time before your food turns cold."

Margaret looks down, and on one of the chairs is Royal's gang of school books. She'd laugh as soon as they'd finish eating since the kitchen would turn automatically into Royal's private study hall. Royal's books and other school-related materials could be seen sprawled out on the kitchen table after dinner. Margaret chuckled to herself. Royal was attending Haverford University but brought along a good chunk of Haverford with him every night.

"As soon as I clear the table. Royal—"

Royal McCloud's quite tall, solidly built, brown-skinned, and ruggedly handsome. Such a mix, customarily, made him the focus of attention in any room he walked into. He was used to such attention, acknowledging it judiciously. He's quite articulate and exceptionally bright.

"Uh, you did say Royal, didn't you, Mag? I did hear you correctly, didn't I?"

"Yes, you did hear me—"

"Am I in trouble or did the angels just part the heavens on my behalf?"

"Ha."

"So … now you're laughing, Mag. A far cry from a second ago, when I got in from Haverford."

"Yes, Royal."

"It's nice to see."

Food was on the kitchen table.

"May we bow our heads in prayer then. To submit ourselves to our Lord and Savior."

Both shut their eyes and bowed their heads for a moment of silence.

"Dear Lord. Dear, dear Father … thank you for this day. Thank you for a day that has been whole, rich, and bountiful. For these simple gifts that lie before us. Simple gifts to nourish us, feed our minds and bodies and our spirit. Gifts to refresh us so that we may have the strength to carry on in faithful submission toward the glory of mankind. Toward the glory of your almighty kingdom, God. Amen."

Margaret opened her eyes. She smiled at Royal.

Royal stands. He's slicing the roast pork with the carving knife. When done, Margaret hands him her plate.

"Enough meat, Mag? Or should I cut more?"

"Fine, Royal. No, it's fine."

They're eating now. It seems it's all they're occupied with. There's a silence, therefore, that has existed between them. Royal looks up from his plate and at Margaret.

"At least you have a good appetite tonight."

"Yes, I do."

"Oh, by the way, how did things go today with Mother Ballad, or need I ask?"

"Darlene, Darlene," Margaret said. "Will it ever change between us, Royal? Ever get better?"

Royal chooses to look down at the mashed potatoes on his plate rather than at Margaret. "The Lord is good. So good in providing that he hasn't run out of miracles—deeds to perform, Mag."

Margaret put her knife and fork down, looking blankly at them. "It'd be nice to believe that, Royal. But …"

"Then, then why don't you, Mag? Let yourself. I do."

"Because Darlene kills miracles, that's why. She … she kills the possibility, the very possibility of them, that's why, Royal."

"She loves Mother Ballad, doesn't she?" Royal replied calmly.

"Yes. Yes, she does."

Royal laughs. "Then she's not the devil incarnate. There's hope, Mag."

"Hope?"

"Yes, if Darlene can love, then there's hope. Miracles, good deeds come from the heart. They're formed there. We both know that." Pause. "If anyone should, we should, Mag."

Margaret's head bows downward to the plate of food. It's as if she wants to count the peas on the plate. It's as if she's demanding some reason for her to do this. To let her mind relax by counting peas on her plate up to the final count. To give the peas focus, attention, and—

"She's taking care of everything for Momma. Everything. Taking charge as … as—"

"You know I was hoping that what we'd planned, you staying on with

Mother Ballad when she was released from St. Bartholomew Hospital, had materialized. For you could be there to help Mother Ballad through her—"

"But Darlene, Darlene dashed that plan, Royal. Of ours, didn't she? Single-handedly. Ha. Good old Darlene. It didn't stand a ... Darlene had her own plans. Set in her mind. And there was nothing Momma or I could do to stop her. Nothing at all once Darlene's mind's made up. As usual."

"Well ... at least Mother Ballad knows we were—"

"But it's not the same. It's just not the same Momma knowing what we hoped, wanted to do, Royal. No ... no ...," Margaret said. "And I won't sit here with you and pretend that it is!"

Her hand slaps hard against the kitchen table.

Royal folds and then unfolds his arms.

"No, it's not. In the least. And yes, I agree: Why should we pretend it's the same."

Margaret's voice builds. "I'm her daughter. Why won't Darlene let me be Momma's daughter? She's my mother, not hers. Why won't she let me do 'daughterly' things for my mother?

"From ... from childhood, when we were children, up to now. But ... but when I ran away from home with ... with you, Royal—"

"It's when Darlene really took over the Ballad household. Seized it," Royal said bluntly. "Took full control."

"When her power really grew over Momma. D-dominated her." Pause. "She became perfect, perfect in every way."

Royal brought the forkful of food up to his mouth and then paused. "I don't know," he said. "I don't know about—"

"And then I became trash! Trash in Mom—"

His fork fell out his hand. "Mother Ballad never said that, told you that. Y-you're—it's ... it's your thinking. You're thinking like—"

"And why shouldn't I think how I'm thinking? The ... the way I'm thinking, am, tell me why?" Margaret said, not backing down. "Why shouldn't I? Oh, Royal, I believe in God, religion, this thing we found in ourselves. Each other. Family, going back to discover what—"

"To our roots. Old roots. To firm roots. To old beginnings. An old religion. To a gospel we all knew as children. Your folk, Mag. My folk. They taught us to love God. The power of his love. The love God has for—"

"It ... it healed us. Helped heal us, Royal."

There's a divinity in Royal's voice. "Took the stench away from us. From our souls. Oh, its healing powers are … are unquenchable if you are ready to receive and not deceive. Healing, Mag. Healing."

"Has cured us—"

"In so many wonderful, profound ways." Royal's face is resplendent. "We are in the gospel's bright fire. In its cure. It has helped to reshape our spirit."

"But Darlene is so formidable."

"And you must not fight her, for she will surely, with all certainty, win."

Margaret sits back in the chair. "And I don't, Royal. I don't fight her. And it makes me feel so—"

"You haven't turned the other cheek, Mag. Don't think for an instant you have."

"Except it's how it feels. Always feels with her. There are times when I just want to take Darlene and … and I … I don't know what I'd do to her, Royal. I don't know what. What!"

"All out of anger."

"Yes, anger, Royal … years and years of anger. Built-up anger."

"And Darlene knows how to use anger, Mag, and don't, for a minute, think otherwise. To her advantage." Royal's voice lowers. "She wants to see anger pour out of every pore you have, if she can.

"And then … she'll use it against you. Try to bring you down to where she operates best. To her level. And then destroy you. She'll be smart enough, oh yes, clever enough to destroy you, Mag, plain and simple. As plain as me sitting in this chair. Me looking at you."

"How, Royal? How? Just—"

"Jealousy. Jealousy." Royal's stroking his chin. "It's how. And she'll flaunt it like she owns it." Pause. "And then you will have served her greatest aim: make herself the victim in the Ballad family. All this conflict."

"Yes, conflict."

"The contest going on, being waged between you and her," Royal continues. "Fighting for Mother Ballad's love. Or how the two of you perceive Mother Ballad's love. For both of you have your own personal, distinct opinion on the subject."

Royal stopped short, as if wanting all of what he'd just said to Margaret to sink in. Not only for Margaret but for his own sake. For it's the first time he and Margaret had spoken so openly, broadly on this subject. Darlene,

Margaret, and Della—their relationship. It's the first time they'd been so candid, frank—to the point, so big and honest and bold in their quest to find the truth in their words and feelings.

But something significant, terrible is taking place in your life right now, Mag, Royal thought. *Your mother's dying, and you trust me. We've gotten this far in our life together because you trust me. It's not like before, in the past, when I was leading myself and you to destruction. On a path so wicked—I did believe in hell. I did! Even then, Mag. That I stood at the gates of hell!*

"S-shall, do you want me to go on with this, Mag?"

"Yes."

"Yes, where was—"

"I wish you hadn't stopped, Royal. There was no reason for you to."

"I thought ..."

"No."

"Then I ... what—"

"Both of us, you said both of us, Darlene and I, have our personal ... how we ... we perceive Momma loves us."

"It's true, Mag. Yes, it's true. You ... you, Mag, think your mother has always loved Darlene more than she loved you, from the day Darlene came to the house to live with you. Your aunt Nettie died, and your mother and father took her in."

"And ... and Darlene, Royal?"

"Well Darlene, Darlene's always been insecure, unsure of herself in this whole quest of hers. It's why Darlene fights o hard, so viciously, perniciously against you, Mag. Fights so hard to hold onto, to maintain her turf. What she's been fighting for ... for all these years.

"The hold she figures, reckons she had over Mother Ballad but ... but is never sure. Ever quite sure of. But will fight to the death. With every fiber that's left in her for."

"Jealously."

"Darlene, she'll never fight fair with you, Mag. And don't expect her to, not when she's been fighting for Mother Ballad's love since she was ... was ..."

"Eight. Eight years old, Royal."

"Mag, it's all Darlene wants," Royal said. "All Darlene will ever need."

"Momma's love."

"Which you already have."

"But … but Darlene does too, Royal. D-Darlene does too. H-has it too," Margaret said as if the words had burst through her.

"I know. I … I know. But all this, all this confusion is about being first in Mother Ballad's heart. Number one. It's all it's about." Royal stood. His hands are linked.

"You see, Mag, you see, our God, our Father is not jealous of any man or any woman. He permits me to love you, for he knows such a love is not equal, cannot compare, cannot be drawn from the same pit of fire that burns inside me, that is his love, solely, his province, exclusively.

"For God knows there is no greater love than that which I have for my father. And there is no greater love than a mother has for her daughter, Mag. No greater love on earth exists. Y-you must understand that, Mag. Be guided in your heart by that. Darlene is loved by Mother Ballad, but a mother's love for her child is … it is unequalled, unparalleled, unrivaled."

"Oh, Royal, Royal. I do believe that. I do. I … I do, Royal."

"Then do believe it, Mag. Do believe it," Royal said. "It's not an abstraction. God's not putting it there for you to serve as an abstraction."

Margaret's withdrawing her hand from her face. "But like today, Royal, not being able to brush Momma's hair. Grease her scalp. Fix Momma's meals. Stay with her. A-attend to her, Royal. Not being able to be there with her. In the house. For … for her. Her daughter."

"Yes."

Her voice sinks. "These are things that—"

"That kill your spirit." Royal is looking down at her. "I do know that, Mag."

"I want to do things for Momma. I want to. Be there for her. F-for Momma. And when I can't, when Darlene won't let me, takes over, takes them from me, I want to cry … cry out, Royal. Say … say, 'Look at me, Momma. Look, look at me, Momma. Look at me!'"

"But it takes control. A certain level of control, Mag—"

"Until I explode, Royal? Just, what, just explode? Is—"

"Then it … it is, it's why … why we must pray on this. It … it's why we … we must pray together, together on this, Mag."

Margaret gets up from the kitchen table. "Not tonight, Royal." Her anger glows.

Quickly he's at her side.

"It's when we're at our weakest point, at our most vulnerable, when we must pray, Mag. We, when we most need prayer. Must turn ourselves to prayer. To God."

"Royal! Royal! No, Royal, no!" Margaret's hands are fists. "I won't pray with you. I won't!"

Singularly, Royal's knees drop down onto the kitchen floor. He doesn't look up at Margaret. His eyes are shut. His hand reaches for hers. "Will you join me in prayer, Mag? Will you?"

Margaret's crying, sobbing, but reaches for Royal's hand eagerly and kneels down beside him.

Both bow their heads in prayer.

CHAPTER 4

Royal McCloud was standing outside the beautiful brick building with both hands stuck deep down inside his coat pockets. His hands were in his pockets, he knew, to try to weigh himself down, because at times like this, he thought he might fly away untethered like some giant balloon free in the sky since he'd already begun to get in his "swoon mood," and who knows, he thought, he might fly away today. He was in love with that big, beautiful brick building at Bayer Street, all right. The store-front building had so such promise for how he wanted to utilize it. It was so ideal. It had space, space, and space—that was the main thing—space.

"It will work. It will definitely work."

When he was in this kind of mood, he didn't want to get too close to the building for fear he might try to give it a bear hug, wrap his arms around it, or something as implausible or dumb as that—squeeze it to death. But he had a meeting with John Houston tomorrow, and they would sit down and talk about the building. He'd found time to squeeze the meeting between everything else he was doing, but it was imperative he have the meeting with John Houston.

"A parking lot on the side of the building, everything. Everything. It's ideal."

Then Royal looked at his car and then at the building, the contrast being obvious.

"My old secondhand car. Hand-me-down. Maybe one day I'll get from there"—he laughed—"wherever 'there' is, to here. It'll be parked in the parking lot on a Sunday morning. M-maybe."

Royal could feel that *swoon thing* coming on, the chill in him, the uneasiness that excitement brings on. But this was what he was after—this store-front building at 20 Bayer Street. This would be another change in his life, another firm, positive foot forward. But each step had to be measured and set solid like concrete. It's how sure he had to be of everything. It's how dedicated to change he had to be—he and Margaret.

"Me and Margaret."

From what they'd come from, from darkness into light. They had so much to lose if they didn't do things the right way. If they weren't dedicated to each day, make it stand for something, count for something, to say at the end of the day, in bed, in the bathroom, somewhere in the apartment, that they'd made progress, could write it down, bookmark it, whether or not it was tangible or intangible, but that it was honest and real and satisfying.

"God, God, you're so good to me, God."

Royal had turned his back to the building. He didn't want to pray for it. He didn't want to drop down on his knees and pray for the building, for he would, he would—it's how much the building meant to him. And he'd said to himself, *If God wants me to have the building, I will have it*—something he'd been saying over and over. He wasn't going to use the power of prayer. He wasn't going to overpower this desire he had with the power of prayer. He'd consciously chosen not to. He didn't know why.

He couldn't answer his own emotions, motivations. It all seemed beyond him, too much of a mystery and a power to rise to, to match, so he fell silent; it felt safe that way. And there were times when he did want to feel safe, that he could overcome disappointment, letdown on the grandest scale—if he had to—that God had brought him and Margaret that far in their journey.

It was cold, and it had snowed only a few days back, and it wasn't a big accumulation, not like the ones that would typically hit Myles Day City; that snowstorm would come in a few weeks—guaranteed. So what snow was still left on the ground on Bayer Street was still mild compared to what snow was ahead down the pike.

Royal was in his car. It was black, long—it looked like a hearse. Royal laughed. When I die, the funeral director will have one less car to think about. Can skip over. "When I die. When I die," Royal said, entering the car.

"What a thought. I'm so young, yet it seems as if I've lived a few lifetimes. Enough for three people. At least three."

He stuck the key in the ignition. "Now start. It's all I ask. It's not that cold."

He thought of Margaret immediately, of how she laughed when he talked to the car Sunday last when they drove to church. It was a colder Sunday than it was today, but he'd said this to the car because it was really a *cold* Sunday, and then the snow came. He'd put antifreeze in the car, so it was good to it—so he wanted it to be good to him. He felt like saying, "Baby, be good," but not at this stage of his life, he thought.

He and Margaret had bought the car just before summer, but it was easy for a car to hold up during the summer months (even though an old car can overheat). But the real test came during the winter, especially in Myles Day City when skis probably offered better transportation for getting around the city than cars and trucks and buses and motorcycles. Royal laughed.

Royal was back in the car seat; the keys dangled out the ignition switch.

"When I die. When I die. Why did I say that? Why?"

Was it because he was thinking of Mother Ballad too much these days? So this kind of thinking was plush in his mind—the foreground? It wouldn't go away, not for a day. There was a pall over the Ballad house: Della Ballad's dying. Or was he thinking about his past, when he'd reached such a desperation, such a low, he'd felt suicidal, could kill himself.

"It scares me now. The thought."

And maybe it scared him then too, when he started to think that way, that he could end it all with a gun, a bullet, just point the gun to his head, blow out his brains and that would be the end of Royal T. McCloud. *Royal Tyrone McCloud.*

"When I die."

This time the three words sprang out his mouth.

*   *   *

Margaret poured the water out the glass and into the iron's spout. She stood by the ironing board and waited for the water to turn to steam, and then she could press her woolen skirt. Did she just hear Royal let out a few precious snores, or … yes, it was him, all right. He deserved to snore as much as he wished, what with his schedule. He was taking a nap at 10:20 p.m., said he had a school exam coming up, so he had wanted to study as much, as hard as he could, into the wee, wee hours of the night. But he was so smart; she didn't worry about him. But he was smart enough to be prepared.

Margaret began pressing the woolen skirt.

The radio was on (on the low side of the volume button). She was humming to the Chi-Lites. There was only one black radio station in Myles Day City, and the radio dial was set on it. It played some great music on that radio station, the kind to iron a dress to at 10:00 p.m.

Darlene, Margaret thought. Darlene was a real force again. She was out of control, totally, completely out of control. Today marked the sixth day Darlene had been in the house, staying in the house, attending to her mother. But she couldn't complain about a thing, anything when it came to how her mother was being managed, taken care of, attended to, her home care. There was never a reason, any reason at all to complain about that.

She had to admire that. Give Darlene high marks, the highest grade possible. Kudos. How could anyone be as keen, as alert, as thorough to her mother's needs as Darlene? She was like a machine, a robot—but with a heart, a soul. She was selfless, unblemished, part hero and part myth. Anything one could say about her was well earned, deserved—came with some duty, obligation to say it right, to beat the drum nonstop no matter how lavish the sound, jarring or earsplitting.

Margaret lined the hem of the woolen skirt up just right and began pressing it with the iron at the bottom.

She'd talked to her mother three times today, and each time, it meant three times she spoke to Darlene, had to go through Darlene, said, "Hello." She said, "Yes, here's Aunt Della." "Thank you. Momma …" Three times. Three times. Three times. Three times she had to talk to Darlene. Go through Darlene. At times it felt like a weight falling down on her, crashing down on top her—at times.

Only, it wasn't as bad as being there, in the house with Darlene, watching her every movement in the house as if she were paid to spy on her, recording everything she did for she could report it later to herself, not to Royal but for her own benefit, for her own purpose.

It was like looking at minutiae in its grandest, most complex and elaborate form. Minutiae. By its grandest, most elaborate example. *This always looking.* This always looking at Darlene as if she could steal her heart. And she was jealous of Darlene. Almost like she could climb inside her skin to be her. To breathe her breath. To have what she had that made everything work for her. That made everything seem possible in the situation both were in. To take hold of a moment and claim it, own it almost as if it were made, created for you. This was what was so masterly about Darlene, Margaret thought—the sheer, stupendous guts she had in her.

"I can't be like that. J-just can't be like that. I … I …"

But Darlene knew that. Maybe it was why she was so bold, ruthless, evocative. Maybe it's why she was so daring and cunning in their personal relationship with one another, how all this had evolved from childhood, from the first day Darlene stepped into the Ballad household to live after her aunt Nellie's death.

Margaret glanced at the clock. Royal had asked to be awakened at 10:40 p.m. He had ten more minutes. Yes, it's 10:20 p.m., and what, it's taken her ten minutes to, so far, to iron this skirt?

"Relax. Relax. You're spinning out of control again. You're spinning out of control again."

She looked at Royal's books and had to laugh at them. There were the usual ones and the ones he said he'd checked out of Haverford University's library. She didn't want to count them; it might be too painful to her eyes. He was all business when he opened those books, all business; his life was so busy, exciting, engaged.

The skirt was pressed.

Margaret entered the bedroom. Royal's body was spread across the bed, and he wasn't snoring now; in fact, she didn't hear a whisper from him. She was going to feel good about waking him. God only knew what he was dreaming of! How many sheep he'd counted by now.

She hung her skirt on the back of the door and then walked back out to the kitchen, looked at the kitchen clock, and knew Royal had eight minutes left to go, and then he'd be up for the next four hours or so, tackling the books on the kitchen table. Then she'd be in bed possibly to evoke her own snores (for she was a snorer too) or be on snooze control. Margaret sat down at the kitchen table.

"Momma …"

If Darlene was waiting on her mother hand and foot, was she getting enough exercise? But her mother said she was—and she had no reason not to believe her, for she was an independent woman who wanted to recover, be fully back on her feet again, who wouldn't settle for anything less. So she wouldn't let Darlene, or anyone for that matter, deprive her of her daily physical therapy essential to her recovery. No, Darlene wouldn't do that to keep her toehold in the house.

"And she wouldn't do that. That was just a sinister, evil thought on my part. Biased and unfair. Darlene doesn't have to further establish her importance or reinforce it. What need is there for that? She knows her mission no matter what our personal relationship is.

"What an awful, indecent thought on my part. Trying to accuse Darlene. She wants Momma to live forever like I do."

But will Momma live through the holidays? Thanksgiving? Christmas? New Year's?"

"Oh … oh, I never thought of that. I … I never thought of that. The holidays. Why haven't I thought of that? Will Momma live through the holidays?"

Margaret looked at the kitchen clock, stood, and walked back into the bedroom. She walked over to the window where the shade was pulled down. She stood there by the window. Royal was down to three more minutes before she awoke him. When she'd looked at the kitchen clock, it said 10:37 p.m. The clock in the bedroom had the same time. She'd wait until it said 10:40 p.m. and then wake him from his sleep. She could see the clock from where she stood by the window.

It was better this way, Margaret thought.

∗　　∗　　∗

Royal came into the kitchen. He was shedding his coat, scarf, hat, and gloves.

"Brrrr … oh, if it isn't c-cold out today! A winter storm is on the horizon, and when it hits, it's not going to be pretty. So gentle, this time around, Mag!" Royal appeared puzzled.

"Why am I taking everything off here, when I have to hang them up in the closet?"

"Maybe to impress me," Margaret laughed.

Royal stood there as if what Margaret had just said made sense. "Y-you think so, Mag?"

"Royal ..."

"Okay, Mag. Okay." Royal ducked back out the room.

"You look strange without your school books."

"It is Saturday!" Royal yelled back.

"Yes, I know"—Margaret giggled—"but you still look strange without them."

"Just because I aced Professor Jonas Rothstein's exam the other day doesn't mean my dedication has diminished any. That I no longer hold higher education in high ex—"

"Hot chocolate?"

"Man, oh man, Mag," Royal said, rubbing his hands, now back in the kitchen. "Hot chocolate's definitely on the menu. What the doctor ordered. For cold days like today."

Royal's gotten over to Margaret. He kisses her.

"Oh, you *are* cold, Royal. Even your lips are cold."

"Ahh ... see, I have no reason to try to impress you. None at all." Then Royal's body spins from Margaret's like a whirling top.

"You must have good news. Good—"

"Do I! Do I ever," Royal said, practically breathless. "If ... if Brother Houston isn't working for the Lord then I'd like to know, ask ... could you tell me who in God's kingdom is? I mean, I mean he's breaking his neck for us, Mag." Pause.

"He's trying his darndest to get this vision of mine off the ground. He wants me to have a church as much, as badly as I do, Mag. I don't care where our church winds up being for now, its home, well ... I do care, but—"

"Ha. But Bayer Street is still in the running. Picture, isn't it, Royal?"

"Bayer Street's still in the running. That's right. At the top of the list. That beautiful building's still—no—it's never been out of the running." Royal grabs her. "Oh, Mag, Mag, that would be a dream come true, Mag. A—it's a store front. Yes. Granted. It's a store front. But we could fix it up, the place up, inside, easy, real easy.

"The brick's still in good shape. It could be something special. We could, you and me, our tiny … small flock of worshippers could turn it into something special—a nice church for folk to come to, worship in every Sunday morning. And there's a parking area on the side of—"

"I know." Margaret laughed.

"Yes, you know, if anybody would, you would."

"Since my bus passes it on the way to work and back every day."

"It's just that—Mag, I want to be a part of that downtown community area. That part of town. Myles Day City. A vital part. The needier the people, the better it is for me. I'm just so glad I have a Christian brother like Brother Houston in my corner.

"Putting forth such effort. His expertise in finance and legal matters, real estate, and … and the sort has—it's been a godsend, Mag. A godsend."

Margaret hands Royal the saucer with the cup of hot chocolate on it.

"Thanks."

"You're welcome."

"I don't know what I'd do without him, honestly." Pause. "Aren't you going to partake of a cup of hot chocolate with me?" Royal asked with a sly smile on his face.

"Uh-uh. I've been out the cold and in the house for a while. My blood … ha… has thawed out by now."

"Yes, it's all I want, Mag—a church. A church. A congregation. Somewhere where you and I, our small flock of worshippers can worship together as a family. Folk who've shown so much faith in me … despite my past transgressions. My past reputation in Myles Day City. Are standing shoulder to shoulder with me."

"And I know that that day is drawing closer and closer for us, Royal."

Royal looked down into the cup of hot chocolate and then drank from it this time.

"Umm … good, Mag. Good. Very … oh, it is, Mag. It is. Closer and closer for us. And I feel it too." Long pause.

"But money, money, Mag, money. That still looms large as a huge hurdle standing in the way. With work and school, I—"

"Royal, I can still take on extra work. A part-time job, if you-you'd like.

My bookkeeping job at International is, after all, just five days a week. I can do part-time work on the weekend."

"Yes, I know that, you can. But the two of us shouldn't work ourselves down to the bone. Where we never get a chance to see each other, and then when we do, at the end of the day"—Royal laughs—"we're so worn out, exhausted, our tongues are dragging the floor."

"Ha."

"Oh, Mag, the Lord is good, but when he who labors too long and hard in God's kingdom, vineyard, becomes only, only a beast of burden, serving no master ... ha ... but himself, then ..."

"Now that, whatever you just said, Royal, I'll pretend I didn't hear!"

"Me, too, Mag, me too!"

Margaret took Royal's hand, and when she did, she looked into his eyes. "You are such a good man, Royal. And I truly love being a part of this mission. With you, Royal. The good work you are trying to do in Myles Day City."

"It's us, Mag. Us. We have come so far. We've done it together, you and me."

"Step by step," she said proudly. "It's what feels so good about it. T-to think one day we'll be able to move from out Mr. Tolletson's basement and into a church. Our own church."

"And it's going to happen, Mag. Will happen for us. It's just down the road. Around the corner. Ahead for us. A matter of time. God hasn't run out of miracles. They haven't dried up. We're going to continue to follow God's light."

They laughed.

"By the way, Royal, I'm taking a baked ham and a dish of macaroni by the house tomorrow night."

"Why ... I know it's not for Mother Ballad."

"No. No, of course not. It's for the rest of us, uh, the family."

"You know, I can't wait to see Mother Ballad. I ... I do feel bad that I have to call her, talk to her by phone every time I do talk to her these days."

"Momma understands."

Royal takes another sip of hot chocolate and then slowly, deliberately, puts the cup back down on top the saucer. "But ... but suppose, Mag, just suppose Mother Ballad was a parishioner of mine, was a shut-in, Mag, my duty, as her pastor, is to call on shut-ins at home. Be there for them in their time of need, crisis. If Mother Ballad were a shut-in in my church, depended on me for spiritual support, restoration … well … you see, I would fall far short of my Christian duty. It's just with my job and the church and school that—"

"Don't tell me, Royal, that I'm the one who's elected to preach to you this evening. Me. The one to give today's sermon … from the Mount. Tell you all about the virtues of—"

"Being patient. Just being patient."

"Yes, patient, Royal. Patient. Not judging yourself for what you cannot do, but only for that which you can."

"Right. Right. You are so right. And spoken by a true Christian woman. Ha."

"And Momma can't wait to see you!"

"And I can't wait to see Mother Ballad. It'll be my second time since she's been out St. Bart's."

Margaret had the empty cup and the saucer; she was carrying them over to the kitchen sink.

"Mag, thanks."

"Royal, you're welcome."

CHAPTER 5

Della's cheeks looked as red as a lollipop.

She was sitting upright in bed, and she looked nothing like she looked when she first got home from St. Bartholomew Hospital. There was every reason for Dr. Ives to send her home then, but now it's as if she'd just had a bad cold, nothing, surely, as serious as a heart attack.

"Oh … Darlene and I had a good walk in the house today. My legs felt strong. Under me. It's what they felt like—under me. Two days now. Two days straight. Yes, under me."

Della could feel her physical strength returning, soaring back. It wasn't 100 percent. It was near 95. But if that wasn't good news, she thought, then a dollar during Depression days was fool's gold. She was really feeling good about her prospects.

The pills were working wonders for her.

"Those pills and Darlene, they're one of a kind! That they are!"

The walker, yes, she still used it in the house to navigate about but wasn't reliant on it. But for safety reasons, for precaution's sake, she hadn't deserted the walker. She wasn't going to be silly about this whole business of recovery, deluding herself to think she was less sick than she was because having heart disease, especially at her age, was serious business; and she knew firsthand how it was to be sick. To feel so weak, that to lift your head from the pillow was a triumph, you'd overcome something pretty awful that day, devastating.

But I'm beyond that now, Della thought. *Far beyond that. I can walk around the house, upstairs and downstairs, and feel confident about it too!*

Her family was such a source of comfort—Margaret, Lee, and seeing Royal once at the house since she's been out the hospital but talking to him on the phone. She felt both lucky and blessed. And she felt Frank. She always felt Frank.

"I always feel, Frank. Frank standing in the shadows. Ain't far off," Della laughed. "No, not my Frank. Not my Frank. That handsome-looking man of mine."

She was waiting for Darlene to—Della heard her come out the bathroom.

"Darlene, I want you to pretty me up tonight. Really pretty me up," Della said, flinging her full set of gray hair like she was eighteen years old again, and Frank Ballad had just knocked on the front door of her parents' house for a date that would culminate into many more dates to come.

"No," Darlene said, "I won't let you look in the mirror until I say so, Aunt Della."

"I can't wait, Darlene. I can't wait!"

"Oh, your hair, your makeup—"

"Do I look like a beauty queen, Darlene?"

"Better than a beauty queen, Aunt Della. You've got class! Plenty of it, Aunt Della!"

"You know, Darlene, when I was young, I would've looked great in a bikini."

"You did have quite a figure, Aunt Della," Darlene said, applying rouge to Della's already-rosy cheeks.

"Yes, your uncle Frank thought so too. But of course, when I was young, growing up, during my time, we were modest about our bodies. Wasn't something to display, like fruit."

"Ha. Aunt Della, now where did that come from? You come up with that?"

"Don't ask me, honey. I must be thinking odder by the day. Getting my oats back."

Darlene stopped what she was doing. "Yes, yes, you are, Aunt Della."

"Me and that walker." The walker was parked at the foot of the bed. "Are gonna get outside soon. Throw on my coat and see how cold it is in Myles Day City these days. Find out if it's cold as everyone marching in here, the house, been saying it is. Ain't lying.

"Just don't think it's nowhere near as cold as it was at the turn of the century ... 1910 ... 1920. As cold as my parents would tell me it was around here during those times."

"My grandparents, Aunt Della."

"Yes, your grandparents, Darlene. Were a strong lot, your grandparents. Had to be strong to be black in Myles Day City. Back then. Those times. Wasn't an easy place for blacks, black people to live in—and had nothing to do with the cold."

"Yes, so ... so I heard, Aunt Della."

"Had to be strong. But we survived it. Didn't get pulled down. Times, things change. There's a good community here. Solid. Valued. Blacks, I mean. Colored folk. Are valued here."

"Grandmother and grandfather—"

"They didn't take no stuff ... wasn't about to—not from the white man, not from, Darlene, you're through, aren't you, with my makeup? And my hair's already been brushed out, so may I—"

Darlene snatches the mirror off the bed and puts it in front of Della's face.

"Darlene! Darlene! Oh, honey! Honey!"

Della was still in her bedroom. She was sitting in an old, comfortable chair in a floral dress and her unfailing house slippers. Her walker stood directly in front of her.

"I'm sitting here all dressed up. But like I have nowhere to go. Standing on a street corner—cars whizzing by. Just whizzing by me. Ha."

But Della knew she was having fun with herself, for this was to be a big evening for her. She was full of extra good cheer, and now that she had assessed her health, she was ready to stand on her own two feet. She looked at the clock on the nightstand.

"Everybody's going to be here in a matter of a few minutes now. Margaret, Royal, and Lee. I'm ready for them. Am I!"

Della not only felt physically strong but mischievous. She felt like a mouse trying to make a cat's life miserable. She felt like she could scoot around the house and squeeze through things, slip her shadow even, if it had the nerve to think it could keep up with her.

Della sniffed the air, for she could smell the foods she and Darlene had cooked this afternoon. And she'd stood on her feet for long, long periods, stretches of time and hadn't felt the least tired or lightheaded. Darlene had remarked about it too, about her sudden improved level of endurance.

"We cooked up a storm, Darlene and me. This afternoon."

She hadn't lost her touch. Who would've ever suggested that she had?

"I've been cooking collard greens, ham hocks, baked macaroni, black-eyed peas. Baking cakes. Coconut layer cake and sweet potato pie and—it's them! It's them!"

Della stood. Then her hands reached out for the metal walker. The lightweight, aluminum walker had rubber wheels on it, so she began rolling it across the floor and toward the bedroom door. In her heart, she felt she really didn't need the walker, but it'd been so good to her—they'd been through so much together, formed such a partnership, friendship, she didn't want to feel as if she were shunning it, devaluing its importance suddenly.

Della was in the hallway. She was moving smoothly, beautifully along. Della and her walker were keeping a good pace in the hall, heading down it.

"Momma! Momma, Royal and I are here!"

Della heard Royal's voice.

"I'm on my way, Margaret. Me and my walker are on our way, honey."

"Lee!"

"Hi, Margaret, Royal!"

"Lee, you just coming through the door too? Behind Margaret and Royal?"

"Yes, Aunt Della. Yes I am, ma'am."

"And where are you, Darlene?"

"Right here, Aunt Della. Right here. About to take Lee's coat and hat and hang them in the closet, Aunt Della."

"Yes, Aunt Della," Lee laughed.

"Don't go too far now. Too far off now, Darlene."

"W-why, Aunt—"

And they saw Della now, she and her walker, for she was at the top of the staircase, looking down at the four of them.

"Momma, you look beautiful."

"Absolutely beautiful, Mother Ballad."

"Yes, Aunt Della."

"You can thank your wife for that, Lee. Darlene for that." And then Della pushed her walker aside. "And … and for this too."

And it's when Della began walking down the staircase, holding firm to the banister.

"Aunt Della!"

"Momma!"

"Mother Ballad!"

"None of you move. Darlene. None of you. Stay put! Where you are. Don't move. Not one of you move. No, no need to worry. To trouble yourselves. I feel as strong as an ox. Don't move an inch. My legs are under me. I'm telling you—my legs are under me …

"Look … look at me!"

The living room had a sense of not only beauty but of peace and harmony. It was a delicate balance to be sure in a room of old, established furniture of classic design and nostalgic grace in its DNA. It was a room Della and Frank Ballad both loved and took especial care in decorating and rendering it character in reflecting their personal tastes. There was a lovely maroon rug anchored by a red throw rug beneath the mahogany coffee table. Colorful lampshades added to the room's old-fashioned, dignified posture, the room's casual, basic reserve. The tall windows were majestic and, when the drapes fully drawn, the bright sun filled the room, breathing in its natural refinement.

The family had moved from the dining room to the living room, and during the transition, Della hadn't lost her position or the spell she'd been casting over her "children." She was the queen bee. Everything revolved around her, like if she sneezed, four tissues would suddenly simultaneously appear, showering her nose. Darlene and Lee and Margaret and Royal would run to her with tissue in hand and tell her to blow as hard as she could into it.

Della couldn't remember when she'd last had so much fun or enjoyed her family more. She was delirious with joy. She'd been laughing, reminiscing, counting days she'd sometimes count like this, family dinners, family gatherings, family holidays. There was a certain thrill in her—in fact, it was making for quite a strong pulse in her.

"My family ..."

"It is a blessing, isn't it, Mother Ballad?"

"It is, Royal. A true, true blessing. And it feels as wonderful looking out at you here in the living room as it did at the dining room table. It just does my heart good. Makes me feel better than those pills Dr. Ives has me taking ... ha ... every day—that's for sure!"

"Now, Aunt Della, don't tell me you're still complaining about those—"

"Lee, Lee, it ... it would do you good, a ... a lot of good to listen to what Aunt Della's has to say. Don't, wouldn't you think, Lee!"

Darlene's sitting next to Della on a smaller sofa off by the fireplace. Darlene's holding Della's hand. Margaret, Lee, and Royal are sitting on the larger sofa, the one with the antique-looking coffee table in front of it. But the living room is huge, so there's a broad path between the coffee table and sofa.

Della's rubbing Darlene's hand. "That's all right. Lee. Me and those elephant pills of mine are ... are still ... ha ... battling it out. Going to battle, Lee. Battling each other morning, noon, and night. Going toe to toe."

"But as long as you're still taking them, Mother Ballad, God has won!"

"Oh yes, Royal. God has won. Indeed!"

"Has already ... ha ... won the Battle of Jericho!"

"God"—Lee laughs—"and Dr. Ives's pills, you mean, Royal! Ha!"

"Oh, yes. Oh yes, indeed, Lee. Indeed!" Royal said.

Darlene glares at Lee.

"Oh, it's a battle all right. Every day it's a battle, I must admit. A battle to end all battles. But ... but I said, well ... I did say I have a surprise for my family, all of you this evening, didn't I?"

"Yes, Momma," Margaret eagerly replied.

Della looked over at Royal. "And, Royal, now we're going to call on the Lord again, you and me. Us two."

"Gladly, Mother Ballad. Gladly."

"For I don't know how I kept this news I've got in me so long, for as long as I have, under my hat. I mean at the dinner table, up to now. I guess, s-suppose it was with God's help that—"

"It was, Mother Ballad. It surely was, Mother Ballad."

Della pats Darlene's hand.

"But I figured us sitting here in the living room, me on Frank's sofa. One built for two, but Frank always sitting on it alone, not like me and Darlene are doing right now, uh, right, Darlene?"

"Yes, Uncle Frank's sofa, Aunt Della. My Uncle Frank's sofa."

"Maybe you can squeeze in three, if all of them are slender, slender like Darlene is."

They laughed.

"But with me sitting in it or Frank, two will do." Della began patting the arm of the chair with her hand. "Yes, a sofa he loved to sit on so much. Was good to him."

"When Daddy would come home from the barber—"

"Shop. His barbershop, Margaret. Yes, honey. Standing on his feet all day. Cutting hair at the shop. Would park himself right here on his lovely sofa we're sitting on some nights for the whole night. Wouldn't make it up to bed. As much as get up to our bedroom. Some nights. Tired as a log."

"I w-would practically wait on Uncle Frank hand and foot, wouldn't I, Aunt Della? Wouldn't I? When … when he got in from the barbershop each night. Wouldn't I, Aunt Della?"

Della sighs. "That you would, Darlene. And your uncle Frank just loved you for it." Della pauses as if to select her words more carefully.

"What you did for your uncle Frank is … is like what you've done for me over the past few days, Darlene … honey." Della's eyes looked into Darlene's with what seemed a deep, personal reverence.

"It's why I've gathered the Ballad family together this evening. Asked you by the house." Pause. "My strength is back. Not all the way, granted, the full 100 percent back, mind you, but … but I … I'd say 95 percent back. If I were to put it on a scale. Where I'd put it for now. And … and that's good enough, quite good enough for me.

"And so I have all of you to thank for that. Margaret, Lee, you Royal, but … but especially Darlene. Darlene. My dear, sweet Darlene."

Pause.

"Was here in the house for me night and day. Night and day. Made sure I didn't want for anything—nothing. That I did everything right. To a tee. Uh … ate right. Slept right. Took my medication right. Washed me. Dressed me. Nothing … nothing was too big or too small for Darlene." Della kisses Darlene's forehead.

"My sweet, sweet Darlene. Was nothing Darlene wouldn't do for her aunt Della. An angel. Darlene was my Florence Nightingale if … ha … there was ever one. You could find one."

"Thank, thank you, Aunt Della," Darlene said, feigning modesty.

"So, Lee," Della said, looking at Lee, "I'm sending Darlene home. Packing her bags and sending her home. Back to her husband. Her husband. Ha!"

"Back home? Back home! But … but, Aunt Del—"

"No buts. No buts. No, there's no need now. No need for you to stay on now, Darlene. Y-you saw how I took those stairs before. Did with them. Came down them. You saw, Darlene. My legs are under me. Under me. Up under me. Saw for yourself. No, there's no need to stay in the house with me any longer. No need at all.

"You can get back to a normal life again. Get back to your normal routine, honey. You and Lee. Your husband. Being a wife, Darlene."

"But, Aunt, Aunt—"

"Momma, Momma, you're, you're sure, Momma?"

"Yes, Mother Ballad, are you sure?"

"I'm con-concerned too, Aunt, Aunt Della. Concerned—"

Della draws her head back and laughs riotously. "Well, you needn't be, Lee. You needn't be. None of should. Uh-uh. Della Ballad's feeling wonderful. Just great. I don't want to pretend any, 'cause when I took those stairs tonight, this evening, that was for show. To demonstrate how far I've come—me and my ticker. Yes, Della Ballad's feeling wonderful, wonderful—her and her old ticker. My heart.

"And Darlene has put me through a number of paces, 'tests,' I've been calling them, me and my walker, haven't you—"

"But I … have you discussed this with, this decision with Dr. Ives, Aunt—"

"Now, now," Della said patiently, "I don't have to do that, Darlene." Della shook her head. "Uh-uh. None of that, Darlene. Not at my age. I know my body by now, honey. Upside down. Much better than Dr. Ives does. At my age. Been living with it long enough."

"No, Momma, I agree with Darlene. Dr. Ives should be consulted. He—"

"For what, Margaret? I take my pills. And I listen to my body. What it tells me to do. For what, Margaret? Tell me."

Royal, who's been looking at Della, looks at Margaret. "Mag, I think Mother Ballad's right. If anyone's attuned to their body, their spirit, why, it's Mother Ballad."

Della's voice really rings out into the room. "Yes, Royal, I am 'attuned' to my body, my spirit, all right, Royal. As you say. It's the one thing I can say for myself at my age. The one thing positive, darling. Oh, you put it so nicely, sweetly, Royal. So lovely for me, Royal."

"You'll … b-but you'll, r-remember everything, Momma?"

"Margaret, honey, what's there to remember?" Della said with an air of conceit.

"The pills, Momma. Why your pills. To take them on schedule. Thirteen pills on schedule, daily, Momma."

"Oh … them," Della laughed with further conceit. "Them. Ha. They're like second nature to me now … r-right, Darlene?"

Haltingly. "I … I guess, yes, Aunt Della."

Haughtily. "Like clockwork now. Like—I could set every one of these clocks in the house by them by now. All of them to the same time."

"Mother Ballad, why I bet you could."

"Aunt Della, Aunt Della, maybe two days. T-two more days? Two more days in the house with you, Aunt—"

"Darlene, now come on, come on—your aunt Della's all right."

Della turns to Royal again. "Royal, the Lord's not calling me home. I don't think, just yet."

"No, not yet. Just yet, Mother Ballad. God knows when. God and only God knows when. The day has come. Is the only one to know that, Mother Ballad."

Suddenly Della's frowning unpleasantly, uncharacteristically. "But if I don't, me and my walker don't get to the bathroom and out of this living room, and fast, I think there could be a small flood that's gonna take place. Happen here, right here in the living room—and it ain't gonna be pretty.

"Darlene, oh, that iced tea of yours was delicious. And I did drink enough of it I think to know!" Darlene gets up with Della, holding onto her hand and then Della's arm. But gently, Della nudges her hand and arm free.

"I can make it to the bathroom all right, Darlene." Della looks at everyone.

"No, uh-uh, there's no need to worry about me. None, none at all. What, whatsoever." Della smiles. "Don't expect me to run the one-hundred-yard dash with anybody, but I can get to the downstairs bathroom all right. With no trouble."

Somewhat slowly, Della heads off for the bathroom (having sat for a while) steadily.

"Just got to get my muscles warmed up good. My bones heated up again," Della said over her right shoulder. "It's about all. Ha. For me to do."

Then the three heard Della stop when she got to the bathroom door. "Della Ballad's doing okay for herself. This old gal. This old gal. No, you can't keep a good woman down. Not me. Ha!"

They all sat in the living room and listened to the bathroom door, located at the back of the hallway, shut. It's when Darlene, Margaret, and Lee, and Royal sat in silence, each seemingly thinking through their own private thoughts in their own personal, particular way. Family, yes, but almost looking like total strangers who'd gathered together only for the sake of someone else not themselves, by some colossal mistake.

Margaret didn't want to look at Darlene, for she could hear what was inside her, was going on inside her, this cranking, shifting through things, gears, mashing of metal, evaluating—some ruptured demon. And then she thought of Royal. He was here beside her, on the same sofa, to protect her from any open warfare with Darlene, any rattling of swords.

Lee was scratching at his head, some mild irritation happening, the only one who felt neutral, not narrowed, not worn down to self-limitation and bias and exhaustion.

"Oh … uh, now they're talking about another storm, another winter storm heading, that's coming, to come our way. Have you heard about it, Royal? Uh, Margaret? Uh yet? Will … will hit us, they … they say, uh in a—"

"How could you! How could you, Lee! How could you be thinking of such a thing? A winter storm, of all things … of all things when Aunt Della's … sometimes, Lee. Sometimes …"

"Sorry, Darlene, sorry … I'm … I'm sorry, I—"

Darlene's eyes seemed to sink into Royal's like a heavy sword.

"And so, and so … how many souls have you saved today, Royal McCloud? How many!"

"D-Darlene, don't—"

"Be quiet, Lee. Be quiet." Darlene turned back to Royal. "How many conversions today, Royal?"

"I preach the gospel, Darlene. The message. God's message. It's for the people to accept God in their hearts. Into their lives. Who are—"

"Attuned to their spirit, as ... as you put it before, Royal. So aptly, r-reasonably put it before. Just now with Aunt Della. Is that it? Is that how it works? Christianity works, Royal?"

Royal glanced at Margaret, whose head was down.

"Yes. Yes, Darlene, to answer your question. Yes, it's how Christianity works. It's how Christianity manifests itself. How God does his work for those who ... who are willing to accept him into their hearts. Want him in their lives as their personal savior."

Darlene stands, stares at Royal, and then sits back down, crossing her leg, her fingers idling with her slacks, and then looks back over at Royal.

"And you're doing all of this conversion business, all of it's being done from where, Royal, from where? Mr. Tolletson's building? In his basement serving as a church? A church ... My ... my God?"

"Darlene, don't—"

"Stay out of this, Lee! I warned you, Lee!"

"Yes, Darlene. Out of Mr. Tolletson's, the basement of Mr. Tolletson's building."

Darlene's body edges forward on the couch. "It's where God is? Where conversions occur, take place? Getting in tune with your body, your spirit, in the basement of—"

"Of ... of Mr. Tolletson's basement. Yes."

"Ha. 'Hands of Christ Church.'"

Long pause.

"Church, church, your church, Royal McCloud's church in the basement of Mr. Tolletson's junk shop! Mr. Tolletson's junk shop! A junk shop!"

Pause.

"Ha."

"You know, Darlene, God loves you."

Darlene stands. She's halfway between the sofa and Lee and Margaret and Royal.

"I'll ... I'll remember what you said to Aunt Della tonight. T-to my aunt

Della tonight. If it's the last thing I remember, Royal McCloud. I'll remember you—and … and if … if anything happens, should happen to … to my aunt Della, my aunt Della's heart, Royal … Royal McCloud, I'll … I'll remember you, you walking into this house, my aunt Della's house, Royal McCloud, and acting as if you're God. God. Like … like you're God!"

"No, Darlene," Royal said softly. "God is God."

"I'll … I'll hold you responsible if … I'll hold you responsible if … if … anything should happen …," Darlene's body's shaking badly. Lee bolts off the sofa.

"Lee, Lee, yes, hold me, Lee. Hold me, Lee!" And Lee held Darlene. "Just … just hold me!"

There's the one light burning in the bedroom. It's easy to reach; it's the lamp on the nightstand. Della's arm can reach it without any strain on its part. She's been lying there, in her bed, just lying on her back with her eyes wide open, her head back on the white-cased pillow, encased in deep thought.

"I'm home alone …"

Della closed her eyes and then reopened them. "Darlene's not here. But she belongs with Lee. Not me. Darlene's done enough." Pause. "I was working so hard with my therapy for me and Darlene. But don't pin any medals on me, no, I don't want anybody to do that. But it's only right that she's back home with Lee. Her husband." Della looks around the room.

"Only how … how it oughta be. Everybody knows that."

But she missed Darlene the moment she left the room, the house, she missed Darlene. As soon as Lee kissed her, went back, and picked up Darlene's suitcase and Darlene kissed her and hugged her hard, so lovingly and angrily both at the same time and then turned, she wanted to call Darlene back. To say, "Stay." *You can stay, Darlene. Stay on with me. In the house. You don't have to go. You can stay with your aunt Della, in the house with me for another day or two, two days like you said, suggested, Darlene*—and then to see the expression on Darlene's face, just to see that …

"My darling, Darlene. My darling, darling, Darlene."

But it wasn't to be, because her mind had been made up, her work had been done, the physical therapy, the mental therapy; but now she was alone in this big house, and she was feeling it and listening to the steam in the radiator pour out, hiss in the room.

"Frank, Frank. I can always talk to you, Frank. Can't I? Can't I, honey? Whenever I want."

It's how it was when Frank died, talking to him, Frank still keeping her company, even though, in the beginning, other people were trying to fill the void, but no one can do that. No one can give you back the best moments of your life when you've built them with someone you love, who's died, but who's still alive in your heart and soul. How do you explain things to people who don't know? How?

"I'm not talking to a ghost. Don't think, don't ever think I'm talking to a ghost … You're real, Frank. Real. Real as you ever were, Frank. So …

"Darlene's gone. She's gone, as you know. And I feel lonely even with you here. Me talking to you now. It's temporary, I know. I'll adjust, ad—always do, always have. You know me, Frank. Ha. Just give me a day or two, no more—and her and Lee and Margaret will still be running in here every day anyway. In and out. Ain't gonna change. Not that, Frank.

"The house. It's just Darlene won't be staying over. She'll still try to convince me different. Go on and on. How that girl is, our darling Darlene. Didn't she do a wonderful job though, Frank? Just … just wonderful."

Della looked over at the clock on the nightstand. She had two pills to take before retiring for the night, and the bottles were clearly labeled. She wasn't going to forget anything, not unless—she giggled, her mind began going nutty on her, and it wasn't her mind that wasn't healthy, it was her heart … and she was going to keep it that way!

She'd turned on the radio, but as soon turned it off. She'd turned it off when Lee's car, she heard it leave from the house. Margaret and Royal left before Lee and Darlene. It's like they knew their place, like Darlene had to be the last to leave the house, unless they'd all still be sitting in the house, probably in her room, till the bitter end, if need be.

"Till the moon went down." Pause. "My girls. My two beautiful girls. I love them so much. Yet … yet, oh Lord, I don't want to think about it now."

Maybe she was—*yes, I was listening to hear Lee's car. I really was. Listening to hear it leave the house. Can't lie to myself.* And when the radio came on, there was music, but then the interruption about the storm, the impending storm as if Myles Day City had never had a snowstorm before, been under attack. Assault before.

"It's when I turned the radio off for good. For good. Ain't nobody gonna scare me!" Della laughed. "How bad can it get … get anyways? Been living in Myles Day all my natural born life. What can they tell me about snow … I won't be trapped in this house a—and even if I am, it only takes one day or two for everything's … the roads and streets are plowed through, and people start getting around good. Things start moving in the city. Back, get back to normal and … and Darlene, I can always count on Darlene. Darlene would move mountains. She'd find a way to get here. To make sure everything's, her aunt Della … Darlene. Darlene, Frank."

But she had plenty of food in the kitchen pantry. The shelves were stocked high with food. It's how most Myles Day folk lived during the winter, prepared for snowstorms when, for a few days, food deliveries stopped, the snow blocked the trucks. And it was tradition, stretched way back to when Myles Day City wasn't as urban as it was today, but more rural, cut from the ground but evolving into today's modern Myles Day City.

Della reached for her pills, and when she looked at the glass of water, she knew it wasn't as cold as when Darlene put it there, that it was at least room temperature by now, since Darlene had been gone, what seemed like a long time now, like she'd felt her first night when Frank died, but he wasn't really gone, and Darlene wasn't either; there was no reason at all for her to think they were, not even for this her first night alone in the house.

The ride in the car had been a chilly one, not because of Myles Day City's cold, because there was ample heat in the car, but because of Darlene. Lee would look at her and knew not to say anything, to keep his thoughts, opinions to himself. To keep them bottled in his mind if only to hold on to his own sanity, peace of mind. But he'd asked himself, *How can I have peace of mind when Darlene's in such a fit, state—my wife?*

He loved her. How he loved her. He understood her. But at times like this it did him no good. It didn't matter; Lee wasn't good enough to pluck the poison out the heart. Their relationship never worked that way.

Lee and Darlene had just entered their smallish kitchen. Lee helped Darlene with her coat; only, Darlene, seemingly, had her own ideas of how her coat should be handled as she wrested the coat from Lee, throwing it to the kitchen floor. She stared at it as if she were going to stomp it into the floor, through the kitchen tiles, crack them—only, she didn't.

"I should be with Aunt Della tonight! I should be with Aunt Della tonight! Not here! Not here! Not in this house!"

Lee bent over. He picked up the coat off the tiled floor.

"Do you hear me, Lee? Do you hear me!"

Darlene's suitcase was by the kitchen door. Lee laid Darlene's overcoat across his arm. Then Lee, whose body looked disjointed, shifted his body weight disproportionately.

"But Aunt Della, I think her mind was already made up, Darlene. It's what I think. How I—"

"Made up? Already made up? Do you think Aunt—"

"And you know how hard it … difficult it is to budge Aunt Della, o-over anything when, once her mind's made up, gets made up about something, Darlene. How stubborn she is, can be. Get. Is … is. Aunt … Aunt Della."

Darlene walked over to the kitchen chair; her body slumps down in it. "It was Royal. That Royal McCloud. It was him. Him. He had to be there tonight. By the house tonight. That Royal McCloud."

Lee approached Darlene, walked forward, and then stopped a few steps short of her. "Maybe Royal did say what … what Aunt Della wanted, just wished to hear, Darlene. Maybe Royal did say—but sometimes you've gotta, have to—Royal was only doing what he thought was right to do, Darlene. B-best.

"When someone's already made up their mind like … like Aunt Della had, then sometimes it's better to go, just go along with them, sort of … sort of with the flow. E-encourage them when … when you know … you know, Darlene, when they're just going to wind up doing it anyway, their way anyway, Darlene. Do it—"

"What do you know, Lee? Lee Winston! What the hell do you know about any of this!"

"I … I—"

"She's my aunt! Aunt Della's my aunt, not yours!" Darlene screamed, banging her fists down on the kitchen table. "My aunt! My aunt! Not, I … I know what's best for my aunt, not … not you or … or a … a Royal McCloud!" Then Darlene catches her breath.

"Had … had to … had to show his face back in Myles Day City again. Didn't he? Didn't he? Him and Margaret. Him and Margaret. Hypocrites! Damned hypocrites! The two of them. The two of them. But … but especially … especially Royal McCloud—passing himself off as a minister. As … as a minister now. T-these days. Rev. Royal McCloud. Rev. Royal McCloud. When we know, when everybody living in Myles Day City … ha … knows … knows what Royal McCloud is. Pimp … pimping for the Lord now. Pimping for—"

"He's trying. Royal's trying, Darlene. The man is h-honestly trying, Darlene," Lee said forcibly.

Darlene scoffs at what Lee said. "Trying. Trying. He … he and Margaret aren't even married. Aren't even married, man and wife. Living under the same roof. Ha. He's married to another woman. H-has a child by her. Royal McCloud's committing adultery in the eyes of God, God and man!"

"You … you can't say that, Darlene. You … you—"

"Why can't I? Why can't I! Why, why the hell can't I! Who—"

"B-because, because of circumstances. The s-situation. W-why Royal's—"

"You think so? You think so, huh? Huh? Well tell that to … ha … the folk who live in Myles Day City. Tell them. They know what a minister is when they see one. Ha. They know what one looks like. How he should look. They know how a minister should conduct his private life, his … his affairs, should live his life—by example. By what's in the Bible, Lee. What Royal McCloud preaches every … every Sunday morning from the Bible. Why should you have to make excuses for a minister, for a man who's supposed to be a man of God. Touched by God. Serving God. Touched by the Holy Spirit. Chosen by God to lead, to represent him. To set an example. Example. To … to be a spiritual leader. Royal McCloud is a hypocrite. Hypocrite living in his own sin. You hear me. You hear me, Lee. Ha. Ha. That's what he's doing. Sin. Sin. Living in his own sea of sin. Self-righteous. Self-righteous. Ooh … how I hate Royal McCloud. How I hate him! And … and if something happens, should happen, if anything should happen to … to Aunt Della … If … if something should happen to Aunt Della, my aunt Della, Lee, he's … he's to blame. Royal McCloud … Royal McCloud's to blame."

Lee steps back and then turns and looks down at the suitcase on the kitchen floor.

"Let … let me take the, this, uh, suitcase up … up to the bedroom, Darlene. I'll—"

Lee bends over to pick up the suitcase.

"Ha ... Royal McCloud. Royal McCloud. Rev. Royal McCloud. Well ... well that'll never happen in Myles Day City. Never, Lee. Never. Ha. And Margaret, Margaret, that fool cousin of mine Margaret, falling in love with someone, a silver-tongued liar ... liar—ph-phony. A con artist like Royal McCloud. Ha. My cousin. My cousin, Lee."

Lee's body's shaking. "It's nice to have you back ... back home, in the house, Darlene. I mean it's nice that Aunt Della no longer needs you to ... Feels she no longer needs you. It's no longer necessary you stay, for you to stay with her at the house now. Any ... anymore."

Darlene looks blankly out into space.

"That church is going to fail. Fail. Fail. Fall on its face. Fold. Fold like tissue paper. Ha. Ha. Ha. I'm telling you, I'm telling you, Lee. It's not going to catch on. Nobody's going to worship there, just that meager bunch of nobodies who go there now. It's going to fail, Lee. Baby." Darlene's looking over at Lee now. "Fail. Wait, you wait and see ... see. Mark my words, Lee. I'm telling you. Mark my words. Just mark ... mark my words. Why ... why it's in a basement. B-basement. A church in a basement. Ha. A basement, Lee. A damned basement, Lee! For god's sake. Worshipping in a base ... beneath a junk shop! Tom Tolletson's junk shop! For God's sake. Ha. Ha. Ha!" Pause. "Everybody knows what it is. Everybody—"

"I know. I ... I know." Lee looks down at the suitcase he's holding, but his hands are still shaking, so the free one he sticks in his pocket.

"Because it's not meant to be, Lee. Not a church. Not a church. None ... none of this is meant to be. None ... none of it's, this ... this is meant to be. Not in God's eyes, Lee. Not in God's eyes. God does, doesn't want it ... it ... t-to find—God in a junk shop, Lee? In a junk shop! B-beneath Tom, Tom Tolletson's junk shop, Lee! Because it's not to be. God doesn't want Royal McCloud to preach to him. Not that church, not Royal McCloud, him a pastor, a spiritual leader. Ha. It's why ... why it doesn't have ..." And it's when Darlene looks at Lee, who's suddenly holding a cigarette in his hand and is about to strike it.

"You've been smoking. You've been smoking. You've been smoking in the house while I've been gone! While I've been gone! Out the house! At Aunt Della's! Staying at Aunt Della's! You've been smoking, haven't you, Lee! Haven't you!"

"Darlene, I ... I—"

"You know you don't smoke in the house! You know you don't smoke in my house. You know that! No smoking in D-Darlene Winston's house! That's law! That's law! It … it's like Aunt Della's house. No smoking in Aunt Della's house. My … my house is run like Aunt Della's house! My house is run like Aunt Della's!" Darlene's fists pound the kitchen table repeatedly, violently. She's crying, sobbing. "My house is run like Aunt Della's. My, my aunt Della's house. My … my aunt Della's house … house …"

Lee turns and opens the kitchen's back door, which leads out onto the short back porch and then the backyard.

Lee closes the kitchen door behind him.

Even when he fell asleep, he didn't want to. And when he'd fall asleep, just for those short, brief periods, times, spurts, it'd become his ally, Darlene would wake him again. It was her movements, her physical movements, not her breathing or any other aspect, only her movements, her physical movements in the bed that would disturb his sleep, wake him back up, only for him to drift back into sleep again. But no words had been exchanged between them. No dialogue, just the two and a half hours they'd been in bed packed in silence.

What could he say, he'd thought. He'd said it all in the kitchen, shot his wad, his load, counting on the words in him to count for something. But even then, before he'd said what he'd said to Darlene, he knew there was no way to win—to come out the other end of this thing, on the other side of the ledger with any kind of victory.

Not against Darlene.

He heard her fingernails scratch into the sheet as if he were in the bed with rats. Lying in the bed with rats beside him. A nest of them. Why he thought of that, made that kind of stark, impressionistic connection, Lee didn't know—had no idea. But it felt, at the time, like some kind of lunacy in the bed, some kind of sickness, perversion, some kind of desperate disorder of the spirit—but that of a human, his wife, not an animal, something as hated, despised, feared as a rat. But his body was rigid at the sound of Darlene's fingernails scratching into the sheet as if he turned to her he would be a part of the same lunacy, he would be acknowledging it, highlighting it, advancing it, owning it as much as her.

Only, he really didn't know his feelings. He loved her. He loved Darlene.

And Darlene was hurting. Hurting bad. And he knew she only needed him when she wanted to need him. When she was on the brink of collapse, but not before. She always felt she had to be strong enough to stand up to the next wave no matter how tall or frightening it was. How hard it hit her. Fight her way. The only way she knew how, found comfortable.

How did he know how she became this way? How?

She stopped. She stopped. She stopped scratching the sheet. Actually stopped. Her fingernails. But for how long? Lee thought. For how long? His body relaxed. He eased his breath out now; he felt better.

His forehead unknotted. He could feel it. *I can touch it. I think I can touch it now. I bet it feels smooth. Yes, yes, it does. It does feel smooth. My forehead does. Maybe I can fall back to sleep now, again, lie here and, I don't know, I mean ... I mean it's what I've been doing for the last, past ... I don't know, I don't care. It doesn't matter. Doesn't even matter. Mr. Baker, the job—I am the best printer he has, like Darlene always says I am. I can say that much about myself, be proud about that. It's nice when your wife thinks like that. Nice. I mean that Darlene should think like that, about me. About her husband.*

She said it again tonight in Aunt Della's dining room, at the dining room table, in front of everyone. Aunt Della and Margaret and Royal. Said I was the best printer Mr. Baker has. Has got. Best one in the shop. That Lee—

"Lee! Lee! I can't sleep with you tonight! I can't sleep in this bed with you tonight, Lee!"

"B-but, Darlene, Darlene," Lee said, shocked, twisting his body in the bed to her.

"Not tonight! Not tonight!" Her voice was shrill. "I can't, cant, I can't, Lee!"

And Lee saw Darlene's slender figure in the dark explode off the bed and watch her snatch her pillow and hug it into her flat-formed chest. She stood there in the dark as if her hair had been mangled, had been blown out its rollers, out the nightcap on her head, her hair standing wild like scared straw if exposed, not satin capped.

"Darlene, Darlene—"

"I can't sleep in this bed with you tonight, Lee. I can't. I-I've got to be alone. I've got to be alone."

And then there was silence between them.

"Yes, yes, Darlene." And Lee turned from Darlene, for he didn't want to see her demons. He could only do so much, he thought, for so long. He just heard her run out the room, not heavy, for she wasn't a heavy-made person, not a person whose bones were made of iron or stone, but light, light as a stick, a switch—as a twig.

Darlene was in the dark, lying on the couch in the house's tight-quartered living room. She was downstairs. She had to get as far away from people, anybody, as she could. Downstairs was her best place, was the best solution. She'd gone to the linen closet and gotten out a sheet and blanket; she already had her pillow. She did this, all of this in the dark. Walked through the house in the dense dark.

"I do that in Aunt Della's house too," Darlene said, lying on her back, her eyes open. "At night, to check on Aunt Della. I … I didn't need a light in the hall, not anywhere. But I did leave a light on in Aunt Della's bedroom. Back … back in the corner of the room. Dim, a mild light in Aunt Della, my aunt Della's bedroom at night."

It's where she was supposed to be from the moment her aunt Della was discharged from St. Bartholomew by Dr. Ives; it's where she was supposed to be, Darlene thought—in her aunt Della's house, taking care of Aunt Della. Taking care of Aunt Della.

It's all she could think of now, taking care of her aunt Della. They were such magic together, were such a team, worked so exquisitely, delightfully together.

Darlene, Darlene, honey.

Yes, Aunt Della. Aunt Della.

No matter the day, the night, they worked exquisitely, delightfully together.

But now it'd been interrupted, the whole damned thing had been interrupted. And she wasn't angry at her aunt Della (how could she be), only at Royal McCloud. Royal McCloud.

"And Margaret, Margaret, weak-kneed Margaret. Why didn't she put Royal McCloud in his place? Why? If … if it were Lee, if it were Lee … She's pathetic, Margaret Ballad's pathetic …"

Darlene rubbed at her eyes.

"I don't want to sleep, why should I? I just want to be with … the first thing in the morning. The first thing in … I'm back, but Lee's still going to have to fix his own breakfast. Yes. Yes, that's right. That's right. I'll be up at five o'clock. Off this couch, damned couch at five o'clock. If I disturb Lee or not, I don't care. He gets up at six thirty. If I make too much noise, I don't care. Why should I? And he won't say anything anyway, Lee. Not Lee. He knows, he'll know. My ... my precious Lee will know. And he won't have to drive me to Aunt Della's. Lee won't have to do that. See, see, Lee, Lee, you won't have to do that, baby. I'll call a taxi. A taxi—it's what I'll do. And Lee can sleep. He'll just have to fix breakfast before he goes to work, Mr. Baker's, I won't fix breakfast for him—but that's something he's been doing since ... since ... Oh, oh, I can't wait until five o'—what time is it now, what time. B-but I can't get up. I ... I can't get up, off my back. I don't have the strength. Right now. Right ... I don't have the strength to. But I don't need to know the time now or ... or need an alarm clock. No, not me. Not me. Ha. Ha. Ha. I'll know when five o'clock comes, a-arrives, comes around. I'll dress, go upstairs and dress and ... and then call the taxi company. Aunt Della gets up around the same time as Lee. It's what's so good about it, never had to adjust to the time. Lee and Aunt Della get up around the same time. It ... it made it easy for me. The whole time I was ... Aunt Della's house. Aunt Della's house. I'll be back in Aunt Della's house. And I'll use my key. She won't even know I'm there, until I come through the bedroom door with breakfast. And then, still after she eats, she'll have to take her three pills, all in a row, in succession. Yes. Yes. And Aunt Della will think I never left the house, that she sent me home with, to be with Lee last night? *You didn't stay in the house? In your room last night, did you? Did you, Darlene? Against my wishes, did you? Did you, Darlene? You did go home to your husband, with Lee, honey.* And I'll say. And I'll say ... I ... I don't know what I'll say. Just what I'll say," Darlene said, closing her eyes. "To my aunt Della when ... when she asks. When ... when the time comes. I don't know what I'll say. I don't. I don't, I ..."

CHAPTER 6

Royal was standing at the back of the room.

"Rev. McCloud, you really heated up the room this morning. Tru-ly."

"Why thanks, Brother James."

"I couldn't agree more with my husband, Rev. McCloud. I was moved."

Royal shook Mr. James and Mrs. James's hand. "I guess when your sermon is centered around your favorite Bible scripture, the one, as a child, meant more to you than any other…"

William James was helping his wife with her fur coat.

"And oh, about the heat, Mr. Tolletson did have it turned up rather high this morning, didn't he?" Royal chuckled.

"Felt downright toasty in here."

Royal chuckles again. "So it just wasn't the sermon, Mrs. James?"

"No"—Irene James laughed— "sometimes my toes do get cold. No matter how well you preach, Rev. McCloud. You heat things up in here."

"But not this morning—"

"Mr. Tolletson's heat warmed your toes, Irene. That's it, huh?"

"Correct, William."

"Praise the Lord!" Royal roared.

"We just love you, Pastor McCloud!"

"Now may I have a piece of him, Sister Irene?" Madeline Steward said. She rushed up to Royal, hugging him. "We do love you, Rev. McCloud."

75

Madeline Steward was a woman in her early seventies, black as coffee, and with a hug Royal still felt in the middle of his spine.

"It's good to have knowledge, education—because books are our best allies—but you still have to get what you've got to say across, communicate it well to people."

Madeline Stewart was very tall, so she said all of what she said practically looking Royal dead in his light-brown eyes. "That hasn't changed since Jesus walked the earth. And from what I hear, my spies tell me"—she winked at Royal—"it's just what he did. Jesus."

Margaret, who stood behind Mrs. Steward along with the Jameses laughed aloud.

"You were born to preach. Communicate the word. Spread God's gospel, Rev. McCloud. Born to do it. Without a doubt in my mind or ... soul either."

And then Madeline Steward looked around the short slender-structured room with no more than thirty chairs lined up in a row, crammed together, six to a row, three on each side of the aisle, five rows. There's enough room though for a raised wooden makeshift platform, where a slim wooden pulpit stands with simplicity and appeal.

"I don't care how small this church is. I've been a part of bigger ones in Myles Day. So it doesn't matter to me, big or small. Good work is good work. And good work is being done here, Rev. McCloud. The kind God likes to see. It feels honest. With no strings attached.

"I like being here every Sunday morning. You and Margaret and the rest of the people here—we're building something. It'll grow. We've just got to keep working at it by doing our part."

"Yes, we—"

"Let me finish, Rev. McCloud, uh, if you will ..."

"Oh, sorry, Mrs.—"

"And I like building things from start to finish. From the ground up. And we're going to build our way out this basement. I have that much faith in God, in what I see is happening in my midst. We're building outward and upward. Expanding our sights. And nobody's going to stop us. I don't see how we can fail, do you, Rev. McCloud!?"

"No, I can't Sister Steward. Not with that ringing endorsemen, I certainly cannot."

"No, there's no doubt in my mind this church will succeed. Is finding its legs."

The Jameses had left the room, but Madeline Steward lingered. She's chatting with Margaret while Royal has apparently gone off to other things in Hands of Christ Church.

"Della, your mother, I spoke to her just Friday."

"Oh, you did, Mrs. Steward? I—"

"You mean she didn't mention it to you?" Mrs. Steward said tongue-in-cheek.

"Uh …"

"Ha. Oh well, she called me. So now I owe Della a call. And she sounded wonderful, even though your mother, Della, always sounds wonderful. Her spirit doesn't seem to change, does it? It's remarkable."

"No, through everything, Momma doesn't let it. It is remarkable, Mrs. Steward."

"It's a special gift she has. I live in a big house too. And most of my family has scattered, is off in other parts of the country on their own. And with Mr. Steward deceased, the similarities of our lives to one another— marriage, family, and our spouses passing on, your mother and I have bonded wonderfully. Through our mutual life experiences."

Margaret agrees.

"It's why … Been in the church all my life, Margaret. Since little. Sunday school. And I've seen ministers come and go. Churches expand, and churches contract. But I was telling Della, your mother, Friday past, that I'm happy here. At Hands of Christ Church."

"And Della says she believes in Rev. McCloud. So much in him too. What he's doing. He's been on the other side of the moon, Margaret. So to speak. One might say. The two of you have. So when he preaches something … it's heartfelt … and meaningful.

"You know it comes from something, from great depth of his understanding of life. Something I was getting at before. When Mr. and Mrs. James were present."

Pause.

"Ha. I told Della how I love how he prays. And she said, 'I don't know if this is right, Madeline, if there's such a word, but Royal's the best "prayer maker" I've ever heard pray. Been in the company of.'"

"Momma … she, Momma said that, Mrs. Steward? That about Royal, Mrs.—"

"Now would I say, make up such a thing, Margaret, if you mother didn't?" Mrs. Steward then leaned into Margaret's ear. "And he's handsome too. To boot. It's another reason why I enjoy coming to church every Sunday morning. Ha. To church."

Margaret and Mrs. Steward turned their heads and looked at Royal, and when he finally noticed them looking at him, he wondered why in the world they were staring at him like they were.

"It doesn't hurt, Margaret, to be handsome and be able to pray and preach either!"

All of this was whispered excitedly, breathlessly, but now Mrs. Steward was back in full charge of her warm contralto voice.

"I'm going to keep trying to bring people to the church, Margaret. Swell up the pews. Force Rev. McCloud out of here through the sheer force of numbers. That's what's going to be my mission, Margaret."

Margaret wasn't going to say anything about Royal and Mr. Houston, the plans brewing with Municipal Union Bank. Even though it was church business, Royal was acting covertly, for there were only two church officers—Mr. Houston and his wife—and Royal didn't want to risk embarrassment if the bank loan at Municipal fell through.

"Well, let me get home. Get started. You see, Margaret, last night, I baked honeyed ham for myself."

"You did, Mrs. Steward?"

"I've got my own recipe—that I'm not sharing!"

"Not even with me, Mrs. Steward? Not—"

"No. No. Ha …" Then Mrs. Steward hugged Margaret. "Does Della know how lucky she is to have a daughter like you?"

Margaret had no idea of how to respond to such a startling comment.

"Then again, it's all she talks about—is you, anyway."

Margaret's body drew back. "S-she, Momma—"

"The snow, it's supposed to get here, hit us, by, oh, uh, this evening, isn't it?"

"I, yes …"

"I believe so. But I wish they could be more specific. More to, up to the minute," Mrs. Steward said. "Not that I'm going anywhere tonight. Not with *60 Minutes* on TV. My television set and I are stuck on CBS. Channel 8 tonight."

Mrs. Steward turned back to Royal. "God bless you, Rev. McCloud."

"God bless you, Sister Steward."

"See you next Sunday. God willing."

"You don't have to worry about that, Mrs. Steward. God doesn't need you in his 'marching band.' Its drum major—not just yet."

"Not with you praying over me, Rev. McCloud."

"Let me walk you to your car, Mrs. Steward."

"Not without your overcoat, Margaret."

Margaret ran for her coat and then was back.

"You know they were wrong the last time out the box. They didn't get it right."

"Uh … pardon me, Mrs. Steward?"

"About the weather. Those 'weather predictors,' Margaret."

"Oh."

"I, you see, I don't call them weathermen anymore. I call them weather predictors—made up a new word for them!" Pause. "I guess you get new words for things when you reach my age. Fuel the imagination. Della coined the word 'prayer maker,' your mother, Margaret, and now I've got 'weather predictor.' Not bad, huh, Margaret?"

Royal stood at the pulpit with the Bible in his hand and looked at the left wall and then over to the basement's right wall, and at times he did feel confined down in Mr. Tolletson's small basement, as if no light would ever shine through, down into the basement—even in the summer. And he was only being honest with himself in the Lord's house, he thought. And he knew God wouldn't mind that, if he chose to be honest with himself. Candid with himself, search his soul.

"After all, I do have a vision to want to serve. Give serious aspiration, outlook to. I have goals. Set in my mind. For … for I have to do, must do more in Myles Day than what I'm doing. And yes, that means touching more souls. Touching more lives. Bring more people to God. Into the church. Into the fold.

"Hands of Christ Church. And people, Christian folk, I don't care who they are, want a more attractive setting, more appealing place to worship than this one. Why shouldn't they? Why shouldn't I? There's no reason for me not to court that thought. Ambition. For me not to trust myself with it."

He didn't want to think that thinking beyond these walls, Mr. Tolletson's basement, was thinking too big. To think that a junk shop above his head was below him. When he preached, he never felt he was in a junk shop, that Mr. Tolletson's storage room was above him, full of current inventory, boxes, equipment, and junk. And above that floor was Mr. Tolletson's official junk shop, not shiny, not new, but a fixture, the store having been there at 69 Sullivan Street for so long. No, when he preached the Gospel on Sunday morning, he never thought of where he was, for he didn't think at all. He was so intense in his preaching, stirred in a spirit of the divine, felt such a spiritual uplift, blissful, such a flurry of words, the comingling of Jesus's hope and God's light, that he, oftentimes, thought he had touched heaven's heart.

It's how he brought himself to each sermon, that it would do as much good for him as it would for the congregants he preached to. That he needed his words, the taste of them, the feel of them, the incantation of those words he preached as much as they did. That he believed in those words as much as they, his congregants, did. He knew he didn't have to stand in a field of gold to feel rich.

"But to be taken seriously," Royal said, sitting in the chair, the pastor's chair just behind the pulpit, "you always have to, must strive to do better than what it seems you're doing."

Royal shut his eyes.

"Tired, Royal?"

Royal hopped out the chair.

"No, Mag, not at all."

"I walked Mrs. Steward to her car, and we—"

"Talked."

"Mostly, uh, Mrs. Steward. But—"

"When you listen to someone like Mrs. Steward, Mag, you're listening to wisdom."

"Experience."

"Earned wisdom." Pause. "And she doesn't lecture, because she's got every confidence in what she's telling you."

"It's why I enjoy talking to her so much."

"Besides her great sense of humor."

"I think people of her generation had a better sense of humor than those of ours do. How do you feel, Royal?"

Royal thought through Margaret's remark.

"You just might be right about that. Hit upon something there, Mag." Then Royal stepped down from the platform. "I wonder why?"

"Humor can be shaped by hardship."

"Yes, and more than that, even appreciation. Sister Steward is a child of the Great Depression—she's seen much worse than the hardships we'll ever see or possibly know."

"It's why I feel so encouraged when she says we'll make it, Royal. What you're doing as a minister in this church."

Margaret walks down the aisle toward Royal.

"She's in our corner, all right. Sister Steward. The few folk who do worship here are in our corner."

Royal's arm's around Margaret's waist and hers around his.

"But Mrs. Steward's faith in us, Royal, is special."

"Ha. Very. It sticks out like a sore thumb." Royal kissed Margaret's cheek. "Just wish …"

"What?"

"I wish Sister Steward had invited us by for Sunday dinner, that's all. That honeyed ham of hers sure sounded mouthwatering."

"It's what I thought when she mentioned it."

"Two empty stomachs think alike, I guess."

"I just hope … ha … Mrs. Steward didn't see my eyes. They didn't betray me any."

"I shut mine when she said it, Mag, and dreamed."

"I couldn't."

"I know."

Pause.

"Oh, by the way, Mrs. Steward thinks you're handsome."

"And I think she's gorgeous."

"Oh, I didn't expect that, Royal. Not that kind, that answer from you."

"Ha."

"I just hope I look as good as Mrs. Steward when I'm her age."

"Don't worry, Mag. You will."

"You really think so?"

"Of course. You'll have Mother Ballad's genes to work with. To thank for that. She'll pass her golden crown from herself to—"

"Royal, I think it's time to—"

"Why, Mag, when I was just getting—"

"Royal, we're having pot roast for dinner."

"It sounded good this morning ..."

"Not until Mrs. Steward—"

"Mentioned her honeyed ham."

"When you start feeling snow in your bones, you know you're getting old."

Della had moved a chair in the bedroom to the bedroom window, and the drape was pushed back, and she was sitting in the chair and looking out the window. Moving the chair to the window was easy on her; she just pushed it along from behind like she was using it as a walker, and it was only maybe ten to twelve feet away—nothing more. This was good stuff, she thought, sitting at the window and waiting for the snow to come. The first snowflake to fall out the sky.

"Oh, I feel alive. I feel alive today. This Sunday evening."

And Darlene and Lee were by the house. She and Darlene cooked. And Margaret had called. And she spoke to Royal. And they prayed together over the phone. Prayed and prayed.

"Oh, it's a good day. A good day for me. And Madeline Steward, she could make a bullfrog sing and sound good. Margaret told me how Madeline just keeps that church going with her positive motivation. Her positive faith in what Royal's doing there. She's been a witness since joining Royal's church. And baked, uh, her honeyed baked ham always sounds better than mine. And to this day, I don't know why. And ain't a reason why, to why, it crosses my mind!"

Della wiggled her backside some more in the chair to make herself feel even more comfortable. She was going to be as stubborn as a hurricane. When that first snowflake fell out the sky, when she made her first sighting, she was going to jump with joy.

"I want to see a real Myles Day storm. Not a timid one. Not the little one, bitty one that crept, sneaked in here before. Just a few weeks back. I want to see a real Myles Day snowstorm. One that means something. Stands for something," Della laughed. "Make you shake in your boots. Ha. Snow boots!"

The wind would have to pick up steam outside though, would really have to begin to blow, and things were mild now, Della thought. Not real storm conditions.

"But the wind can pick up at any time. Start stirring things around out there. Come from out the northeast pretty good. Uh, fast.

"Oh, Frank, Frank would run out there, in and out the garage—get an early start on things, the walkway with his shovel, but when he came back in the house, he looked like a snowman. White as a ghost!" Pause. "Then go back out for more. To shovel the driveway."

Those were the good old days, Della thought. Frank and her and Myles Day City winters. Cold winters, snowy winters, part and parcel of living in Myles Day, a part of the landscape. And here she was, about to witness another Myles Day City storm. To have lived so long. To now live each day so powerfully, so wonderfully.

Two pills to go, and then she'd fulfill her thirteen-pill quota for the day. Those pills were still keeping her alive. Her family, the pills, knowing Myles Day City was still in charge of herself, in command of tradition—this sure, balanced rhythm, continuum.

It made her feel strong, as positive as Madeline Steward, Della thought. Winters don't defeat you, only your mind, your spirit. There's the challenge, she thought. To keep the mind focused on each day as though it promised you something. As though it had your name on it and would rise or fall as dreams or failures do. For she was trying to erect events out of her days, occasions. Grabbing on to them like wildflowers, for they couldn't defeat her. For one wouldn't look like the other, lose their color, for they wouldn't look as pale as ghosts. This was her great fear in getting old. This is what haunted her mind in St. Bartholomew Hospital's hospital bed. When she was weak, she thought, if she lived, recovered, pulled through, she'd become an invalid, beyond repair, disabled to a point where she would have a fear of living and it would weaken her more, like a disease.

She felt like a fox with a plan, always a plan, always a way to make the days softer, kinder for herself. She was so close to something, and she could feel it, but she wanted to fight this battle to the end, stand up to it, challenge it—even though she knew she wouldn't, couldn't win. And the fight removed the fear, not the reality. And it's all she could hope for, she thought. All—

"Come on, snow. Come on. If you're coming. Hurry up and get here. I'm ready for you. I can't wait all night. Sit here in the chair and wait for you all night now." Pause. "To fall. Fall ..."

"Nine days before Thanksgiving. Nine more days and it'll be here. Another Thanksgiving with ... spent with my family. Another one to snatch off the calendar. Ain't that something, Frank? Ain't that something? Oh ... Frank ... Ha ..."

Della was at the window asleep in the chair. Snow fell fast and furious out the sky. A strong wind blew in Myles Day City, outside the house's windows. The city's really bad winter storms were accompanied by brutal, pulverizing winds. Winds that rattled windows, turning the city, in general, into a wind tunnel—a dangerous landscape during its relentless fury.

But Della was sleeping through this fast-developing, nimble white beast, wasn't awake to see the first snowflake descend from the sky. She'd waited and waited. But it was snowing now for the past fifteen minutes. Maybe she would sleep in the armchair she was in for the night, not wake until daybreak, daylight.

But then there was a huge ruckus in the house.

"Aunt Della!" Darlene screamed. "Aunt Della! I'm here, Aunt Della! I'm here, Aunt Della!"

Della's head, which was slumped, snapped out of it. "Who ... what ... uh ... huh ...?"

"Aunt Della! Aunt Della!"

Della looked out the window and saw the fat snowflakes slashing across the window and then recognized Darlene's voice again, for she'd called her name again, her voice drawing nearer her, Della now realizing she'd fallen asleep—plain and simple.

"Aunt Della! Aunt Della, there you are, Aunt Della!"

Darlene ran over to Della. Della extended her arms out in receiving her.

"We got here as fast as we could, Aunt Della. As fast as we could, me and Darlene, Aunt Della."

"Thank you, Lee. Thank you."

"Oh, Aunt Della. Aunt Della. I ... I was so ... wor—I ... I ... I came as soon as the first snowflake fell—fell out the sky, Aunt Della."

"The one I wanted to see so bad," Della laughed. "Was sitting in my chair waiting for."

"It's why you're sitting in front of the window, Aunt Della? The reason why, Aunt—"

"It's obvious, Lee. It's obvious, isn't it?"

"Yes, Lee, my sweet peach. Uh-huh." Pause. "Come over. Let me hug you."

"Aunt Della, Lee's full of snow. Look at him ..."

"Uh ..."

"He's full of snow. His coat. Hat."

"Sh-should've taken it off down—"

"But you're not staying. You've got to get back. Back to the house, Lee."

"But, Darlene, it's dangerous out there, the way the wind's blowing, howling and all, honey."

"It's ... it looks worse than it is, Aunt Della. Really is. Much," Darlene said, walking over to the window, looking out.

"Oh."

"Darlene's right. There's no need to worry about me, Aunt Della. It's in, the storm's in its early stages. It's—"

"Aunt Della. Aunt Della. Your pills, Aunt Della—did you sleep through your pills? D-did you?"

"Oops," Della said, covering her mouth. "Sure did, Darlene. S-sure did."

"Aunt Della ..."

"Was waiting for the snow," Della said, looking at Lee, begging his sympathy. "Must've gotten too comfortable in the chair, Lee."

"That can hap—"

"Well, I'm going to make sure you take them. Lee, can you go and get Aunt Della a glass of water? Out the bathroom, baby. Do that for me."

"Gladly, Darlene. Gladly, Darlene, Aunt Della."

"Thanks, Lee."

Darlene smiles at Della. "You were waiting for the snow to fall, Aunt Della? Really?"

"Ha. Dead set on it. How I was—it's what I was doing. Looking forward to it. As long as I don't have to shovel it, I—"

"Lee'll do that."

"What will I do?" Lee said, getting back into the room. "Darlene?"

"Shovel the snow."

"Gladly. Oh, gladly. As usual," Lee said, handing Darlene the glass of water. "I love that snowmobile in the garage, Aunt Della."

"Bought it just for you, Lee. Especially for you."

"Can't wait to crank it up. Get it going."

"Now here, Aunt Della."

"Thanks, Darlene," Della said, taking the pills.

"Three."

"Three."

"Lee," Darlene said, turning to Lee, "the suitcase is in my room? You put it there?"

"You bet, Darlene."

"You'd better get going then. I don't want anything to happen to my baby. Out there on the wet roads tonight. All that snow coming down. On the roads."

"There won't. You know I know how to drive, maneuver around in the snow. And the car's been winterized. Took care of …"

Della was swallowing her third pill.

"… that two weeks ago. I—"

"That' right, baby," Darlene said, kissing Lee's cheek. "Lee."

"And now you come over here, Lee. Sweet peach."

"But … but, Aunt Della. Lee's not dry. He's—"

"Lee's dry enough for me. For my liking—right, Lee? Sweet peach?"

"Right, Aunt Della. Right."

"Just want him to kiss me, Darlene." Della laughs. "He doesn't have to grab me. Hold onto me tight, right, Lee?" Pause. "Right here," Della said, pointing to her forehead. "And if you drip a little snow on me, it's all right—won't mind a bit. Not a bit, Lee."

Lee stood in front of Della, leaned over, and kissed her forehead. "Now that's the best I've felt all day. All day!"

"Me too, Aunt Della. Me too."

"Had no idea who was coming into the house. Was out of it. Flat out of it. Fell asleep right here in the chair. And when I heard your voice, thought I was hearing angels singing, Darlene."

"But it wasn't … ha … I was yelling, Aunt Della. Aunt Della. My voice was shrill. It—"

"Well it sounded like angels to me, not till I came around, my head cleared—saw you and Lee charging in here. The bedroom. At me."

Della takes Lee's hand, looks out the window again, and then up to Lee.

"And, Lee, you'd better get on home in the car like Darlene said. The snow is beginning to quarrel, talking about angels, with the angels. It's waging a furious battle out there!"

Lee's over with Darlene. "Forehead, Lee. Forehead, like you did, uh, just did Aunt Della. Forehead, Lee. My forehead."

Lee kisses Darlene's forehead.

"Now you call, sweet peach. You call. As soon as you get in. Know you got home safe."

"Yes, ma'am. Yes, Aunt Della. I'll call. Call right away, Aunt Della. Soon as I—"

"Soon as you open the door. Foot hits the floor."

"Just as soon, Aunt Della."

"Ha."

"Even though you're going to be in bed, Aunt Della. By then. You'll be tucked in bed good and tight by then."

"No, Darlene, no, no, I—"

"No, Aunt Della, y-you should be in bed. At this hour of the night. You should be in bed getting your rest—nowhere else."

"Good night."

"Good night, Lee," Della said.

"Good night."

"Y-yes, good night."

Lee exits the room.

Darlene's over with Della. Della struggles to stand (she was sitting in the chair for so long). Darlene hugs her, not as if she were steadying her, just sweetly.

"It's a good thing I came. Had Lee drive me to the house. Got here, Aunt Della."

"Yes."

"Those three pills are important."

"Very, Darlene. Very. And who knows when I would've awoken," Della said. She and Darlene walked over to the bed. "And listen to that wind, the windows. Whoa ... sounds like a Myles Day City winter storm all right. Brewing. Building steam. Up steam."

Della's helped into bed.

"Oh ..."

The phone rings. Both turn to look at it.

"Lee couldn't've gotten home that fast, no matter how much he winterized the car."

"No, Aunt Della. No."

Darlene braces herself and picks up the phone.

"Hello ... Margaret. Yes, I had Lee drive me over to the house. I'm here. Here with Aunt Della. Hold on. Hold on. Aunt Della ..."

Darlene hands Della the telephone.

*   *   *

The great snowstorm had dumped thirty-three inches of fresh snow on Myles Day City's grounds in three quarters of a day of remarkable snow-making. But between Mother Nature and her cleanup abilities and Myles Day City's crack Department of Sanitation, the snow, after one week, was a mild memory for Myles Day City's citizenry. And so now they would brace themselves once more for the two or three more grand-scale snowstorms to hit Myles Day City before March winds blew in spring's fragrant flowers.

A lot had happened since the night of the snowstorm. For instance, Mr. Houston had restructured the loan request at Municipal Union Bank via the bank's recommendation. The loan amount was reduced upon the advice of the bank, and Mr. Houston, John Houston himself, had signed as a cosigner for the loan, subjecting his personal assets to possible lien status.

Royal was annoyed but decided to keep the faith. That it was all he could do, was keep the faith. And now he would have to wait again, keep keeping his hopes alive.

And Thanksgiving dinner had been celebrated at the Ballad house. There was a lot of picture taking and great fun. Della had turkey and gravy and mixed vegetables and a glass of sparkling wine and thumbed through the family album for the twentieth time since she'd been out St. Bart's, at least it's what she'd said. She'd been counting, she'd said, making sure not to inflate the number any, to think they might think she'd fudged the final figure slightly.

It was early Sunday morning, before church service. Margaret was over at the stove.

"Brrr …," Royal said. He'd run into the house.

"I told you not to go outside without your coat."

"Hot chocolate, Mag. Hot chocolate. You've got to—"

"Coming up. I knew you wouldn't be out there too long without your coat."

"Just kicked the tires a few times. The four of them."

"I'm surprised they didn't kick back."

"I can't rotate them anymore, Mag—they're shot. I'll be hunting for a bargain. A tire sale. For four new tires. The storm wasn't kind to them. Beat them up pretty bad, Mag. Pretty, pretty bad."

"Well, it's better to be safe than sorry," Margaret said, handing Royal his cup of hot chocolate.

"And how are my bacon and eggs and waffles coming along?"

Margaret laughed. "Coming …" Margaret stooped over and kissed Royal.

"I'm surprised you did that, Mag—my cheeks are cold."

"Maybe that'll warm them."

"Getting real sexy, huh?"

Margaret blushed and then walked back over to the stove. "You'll have your eggs … everything in a few minutes."

Royal ducked his head under the table, looked at his school books on the opposite chair, and then his head jerked back up. "Uh …"

Margaret was in a pink cloth robe. "Yes, Royal," Margaret said, turning the spatula in her right hand.

"The tires, the car tires, I was going to complain about the car tires again but caught myself. Uh—"

"Royal, Momma … Momma will make it to Christmas, won't she?"

"Wow, uh, wow, Mag, t-that one came out, from out the blue. Wow, Mag …"

"I'm sorry, but—"

"It's why you've been on edge lately? Your body's been so tense? I've no—"

"Yes."

"I thought so, but—"

"We had such a great time, wonderful Thanksgiving together."

"Great … yes, wonderful."

"And Momma—"

"She's going to make it, Mag. Christmas, New Year's. Mother Ballad's going to make it."

"I … I know there're no guarantees, Royal."

"None. No … not a one."

"But … but doesn't she look healthy?"

"Yes, she does."

"I think so, Royal. And I try not to imagine things that aren't there. I know we can be guilty of that. Someone who's too close to the situation. But I think she looks healthy. Living in the house alone, by herself, it hasn't hurt Momma any. Created problems any for her."

"None that I can see."

"That was my greatest source of worry."

"Everyone's Mag. Yours, mine, Darlene's, Lee's. Everyone's."

"Momma keeps on fighting on."

"All the way to Christmas and then the new year."

Margaret took Royal's plate from in front of him.

"Now, it's time to level with you, Mag. Confess something to you."

"Me, Royal?"

"Can you hold off on the … on everything for a minute or two? We have enough time before we take off for Hands of Christ," Royal said checking the time.

Margaret sits at the kitchen table. "I'll … I'll reheat everything, Royal. Don't worry."

"Thanks."

Suddenly tears are rolling out Royal's eyes.

"Marshall, I've been thinking of Marshall, Mag. My son a lot lately."

Margaret smiles.

"You know it hits me, it hits me really hard around this time of year.

I just wonder if it bothers him, Mag. Or if he's forgotten, totally forgotten about me."

Pause.

"I mean, he hardly knows me. What Eve and I had was a farce, a sham—we were no more man and wife than … Why get angry when I brought it on myself. I'll take full blame, responsibility—don't have to point a finger at anyone but me, when I'm as guilty as anyone."

"You still forgive her, don't you, Royal? Eve?"

"I just don't know why she did what she did, Mag. Have no idea. D-does she hate me that much? Despise me that much? To run off with my child. From Detroit. So there's been no trace of him. None. For so long, Mag. Not a trace that she'd ever been there. What's she done with my son? Tell me, tell … What's Eve done with Marshall!"

Margaret looks on nervously, knowing how Royal's anger used to ignite, boil, burn—but day by day the two were drawing closer to God. She and Royal turning more of their problems over to God, for they could find peace, cleanse their souls of their past sins, their past wretchedness so that they might make a way for themselves that was good and solid and steadfast and triumphal.

It's the way they had to think, the way you pull yourself out the cesspool, and at least get back on your feet again, back on track, and then drop down on your knees and pray to God, the Savior, the Almighty, who you brought into your life with open arms and an open heart, whom you're asking to turn it around for the better, to let it last—for substance and sustenance and revival.

"Eve loved you, Royal."

"But I didn't love her. I never loved her," Royal said with red in his eyes.

"But she loved you—regardless."

"And … and what, so what are you saying, Mag?"

"It's what women do. Sometimes do. Take drastic steps. Measures. She knew she'd hurt you as much as you hurt her if she ran away with Marshall. Took him from you."

"Yes. I'm fighting windmills. I … I know what this is all about. And when we were in touch, when she was in Detroit, I told her how well things were going in Myles Day for me. But I was only telling her the truth. Not to hurt her. So much for the truth."

"It-it's something, I'm sure, Royal, Eve didn't want to know about. How well—"

"Of course, since I mentioned you too. Your name came up."

"She hates me."

"Of course."

Long pause.

"If … if only I could see him. Marshall. My son. If only I could see him, Mag."

Margaret's back on her feet. She's at the oven.

"There's always so much going on just below the surface of a person's life, is, isn't there, Mag? So much tension, chaos. At the edges, yes, surface of so many people's lives."

"Momma. Sometimes I wish I could get into Momma's mind. There are so many times I think that. Momma's head."

"We try so hard, Mag."

"I guess so, Royal."

Pause.

"He looks like Eve."

"Yes, he does."

"The spitting image of her." Pause. "But when he looks in the mirror, what does Marshall think, Mag? What goes through his mind? He sees his mother, but does he think of me? I mean, does it happen, ever happen that way, Mag? Marshall … he … he thinks of me?"

Startled by the suddenness of Royal's words, Margaret's head turns slowly to him sitting at the kitchen table.

*   *   *

December 5

Della's just shut the bathroom door. She was in the hallway and then in the bedroom and was now back in bed. She'd eaten breakfast, fixed it for herself, had eaten well. She was supposed to exercise but, for now, didn't feel much in the mood for it. Yesterday, her mind was scattered, was everywhere, and today it seemed her mind hadn't yet recovered, was still scattered everywhere.

It was sudden. Suddenly it was beginning to feel as if the walls were starting to close in on her. She hadn't intimated this to Darlene nor to Margaret (not them, surely not them), but it's how it was beginning to feel for her, as if the walls in the house were beginning to close in on her.

She was beginning to feel trapped, she thought—trapped in a house she and Frank loved, spent their married life in, raised a daughter, had a niece (though through tragic circumstances), they gave a home to. But now the house was the only place to find her. The only place where Della Ballad spent her days from morning to night. The house. This house.

And no one was offering her time out the house, not Darlene or Margaret. Everyone, it seemed, had settled for her staying in the house as if it were the only place for her, where a person her age, with her disease, belonged, must spend her days and nights—in the house.

And maybe, Della thought, she was as much to blame as anyone. That the blame lay with her, just as well. At one time she'd thought about going out the house, thought about it—but then the big snowstorm came, hit Myles Day City, blanketed it with snow; and its timing seemed to work like this big clock in the sky that stopped, made time stand still and, with it, her inability to restart it, get it to race ahead, its hands, once again, move tirelessly inside the clock's circumference.

And now she was thinking of spring, of summer—when it's warmer, more pleasant. It's when she would go out the house—resurface. But none of this, this issue of hers, had to do with how she was being treated. There were times, she admitted, she felt she must be the most important citizen living in Myles Day City, alive. Darlene was always at the house. Margaret was always calling her on the telephone. These were beautiful routines in the day.

When Della got back from the bathroom, she held onto a glass of water. The water wasn't filled to the top, its brim, but not one drop of water had hit the floor during the travel from bathroom to bedroom.

"Pretty good, Della. Pretty darn good balancing act, Della Ballad."

Three pills for now, she said, the three pills in her palm. Then rearing her head back, there was the taste of water and then the swallow and then the feel of each pill navigate through her system. One at a time. Always one at a time—until there were thirteen in total to swallow each day to wind their way through her system.

"But I'm tired. Tired. Getting tired. My mind. I'm getting tired. Down. Down on myself."

But I do understand their worry over me. How Darlene and Margaret worry over me. Why we go through it with our loved ones at one time or another. Our parents, relatives—all of us do. It is a sad thing to watch. Don't … don't think, you think for a minute I don't know that it is, when you, yourself, have been through it with others.

Ha. Darlene and Margaret would like to keep me young forever. But it doesn't work that way. Like that. Nobody can accomplish that. No human being can. The body starts breaking down, losing its effectiveness. You fight it, but it … it takes so much energy for you to. To do so, w-what's left over. I'm finding out more and more, isn't very much left for anyone to use.

"I … I just don't want to be a burden to either of them. One of them. My girls. It's just that you reach, get to that point. How you start to feel about this age issue, situation you're in I think once you're in it. Need them for this and … and then that—for that … ha. Got them jumping like crazy. Ha. Through hoops. Seems, begins to feel like for everything. Everything under the sun—big or small."

Della looked toward the window, and there was a sun in the sky, and it was shifting its way northward, would be sitting in her window fat and lazy any minute now, and if you didn't know better, you'd think it summer, not winter, that there wasn't a cold snap that gripped Myles Day City for the past three days.

"Oh … Lord, it must be cold out today!"

Della snuggled up under her quilted comforter, her body recalling those cold days like icicles were stuck in her socks.

"But of course neither Darlene or, nor …" Her mind, it felt so focused, suddenly, she thought, not scattered to the wind. "As long as they don't think of me as a burden to them. But I bet the thought hasn't even crossed their minds. But it's the only fight I can fight for now. Not to be a burden to them." Pause.

"Margaret and Royal, their lives are such a wonder now. So splendid. And as for Darlene and Lee, well, they were always on track. The right track. Always there. They never fell from grace. Took to the wrong path like Royal and Margaret. Not for a day."

Della caught her breath.

"There are times, I mean there are so many times when I wish Frank could see what Margaret and Royal have done with their lives. They've turned things around. Ain't that the truth. Why, why," Della gasped, "it's nothing short of a miracle.

"Hope, just hope Royal's little church in Mr. Tolletson's basement keeps growing, prospering. It's what I hope. One step at a time. Uh-huh. You don't have to do more than that, as I always say. And they don't have to be such big steps. As long as you're stepping. You keep stepping. Stepping along. Ha.

"And Royal doesn't seem to be rushing to the end. Not at all—in the least. Royal's moving … Why it seems he's moving in a flow of absolute grace, doesn't he? Of absolute grace. He's taken himself from disgrace to glory, Frank. Frank."

Della appears annoyed.

"And to think, to think there was hate at one time in my heart for Royal. For Royal McCloud. A hate I never knew, thought I could have—held for anyone but Royal McCloud. Never knew anything like it before. Could be so strong in me. Powerful. Come out of nowhere. Yes, and it was all because of Royal … Royal," Della said, shuddering.

"My, my, how God works. My how he works. Times when I prayed to God to have him die. Die there in Detroit. Detroit Streets. Let someone kill him. Kill Royal McCloud. It's how you fight evil. What to do with evil. How you, it's how … j-just leave my daughter … Just … just leave my daughter alone. For … for he would not continue to lead her soul down the path of wickedness. Oh, oh, how I prayed. Prayed! Prayed!"

Della felt the shock and the memory of the past.

"But then … why am I going back to those days? Those dark days and hours? When … when I thought Royal was … was the devil himself walking the earth. The devil himself." Pause. "I … I do believe in him … Royal … I—not for one second do I not, not …"

Her voice tailed off. She had to think. She had to retread past memories.

She'd been thinking for a few minutes, when she felt the urge.

"Those darn pills and the water I've got to take along with them," Della laughed. "Uh … for a lack of a better word. Acting on me. They're acting up on me. Ha. But I'm not gonna curse, Frank. In the house. Ain't gonna do that—even at my age—if I don't have to!"

And at the side of the bed she looked at her walker, disdainfully, but then smiled.

"I have to go, but you ain't going with me—not to the bathroom this trip. Haven't exercised today. So maybe making it to the bathroom without you will do me some good. I've learned how to steer you with one hand and carry a glass of water without spilling it, even if I don't fill it all the way to the top. Haven't I?"

(One day, Della thought, that walker of hers was going to answer her, and then you'd really see how fast she'd light out the house!)

Della was back in the hallway, out the bathroom, but the more steps toward the bedroom she took, the more out of focus her eyes were, and this had nothing to do, it seemed, with her having or not having the walker with her.

And then once in the bedroom trying to reach the bed, without warning, she fell thunderously to the floor and felt this horrible thing in her chest, pound it, so big, so large. It's as if someone hit her with a sledgehammer, and now she felt the blow's power increase, and she lay on the floor numb, her eyes swollen and pleading desperately for help.

Darlene tipped the taxicab driver and turned and looked down at the ice on the ground and sniffed the half-dozen beautiful red roses wrapped in paper. The taxi was toasty, but immediately, Darlene felt the cold. Today the wind was blasting Miles Day City nonstop. But she stood looking at the house, seemingly harnessing her energy, happiest, she always was, when she looked at her aunt Della and uncle Frank's house, remembering how she first stood and looked at it when she came there to live, her uncle Frank holding her hand and her suitcase and her holding onto the little toy horse, Tanya, her favorite toy back then—the weather in Myles Day City like today's but knowing her aunt Della and uncle Frank's house was always warm and toasty and that her aunt Della and Margaret were inside the house, her uncle Frank had told her that, that her aunt Della had fried chicken and there'd be smothered gravy for her, something she really liked at that age, and Uncle Frank said everything would be all right, he and Aunt Della would make everything all right, that she still has family despite her mother's death, the car accident that took her.

She was so happy that day.

"Here I come, Aunt Della. Here I come. Red roses and all, honey. I'm here, Aunt Della."

Darlene rushed to the front of the house as if she were competing with the blast of wind at her tail; she drew out her keys.

"Aunt Della." Darlene put the roses on the hall table, hurried with her coat, hanging it in the hall closet, and then picked the roses back up off the table.

"Guess what I have, have for you, bought for you, Aunt Della? What's in my, uh, cold hands … Well, they'll be warm in no time. Especially in this house. The way you keep it warm."

Darlene was on the second-floor landing. In the hallway. She'd smelled the smells from the kitchen, knew what Della had done, had cooked, as usual.

"Now close your eyes, Aunt Della. Close your—don't tell me you're sleeping. Napping. Because I know your ears. I know you should've heard me by now, Aunt—"

Darlene was in the bedroom.

"Aunt Della! Aunt Della! No! No, Aunt Della!"

Della was lying on the bedroom floor.

Darlene dropped the flowers and rushed to her, hoping she was still alive.

"Aunt Della! Aunt Della!"

CHAPTER 7

Three days later.

Royal and Lee are in St. Bartholomew Hospital. Margaret and Darlene are inside Della's room. The four had, earlier, been in consultation with Dr. Ives, who was about to go into Della's hospital room any minute now to tell Della what he'd told the family.

Lee and Royal just seemed to need this respite, to be able to sit outside the room, on a bench in the hospital's hallway.

Lee looks at his hands. They're jumpy.

"It's times like these, Royal, when I wish … when I wish I didn't have the habit. Nicotine habit. 'Cause I need a cigarette. A smoke. And bad. But I'm fighting it. T-trying not to give in to it, Royal. It get … gets the best of me."

Royal smiled. "Well, if it would relax you, Lee, then by all means. I mean I see no harm—"

"I know. I know, Royal. But I don't think a cigarette will … will for now. Aunt Della came so close. S-so close to … to …"

Royal pat Lee on the back. "It's hard to say, isn't it, Lee? Dying? Death. Especially when it comes to saying it about Mother Ballad." Pause.

"Yes. Yes, Royal," Lee said, shaking his head. "Yes."

"God bless Darlene. God bless her."

"G-getting there, to the house when she did, Royal. The … the way she did."

"Yes. Uh-huh, that Darlene got there. To the house. And everything working like clockwork. The ambulance getting to the house, arriving there when it did. The medics. The emergency room. God was certainly at work. Was right on time for Mother Ballad."

"I—yes, he was, Royal. God, God was. Certainly was, Royal." Lee tugged on his socks, first the left one and then the right one, and then straightened his body back up. "Dr. ... Dr. Ives, he's going to tell Aunt Della. E-everything he told you, me, Darlene, and Margaret in his office."

"Yes."

"Aunt Della's last days ..."

"They should be spent at home, Lee. In Mother Ballad's house. In her bed. At peace. Quiet, restful days, Lee."

"Oh yes. Oh yes." Lee stands. "There's nothing we can do for her now, Royal. Aunt, Aunt Della. N-nothing."

Royal stands. "He's a good doctor, Dr. Ives. To admit that. To let Mother Ballad's last days be spent with her family. Away from ... from this kind of environment. In the continual presence of loving family. Surrounded by love."

"It's going to make Aunt Della happy. H-happy, Royal."

"Extremely, Lee. Joyful. It'll make things much easier for her."

"Oh, oh, Royal. Royal!" Lee's body was shaking. Royal grabbed him. Lee's crying. "Oh, oh, Aunt Della. Aunt Della, Royal. I ... I love her so much, Royal, so ..."

"We all do. We all love Mother Ballad with such a powerful love. Unbelievable love."

Royal walks Lee back over to the bench.

"Thanks. Thanks, Royal." Pause. "Royal ..."

"Yes?"

Lee looks Royal dead set in his eyes. "Royal, Darl—Darlene's already blamed you. B-blamed you for all of this. In ... in her heart. In ... in her mind."

"I know, Lee."

"You're to blame for what happened to Aunt Della."

"Yes."

"Dr. Ives, he made it clear Aunt Della was living on borrowed time. Nothing more than borrowed time. Even with the pills Aunt Della's taking and all. They can only do, help but so much. But so long. Forestall the inevitable."

"Yes."

"Dr. Ives made it clear. That ... that this could've happened at anytime. At anytime, Royal—whether there was someone in the house with Aunt Della that day or not ... There's nobody to blame. There's nobody who sees it any different but ... but Darlene. I ... I know she thinks if she was with Aunt Della in the house, Aunt Della wasn't there alone in the house, doing for herself—"

"That this wouldn't've happened. She wouldn't be here in the hospital."

"Uh-huh. Uh-huh, Royal. Darlene believes that."

"I know." Pause. "Thank you for sharing that with me, but I know what I'm up against with Darlene. Her feelings about me. But at least she's truthful about them. Doesn't hide them. Always lets me know exactly where I stand with her."

"But it's not fair, Royal. Not fair at all. I ... I was there that night." Lee's angular face is stern and angry. "You did nothing wrong, Royal. Nothing."

"No, I feel I did nothing wrong either."

"Aunt Della had her mind made up. It was all set. Nobody was going to change it."

"I agree, Lee. Mother Ballad did."

"And—but ... but can you forgive her? Darlene, Royal? Can you find it in your h—"

"Oh yes. Oh yes, Lee. Of course. I can. With no hesitation whatsoever." Pause. "I won't fight her, if that's what you mean. For ... for no reason would I fight Darlene."

"Maybe ... maybe, Royal, there are times when I should. Fight Darlene. Stand up to her. I know sometimes you and Margaret must think I'm less than a man. Don't have much .... a backbone." Lee sighs. "I ... I know that, Royal. Don't think I don't know that."

"Lee, it's not for Margaret and I to judge, Lee. What relationship you have with Darlene is yours. Private. A husband and wife's. Margaret and I, our relationship is—"

"It's only family. Around family that she acts that way. Darlene. Like that. The way she does," Lee said like he had to get it off his chest. "H-humiliates me ... I ... I don't know why. I don't know why. Always around family ...."

Royal was looking intently at Lee.

"I don't want to fight her, Royal. I, you see—I ... I saw too much—my parents ... in ... in my family—they always fought. Went at it. I ... I don't want to fight Darlene. She's good to me. Does things other people don't see. Don't know about—just me, her husband.

"And she loves me. And I ... I understand her, Royal. Understand Darlene like Aunt, Aunt Della does."

"And Mother Ballad loves Darlene. Has always loved Darlene, Lee."

"Always. Always. Yes. Yes, loves Darlene, Royal. I love her too. Aunt Della and I love Darlene. We're the only two people who ... who she knows do ... do love her. W-who can trust us with that."

"And that's a blessing, Lee. A true blessing. For two people to truly, genuinely love you in this world—that's a blessing."

Lee's hand was on Royal's shoulder.

"So ... so forgive her, Royal. W-would you? Please. F-forgive Darlene for what she might say or ... or do a-against you, Royal."

"I already have, Lee."

Lee stands. "Royal, I feel a lot ... a lot better." Lee laughed. "I ... I do. But I still think ... still think I need a cigarette. Ha. Smoke. Nicotine's getting the ... getting the best of me again. O-overtaking me. My ... my will power. So I'm going to step outside the building for a minute.

"When Dr. Ives comes, a-arrives, will ... will you, uh, come and get me, Royal?"

"Of course, Lee."

"To be with Margaret and Darlene. T-to be with them and ... and Aunt Della."

When Royal saw Dr. Ives approaching the hospital room, he was up off the bench.

"Rev. McCloud, we're all set."

"Yes."

"Ready to go in? Mrs. Winston and Margaret and—"

"Mr. Winston for ... well, he stepped outside. I won't, uh, tell you what for, Dr. Ives, but ...," Royal laughed.

"You wouldn't surprise me, Rev. McCloud, not at all. Mr. Winston, he's a smoker. I can see it in his eyes and his fingertips. I've been meaning to talk to him."

"Ha."

"Ha."

"Lee asked me to get him. Would you—"

"No problem. Nurse Myers is on her way. I won't get started until both of you are in the room."

"I'll be back in a jiffy, Dr. Ives."

Royal took a big breath outside the hospital door. So did Lee.

"Like I said, I do feel better, Royal."

"Good, Lee."

"That smoke did do me some good."

"Ready?"

"Uh, yes. Uh, sure."

When Royal and Lee walked into the room, there they were: Dr. Ives, Nurse Myers, and Margaret. Darlene, as soon as she saw Royal, turned her back to him; it'd been the same in Dr. Ives's office too during the brief family consultation.

"Is everyone ready?"

"Are you asking me, Joseph, because if you are, there's no place I can go—so I'd better be ready."

Everyone laughed.

Della's hair was knotted in braids. This was her third day in St. Bart's. Darlene had put her hair back in braids yesterday morning when she got there. Della's voice was stronger today than yesterday and the day before. She was in a short coma, came out of it after about six hours. She had some memory of what'd happened, her going to the bathroom and then coming out, but everything after that, she drew a blank on. But Della knew there wouldn't be much for her to tell anyone anyway. There wasn't much distance from the bathroom to the bedroom, ground to cover.

"Mrs. Ballad …"

"Yes, Joseph?"

"I was hoping I'd see that lovely twinkle in your eye. And you didn't disappoint me."

"Glad about that."

Margaret sneezed.

"God bless you," everyone said.

"Margaret, you're not coming down with a cold, are you?"

"No, Momma, I—"

"I don't want you in this hospital bed next."

"But just in case, Margaret, see Nurse Myers. She'll give you a shot for—"

"Dr. Ives," Darlene interrupted, "my aunt, you're here … we're here for my aunt Della."

"Oh, I'm sorry, Mrs. Winston. Of course. Mrs. Ballad, of course. My dear Mrs. Ballad. I, well, I figure two more days here in good old cheerful St. Bart's, Mrs. Ballad. Ha. And then you're free to leave. Go home to be with your family."

"I am getting stronger. Feel it."

"Your strength, yes, it's coming back. Sooner than expected. There has been steady improvement on your part."

"So you're going to boot me out again."

"Now, Aunt Della …"

"It's what they're gonna do, Lee. It's what they're up to. How they're figuring it."

"But this time, Mrs. Ballad, you have to be under twenty-four-hour care. Supervision, again."

"And that means me, Aunt Della. Me."

"Yes, Mrs. Winston, Mrs. Ballad. Your niece. There has to a presence in the house at all times. You can no longer be in the house on you own. And it's something I'm sure you wouldn't want either, Mrs. Ballad."

Della shook her head in the positive.

"As your physician, I mean, I've been honest with the … your family, Mrs. Ballad. I—"

"I know what you're getting at, Joseph. Don't get yourself upset," Della said, looking at Nurse Myers. "Oh, both of you have been so splendid, wonderful to me. I've been so downright lucky," Della said, reaching for Dr. Ives's hand and then Nurse Myers's. "So don't you …"

"We've been a great team, Mrs. Ballad."

"A great team," Della said, her face glowing.

"Uh … uh, tomorrow, Aunt Della. I'll move in the house tomorrow. F-first thing, Aunt Della."

Della takes her attention off Dr. Ives and Nurse Myers.

"Why in such a rush, honey? D—"

"You … well …"

"Uh, but that's o-okay, all right, Darlene. Honey. You do what you want, uh, wish, honey. What you think's best."

"Darlene—"

"Not now, Lee. Not now."

"So everything's settled, Mrs. Ballad."

"Joseph … so no new pills? Elephant pills?"

"Ha. I'm afraid not, Mrs. Ballad. No, not at all, you can stick with the ones you've got. I'm letting you off scot-free."

"Good."

"Thirteen, right, Mrs. Ballad?" Ives said.

"Oh, I could put them in a poem. Make them sing like a song."

Ives bid everyone good day. Then he and Nurse Myers headed for the door.

"You're a lovely man, Joseph."

Ives turned. "The feeling's mutual, Mrs. Ballad."

When the door shut, silence ensued.

Royal was holding Margaret's hand, and Lee was standing next to Margaret, and Darlene had moved back to the bed and sat beside Della. Darlene put her hand inside Della's and rocked it easily from side to side. There were tears in her eyes that Della began brushing away with her hand.

"Now don't you worry, Darlene. Don't you worry any. I—"

"Momma, I'm going to stay with you too this time," Margaret said, pressing Royal's hand. "At the house, Momma."

It sounded like a shot out the blue.

"R-Royal …"

*　　*　　*

Margaret was going to move into the house a day before Della was released from the hospital too. Her bags were packed. Because of a prior commitment (it was school related), Royal couldn't drive her to the house.

Royal entered the kitchen. "The taxi's on its way. Should be here any minute now."

"Thank you, Royal."

"I'm going to miss you, baby," Royal said, kissing her.

"Now if that doesn't sound like a pastor talking."

"You know, I haven't used that word in a long time, have I, Mag?"

"'Baby'? No, Royal. No, you haven't. Not 'baby.'"

Royal leans his body against the refrigerator door.

"I … uh … remember when there was a time it's all I'd use. Baby. To be cool. Then sometimes distant. Cold, or detached or aloof. To maintain my control over you. My authority back then, Mag." Royal scratched his arm.

"Guess the word, back then, took on a certain kind of psychological dynamic for me. It was played for high stakes, very high stakes at the time, Mag."

Margaret went over to Royal and pulled him off the refrigerator door. She swung around, for he could hold her from behind. "Well, it sounded perfectly suited for now. For this occasion, Royal." Pause. "Royal, my suit—"

"Don't worry, I parked it at the front door." Royal nuzzled the back of her neck.

"Y-you do understand, don't … don't you, Royal? A-about me staying at the house? W-with Momma?" Margaret asked cautiously. "I did explain everything, my feelings about everything for—"

"Mag, now why would you ask me that … that for?"

Margaret's body tensed.

"It's just—no, Royal, Darlene wasn't going to get away with it this time. F-for a second time. Staying with Momma. Exclusively. Shutting me out again."

He let go of her. He walked over to the doorway connecting the kitchen to the short hallway. He leaned his back against the doorway's wooden frame.

"What, Royal, what?" Margaret said. Royal didn't turn to her immediately.

"It's just that, I just hope you and Darlene—the two of you can … can—"

"Coexist?"

"Yes. Yes, Mag, coexist. Darlene and … Mother Ballad's last days in her house, Mag, must, they must be peaceful days. Restful days. It's the only reason why Dr. Ives has sent Mother Ballad home."

"Don't you think I know that, Royal? Am fully aware of that?"

"Okay. All right, but my only fear I have, and it is a fear, Mag, a real one, is—you are only human. You're not a saint. No one is. There may be times in the house when Mother Ballad's needs might be such that you and Darlene openly clash, that it turns into a competition of wills and egos between the two of you, and instead of, the two of you doing what's best for Mother Ballad, keeping her first and foremost, at the heart of this, you both lose sight as to why you're there, in the house, in the first place. What purpose you're there to serve." Pause.

"It's my only worry and real fear, Mag."

Margaret clenches her fist, flexing it over and over, only to soon calm herself. "Yes, I see what you mean, Royal. Someone will have to back off. D-down."

"Withdraw themselves. Plain and simple."

"And it's always been me in our relationship. My role. Not Darlene's. Not ever, Roy—"

"Mag, can you continue to do that? Can't you? Have the strength to?"

"And … and it's the question I've been asking myself too, Royal. In bed last night. Over and over, since things are so accentuated between me and Darlene now. High stakes—like you said before. I … I prayed to God. Prayed on it alone. That he'll give me the strength to."

"Good." Royal went back to Margaret; he held her. "Prayer is good. But even I know so much depends upon ourselves. Rests on our shoulders We can pray for the strength, and even if God should provide it, we still must use it. Have the will to carry it out for ourselves."

"Darlene will—"

"She'll test you in every way she can. At every turn."

"Oh, Royal, I want to be the last one to hold Momma's hand. The last one to tell her I love her. T-to be there when she closes her eyes. When … when …"

"Our Father calls Mother Ballad home to his kingdom. The last one Mother Ballad sees before she—"

"Dies. Yes. Yes, Royal. Momma dies."

And for them it felt as if a ban of silence had been broken and a new bond built.

"The taxi, Mag. Let's get to the front door. It should be here any minute now."

They're heading for the front door. "You'll be okay, Royal? Here in the apartment?"

"Let me see," Royal said, exaggerating each physical gesture he made, "I have to turn the knob to the right clockwise on the stove when I want to turn it on. Right?"

"Ha. And to the left, counterclockwise, when you want to turn it off!"

"Then I think I'll be all right since that's all I have to do. There is for me to figure out."

They're at the door. It's when they kiss.

Margaret was in her old room. She'd settled in. She'd already called Royal to tell him, let him know everything was okay. He was out the house, as expected, but she left a message for him on the telephone's message unit. Darlene was in the house before her. In fact, Darlene had been in the house all day. She didn't know the exact time she'd gotten to the house, but she knew it'd been all day since Darlene knew she'd be coming to the house, even if she did have to get off work from International Retailers first before getting there. She certainly wasn't going to drop her personal belongings off first, before going to work.

In fact, it was the dinner arrangement, cooking, eating in the house—it'd be easy with just her and her mother in the house, but with her and Darlene, it hadn't been. They'd eaten, yes, but at separate times, cooked different meals. It'd been difficult—even if it was for just one night, Margaret thought. Difficult. Then she laughed. "'Just One Night.' Isn't that a Lionel Ritchie hit—song, or am I mistaken?"

The reception was chilly. If she thought it was cold outside, well inside … inside the house … But now it seemed both listened for footsteps, something both were acquainted with, accustomed to doing; they'd lived like this, in the house together for so long. For right now, at this moment, Darlene was in her room. In order of rooms, it was Darlene's room and then her mother's and then hers, but opposite the bathroom, not on the same side of the floor—and a linen closet separated her mother and father's bedroom from Darlene's bedroom, a big linen closet, built for a lot of linen, et cetera. Still, when she went to the bathroom a short while back, she heard Darlene's sewing machine (her mother's, actually) whirring. It's what Darlene, of course, had been doing most of her day. She was a hard worker and a great seamstress like Momma, Margaret thought. The best. The best you could find in Myles Day City.

It's a talent she never had nor pretended to have—her mother's gift. But Darlene had it. She was meticulous, creative, and was sparked by an unbelievable energy to make sure her work was exemplary. She kept her standards so high. So very high.

"I'll give Darlene credit for that much. Y-you have to give her credit for that much."

There was no television in her old bedroom, but there didn't have to be. She carried her books with her, and if she wanted to watch TV, entertain herself that way, she could. There was a TV in the living room. And she didn't have to worry about Darlene. Darlene had her sewing, her dedication to it. She rarely watched TV. She was, again, like her mother when sewing was her mother's life, when it's all she did morning, noon, and night.

"Until the stars came out," Margaret laughed. "Oh, how I remember it. Remember it so well, Momma. Daddy cutting hair all day and Momma cutting out patterns. Matching, shaping up this with that, her eyes so sharp then—it's why it's so hard, so hard to see her this way. Now. What's become of Momma now. What's become of her."

When do you start thinking about old age? At my age? At my age? It's when you start thinking about it—or is it too early to do that? Am I too young? But it's what's down the road eventually. I can't very well cancel it out. Daddy ... now Momma.

"Daddy was a shell of himself. Daddy was a shell of himself though. The last three months, they say. The last three months, he was a shell of himself."

But she wasn't in Myles Day City; she was in Detroit, with Royal. Things were different back then, five years ago, between her and her parents when she lived in Detroit with Royal.

"Just seeing Daddy in his casket. It wasn't him. It wasn't his body that was in that casket at the funeral."

But she was there for the funeral. The funeral she came for but without Royal. Royal didn't fly in with her, saw no need to; he couldn't take the time, not in Detroit—he was too busy, it wasn't good for business. And then she left the funeral, flew back to Detroit, didn't stay for her father's repast. She had to get back to Royal. Royal needed her back in Detroit.

Margaret came off the bed. She felt like leaving the room. And she didn't feel like a prisoner, no, no, not even with Darlene in the house, around, for even walking out her room, she'd still have things to iron out, mend in her mind no matter the room she was in; the encroaching doom no matter how peaceful and restful she was going to try to make her mother's final days, at the tip end of everything, of every word, gesture, was death. It would be in the house, sunk in its marrow, in its old creaking wood. Nobody could pray it away, exorcise it out the house, or make up a religion that wouldn't demand the same final price for living.

But each day she must rise above the house, above the creaks. No matter how many times she heard them or how loud they were, she must pray anyway, find courage through faith. Dr. Ives, in the hospital, standing there in the room, his splash of handsome gray hair, didn't look grim but resigned. Is this how she must carry herself, her courage by his example? Is this how she must face up to her mother's death?

She paused, for she heard familiar footsteps. They were Darlene's footsteps leaving the room. She was out in the hallway, near the bathroom now. The bathroom door was open. Margaret would wait for it to close. And when it did, Margaret breathed a big sigh of relief.

She hadn't realized that she had—but she did.

Darlene had been in the bathroom, came out, went into her aunt Della's room, looked around it just to make sure everything was all right, and then went back into her room. It's where she was now, sitting down in front of the sewing machine, material in hand, about to turn the sewing machine on (she'd moved the sewing machine into her room from Della's sewing room during her first day in the house), but her hand was shaking now like if she tried to sew, her hand would become a part of the fabric she was holding, and the sewing machine's needle would stitch her skin, her hand too.

Darlene threw the material at the wall.

"Damn her! Damn her! She doesn't belong here. In this house!"

It's all she'd been thinking since Margaret arrived at the house, walked through the front door of the house with her bags in tow; she'd heard the key inserted into the door and was sure to be standing there when she got there, stare her down until she hoped she would shrink, evaporate, or run from the house.

"But not Margaret Ballad. Not Margaret Ballad. No, no … no, not her, not her …"

But she let her know who belonged there, in the house, even if she didn't say anything to her. She let her know she wouldn't hide from her, not under any circumstance, situation. That she was the intruder, interloper, not her. That the house was hers, her territory.

"There's no reason for her to be here. In the house. Insinuate her … damn you, Margaret Ballad. Damn you!"

But she would assume her same duties, her caring for her aunt Della as before, as if uninterrupted, unimpeded, those days never having gotten in her way, squeezed her out, having put a wall between her and her aunt Della—ever existing.

"There's nothing to think out. Nothing to plan."

And then a calm fell over Darlene like a cool curtain of rain.

"So why am I getting so upset? S-so what if Margaret's here? So what if she's here?" Darlene got up and picked up the material off the floor.

"Things won't change. They'll be as they were before," Darlene said under even better, tighter control. "Always have been."

"I will run things, plain and simple. The things I can't do, maybe, for the moment, if I'm too busy at the time to do them, I'll delegate to Margaret—that's all. It's how I'll handle it. The situation. Run things—the household. Small things. Insignificant things. Matters."

Darlene sat back down in front of the old Singer sewing machine.

"Margaret's here but …Ha. Ha. Ha …"

Darlene's hand covers her mouth; she didn't want to laugh too loud, hard, Margaret might hear her. "Ha. Ha. Ha …"

Darlene started the machine back up; the whirring sound was back in her ears. She loved that sound, how it made itself, produced itself, even though, when she'd think at the machine, while sewing, she'd never hear it. But now she didn't have to think, and she could listen to the sound, to the whirring sound the Singer sewing machine produced.

"Aunt Della still loves to hear it too. She can hear it from her bedroom, but sometimes she'd come in here with her walker and sit in the chair. That chair over there, over there and just listen. Shut her eyes and listen to me sew." Pause. "Like it was music, music to her ears.

"Yesterday you were up on your feet, Aunt Della. In the hospital.

Tomorrow, it might take a little time to get up the staircase, but you will. Just take your time, Aunt Della. Lee and I will be right there for you. There's no rush."

The sewing machine was whirring rapidly.

"Ha. Ha. Ha …" Darlene laughed, tearing fabric with her teeth; she'd just thought of Margaret. "Ha. Ha. Ha." She laughed, laying the material flat, pressing down hard on it with her right hand.

CHAPTER 8

Della awoke in St. Bart's this morning knowing this was the day she was to go home. Awaking, happy to be alive, happy to know her family was coming for her. Happy to know she was going home, would die, if not in bed, something she hoped with all her heart, prayed she would, then in the house. But she wanted to die in her bed as Frank had died. She wanted to have that much in common with his dying.

It sounded morbid, she knew, but there was nothing morbid about reality, she'd discovered, once you reach the stage where she was. And she was at a stage where she could make wishes for herself, little kept, little held secrets. She had a right to have them, to hold onto them, what now lifted her spirits.

She had a good idea as to the time, and if she wanted to find out, all she had to do was look to her right, and the clock was there—but she didn't. In a few minutes, the nurse's aide, Irene, would come into the room with her breakfast. She couldn't take her first round of pills on an empty stomach. First and foremost, she had to have something solid in her stomach.

"Darlene, Margaret."

A sweat swept over her face. She became more bright and alert and fearful.

"They spent last night in the house together."

Last night before falling asleep, it's all she thought about. It's a miracle she didn't have a nightmare about it last night, but she couldn't recall one now.

She couldn't remember one or waking up—not anything about last night. But she was happy as pink to have Margaret in the house, even though she had to leave the house during the day to go off to work, her job—at least she'd be there in the evening with her.

"I was all for it. The moment you said it, Margaret. It's just Royal I was thinking of, honey. Royal, no one else. I want you in the house with me. I want you to be with me as much as you can, Margaret, not just Darlene, honey, but you too."

But last night, knowing the two of them were in the house together, not under any supervision, with no common purpose (her) to keep peace between them some core of civility.

"I wish it could be different, but it can't. I know how Darlene came to me and Frank. Her emotional state. What it was. I know how—and it ain't changed from then to now. Over the years. Darlene's still emotionally unstable no matter what Frank and I tried to do to change it. Help her with it. No matter, no matter …

"But I'm going home today. Welcome it … ha. It's all I can say. Welcome it. Lee's taking another day from, off work, and so is Margaret. All of this for me. On my account. Yours truly. It's gonna go well in the house. Darlene has the whole routine down pat.

"There'll be no burden on Margaret. She can come and go as she pleases. Darlene, my darling Darlene, always wants to carry the load. Can't stop her from doing that. Nobody can. It's a part of Darlene's personality. Something you just gotta accept."

Della's hand patted the mattress.

"It's gonna feel good to sleep in my own bed tonight. I'll have Darlene cook me some salmon. There's plenty put away in the freezer. Darlene'll make the sauce I taught her to make especially for my salmon, my secret recipe, just Darlene and me know, know how it's concocted.

"And she'll spread the sauce, spread it over the cooked salmon, smother it in sauce, there's no reason to be … Oh, I can't wait for my family to get here this morning. Darlene, Margaret, and Lee. To ride in the car today and get home, to the house. I can't wait.

"Ha. Yes, yes—Lee'll be driving, and Margaret will be in the front seat, turning around to keep an eye on me. And … ha … me and Darlene will be in the backseat holding hands, keeping me steady, making sure everything's all right. Like she always does."

Irene, the nurse's aide, made her entrance into the room.

"Good morning, Mrs. Ballad!"

"Good morning, Irene!"

"Ready for breakfast, Mrs. Ballad?"

"What's for breakfast?"

"The usual, Mrs. Ballad. Nothing new, ma'am."

"Won't be able to say that for dinner though, Irene."

"How come, Mrs. Ballad?"

"My niece is gonna cook salmon for me tonight."

"Mrs. Winston?" Irene said, putting the tray down and then tucking the napkin along the edges of Della's nightgown.

"With my secret sauce. Recipe, Irene."

"Mmmm … sounds good. Delicious, Mrs. Ballad."

"It is, Irene, it is. It's mouthwatering. The way it comes out. And Darlene cooks it just like me. Exactly like me."

Irene nodded her head and then lifted the spoon and then dipped it in the bran cereal soaked in skim milk, the way Della liked it.

Everyone was laughing like they were up on the balls of their feet and weren't coming down.

"And ha … Don't you go and tell me how I looked going up those stairs before, 'cause I know you wanted to push me up from behind. I was going up them so slow. So don't tell me!"

"No, Aunt Della. No, Aunt Della. I don't know about Darlene or Margaret, but it never crossed my mind to, Aunt Della!"

"Now, Lee, sweet peach, your halo's about to crack."

"It … it is, Aunt Della? M-Margaret?"

"It is, Lee. Like Momma said."

"No, you're wrong, Aunt Della, Margaret, you're wrong!"

"Almost caught you, Lee."

"Almost, Aunt Della. Al—"

"And now, I'm going down, going down to the kitchen and prepare—"

"The salmon, Darlene."

"And our special sauce, Aunt Della."

"Mmmm …"

"I think I'll—"

"You'll do nothing of the sort, Lee. Your meal's fixed for the next three nights at the house. And then you're on your own until I can get by the house again."

"Right, Darlene. Uh, uh right."

"But don't you worry, baby. I'll try my best to get by. By the house."

Lee and Margaret were sitting in chairs. Darlene was on top the bed, sitting next to Della.

"So, uh, let me get up from here. Get down to the kitchen. Mustn't delay. Mustn't delay."

"No, no, you mustn't, Darlene."

Darlene studied Della. "You, you're all right, Aunt Della?" But before Della could answer, Darlene said. "But of course you are, Aunt Della. You're home." Darlene leaned over and kissed Della. "Home in … in the house. With me."

"Mmmm …," Della said.

"Lee …," Darlene said, looking at Lee.

"Uh … I'm gonna stay a little longer with Aunt Della and Margaret. Uh … in the room, Darlene. For a bit. A bit longer."

"Do as you wish, Lee. Do as you wish. Just don't stay too long. Aunt Della needs her rest. Her strength. The staircase, well, it wasn't easy … easy for her, Lee."

"I huffed and puffed, but—I could've blown the candles off a birthday cake!"

Darlene trembled. "You, Aunt Della, you … you shouldn't joke like that, Aunt Della. I don't think you should joke like that."

Della was about to laugh but didn't, smiling awkwardly, woodenly instead. "No, no, I shouldn't, Darlene."

Darlene left the room. There was a quiet, as if Della and Lee and Margaret were waiting for Darlene to clear the second-floor landing. To keep the silence between them for at least that long. So at least thirty or forty seconds passed without any words passing between them.

"So … Aunt Della, Christmas is coming."

"So … that it is, Lee. And then the new year."

"Can't wait, Aunt Della." Lee turned to Margaret. "What about you, Margaret?"

"Oh, I … I can't wait either, Lee."

"Already been looking around for things for Darlene. Get an early start."

"What about me, Lee?"

"Oh, Aunt Della, you come first."

"Oh, you can pitch a line, can't you, Lee?"

"I … I can, Aunt Della?"

"Now you know you can, know full well you can, sweet peach. I don't have to tell you that. Something you already know."

"No, uh, no, you don't, Aunt Della. You don't."

"Margaret, honey, what about you?"

"Me, Momma?"

"For Royal. Got anything in mind for Royal this Christmas? What you're buying him?"

"Oh, uh, I haven't been—"

"So where's your mind, if it's not on the holidays? It has a tendency of sneaking up on you before you can turn your head. You'll be right smack in the middle of it, honey."

"I … I know, Momma."

"So you'd better start looking in those store windows or catalogues."

"We get a million of them, Aunt Della. Catalogues delivered to us. With Darlene's line of work, we—"

"Tell me about it, Lee," Della laughed. "Since we seamstresses have to keep up with the latest fashion. Keep a step ahead of—"

"Momma, I'm going to call Royal. Tell him everything went well today."

"Tell him for me, I—"

"You know he'll call you later."

"For 'phone prayer.'"

They laughed.

It was just Lee and Della now, alone in Della's bedroom. Lee was over by the fireplace, had just naturally drifted there.

"Lee, come over here, on over here, Lee. Sit by me."

Lee came over. He looked down at Della like a child whose aunt just beckoned him and was holding out a shiny red lollipop to him to lick.

"Give me a kiss, sweet peach."

"Gladly. Gladly, Aunt Della."

Lee kissed the top of Della's forehead. Della took hold of Lee's hand.

"Thanks for everything, Lee. You've been so good. So patient."

"Anything for—"

"Now, now hush, Lee. Hush. I just want to tell you my appreciation. You have sacrificed a lot for this family, and I just want you to know it. Have it come from my mouth. Nobody else's. It … it can't always be so easy for … on you, honey. I know that, Lee."

"Uh … uh, no, no it … sometimes it isn't, Aunt Della."

"You make it look easy. You are a strong person, even if people who don't know you like Margaret and Royal and I do might not always think so. Uh … that you are."

"I just don't try to get in Darlene's way, Aunt Della. That's all."

"I know, Lee."

"I have something good. I know I do." Pause. "If I was in this bed and not you, Aunt Della, Darlene would be by my side twenty-four hours a day too. I know that, Aunt Della. T-that Darlene would for a fact."

"Twenty-four hours, Lee. W-without fail, honey. My darling Darlene."

"Darlene wouldn't complain either, Aunt Della."

"Uh-uh. Not a once."

"She'd show me all the love I needed to have, Aunt Della. Wanted."

"That she'd do, sure would, Lee."

"It got lonely before without her. Back at the house. C-coming home from work. Mr. Baker's shop. But it's all right, Aunt Della. It's all right."

"Just don't, didn't want you to feel invisible, like you're not here. Like you're a shadow on the wall, Lee. Sweet peach. Uh-uh. When you ain't. You mean just as much to this family, what's going on with me as Darlene does. Know you're contributing as much. Doing your part. Just want you to know that, honey."

"Thanks, Aunt Della. And I feel I do—Margaret too."

"And Margaret too. Yes, Lee." Pause. "Now let me hug you, 'cause I'm gonna take a nap. Get some rest—don't care what anybody says. Ain't booting you out now but …"

"No, Aunt Della. Ha. Oh … uh, no, Aunt Della."

"Just feel a little winded … Guess those stairs are telling on me. Finally got my number."

Lee hugged Della.

"Uh, Lee ..."

"Yes, Aunt Della ..."

"I'm gonna, just between you and me, I'll save you some of that salmon of mine. The sauce and all too."

"But you don't have to, Aunt—"

"I'll find a way. Don't worry, I'll find a way. Still can outfox those girls of mine, Darlene and Margaret. Still got tricks they don't know about. You'll have smoked salmon tomorrow night for dinner, Lee. With the sauce. Don't worry. Salmon staring up at you from your plate.

"Staring straight up at you like ... ha ... I cooked it. Just came fresh out the oven!"

*   *   *

Sorting mail in the mail room of Myles Day City's post office wasn't boring for Royal. He had things in mind for himself, much bigger. A lot of workers looked up at the clock on the wall, either for checking how much time it was before coffee break, lunch break, or, of course, quitting time. Royal never did—he laughed—he let them do that for him. But taking the mail from here (envelopes, packages, small boxes, etc.) and putting it there, whereas mindless to a degree, kept him physically active; and there were a lot of talkers on the job, and he liked to talk too, so there was compatibility and a mutuality while he worked that made the job mostly pleasant.

His coworkers called him Royal, even though at times they'd call him Preach or Preacherman just to tease him, something he took in stride and in good fun. In his past life, he would tease and rib people unmercifully about pretty much anything and everything under the sun (pretty much nothing was off-limits), but no more. His change of attitude came about pretty much on the heels of his religious conversion, and so he no longer chose to be loose and frivolous with people. He chose, instead, to stay within a certain strict code of conduct, respectability—maintain his sense of humor without exception, yes, but let him be the butt of jokes, not him on the other end of the joke, initiating it.

Walter Towers had just looked up at the clock. Royal had caught him in the act.

"Hey, Royal, man, it's that time of day."

"Lunch time."

"You got it. Time to chow down. Get down with my roast beef on rye Joanne packed me for lunch this morning."

"Good for you, Walt."

"What? What about Margaret?"

"Margaret ... she's still with Mrs. Ballad. Her mother."

Walt nods his head.

"Guess with your schedule, man, you hardly miss her at all."

"Oh no, I miss her all right. Can't say I don't."

"See you inside."

"Okay."

Of course what Walt meant by "inside" was the building's lunchroom. Royal was going to get there, but first, he was going to call Margaret. He had some news to pass onto her, plus, he was being bugged by something. Maybe "bugged" wasn't a good word, the best he could come up with, but it was the best he could do for now.

First off, he was going to tell Margaret he would get a letter from the bank either tomorrow or the next day, he'd found out. It was regarding the bank loan. So that it, that alone, was scaring the pants off him. And it was funny how Municipal Union Bank did business. All the times before, he'd sat down with Mr. Darling, one of Municipal's chief loan officers, to discuss things, all aspects of the loan and the bank's policies; but when it came to finding out the final verdict of the loan request, he would be engaged by mail, like human contact had, suddenly, been cut entirely out of the equation.

It made Royal feel strange, like he had been knocked down a peg or two, no matter the loan's outcome.

"Maybe I'm too sensitive. My guard's always up. I can't bring it down. Not for a second. I'm too afraid to."

He was standing at the pay phone in the post office's noisy hallway. He deposited a quarter into the phone's coin slot and laughed, for Royal remembered when it cost a dime for local calls. *How long ago was that?* he thought. He was calling Margaret on the job, so there was no worry. When he called her at the house, there was plenty of worry. But he was used to Darlene's icy voice by now—layered with all her toxic feelings toward him.

And Darlene was the one who would pick up the phone at the house the majority of the time when he called Margaret and Mother Ballad.

"Hi, Mag. How's your day been going?"

"Oh, fine, Royal."

"Hope it's been as good as mine."

"I look at numbers all day, you look at mail."

"Ha. I know. Talk about being on opposite ends of the spectrum."

"What did you fix for lunch?"

"Oh, a baloney sandwich. Uh, by the way, Walt Towers, his wife, Joanne, packed roast beef on rye for him for—"

"Don't worry, Royal. I'll make it up to you."

"Ha."

"Seriously, are you doing all right?"

"Besides missing you like crazy, Mag, I'm doing fine."

"I miss you too, Royal. This has been quite an experience. At times … at times I feel like a little girl in my parents' house, and other times like the adult I am, should be, out the house. It's weird, Royal. Really weird. The two extremes."

"But none of that, uh, your feelings mean anything when you put them in context."

"Oh no, no, not at all. It's just idle thinking. Thoughts then. At that point."

"Listen, why I called, besides to tell you how much I love you, is—"

"Aren't you going to let me say it back to you … Royal?"

"Mag, I'm no fool."

Margaret went for the dramatic. There was a cushion of silence.

"I love you, Royal."

"I'm glad to see that absence does make the heart grow fonder. That it's not an empty cliché." Pause.

"Now …"

"Right. Right. The loan, the bank loan with Municipal Union. The answer's coming, forthcoming in the mail—either tomorrow or Wednesday, Mag. But I'm guaranteed an answer by then, and I'm scared to death."

"S-so am I."

"There's a lot riding on this. The outcome."

Pause.

"It seems like forever I've been waiting. Brother Houston and I. But it hasn't been as long as it seems. I guess when they bounced the loan back to us the first time, told us to drop the loan amount, well ... well that should mean something, shouldn't it, shouldn't it, Mag?"

"Yes, yes," Margaret said hastily, as if obligated to.

"It's in God's hands now."

And even as Royal said it, Margaret felt Royal's tenseness.

"Mag, I'm going to let you get back to work—"

"Don't worry, I'm working while we're talking."

"How do you do that? Dealing with figures, numbers too?"

"I don't know, Royal. I guess if you've seen one number, you've seen them all."

"Okay, I think I'll just leave that one alone. But it still amazes me."

Margaret waited.

"Mag, I'm really getting pangs of pain this year."

"Pangs of—"

"Let me explain. It's Marshall, Mag. It's Marshall. My son."

"Oh ... oh, uh, Royal, can I call you back? Phyllis, my supervisor, wants me. She's paging me. You know I know the number there."

"Yes."

"I'll call you right back."

"Sure, Mag. Sure."

Royal stood by the pay phone as if he were going to strong-arm it at any second. But no one else wanted to use the phone, so he was lucky. Christmas, the holidays were peak times when his coworkers would compete for the lone phone in the hallway, Royal thought. But right—

Ring.

"Mag?"

"Yes."

"It's been bugging me," Royal said, picking the conversation back up where he'd left it without missing a beat. "Really ... especially this year, Mag, for some odd reason. So I was thinking, thinking if it would be possible. Mag, I want to call in a private investigator and have him look for Eve and Marshall.

"See if a private investigator can find ... locate them. Be of help. I ... I don't know how much it would cost, the expense involved, what it would be, but …"

"Royal, there shouldn't be any buts. You must do it. Go ahead and do it."

"Where is he? What's he doing? How is he being treated, being taken care of? I have all these questions. I … I mean I have to know, Mag. I have all these questions that go, remain … are unanswered and I have to know.

"You see, the questions that used to nag me before, they're killing me now. I mean it's been bad. Hard for me to deal with, Mag."

"That's why you must get to the bottom of it, Royal."

"When the holidays come, roll around, Marshall barely knows me."

Margaret's mum.

"I'm not a father spiritually or … or financially. I'm not there to provide for any of his needs. I'm not there, Mag—and it hurts. Is a constant source of pain for me." Pause. "Here I am looking for a loan from—"

"But it's for the church, Royal, not us. Hands of Christ Church. We're not living on a shoestring. Hand to mouth. We're responsible with our money."

"But … but I just don't want to look at a big expense, Mag. Layout. Of … of money."

"Just call, Royal. Call down to Detroit. Don't make it … please don't make it any more difficult than it already is."

"No, I'm not trying to do that. I … I can assure you of that, I'm not—not at all."

"Royal, I've got to go. Hang up."

"So do I. Ha. My baloney sandwich in the lunchroom's refrigerator's getting cold. I'll call the house tonight."

"I'll try to pick up."

"You notice I call—"

"At the exact time each night."

"Hoping Darlene will get the hint. By now."

"But she hasn't. She's determined to be in control. All the time, Royal."

"Talk to you."

"Okay."

Royal hung up the phone and then dug into his pockets.

"You're worth every cent I've got, Marshall. Every penny."

Darlene and Margaret are in Della's bedroom. It's 9:38 p.m. Darlene and Margaret stood to the left of Della's bed.

"Aunt Della's fast asleep." Pause. "She ... Aunt Della looks comfortable."

"Yes, Momma does."

"So comfortable."

"You gave Momma—"

"Her last two pills. While you were downstairs tidying up the kitchen—I took care of everything." Darlene crossed her arms in front of her thin frame. "Aunt Della had such a beautiful smile on her face when I did."

Margaret stepped over to the bed. She kisses Della's forehead. "Good night, Momma."

Darlene watches. Now she steps forward as Margaret steps back, and she kisses Della on her lips. "Good ... good night, Aunt Della. Good night. I love you, honey." Darlene steps back.

Margaret's about to turn off the lamp at the far end of the room.

"You haven't caught on yet, have you, Margaret? Not at all. Not one bit. You know I keep that light on, burning overnight just in case I have to come in here at night for Aunt Della, for anything, need—then I won't have to turn the ceiling light on to feel my way across the room. The ceiling light's too harsh, harsh on the eyes."

She looks at Margaret, who's still across the room, with disdain, contempt. "Especially Aunt Della's."

Pause.

"When are you going to catch on? Learn? When? Tell me, Margaret?"

Margaret steps away from the lamp.

"Of course I took care of Aunt Della before, without your help. I learned all the tricks. Tricks of the trade. I'm sure it's something you've noticed, picked up on by now. How I run things. In the house. Make certain, sure there's nothing taken for granted, overlooked.

"And of course, as you've seen over the past several days you've been here, in the house, Aunt Della has, she has every confidence in me, Margaret. It's why I keep wondering why, I don't know why you're—"

"Here, Darlene? In the house, Darlene?"

"I have no clue. Idea. None whatsoever."

"I'm going to my room. Good—"

"Why, Margaret, when we have to talk. You and me. Must talk."

"Talk?"

"Yes, talk. Go to your room for whatever you have to do. Then come down to the living room. I'll be there."

They were out of Della's bedroom, out in the hallway.

"On neutral ground."

"No, I'm not going to—"

"Come, Margaret," Darlene said, goading her. "You knew it was inevitable. Between us." Pause. "The two of us staying, occupying this house together with one aim, one purpose in mind, the only thing that would bring us together under the same—"

"Momma."

"Aunt Della. The only reason to put ... set our personal differences aside, but we still must talk ... talk, Margaret. We still must talk, you know that. Ha. Ha. Margaret."

Then Darlene walked off, smugly.

Darlene's in the living room sitting on her uncle Frank's sofa.

"I'm here, Darlene. Of course you knew I would be."

"Don't look at me like that, Margaret. When you know we have to talk."

Margaret sat.

"Yes, sit, Margaret. Sit. Make yourself comfortable—even though what I have to say won't take long. It never does between you and me. Does it?"

"If you think I came down here to fight. To fight with—"

"Fight? You fight with me? No, Margaret, you've never been a fighter. You've never had to fight, fight for anything. I'm the one who knows how to fight, not you."

Pause.

"We've been forced together under the same roof, haven't we? Been brought back together like this. Into this house. Yes, we should've had this talk, discussion the first night you arrived, stepped foot into my aunt Della and uncle Frank's house."

"We're here, back in my parents' house for ... for the sake of Momma."

"What else, Margaret? Tell me? Of course, what else would we have in common? W-would there be? But that?"

"We … we are cousins, Darlene," Margaret said.

"Cousins? Cousins? What, that should matter? Being cousins?"

"I'm … I'm Momma's daughter—it's all I want you to understand. Know, Darlene. Comprehend. Realize, I'm—"

"Ha, daughter … daughter, why don't make me laugh, Margaret. Daughter? Don't make me laugh."

"Laugh? I—"

"Laugh. Yes, laugh. Laugh. You relinquished that right, privilege a long time ago. A long, long time ago. Remember? Remember?"

"I—"

"And now you want it back? Now? Now? Ha. Ha. Well, you can't have it back, Margaret. You can't. Because I'm Aunt Della's daughter. I'm Aunt Della's daughter now. The only daughter Aunt Della has. Wants. Let's get that straight. That's one thing let's get straight right now."

Margaret wasn't surprised, not at all by what Darlene said. She looks at her, and since her heart's been healed of hate and jealousy toward Darlene with one prayer after the other and thinking only of the resurrection of her own life and Royal's, having cleared away so many demons put in her path, she steadies herself—what has worked as her *living anchor*.

"It's what you wanted, all you've ever wanted to be from the day, the first day you moved into the house, isn't it, Darlene? Momma's daughter? My … my mother's daughter. The day Aunt Nettie died."

"And I am. I am. I am that. And Aunt Della, Aunt Della knows I am. That … that I am. I've earned it. She loves me more than she does you. She loves me more than she does you. You … you hear that, Margaret? Much, much more. Loves me more than she loves her own daughter—more than she could … could love her own daughter. You and Royal McCloud," Darlene said with disgust, seething. "You and Royal McCloud. What you … you and that—"

"Say it, Darlene. Say it," Margaret said, now goading Darlene.

"Will I … will I," Darlene said, seemingly relishing the moment. "That … that phony minister of yours. That, oh … he's a phony. A phony all—"

"And you were ready to step in. Fill the void when I was gone. When I r-ran off to Detroit with Royal."

Darlene's eyes squinted, and she laughs. "Ha. Ha. Do you blame me, Margaret? Tell me, do you blame me? Ha. Ha. Yes, 'step in,' Margaret. Step in, as you call it. Say. F-fill in the void. Was ... I was right by Aunt Della's side. The whole time. Sharing ... sharing in Aunt Della's anguish. Her grief. Her pain. Aunt Della's ... I ... I—all of Aunt Della's anguish. This noble, fine, splendid ... splendid, beautiful woman, human being who didn't deserve this ... this kind of—I hated you, Margaret. Yes, yes, I hated you, loathed you, I—"

"And—"

"Now you want to be what, Margaret? What? The perfect daughter?" Darlene charged to her feet. "The perfect daughter? Well, you can't. You can't. You can never be. For I'm the perfect daughter. Aunt Della's perfect daughter! Aunt Della only has one daughter, and it's me, Margaret. Me. It's the only daughter she needs, wants."

"God help you, Darlene, God—"

"Shut up! Shut up! Shut up w-with—you think God can ... can save you and Royal McCloud from ... from your sins? Past sins? Trans—past transgressions? Ha. Ha. That's what you think? That's what you think? Think? Now after what the two of you did in Detroit!"

Margaret stood, and her body brushed past Darlene's. Now she's in the middle of the living room floor. Margaret looks harried, put upon, unsure of herself, wobbly, of what to do next—just where to go.

"R-Royal and I have r-repented. Have repented for our sins. W-we've moved beyond our past. B-beyond what happened in Detroit. The past. The past. We've—"

"Ha. Ha. John Houston. John Houston. So now ... so now John Houston's gone to the bank, Union Municipal Bank, for Royal, huh, Margaret? The church? Ha. Ha. Is that it? Is that it? Ha. Ha. Word gets around, Margaret," Darlene said, looking at Margaret's shocked, stunned face. "Word gets around fast in Myles Day, Margaret. Or haven't you heard? He still wants that location on 20 Bayer Street. Over on Bayer Street. Royal McCloud. Wants the bank to do what? Finance it for him? It ... that's what Royal McCloud—"

"Yes. Yes, R—"

Darlene rolls her tongue. "Finance it. Yes, finance it, uh-huh. For Royal McCloud, Royal McCloud can have himself a church. Ha. Ha. Save people. Royal McCloud. Pull them up, out their misery." Pause. "Royal McCloud. And John Houston thinks—why would anyone, a bank finance anything for Royal McCloud? Why? In God's name—"

Margaret backed away. "I'm—good … good night, Darlene. I—"

"Royal McCloud belongs in the basement. That basement of his. A church in the basement. Hands of Christ Church. Ha. Ha. A church in the basement of Tom Tolletson's old junk shop with his kind of religion. Down there on Sullivan Street. Sullivan Street. Brand of religion. Ha Ha. What Royal McCloud preaches from his pulpit. With his—"

"Stop it! Stop it! I-I've had enough! Heard enough! Enough, Darlene, enough!"

Darlene runs at Margaret, grabs both her wrists, roughly, violently.

"You sinned against your mother! You sinned against your father! The final stone has not been cast. The final stone has not been cast, Margaret Ballad. Is that how you talk? Is … is that how you and Royal McCloud talk! Your religion? Your religion!"

Margaret and Darlene struggle with each other, but Margaret breaks free. She runs out the living room and toward the staircase with Darlene chasing her down from behind.

"Leave me alone, Darlene! Leave me alone! Leave … leave me alone!"

Margaret's ascending the staircase. Darlene's at the bottom of the staircase.

"Not yet, Margaret Ballad. Not … not yet, Margaret Ballad. Not yet!"

Margaret's in her bathrobe. It was late. So much had happened in one day. She was in the kitchen, at the wall phone. Her head felt like it would split open.

"Royal."

"Mag?"

"Yes, it's me, Royal."

"Mag, uh, why so late? Everything's—"

"M-Momma's fine."

"Oh … oh I suddenly got worried. Worried for … for Mother Ballad. But if—"

"It's not that … at all, Royal."

"Then what? What, Mag?"

"Darlene and I—"

"No, no."

"Yes, we had a flare-up. A blowout."

"Not in front of Mother—"

"It was in the living room. We'd put Momma to bed. Just after … after we did."

"What did Darlene—what did she say?"

"It was about us … us—but what's new?"

Royal shakes his head.

"B-but I don't want to go into it, Royal. It's not why I called."

Royal waited.

"Royal …"

"Yes."

"I'm going to have to be more … more—how should I put it—more present, available for Momma."

"Aren't you now?"

"No. Not enough. You see, I have days coming on the job."

"I know."

"And I think it's time to use them. I've been saving them for … with Momma's condition, I made sure I didn't take them or my vacation time."

"But now you feel it's time. The right time."

"I have to, must … must establish myself more in the house. My presence, yes, my …"

"It's what Darlene—"

"Rantings. Rantings. It's all they are, were, Royal."

"Yes, rantings, I agree, Mag. But sometimes … sometimes she scares you with how accurate, on target she can be with her barbs. Jibes."

Royal's comment knocked the breath out Margaret.

"W-will, uh—do you think there'll be a problem with the job?"

"No."

"No, of course not. Why'd I bother to ask?"

"Starting Wednesday, I'll be in the house with Momma all day."

Long pause.

"I haven't called yet."

"You …"

"Down to Detroit. The private investigator yet."

"Oh, t-tomorrow then."

"Yes, tomorrow. But I'm disappointed in myself. I picked up the phone to. I got the information I needed and all, e-everything, but I …"

"That's all right, Royal."

"Chickened out."

"You didn't chicken—"

"I didn't want to put a price tag on Marshall, Mag. On my son. The private investigation business ... they're just in it for the money. They don't gain anything to benefit them spiritually in any way by bringing families back together.

"It's just a business for them. Money. A ... a payday, Mag. A good payday."

Pause.

"I'll try tomorrow. I'll ... I'll try, give it a try again tomorrow. See how far I get with it. What happens."

Longer pause.

"Did you kiss Mother Ballad for me tonight?"

"For you and for me both."

"I'll call you from the job tomorrow."

"Okay."

Royal threw Margaret a "phone kiss." In turn, Margaret threw him one back.

"And as for Darlene, we'll continue to pray for her, Mag."

"It's just ... that she's so good, capable at what she does."

"Yes, good at it, I know. But God loves her, and so do I."

"I don't."

"Then God and I will pray for you, Mag."

"You don't give up, do you, Royal?"

Pause.

"No answer? Reply?"

"Ha."

"And we'll find Marshall. We will, Royal. We will!"

"If we ran a card business, Mag, we'd run Hallmark out of business. And fast."

"I love you, Royal."

"I love you."

"Good night."

"Good night."

CHAPTER 9

Della's in bed. She's slow in waking, in responding to stimuli around her. Then her eyes begin to focus to see things much clearer. She sees Darlene across the bedroom doing something.

"D-Darlene."

"Aunt Della, y-you're awake." Darlene gets over to the bed. "Good morning, Aunt Della."

"Good ... good morning, honey. I ... I didn't oversleep, did I?" Della asked, not bothering to look at the clock on the nightstand. "I ... I do feel tired."

"You do? No, Aunt Della, you're pretty much on schedule. Only ten minutes off."

"That's not bad. Thought it was worse." Della looks at the clock. "Oh yes, about ten minutes. Do feel tired though. Still."

"We all have days like that, Aunt Della."

"Right, Darlene. Can't blame it on age," Della said cheerily. "Use that as an alibi."

Della's had breakfast.

"Look how the time flies, Aunt Della. It's time for your pills."

"Pill time," Della laughed. She clapped her hands. "Get them, Darlene, 'cause I'm ready to go. To take them on. Go to battle!"

"That's right, Aunt Della. That's right." Darlene took the empty glass off the tray. "Off to the bathroom I go for the water, Aunt Della."

"Ha. Off you go, Darlene."

Margaret was in the kitchen. She'd beaten Darlene into the kitchen this morning. It felt good. She knew Darlene didn't expect her to be there, in the kitchen. She saw the shock, how it registered on Darlene's face. She made the breakfast this morning for her mother. And it did feel good, Margaret thought, to surprise Darlene, shock her the way she did; she wasn't going to lie to herself that it didn't feel good when it happened.

It was the second shock she'd given Darlene in the past twenty-four hours since announcing in front of her and her mother—even though she was talking directly to her mother, not Darlene, but, of course, it being meant for Darlene too—that she had taken a number of vacation days from the job and that she would be in the house, how did she put it, *around the clock.* And then when her mother took her eyes off her and turned to other things after expressing her great surprise and pleasure, it's when she turned to Darlene to look at her face, what, she knew, would be of great contrast to that of her mother's.

But this felt good, her decision to take vacation time, in the morning, not having to head off to her job. Not coming in from work, feeling as if she were visiting, not living in the house—uninvolved in the house's network of activities. Better still, being there if, God forbid, something should happen to her mother. Could she trust Darlene? How soon would she get the news about her mother? Would Darlene's hatred for her skewer her judgment, or would she be in such a panic, hysteria, that almost anything would be overlooked, not taken into clear, thorough account?

When she prepared breakfast this morning, she had her mother's favorite apron tied to her waist. She felt in control for a change, in charge for a change.

"It does feel good."

Maybe it was an open challenge she'd thrown down to Darlene. Or maybe it wasn't—even she was ambivalent as how to interpret it. But it didn't matter her take on it; it only mattered how Darlene interpreted it. And maybe it didn't even matter then, Margaret thought. She never had to find ways to provoke Darlene anyway. Their relationship was fraught enough, didn't have to depend on such device or artifice.

"But I'm here. In the house, at least through Christmas. At least till then."

"Ha. Well … looks like I've made it through another day, Frank. Another day in my bed, honey." Della looks up at the ceiling. "When I woke up this morning, everything was fuzzy, blurry, kind of, slightly out of focus … ha. Thought I had reached St. Peter's Gate, but I soon realized I was lying on my back—that you don't gain admittance by …"

And what's now weighing on Della's mind produces a profound panic.

Darlene's back in the room; she's looking at Della.

"Aunt Della, Aunt Della. What's … what's wrong, Aunt Della? What's wrong! Y-you feel all right, don't you! Don't—"

"My will. My will, Darlene. My will. I … I have to see Attorney Robinson. My lawyer. About my will. My will."

"Your will, Aunt Della? Your will?"

"Yes, Darlene, yes, my will. My will. I … I must see Attorney Robinson. I must. I must."

"Yes, Aunt Della. You … you must, Aunt Della. You must," Darlene said, repeating it herself too.

"You must call him, Darlene. Call him," Della said, pointing to the phone. "I must see Attorney Robinson, speak to him as soon as possible. Soon as I can. Is … is—"

"But first your … your pills, Aunt Della. Y—"

"Yes, yes, my pills. My pills, Darlene."

"Darlene …"

"Lee … get—you must get over here tonight, Lee. Tonight!"

"What's—"

"Don't ask. Don't you dare ask. After work. As soon as you get off work. Leave, you … you leave Mr. Baker's print shop. You get over here, Lee. I have to talk to you. You hear. I have to talk to somebody. I have to talk to somebody, Lee. You're … you're—t-to somebody, Lee…"

Darlene hangs up the phone and begins crying but feels like she's dying; she's close to dying.

The doorbell rang.

Darlene, from the living room, ran to the front door. The living room door opens and closes. Having grabbed Lee's hand, Darlene rushes into the living room. When in the living room, Darlene wheels around to him. While holding her, Darlene's head grips Lee's chest as if she's listening to hear if Lee's heart's beating as loud and as rapid as hers.

"Oh, Lee. Lee."

"I … I came straight from work. Like you said, Darlene. Like you said, Darlene."

"I know you did, baby. I know you did."

"Straight over from the shop, Darlene. Mr. Baker said—"

"Thank you, Lee. Thank you."

Darlene steps back from Lee. There's a nasty look on her face. "They won't get it! They won't get it!"

Lee's at a loss.

"What, Darlene? What? Who? Who won't get—"

"The house, Lee! The house! What else! What else! They won't get the house! I won't let them! I won't let them!"

"The … the house?"

"This house, Lee. Aunt Della's house, Lee!"

"Darl—"

"I … I called Attorney Robinson, Lee. A-about Aunt Della's—"

"Aunt … Aunt Della's—"

"Lawyer. Lawyer. Aunt Della's lawyer. You know that. You know, who he is, Lee." Darlene's eyes scan the room. "This house belongs to me. I … I worked for it. I … I worked hard for this house … e-earned it. Aunt … Aunt Della, my aunt Della owes it to me. She has to leave it to me, Lee. Aunt Della has to leave it to me, Lee! Leave this house to me, Lee!"

"The … the house? Why do … do you think Aunt Della, that she's seeing Attorney Robinson about the—"

"The house. It's the house. What else, Lee? What else do you think, possibly, what else do you think she has left, a-assets left—but the house. T-this old house. Glorious old house. What else, Lee!"

"Yes. Yes," Lee said, agreeing with Darlene. Lee took another step forward as if his intention was to hug Darlene again, but Darlene took to her uncle Frank's sofa, so Lee turned and walked over to the bigger sofa to sit.

Darlene sat on the sofa, her body hardening, looking like it could explode like the sofa seat she sat on of springs and stuffing. She sat there fuming, her anger building up from her shoulder blades and then rising to above her head. Lee, across the room, enveloped in his own tension, emotional war—but he was not angry, only worried about Darlene, only hoping some relief might come for her, that it might be shorter, quicker than in past times before for them.

"Attorney … Attorney Robinson's out of town though. Out—he'll be back in two days. His secretary said he could see Aunt Della Thursday, at two o'clock this Thursday if … if Aunt Della … if Aunt Della lives that long, Lee. If she lives that long."

"How … how's Aunt Della doing today?"

"Alert. Alert."

"Oh, good to hear. Good to hear, D—"

"Did you hear what I said, Lee? Did you hear what I said!"

"Yes, yes, the house, Darlene. The house. But we have a—"

"That house! That measly little house! Small thing. N-nothing of a house. It's not a house. Is it? Is it? It's not my aunt Della and uncle Frank's house. Is it? I want this house. I desire it. I've earned it. Worked hard … By right—I've earned it, Lee."

Pause.

"What … what could Aunt Della be thinking? What? What? What could Aunt Della be—"

"M-maybe it's just a minor detail, ad-adjustment she has to work out, that has to be ironed out with Attorney Robinson, D-Darlene. R-regarding the will. The will. Minor."

"Something Aunt Della f-forgot about. F-forgot about until now. B-before."

Darlene's tapping her finger stiffly against her cheek. "C-could be. It could be. Yes, maybe, Lee. Yes, m-maybe."

"Yes, that could be it, Darlene," Lee said, gaining confidence. "Between Aunt Della and Mr., uh, Attorney Robinson. Some, some minor detail. Something that maybe, that Aunt Della maybe overlooked. Have ironed out. Have clarified with Mr., uh, Attorney Robinson, Darlene."

"Margaret Ballad. Royal McCloud. Ha. Aunt Della's not fooled by them, Lee. Not for a second, an instant. In the least. Not by them. Uh … but … but I have to make sure. Make sure, Lee. I … I can't take any chances, anything for granted, not with, not with those two. Margaret Ballad and Royal McCloud. Be sure, Lee. They're dangerous. Too dangerous."

Darlene tensed.

"Aunt Della she … she's … I, Margaret might try to take advantage of her. The … the two of them. Two … two of them. Margaret … Margaret and Royal McCloud."

Lee shut his eyes; he looks put upon.

"Aunt Della, she can't think for herself now, Lee. With … with her illness, Lee. Clearly for herself. Her condition affecting the way, the way it is, to such a degree, extent, Lee. She, my aunt Della can't think for herself, clearly. And … and Royal McCloud's loan at the bank, the one I told you about, Lee … ha…"

Lee shook his head up and down.

"It's … it's not going through. No. Uh-uh. Uh-uh. Municipal Union Bank won't approve it no matter how hard John Houston tries to get it pushed through. For the bank to … Ha. Ha. Not … not on a wing and a prayer. A wing and a prayer, Lee. Ha. Ha."

Pause.

"And … and there's nothing better Royal McCloud would like to do better than … than turn this house, Aunt Della's house—"

Darlene got up and walked the living room floor, every inch of it, board of it, it seemed.

"Uncle Frank and Aunt Della's house, c-convert it into a church." Pause. "A … a …c-convert it into a church, Lee. A church!"

"A church? A church!"

"A church, Lee. Yes, yes, a church! You heard what I said, Lee! You heard me. You heard me. What I said!"

Lee, his emotions are tumbling out him. "H-how did you come up, by, to … to—"

"Ha. Ha. Oh yes, Lee. Oh yes. A church! A church! T-those sinners of Royal McCloud will march themselves in here, all right, in here—straight through the front door, here with, like a marching band with Royal McCloud and Margaret Ballad leading them, the way, all … all right.

"R-right into Aunt Della's house. Ha. Ha. T-those damned heathens of Royal McCloud's."

If Lee were standing he'd probably be stumbling, for he was unsteady, was toppling from everything Darlene was saying.

"Darlene—"

"Go … go now, go home now, Lee. Go … go home now. To the house. I … I don't need you now, Lee. Any, anymore, Lee. Go … go home, Lee." Darlene was walking away.

"I'm, I'm going upstairs to be with, with my aunt Della, Lee. M-Margaret's been up there too long with her. Already. My, my aunt Della." Pause. "Ha Ha. A, a church, Lee. A church. Just think. Just think. I'm telling—imagine? Can, can you imagine that? Just imagine that? I'm telling you, Lee. I'm, I'm telling you…"

Lee stands. "Yes, Darlene. Yes."

$$* \quad * \quad *$$

"Here goes, here goes," Royal said, sitting on the stool by the side of the phone. He was making the call to a private investigator. He'd gotten the information he needed, and now it was just a matter of luck and getting the right person at the right price to conduct the operation.

"Operation, why did I say 'operation'? It's not an operation, it … it's a search for my son, and … and that means I, this investigation has to find Eve. She's the key to the hunt, search for … I'm beginning to get hung up on too many words, tangled up on too many words, making it sound so complicated, s-so prolix." Royal stopped.

"But it is, isn't it? It is, when you haven't heard from someone in over three years. When my son is eight years old now. It is complicated. It isn't something simple. S-so simple, w-without complication."

Royal looked at the private investigator's number on the slip of paper he'd jotted it on. "Missing Persons." It said he could find missing persons. "Vincent Perrone Investigative Agency." Private investigator. *I don't know what to think right now.*

"Search, hunt … he's my son. I just want to hear his voice, Marshall's voice."

Royal hung up the phone.

"That's the reality. Ha …," Royal laughed mockingly. "That's the reality. I finally brushed up against the cold reality of … of …"

Vincent Perrone was asking for too much money. Plain and simple. It was a high price tag to pay to find someone. It was a high cost. It didn't come cheap. And then Mr. Perrone told him, "There're no guarantees I'll find Eve McCloud, Mr. McCloud. So I ain't gonna lie to you, sir. This kind of work's unpredictable as hell."

"I … I … I just can't afford it. I had no idea it'd be that expensive. Cost so much money."

Royal got up from the stool. He looked over at his school books. He still had studying to do, but he was going into the bedroom, lie down, meditate— just close his eyes to look for some peace in him—make that his single goal.

He was on the bed, lying across it, thinking of Margaret, thinking of anything he could to make this oppressive feeling he had leave, a feeling of inadequacy, a feeling of underachieving, a feeling of all those wasted years in Detroit, of not being smart enough to figure out his life, not until God came along, not until spiritually, as a person, he'd hit rock bottom, became spiritually bankrupt; and he was searching then for himself, having already paid the high price, cost, for who he was.

"I couldn't hire someone to do the work I had to do. P-pay them. It … it wasn't possible. Just wasn't possible for me to do."

He couldn't clear his mind of what had just happened. It was just impossible to do. The ache in his heart. Of not knowing where Marshall was living, the kind of life he was living. And him being this lay minister, this minister without shining credentials, ordinations, or the like. All he could say to any follower, to his faithful, was that he was chosen by God to do good. To do good in the world. And his principles, as strong as faith, was as strong as religion—this principle to guide him, uphold him, that had changed his life.

Yet in his personal life, he thought, he couldn't do any good for his son, for Marshall. This was what was eating at him now. *The shepherd amongst the sheep, in the field, but a baby sheep lost in the wilderness.*

"My son. My son."

And he had no reason to believe Eve's life would be better since Detroit. Oh, how he wanted to believe it, wished to believe it, that there was a chord in the universe, some striking of instruments, of cymbals that made great sound in the sky and could turn lives around as his and Margaret's had been turned around by God, religion, trumpets.

"But. But. Oh, I want to have faith. Say, I want to say Eve can do it too. That she can find a voice inside herself. Or … or it can find her as it found me. Spoke to me. M-made me listen. That there's a miracle inside all of …"

Royal opened his eyes, for he knew this was doing him no good. It was making him more anxious, getting him more down, depressed. It wasn't helping. Lying on his back on his bed this way. Thinking of sheep and shepherds and cymbals and instruments striking in the universe like some lost, ancient, archaic evangelist caught in a modern-day fire-and-brimstone sermon. Sometimes he wished he could preach that way, the old-time religion, use his tongue to cut evil down to its knees, purge it from humanity, only he had to find both an elegance and eloquence in the modern language, verse, poetry, prose, in the language of his time, and tell sinners they would burn in *hell* but make sure they never got to *hell* in the first place.

And Royal was back in the kitchen, out the bedroom. He didn't know what made him think like he did in the bedroom, on top the bed. But he had assigned religion to the power of protecting him. And if it could protect him, it would protect others, he thought. It would elevate their lives to a level of good and good will. *I think it's what I'm trying to say. I'm trying to do. Where I am now in my faith. My God has taken me. Religion.*

Religious power was in its responsibility. He looked at the books on the kitchen table, and why he was going to college was because he wanted a better job, more earning power, more money, and yes, yes, maybe more personal satisfaction for himself, from his job too.

And after some time, contemplation, Royal snapped his fingers.

"I … why … why didn't I think of it before … R-Ronny Bowers. He's still in Detroit. Living there. Maybe … maybe he can do me a favor, help me out. I don't know … I don't know—it's worth a try, isn't it? If I ask him. R-Ronny. I didn't burn all my bridges in Detroit. B-behind me."

Christmas break was coming, granted, Royal laughed, feeling better, but he still had to study. He sat down at the kitchen table and cracked open a book and then another. All of a sudden, it felt like a breath of fresh air for him. Then he paused.

"I never want to take myself too seriously. I don't. Just what I believe in.

The words I put in my sermons. What comes out the Bible and from me. It's what makes me modern, what I hope makes me valuable to God. It's how I want to serve him."

Royal felt relieved. He picked up the bright-yellow highlight marker. He knew there was something of importance in the sentence he'd just read that might come up in Professor Kinney's examination two days from today.

CHAPTER 10

It was late afternoon.

Margaret was food shopping. She would take the bus to the supermarket and return by taxi. The pantry was full of food, but in reality, she was shopping for Darlene and her needs, not Della's.

Darlene and Della are in the bedroom together, alone. Darlene sat at the right side of the bed. Her hand was stroking Della's hair. Della's eyes were shut, restful.

"I feel like a baby, Darlene. No older than one."

Darlene laughed. "Only difference, Aunt Della, is a baby doesn't remember things that happen at that age. So young, to them. But you'll always remember these moments. Precious moments, Aunt Della, won't you?"

Della impeded Darlene's hand. "Always. Always, Darlene." Della let go of Darlene's hand so Darlene could continue the smooth, seamless stroking of her hair.

"Aunt Della," Darlene said coolly, "how much of the past has remained? Has stayed with you over the years?"

Della smiled. "The past, honey? Why ... why I haven't forgotten anything about the past, Darlene. Not a thing. Nothing."

"Neither have I, Aunt Della."

"Why, uh, why the heavyhearted sigh, honey? Ha."

"Oh ... nothing."

"Only think of good times when I think of things now, thoughts, Darlene. Good—"

"The good times, not the bad, Aunt Della?" Darlene's hand stops stroking Della's hair.

"Don't stop, Darlene. D-don't you dare stop what you were doing, Darlene. Keep on. Keep on. Not a bit."

"Oh, oh sorry, Aunt Della. Sorry."

"Mmmm …," Della said soothingly. "No, don't stop what you're doing, honey. Feels so good."

"Aunt Della, it's what you do these days—only think of, uh, good days, not the bad?"

"Try to, Darlene. With age comes wisdom." Della takes Darlene's other hand. "Think I practiced this, don't you? Rehearsed it."

"No. No."

"But I didn't. Wisdom, Darlene. To use those bad times that were given you to turn into the good that eventually comes out of—"

"L-like what Margaret and Royal McCloud did to this family, Aunt Della, when they tore … uh, ripped it apart? The Ballad family when they ran off to Detroit together so Margaret could become Royal McCloud's whore. And … and Royal McCloud her pimp, Aunt Della!?"

Della's gasping for air. "Why? Why, Darlene? Why?"

"Margaret Ballad, Margaret Ballad a prostitute in Detroit. Royal McCloud her pimp! His prostitute! Pimping Margaret's body for money! For money in Detroit, Aunt Della!!"

"Oh, oh I … I—why now, Darlene? Today? Why … why are you bringing this up—"

"Do you remember, Aunt Della? Do you … do you, Aunt Della, remember, Aunt Della!?"

Alarmed, Della's shaking her head back and forth. "Yes, yes. Why … why of course I do, Darlene. Of—"

"Your daughter, Aunt Della. Your daughter. Running off to Detroit. Royal McCloud selling drugs. W-what he was doing in Myles Day City before he left. Margaret b-becoming—"

"Why now, Darlene? Why now? Today!"

Darlene stood. She fiddled with the bottle of pills on the top the tray. "I … I don't want to upset you, Aunt Della." Her voice had softened, losing some of its sting. "But ... but I don't want you to forget either. Ever forget those times either. You ... you mustn't f-forget them, Aunt Della. Those bad times in this house, Aunt Della. The gloom in this house. The pall that fell over the house. The—"

"It ... it was heavy. Yes, yes, it was—"

"What you and Uncle Frank went through it. Were put through. Went, but ... but I was there for you, Aunt Della. H-here—"

"Yes, yes, honey. It was your cheer. Your good cheer that Uncle Frank and I would look forward to every day after a while, Darlene. To help pull us through. H-help us, Darlene."

"Yes, Aunt Della, to pull you, to help pull you and Uncle Frank through."

"You running bathwater for your uncle Frank and me at night. Cook when—"

"You were having your bad days, Aunt Della. Were unable to. Were ... were too depressed to."

"So many bad days. Piled one on top the other. Days I was so depressed. D-down."

"Margaret, Margaret—Royal McCloud's prostitute. Whore."

"S-so many bad days, Darlene. So many."

"Then Margaret having the nerve to come back home. Running away from him, only to ... only to—"

"Run. Run off again. Run off to Detroit to ... to Royal again. A second time. M-Myles Day City to ... to Detroit. Darlene. A—"

"Yes, again, Aunt Della. Again. A second time, Aunt Della. To break your heart a second time, Aunt Della."

Pause.

Darlene stood at the side of the bed like a dark figure from the past.

"And then to spite her. To spite her by marrying that woman, that other woman—"

"Eve. Eve McCloud."

"And for her to have a child. S-son. By him. M-Marshall McCloud."

"Marshall McCloud. Marshall McCloud."

"And he and Margaret living under the same roof, Aunt Della. Then. Now. They aren't even—"

"But ... but they can't find her—E-Eve, Royal's—"

"The other prostitute. The one he, Royal McCloud, had pimping for him in Detroit. Then married, Aunt Della."

"Such words, Darlene. S-such words I used too when I—"

"Hated them, Aunt Della. Eve and Marshall McCloud and Royal McCloud. Hated them, Aunt Della."

"But he's tried … tried to find them, R-Royal. His family. Royal's tried to find his wife and his son so he can divorce her. But she ran away from Detroit. Nobody knows where she and—"

"But how hard, Aunt Della? How hard has Royal McCloud tried? Really, really tried to find—"

"Margaret says, Margaret says—"

"But Margaret will say anything, Aunt Della. Anything. She's under his spell. Royal McCloud's spell, c-control, night and day, Aunt Della. Night and … only, it's religion this time, Aunt Della. Controlling Margaret through religion, using religion this time. God, Aunt Della. God this time."

"No, Darlene. No, I—"

"Don't be confused, Aunt Della. Please don't be confused," Darlene said, her words rushing at Della. "This is no time to be confused. F-for confusion, Aunt Della. Not by Margaret, or … or by Royal McCloud, Aunt Della." Pause.

"You're to see Attorney Robinson tomorrow afternoon, Aunt Della. Your lawyer. It … it's about the house is … isn't it, Aunt Della? The house. This house. Isn't it? Isn't it?"

Slowly. "Yes."

"Who should get the house when … when—"

"I die, Darlene. Die."

Darlene grabs Della. "D-don't say that, Aunt Della. Don't say that. I … I don't want you to die, Aunt Della. I … I don't want you to die!"

"But … but I will, honey. But … but I will die. I'm reconciled to it. God knows I'm reconciled to it. And … and I've got decisions to make. Big, huge decisions to make, Darlene."

"About the house."

"The house. Uh-huh. The house, Darlene."

"The … the house," Darlene said like she was about to lose control. "The house. T-this glorious old house, Aunt Della."

"It's ... it's all I must think of now, Darlene. Nothing else. This is the most important thing I'll do b-before I die."

"You know I love this house, Aunt Della. You know that. Love, love this beautiful old house. Cherish it."

"How I know it, honey. How ever do I, do I know it."

Darlene's body turns 360 degrees. "This place. This place, Aunt Della. This house, Aunt Della!"

"Your uncle Frank and I thought it the most beautiful house, sight—we were so lucky ..."

"To be able to buy it. E-especially a colored person back—"

"In ... in Myles Day City back then, honey. Oh yes. We wasn't nothing back then. A colored person wasn't n—"

"Lucky, Aunt Della. Lucky."

"Guess some white people thought it time for coloreds to buy around here. Part of town. But had trouble in the beginning. Our share of it with white folk. Wasn't easy, easy sledding then. Didn't want us here. Living around here. Coloreds. In this area of town—no way. Myles Day City, Darlene.

"Come a long way. Not one day of those days was easy. But things worked out for the Ballad family. Thought at the time there'd be more than just Margaret running around this—"

"But there was room for me, Aunt Della. Plenty. A room was waiting for me when Momma died. D-down the hall from your and Uncle Frank's room, Aunt Della."

"Yes, for my darling Darlene."

Darlene's stopped spinning around the room. "They'll convert it, the house into a church, Aunt Della. You know that, you know that—Royal McCloud and ... and—"

"Margaret? Royal!" Della looks terrified. "This ... this house, D-Darlene? This house!"

Darlene walks to the front of the bed; her back's to Della. She turns sharply to her. "It's what they'll do. Of course. Of course. Those two. It'll be a church. Hands of Christ Church, not ... not a house, Aunt Della. It's what Lee and I think."

"Lee? Lee!"

"At first we, Lee and I, thought they might sell it if ... if—"

"I left it to them in—"

"Your will, Aunt Della. Your final, last will and testament, Aunt Della. You see ... because Royal's waiting for an answer on a loan from Municipal Union Bank. He wants the location on Bayer Street, at 20 Bayer Street, but that'll fall through. Fail. Fall on its face for sure, Aunt Della. The bank, Union Bank's too smart for that, Aunt Della. Oh yes. Then ... then Royal McCloud and Margaret will just as soon turn this house into a church. Why not? Convert it into a church. There's enough room to. People coming ... coming and going, coming and going, marching in and out, marching in and ou the house like a band, Aunt Della. All ... all the time, all hours of the day and night with their meetings, church meetings, church functions, church ac-activities."

"No. No. M-Margaret and Royal—"

"In and out. In and out. Who knows. Who's to know what they'll do. With this newfound religion they've got. Them and ... and this religion of theirs. E-especially Royal McCloud. Especially him. You've had your doubts about Royal McCloud all along. Aunt Della."

"But—"

Darlene feels as if she's finally overpowering Della, has overwhelmed her.

"One day a sinner, the next day a saint? Sinner to saint? Pimp to preacher? What's the difference, Aunt Della? Royal McCloud's still a con man, a con artist. Preaching a, preaching for people to follow him, for he can take ... manipulate them, Aunt Della. The same old Royal McCloud. He hasn't changed any. Ha Ha. He—c-control them for he can take, one ... one day take what, whatever money he can from them. G-get from them and run off with it. Back to Detroit. Off to Detroit like he did b-before. Steal their money. Steal their money right out their pockets or ... ha ... t-that church's collection plate this time, Aunt Della. This—but the house will do for now. Will do just fine for Royal McCloud now, Aunt Della. His taste, liking now, Aunt Della. The house. This beautiful, glorious old house, Aunt Della."

"F-for now, Darlene? For now?"

Suddenly. "Oh, your pills, Aunt Della. Y-your pills."

"I—"

"Ha." Darlene runs over to the tray. "It's five o'clock after all. It's five o'clock." Darlene looks at her watch. "It's five o'clock after all."

"Three, three, Darlene. Three pills at five o'clock. Three."

Darlene, animated. "Three pills. Three pills down the hatch, Aunt Della. Three pills down the hatch."

"My, my—"

"Elephant pills. Elephant pills, Aunt Della. I'll get the water. Go get the water. Out the bathroom. Ha. We were talking so—but nothing's more important right now than—"

"My pills, Darlene. El-elephant pills."

"Your pills, your pills. Your … your pills. Your elephant pills, Aunt Della." Darlene's headed for the bathroom. "I'll … I'll always r-remember what you called them, that saying, Aunt Della. Ex-expression. You used. Always. I'll never forget. I'll never forget, Aunt Della."

Della looks over to her left, and they were still there—the sponge and the "small tub of water" (as she called it) on the chair. They'd been there from this morning, and no one had removed them (neither Darlene nor Margaret). She was always sponge bathed right after she ate breakfast. It's the first it'd happened, what she saw, and she'd kept forgetting to tell either Darlene or Margaret about it, so she was as guilty as they about the sponge and small tub of water. She couldn't remember when last she'd had a *real* bath.

"If I say I remember, I might as well be lying." Della chuckled. "Don't always have my facts straight. In good order. Get them mixed up now and then nowadays."

Della was in the room alone. She had such periods even with Darlene and Margaret in the house. With Darlene, the sewing machine would go day and night, something that was real comforting for her, to hear that Singer sewing machine going. And Margaret, it was as if it were deliberate, like she wanted to give her time to herself, not press up on her all day long now that she was off from work, in the house all day; Margaret was considerate that way with her.

Della looked back over to what was on the chair, and it's when she looked at the items on the chair, and it affected her, troubled her, and she didn't know why. And then she looked around the room as Darlene had earlier.

"This house. Our house, Frank."

No, she hadn't recovered from the shock of Darlene's words, her opinion of what might happen to the house if it was willed to Margaret and not Darlene. The things Darlene said would happen to it.

"A church. A church. A church for Royal. Converting this house into a church. Christ of Hands Church."

Darlene was in the kitchen cooking. Where Margaret was, Della had no idea. But Margaret would drop in and check on her. It'd be any minute now. It was always an ideal time for her to, when Darlene was in the kitchen cooking, taking a lot of time with something; both were clever about their movement and maneuverings in the house, Della thought.

"I'm gonna have Margaret get rid of that sponge and washtub on …"

Then Della was struck by her own anxiety, like she was when Darlene was in the room with her and she was saying all those things, digging the past back up, dredging it up. "Prostitute," "pimp"—words she used, learned to use to describe her daughter and Royal at one time. The two of them living their life of sin in Detroit, and she and Frank dying every day, not one day buttressed by peace or hope, not one day sure, safe, always thinking the worse— Margaret winding up on Detroit streets dead. Royal McCloud responsible for her daughter's death.

A shiver shot through her. It really hadn't left since Darlene went downstairs to cook dinner. It was in her and with it painful, agonizing thoughts.

"No telephone calls. No telephone calls. No nothing. It was like she had no mother or father. And then, after so much time, she came back, was back on our doorstep like she was a lost child coming back home to us. And … and me and Frank, me … me and Frank thought it was over—the worse was over.

"But Royal came back for her. He … he came back to Myles Day City too and found a way to … Oh … oh, Darlene, Darlene … what did she do …"

It's when Margaret went back to Detroit, was when she found out Royal, for spite, married Eve. And it was months later when Eve said she was pregnant with Royal's child, was carrying it, but Royal was back with Margaret.

"There was such evil in Royal's heart then. Those days. Would do it over and over. Lord, Lord.

"And now the house. The house. Who should get the house, Frank? Darlene or Margaret? Darlene or Margaret? Help me. Help me, Frank. Help me."

"Momma …"

"Margaret, Margaret …," Della said, looking up; she pawed at her eyes. "I was waiting for you to drop by."

Margaret giggled.

"But I must've dropped off. Was catching a catnap."

"I called the job. Betty, my new supervisor in the new division I'm in, said they really miss me. A lot."

Della perked up. "And why shouldn't they, Margaret? Tell me, why not?"

"Yes, why shouldn't they!" Margaret laughed again.

"You're so delicate, aren't you, Margaret? Honey?"

"Momma, what do y-you mean? What—"

"Oh … uh, never mind, honey. Never mind."

"But—"

"Know Royal misses you too. Royal doesn't mind … mind you staying here any, does he?"

"Mind? Royal? Royal, Momma? You know better, Momma. Better than to ask that."

"Uh, yes, yes, I do, don't I, Margaret? I do."

Then Margaret looks to her right. "Oh, Momma, the sponge and washtub, it's—"

"Margaret, uh, Margaret, never mind that for the moment, Margaret. The time being 'cause … 'cause I've … I must tell you something, honey. I …"

"Yes, yes, Momma?"

Silence.

"Momma, you have had a good day, I hope, haven't—"

"Oh yes, uh-huh. Oh yes, Margaret. I've … I've had a good day. An excellent day. The best. Oh yes."

There's relief on Margaret's face.

"Margaret, I'm seeing Attorney Robinson tomorrow."

"Attorney … Attorney Robinson, Momma? Y-your lawyer?"

Della lowers her head and then raises it.

"Going to see him tomorrow." Della begins scratching at her hair."At the house at two o'clock. Was done yesterday. The appointment, that is. Meant to tell you. But didn't."

Margaret couldn't restrain herself. "But Darlene knows, knows about it, doesn't she, Momma? The meeting with Attorney Robinson, doesn't she?"

"Uh-huh. Darlene knows all right. She's the one who—"

"Called Attorney Robinson for you."

Della hears the resentment in Margaret's voice. "I—it just happened that way, Wasn't planned out. Just happened—yesterday morning when I woke, came out the clear blue sky, honey. You were in the house doing something … something at the time, Darlene said."

Pause.

"It … it hit me. Just hit me like a ton of bricks. I've … I've got to see Attorney Robinson, I thought. I've got to see—"

"About what, Momma? What exactly?"

"My will, honey. My final will and testament."

"Yes, Momma, your—"

"The house, Margaret."

Margaret trembled. "The house, Momma?"

"Yes, honey, the house. Got … got decisions to make, Margaret. About the house."

Margaret really studies Della but finds no clear emotional sign on her face to draw any conclusions from.

"Regarding Darlene and me, Momma?"

"Yes."

"It … it's all right, Momma. Don't worry. Your last days, I want them to be peace—"

"It ain't that easy, Margaret. Ain't—is never that easy when it comes to family. To the people you love … Who love you. Isn't that easy at any age. I've got a decision to make about the house, Margaret. One I can't run away from, honey."

"No. No. Momma. You—"

"If it wasn't for me to do, it would've been for your father to do if he outlived me, for Frank to do—the house isn't going anywhere. Is-isn't going to disappear. Vanish into thin air."

"No, no, it isn't," Margaret said nervously.

"But first, Margaret, we've gotta talk."

Margaret, who'd been standing all the time, sits, drawing the chair nearer Della's bed.

Della swallows her saliva with difficulty.

"A talk I should've had with you a long time ago." Pause. "But how do I begin? Where? At the beginning? I guess." Della looks frazzled. "When, how Darlene came in here, this house.

"The circumstances. under which Darlene came to us, your father and me."

"Aunt Nettie's death," Margaret said.

"My sister dying sudden. Darlene … y-your cousin losing her world at age eight, so young. Her father long gone. High-hightailing it out of Myles Day City not long after she was born. Eddie Lyles. Never marrying your aunt. Aunt Nettie. Her death such a tragedy."

"Yes, I remember how it was for Darlene," Margaret said, indeed remembering.

"You were seven months older than her, Margaret. What you were. Was so much happening to that little child's life … my niece." Della looked point-blank at Margaret.

"Margaret, she was hungry for love." Pause. "Your father used to say she starved for it like an animal in the wild. And she did. But it couldn't come from you, oh … oh how you tried, honey. Tried with all your heart. Worked at it. Saw, Frank, your father and I saw how you tried to be like a sister to Darlene. Love her. How Darlene rejected it." Pause. "Flat out …

"'C-cause it could only come from a mother, a father, for Darlene, not anybody else, what Darlene had lost. Nobody else would do. Was capable. Was, just was no other substitute for her, Margaret. None in the world.

"Only, she got hungrier and hungrier. Greedier and greedier. The older she got. She clung to me, Margaret. To her aunt Della as if … if she didn't, she would die. Just die. Poor little thing. The … the world, Margaret, would just stop for her. Or … or something like that in her mind, and she would just die. I don't know how it got in her heart and head that way. Darlene figured it that way. Not to this day. But it was there, and your father and I had to … t-to—"

"Deal with it, Momma. You and Daddy had to deal with—"

"As best we could, honey. Almost to the point where it hurt the relationship we had with our own daughter, Margaret. Flesh and blood. With you. I … I didn't know Darlene was out to destroy you, Margaret. It's why your father and I eventually felt responsible for—"

"Royal?"

"We let Darlene get away with too much, Margaret. Indulged her too much. Put up with too much. We—"

"Yes. I felt, I did feel … Oh, Momma, Momma, I didn't expect this talk. This conversation with you just now. You caught me totally off guard. Un-unprepared, but—"

"Your … your running away from home …"

Margaret collected herself. "Maybe I was seeking love. A different kind of love. S-someone I … I didn't have to share."

"Weren't uncertain—"

"Of?" Margaret said, cutting Della off. "No, Momma, I've always been certain. Certain of how you love me."

"But I could've stepped in more often with Darlene. Taken your side. Taken up for you. Fought for you. Up to, even up to now, this day, very day, I … I—"

"But still, Momma, still—a lot had to do with Royal. The promise of love and then being afraid of losing it. Finding I … I would do anything for it. To hold onto it, Momma. Anything, Momma. It was the power Royal had over me, Momma. The power."

"It … it's what Darlene said. What she said. Exactly, Margaret. Exactly."

"Darlene? Darlene? Y-you discussed this with—"

"The house, Margaret."

"Yes, Momma. The house."

"It, if I leave it to you in the will, the house, she, Darlene thinks—"

"I'll sell it? Sell the house, Momma?"

Della drew her body up in the bed. "Was what she thought, honey. Before. Was what Darlene—was o-originally."

"Was? Was, Momma?"

"Thinks, thinks now that you'll convert the house, you and Royal, will convert the house into a church when I die. If I leave the house to you in the will. Will and testament. The house will be a church for you and Royal, Margaret. Hands of Christ Church."

"Oh, Momma! Momma!"

Della knew she must press on with this no matter the difficulty, no matter the moment's apparent cruelty, she must press on; she must not stop now that she'd driven this thing this far.

"Thinks Royal's loan at Municipal Union Bank won't go through for him. C-certain not to go through the bank. What's pending there. What Darlene thinks."

"The ... the loan—"

"And when it doesn't—that ... that the power Royal has over you like—"

"Before. Before, when I sold my body for him. For Royal. Detroit, Momma. In Detroit. W-was a prostitute. A ... a prostitute in Detroit, Momma."

"Yes, honey. Yes."

Coldly. "Then ... then I can't help you, Momma," Margaret said, getting up, her arms reining her in. "I can't help you then."

"Margaret, I—"

Margaret looks down at Della. "Darlene, she has a power over you too, Momma."

"S-she does, Margaret," Della said sadly, her head dropping. "Darlene does. I ... I know."

"But ... but you're not to be blamed. You nor Daddy are to be blamed, Momma. And certainly not for me, my life, what Royal and I did in Detroit. Me turning to prostitution. I-I've forgiven myself, Momma. At last."

"Yes, I know, Margaret."

"I-I've forgiven myself, Momma," Margaret said, echoing herself.

"And I ... I..."

"Momma, please, you don't have to say anymore. Nothing more to explain yourself."

"But, M—"

"You have to make a decision about this house—who you will leave it to. Me or—"

"Dar—"

"You'll be seeing Attorney Robinson tomorrow."

"At two o'clock. Yes, Margaret."

"And it will be your decision to make. Yours, Momma. Not mine. Not Darlene's but yours, Momma. As it should be. For the Ballad family. You and Daddy, Momma, w-who you think this beautiful old house should be left to in your will."

Margaret walks over to the chair and picks up the sponge and the small tub and then walks out the room.

Royal's in the kitchen. His head's down on top the kitchen table, his body depressed. A letter's in his hand. His head pops up.

"Mag!"

"Royal, what's wrong? T-the matter?"

Royal's up from the table. "I was going to call you, Mag. Honest. Honest. The loan—they turned it down. Municipal Union Bank. The letter came in the mail today."

Margaret's hugging him.

"Oh, Royal. Royal."

"I, guess … I guess it wasn't meant to be. To happen. But Brother Houston tried, oh how he tried. He really, really tried. I … I thank God for him trying so hard."

"Yes."

Both sat down at the kitchen table.

"But I was going to call you at the house. Honest. It was just that I had to get over my disappointment first, I guess. Felt I—my heart, Mag, it never beat so fast when I saw the envelope, the bank's name inscribed on it, and when I opened it … well …"

"It … it doesn't mean it's, that's the end though, Royal. Our trying."

"Oh no, Mag. No. You know me better than that. Not by a long shot. Uh-uh, not at all."

"Good."

Royal laughed. "We've only been sidetracked tem-temporarily. Nothing, no more than that. Not permanently. I'm still going to pray on it. Still going to … ha … keep the faith. God will provide in some way, I'm sure. Even mysterious unto me." Then Royal looked into Margaret's eyes, seems to be piercing them.

"Only, you're home."

"Took a taxi," Margaret laughed.

"Was smart enough to figure that out. On my own. I didn't drive you … What are you doing home? Clothes … clothes, you need a fresh supply of—"

"Momma. Momma meets with Attorney Robinson—"

"Morgan Robinson? Mother Ballad's lawyer, Mag?"

"Yes, Royal. Momma's lawyer. They're meeting tomorrow. Tomorrow afternoon at two o'clock in the house, Royal."

Royal sucks in the air. "What? About Mother Ballad's will?"

"More specifically, a-about the house, Royal. Momma's house."

"Yes, the house, the house," Royal said seemingly to let it sink in, all sink in, the information. "I ... I—why I should've seen this coming, Mag."

"Momma has to make a decision about the house."

Royal's not looking at her. "Yes, I know. It involves you and Darlene, who should get the house. You or Darlene."

"Royal, where have I been? All this time? My mind? I ... I never thought of it, Royal. Never—"

"Y-you mean you haven't?"

"You have, Royal? You mean y-you've thought of it?"

What had been his smooth movements before now were jerky. "Yes, yes, I have, Mag."

"Oh, oh I ... I didn't know."

"Yes, I have."

Silence.

Margaret's regained her composure.

"Well tomorrow at two o'clock, Momma's to inform Attorney Robinson what she wants to do with the house."

"Two o'clock?"

"Yes."

Royal glares at the bank's letter. "Yes, yes, Brother Houston tried his best for us, Mag."

Pause.

"I ... I had to get out of there, out the house, Royal. I had to."

"W-why, Mag?"

"Darlene. Darlene. I, to get from around Darlene. S-she's been poisoning Momma's mind with all kinds of things. I-ideas. So I called a taxi. I'm going to eat dinner here tonight. With you, Royal, if it's all right—you don't mind."

"Fine. Fine. You know, I'd love that. To have your company."

"And then I'll go back ... back to the house to be with Momma. But I had to get away from Darlene, Royal. I had to. I ... I felt contaminated by her."

"Mag ... but what kind of things is Darlene saying to Mother Ballad? How's she been p-poisoning Mother Ballad's mind?"

"With all kinds of things, Royal. Saying all ... all kinds of terrible, awful things."

"I know you're—but, Mag, can't you be clearer? More—"

"It's us, Royal. Us. Our past. And … and what we are to each other now."

"We love each other. Is there something wrong with that? All of a sudden? Is it a crime suddenly? A man and a woman who love each other?"

"The past has been thrown, tossed back into Momma's face—"

"By Darlene."

"If the house is willed over to me—"

"Then you will do what … what with it, Mag, s-sell it? Sell the house? It's what, is that what Darlene's telling, saying—sprung on Mother Ballad?"

Viciously. "No, no, that was the original scenario. The original one Darlene used. There's a new one. A new one Darlene's hatched. More sinister. The new one that …"

Margaret stops.

"What? What's the new one, Mag? Scenario? What!"

Margaret's body was coiled.

"That you and I, you and I, Royal …"

"Yes, yes. You and I, you and I would do what, what with the—"

"Convert it. Convert it. Convert Momma's house in, into …"

"What, Mag? What!"

"A church. A church, Royal. A church. Hands of Christ Church!"

"A church? Hands of Christ Church!"

"Yes. Yes. D-Darlene knew about the loan pending at Municipal Bank. And … and she said it would be rejected, t-turned down, Royal. Turned—"

"D-Darlene knew that? She knew that? Darlene knew that?"

"She knew. Yes, she knew."

Royal picks Municipal Union's Bank's letter back up and begins waving it in front of him like a desperate man.

"And … and if Momma leaves the house to me, that—"

"Royal McCloud, Royal McCloud will convert the old house into a church. Use it as a church. Hands of Christ Church."

"Yes, a church, Royal. A … a church. Hands of—th-that people will be coming in and out of the house day and night. All hours of the day. All hours of the day and night, Royal."

Royal bows his head and clasps his hands in what seems an act of total submission.

"I want to pray for Darlene. Pray for her." He's standing again. "I always want to pray for my enemies, Mag. Those who stand against me. Those formidable foes who line up against me. Assail me. I … I let them take their shots at me, Mag. I let them take their shots at me, and I still know I will continue to carry the cross high up on my shoulders and then sink down to my knees, get down on my knees to pray for them, Mag. Pray for them. Their souls.

"But today, right now, I don't want to pray for Darlene Winston but … but damn her, Mag. Damn her!"

Pause.

"Sweet, sweet Darlene. Sweet, sweet Darlene. And God, yes, forgive me. Forgive me for what I just said in your presence. F-forgive me for what's, what you know is in my heart. Deep down inside my heart. God. God, forgive me." Royal sinks to the kitchen floor, is on his knees.

"P-please forgive me …"

"She's wrong, isn't she, Royal?" Margaret asks frantically. "B-but Darlene is wrong, wrong a-about the house, is-isn't she, Royal? If … if it's left to us, Royal—isn't she?"

Royal drove Margaret back to the house under Margaret's strong protest. But he wasn't going to have her take a taxi, not under any circumstance. Yes, there were a lot of things on his mind, on their minds, but they weren't going to block him from what he knew was right.

The car had been pretty much cloaked in silence and doom the whole trip to the house, from start to finish. But it was expected—they'd both been impacted. They'd both been hit by a hard savage blow; they'd been ambushed. It had come from out of nowhere, a bolt from out the blue. It'd hit its mark though, directly, square center, bull's-eye, and it hurt; there was no denying that, getting around that. It hurt. And he wasn't going back to the apartment to lick his wounds; no, it was more elevated, serious than that, for he had to find solace, a place where he could really think, meditate, examine his feelings like they had to be put up to the most severe light, receive the most harsh scrutiny even if it was down in the basement of Tom Tolletson's junk shop, where no light, no sunlit days, could ever possibly come from.

It's where he was. The place he'd driven the car to, a place he had to be, down in the basement of his church. Hands of Christ Church. This place where he preached. This place where he dreamed. This place where he tried to be a shining example, open the book of truth and find scriptures and parables to live a good life, Christian life, by. Where his faith was. He had to be there. It's the only place he could be right now.

He felt like a thief in the night, because he'd snuck himself into Hands of Christ Church's basement. Even with these feelings squarely inside him, there was an awkwardness in his thinking. His head led him there, but his mind had yet to catch up, because he was trying to think everything through even though it looked so simple; but for him, what he'd been through, an ex–drug dealer, pimp, someone who worshipped money, adored fine clothes and jewelry and cars—not God—he had to examine any thought complex, any breach that might tie him to his past, cling him to it like barnacles, first in Myles Day City, and then Detroit—somewhere where he went to for bigger game and fame.

And so Royal, having turned on the light in the church basement and now walking up to the pulpit and picking the Bible up off the pulpit and letting the book's spine fit comfortably in his hand, looked up at the cracked ceiling as if looking up at a piece of heaven.

"I've come to you heavenly Father tonight, for life is back in the thick of me. Back raging as it's not raged before. The … the forces of good and evil, they are converging … Are converging in Mother Ballad's house and, now, in my heart. W-why did I think of Mother Ballad's house, the old house, and not Mag, her daughter, her own daughter? But it was me, dear Father, me who thought of Mother Ballad's house, and why? Why, Lord, why?

"Am … am I the devil incarnate, now disguised in lamb's wool? Lamb's clothing? Am I so … so simply shaped, crafted in evil, deception, so wicked— have I not thought of Mother Ballad's house. Have I not?"

Royal put the Bible down. His head moved downward with his hand, but once the Bible's back atop the pulpit, Royal raises his head once again; his eyes are back looking up at the cracked ceiling as if he's looking at heaven.

"It was my dream to have a church. My own church. My vision. But God … God, why don't I … why do I no longer trust myself? My own heart. My own soul. My intentions. Why … why I am standing here … here at the altar with self-doubt? Someone who no longer feels like a man but is a man. Knows he is a man. How much has been stripped from …The loan! The loan!

How much of me does ... does Darlene know? D-Darlene Winston know of Royal McCloud!"

Powerfully, Royal clasps his hands together, and his head shakes as if trying to shake the tears free from his eyes.

"I ... I was ... yes, I was a pimp. Dealt drugs in Myles Day and Detroit. Killed young men's and women's souls. It's what I did. What I—yes, me. Me. Who ... who I was then. Back then. Pimp to preacher. Pimp to preacher. It's what they say in Myles Day City about me. About Royal McCloud. Call me. I know. Darlene is ... is not alone. Is not the only one to call me it to my face. Pimp to preacher. Darlene Winston is not alone. S-set outside the margins of judgment. No, she's not the only one."

Royal's body stiffens and then hurls itself forward.

"M-Mag said I have a power over her. Had it then in ... in Detroit. Turned her ... turned her into a ... But then I ... I—wasn't I the one who helped give her God too? Too? You ... you too, God, when I found you. She ... she, her soul was not so lost, so tattered and ... and frayed that she couldn't turn to you too." Pause.

"But ... but it was still my power. By my power. My will. Determination. Admittedly. Admittedly. Royal ... Royal McCloud's power over her was ... wasn't it, God? Wasn't it?

"And now the house. Mother Ballad's old house has come into question, and I, un-under suspicion. Sell the house? Sell it so I could get the Bayer Street store front, property ... Or ... or convert, what, t-the house into a church? A church! For I could do better than this? W-what I'm now doing?"

Royal looks around the basement.

"The power. The power I have. This power of Royal McCloud. Of ... of Royal McCloud. What is it? What is it? What ... what is its good? Ex- exactly its good. The ... the nature of its good? What good does it serve? Or ... or am I still a pimp? A Detroit pimp? A devil? Pimp to preacher. Pimp to preacher. Still in Detroit pimping Margaret's soul? Saved by the Holy Ghost but to be accursed by my own wretchedness. Heathen heart. My ... my ..."

Royal lays his head back down on top the Bible and shuts his eyes and stands there as if hoping God's spiritual power will enter in him, through his fingertips, hand, and then for it to surge into his veins, his body, the rest of him.

Royal's still anchored to the pulpit, has not moved, is shimmering now as if in some spiritual fire, an illumination, a manifestation of spirit, feeling as though it could steady the ground he's standing on, unify it, keep it from shifting beneath him. "Thank you, Lord. Thank you, Lord, for listening to me, Father. Hearing … hearing me out, Heavenly Father."

Royal walks away from the pulpit. He stands in the middle of the basement's aisle.

"This is where my small flock gathers every Sunday morning to praise your name. In this holy sanctuary we call church. It is our home for now. The ground on which we stand. God's ground. There will be another home for us in the future, one day—there will be, Lord, there will be. I know there will be. I do have the faith. I do have the faith."

Royal's at the basement door and then looks back into the room.

"Royal McCloud. Rev. Royal McCloud. I stand right up … ha … up there at the pulpit every Sunday morning and preach whatever sermon I have prepared during the week for those people to hear on that designated Sunday. I do. Royal McCloud does." Royal smiles. "Rev. Royal McCloud does.

"There will be a church. One day, there will be a church. Sacred ground for one. And I will be its pastor. Its leader. Rev. Royal McCloud will be its spiritual leader. We will have a church home. A sanctuary."

Royal turns off the basement light and stands there as the room quickly darkens.

"For God … God—for he does move in mysterious ways, even unto me."

Royal's eager to get into the apartment, yet he's sitting in the car directly outside the apartment building, letting the engine idle, keeping the car's heater on, a heater that delivers heat and then dies, something needing mechanical attention. It was too cold outside to shut the heater off, for someone to sit in an unheated car. He was just sitting there eager to get into the house but not finished with his soul searching, not totally mitigating it. For he was thinking of those he'd killed, poisoned with the drugs he'd sold in Detroit. They were still casualties he carried inside him, his eyes and his heart every day. Every day he thought of them, strung out, eyes vacant, the needle, the drug offering no hope for them but keeping them alive while, ironically, killing them slowly.

"I see them every day. Those drug addicts. I can't forget them. I won't forget them. There were so many of them."

They were Latino and white but mostly black he sold to. He'd killed mostly black drug addicts, users in Detroit (his own black brothers and sisters, his own kind). And so many he killed were so young. It's why he thought of Marshall so much, besides the holidays (yes, it increased then). He had a son, and to think that someday some drug dealer could do it to Marshall, what he'd done to others, it would surely be the devil's revenge, the evil he'd perpetuated onto others *coming home to roost*, coming back now to put a curse on his house.

Royal shut off the car engine. Once again he was eager to get into the apartment, to call Margaret, tell her he'd gotten in touch with Ronny Bowers, something he did not tell her, not with the startling news, the startling circumstances, the mess with Darlene and the house, which just came out of nowhere, sprang up. For Ronny said he could help him with the investigation, that he would put him in touch with someone in Detroit who was good at finding missing persons, a real pro, who knew his stuff, who didn't work cheap, for nothing, but was reasonably priced.

Royal shut the car door. Immediately he felt the cold blast of air on his face, right away. But he was bundled up for the short walk to the apartment. Royal blew on his hands. He wanted to talk to Margaret anyway. Tomorrow was to be a big day for the Ballad family with Attorney Robinson coming to the house. He still wanted to relax her. Help her clear her head, wind herself down.

"Everything's going to work out. It'll work out okay. One day at a time. One day at a time. We'll handle it one day at a time, Mag."

CHAPTER 11

Next day.

Darlene knew Margaret knew about Attorney Robinson coming to the house at two o'clock. In fact, she was the one to tell her she did, and Margaret had nodded her head, showing no surprise by the news. *You spoke to Aunt Della. Aunt Della told you. Yes.* And so that was that—end of conversation, for she had no more to say to Margaret, nothing more than what she'd said.

Darlene was sitting in the living room. She felt sick. She was sitting in the living room, anticipating the worse—Attorney Robinson coming to the house, looking official, carrying that dark-brown briefcase that bulged with legal papers, with legal documents it could barely hold.

She couldn't sleep last night. And then Royal called, and it upset her more, worse, and it bothered her that he called the house late to talk to Margaret. *She had seethed.*

"My whole night upset. Upset, upset. I was going to call Lee, but … but …"

What time is it? Darlene thought. *What time is it now?*

It's why she was sitting in the living room, wasn't it? Because it was almost two o'clock; it was almost two o'clock—a time she'd been anticipating the whole day.

But why am I worried? Why am I worried when it's Margaret who should be worried? Margaret, Margaret, not me, she thought. Margaret Ballad. It's why Royal called her so late last night. It had to be, it had to be. They were already anticipating the worse, defeated, defenseless, knowing the reason why Attorney Robinson was coming to the house today was because her aunt's will would deny them the house, would refuse them the house, that her uncle and aunt's house would be willed over to her today, that those papers of Attorney Robinson's in his briefcase would seal their fate. It's why she was in the living room and Margaret was upstairs in the bedroom with her aunt Della. She'd told her aunt Della she would receive Attorney Robinson, let him in the house, escort him up to her bedroom as soon as he got in, arrived, and now she was sitting on her uncle Frank's couch, waiting for him, sick to her stomach, having lost sleep last night, almost, practically calling Lee, but not doing that, so, not needing Lee that much, not needing anyone, just making it through the night, through the day by her own resources, strength, able to do so by her own internal engine.

Yes. Yes. Y—

Ring.

"It's him! Attorney Robinson!"

Darlene leaped off the couch. She was running to the door but then stopped.

"Why, why am I doing … doing this for? Running?"

She smiled and then flipped back her soft hair. Then she walked to the front door and smiled again and then opened the door.

"Attorney Robinson."

"Good afternoon, Mrs. Winston."

"Come in. Come in. My aunt's been expecting you."

"Thank you, Mrs. Winston."

Attorney Robinson was short, slender. He was dark skinned. He was in scarf and overcoat and hat, and Darlene was taking them in hand as he removed them article by article, putting the dark-brown bulged briefcase on top the rug.

"Thank you, Mrs. Winston. So much."

Darlene hung the articles of clothing in the closet. Attorney Robinson walked to the bottom of the staircase. He had a distinguished smile. He looked like a legal beagle.

"After you, Mrs. Winston," Robinson said when Darlene joined him at the foot of the staircase. It's when Darlene paused, looked at the briefcase, and then breezed past him.

"Aunt Della can't wait to see you. To clear this whole will business up."

"Ha. It's always a special joy just to see your aunt, Mrs. Winston. Whenever and wherever possible."

They were on the house's second-floor landing. Hurriedly Darlene walked with Attorney Robinson, Robinson following her with equal pace.

"Aunt Della, Aunt Della, Attorney Robinson's here. Attorney—"

And Margaret was at the bedroom door, and Darlene glared at her.

"Good afternoon, Margaret."

"Good afternoon, Attorney Robinson."

Margaret and Attorney Robinson shook hands.

"Good afternoon, Morgan."

"Oh … good afternoon, Mrs. Ballad," Attorney Robinson said, rushing headlong into the room. "It's so good … good to see you, Mrs. Ballad."

"Likewise, Morgan."

"And do you look good, ever look so wonderfully well."

Della extended her hand, and Attorney Robinson kissed it.

"Chivalry's not dead, after all—I see, Morgan."

"Not when it comes to you, Mrs. Ballad, I'm delighted to say."

"Well, thank you, Morgan. Thank you. It's always nice for a girl to hear."

Then the air seemed to flatten, rise no more than the room's carpet.

"Uh, pull up a chair," Della finally said. "And let's get down to business. Shall we, Morgan?"

Attorney Robinson sought the nearest chair; he put the fat briefcase down on the floor.

"Uh, Momma …"

"See you later, honey."

Margaret left the room.

Darlene stood there, in the bedroom, rooted in place.

"Uh, Darlene, honey … uh …"

Attorney Robinson's hand had dug down inside the briefcase; he was pulling out a slew of papers. And now his hand had gone inside his suit jacket to retrieve his polished blue pen.

"Yes, yes, Aunt Della?"

"You may close … uh, shut the door, honey. Behind you."

"Of … of …"

"Morgan and I want to be alone."

"A … a—"

"What do you have for me, Morgan?"

"Well, Mrs. Ballad …"

Darlene shut the bedroom door.

Darlene was back in the living room. Attorney Robinson had been in the bedroom, behind the door what now was some twenty-eight minutes. Darlene had been counting, keeping track. How much time was on business, being spent on business, the will and testament, and how much on the social side she didn't know … But he was out his office. *He does have a work schedule to fulfill, doesn't he?* This question she'd been asking herself, this question and only this question.

But here she was, waiting for the bedroom door to open, timing, with her watch, just how long it'd been closed, not knowing how to think, how to come up with answers that might fit, provide something other than chance and confusion and this sick stomach of hers, that wouldn't quiet, quit, stop, causing her to stop just short of grabbing it, pressing it, demandingly, making her feel more nauseated, close to throwing up her breakfast and lunch.

Except she was the strong one, the rooted one, not Margaret. She had to compare everything against Margaret—it was her measuring stick. *Margaret. Margaret.* Margaret couldn't come close to her, not even close—couldn't touch her.

God only knew what she'd been doing in her room, Margaret (Darlene glanced at her watch—thirty minutes now. What, two minutes had passed that quickly?).

"Ha Ha. God only knows. She must be in so … there must be, she must be agonizing so much. So much. I just feel … feel …"

She was sweating. She was sweating.

"I … I mustn't sweat! I mustn't sweat!"

Darlene got up from the couch and ran into the downstairs bathroom and then back into the living room.

"There. There."

There was sweat atop her forehead, her hands, both hands, the fine hairs on her arms.

"I …"

And the bedroom door opened.

"I'll do that, Mrs. Ballad—drive safely, don't worry. Thank you so much."

"He's out the bedroom. Out Aunt Della's bedroom. It-it's a good thing I ran in and out the bathroom like I did—did, didn't take long!"

"Oh, you too, Margaret. It's always good to see you too, whenever I can."

Margaret!

"Good afternoon."

"Darlene's waiting for you downstairs, Morgan."

"Yes, I know, Mrs. Ballad. Mrs. Winston is."

It's over! It's finally over. *Margaret's fate is sealed!*

"Mrs. Winston, well, I'm on my way."

"I trust things went well, Attorney Robinson?"

"Yes, wonderfully well. And to be honest, Mrs. Winston, with you," Robinson whispered, "I didn't expect Mrs. Ballad to look, well … to look so, in such splendid health. I was particularly pleased. Bowled over, to be honest." Pause.

Darlene was handing Robinson his scarf and hat.

"She says she owes it all to her family, but I must admit"—Robinson smiled—"your name did pop up quite a bit, a great deal, Mrs. Winston—in conversation."

"I try to do my best, Attorney Robinson. I do love my aunt Della more than anyone in the whole, whole wide world."

"Who wouldn't? Oh, thank you"—Darlene was helping Robinson with his coat—"there are such strong, splendid black women in our—"

"It's why this whole will business, this whole legal wrangling—"

"Well, you do want your assets, hard-earned valuables obtained during your lifetime to wind up in the right hands. Don't you, Mrs. Winston? Your possessions safeguarded. A legal justice system, as an instrument, does that. Provides that benefit for you. As a lawyer, it makes me feel especially good too to see people's lifelong possessions properly protected by law.

"Disposed of and, as I said before, wind up in the right hands. And me serving as a legal custodian for my clients during the process."

There's no reply from Darlene, just her escorting Attorney Robinson to the house's front door, opening it.

"Thank you. Well, I'll be seeing you then, Mrs. Winston. Good day."

"Yes. Good day."

Darlene shut the door. She stood behind it, leaning her back against it for solid support and then thought she'd better get upstairs. It was important she do so. Maybe she could read her aunt Della's face, even though it was Margaret who still must be in an inordinate state of agony, pain, she thought.

And as she walked the hallway, she heard the two voices.

"It's done, Margaret. Over with."

"Yes, Momma. And I know you did the right thing. What was, you thought, appropriate."

And Darlene heard that, and it twisted her stomach, and now she really wanted to throw up.

"I did what I thought best for the family, Margaret. Our family. All of us. You and Darlene. The Ballad family, honey."

It was 8:30 p.m.

The doorbell rang. Darlene ran out the kitchen. She had a good mind as to who it was at the front door ringing the doorbell at 8:30 p.m. at night.

Darlene flung the front door open.

Hysterical. "I told you not to come! I told you over the telephone not to come by the house, Lee!"

Lee's rake-thin body looks trapped in his heavy wool coat. He's removing it.

"Don't you dare stay! Don't you—"

"I had to come, Darlene. After hearing you w-when we got off the phone ... I had to come."

Darlene blew into the living room. Lee followed her.

"Y-you sounded like you ... you needed me, Darlene. You—"

Darlene was about to sit, when she turned to Lee. "Need you? That I need you? That I need you? You? You, Lee, you—I don't need anyone! I don't need anyone!"

Lee's holding his hat and gloves in his hands.

"D-don't say that, Darlene. Don't say that. Not tonight, Darlene. Not tonight."

Darlene's hand gripped the chair's hand-carved wood.

"I ... I know how it must feel. How it must feel for you, D—"

"Feel? Feel?" Darlene's eyes bulged. "Ha. How do you know how it feels—must feel? How, Lee? How? Nobody does. N-nobody does." Pause. "I ... I ...," Darlene tried to get up, to stand, but couldn't.

Lee sits across from her; he leans forward. "Aunt Della wants, she wants, wishes to do it her way, Darlene. That's all, Darlene. She has the right to. Aunt ... Aunt Della."

"Just tell the woman. Tell her, Lee! And get it over with! Plain out and out tell her, Lee!"

"It ... it's not Aunt Della's way. It's never been Aunt D—"

"It's the first time I ... I've been angry with her, upset with Aunt Della. M-my aunt Della. T-today. This afternoon when Aunt Della told me and ... and ..."

"Margaret, Darlene. M—"

"That woman. That woman. T-trying to make herself equal to me, us equal, when she knows we're not. W-when Aunt Della knows she loves me more than she loves her. More, more, so much more—far more than she loves her. Wait. Wait. Is what Aunt Della told us. We were in the room together after Attorney ... he left the house this afternoon ... wait. Wait. Wait. It's what Aunt Della told us. Wait until she dies, and then Attorney Robinson will read the will for all of us to find out who, who gets the house. This ... who gets the house, Lee."

Darlene brushed her arm across her mouth.

"Why? Why? Tell me why I should wait, have to wait when ... when everyone knows, Lee. Knows. Everyone, Lee. Everyone. Me. It's me. Aunt Della loves me, n-not Margaret Ballad. Me. I own Aunt Della's house, not her." Darlene's sobbing.

"Not her ... not her ... I ... I don't want to be mad, angry, upset with ... with Aunt Della. I don't want to be."

Lee was frozen.

"I've never been angry at my aunt Della. Not ever, Lee. Not ever in my life, Lee. Not ever in my life ..."

"It ... it'll pass, Darlene. The anger. Y-your anger will—"

"Yes. Yes, I, why … why I already feel better … better, feel b—"

"See, see, Darlene, see."

"Yes, yes. I'm already feeling better. Yes, let … let Aunt Della do it this way. Her way. How she's chosen to do it. Let her. Let her, Lee. It's … it's Margaret … Margaret who it's upsetting, r-really upsetting … Who's suffering, Lee. Ha. Ha Not me, Lee. Ha. Ha. But M-Margaret and Royal. Ha. Ha. Royal McCloud. It must be torture for them. Torture for them.

"Waiting. Waiting. Pure torture for them. Hell. Hell. This waiting. Waiting, Lee."

A rueful look crosses Lee's face when he looks across the living room floor at Darlene.

"I … I told you he came over here, baby, here, over the phone. Royal McCloud was here, here in the house, this evening."

"Yes," Lee said. "Uh … you did. O-over the phone."

"I had to leave the room, Lee. Leave the room, Lee," Darlene said like she meant for Lee to see every step taken out the room. See it and feel it. "Get out that damned room, Lee. I had to Lee. Unless I think I would've thrown up. Royal, Royal McCloud wanted to pray with Aunt Della, Lee, can … can you believe that? Imagine that, Lee? Ha. Ha. Well, Aunt Della fooled him. The deed's been done, done. The will's in Attorney Robinson's office now, right now, Lee. At two o'clock the deed … was done, Lee, done. It's done, final. I don't care how hard Royal McCloud and Margaret Ballad try now. They can't change it, any of it, anything in it, Lee. Nothing, Lee. Not one damned thing. Word in it. Ha. Ha. It-it's done."

Darlene rubs her hands together.

"Done with. Over." Now she's able to stand. "This house is mine. Mine. Lee. Finally. Finally, baby. It's always been mine. This … this beautiful old house. I love Aunt Della. I love Aunt Della, Lee. I love my aunt Della. And she loves me. She loves me, Lee!"

Lee stands. "I … I think I'll go upstairs and see Aunt Della since I'm here, Darlene. Over here—"

"No, no, not tonight, Lee." Darlene glances at her watch. "It's late. Too late to visit Aunt Della now. I have to give my aunt Della her sponge bath now."

"Darlene, just for a—"

"Did you hear what I said, Lee? Just said? Told you? Aunt Della gets her sponge bath now. It's new. New. Something n-new I've added. I give Aunt Della her sponge bath twice a day now. She must have her sponge bath now. Aunt Della loves it. Just—"

"Sure, sure, Darlene. S-sure …"

"Besides, Lee," Darlene said sweetly, "it's been such a long day for Aunt Della. Tiring, Lee. You can imagine—can understand, can't you, baby? I mean you can well … well imagine with people coming in and out the house all day. Tiring Aunt Della, Lee."

"Oh yes, yes. Sure, Darlene. Sure."

"Ha. Ha …" Darlene laughed spontaneously. "Ha. Ha …"

"What, Darlene, what?"

"Just that Royal McCloud. That Royal McCloud. The thought of him."

"What about Royal? Him, Darlene?" Lee asked while fumbling with his hat.

"I … I know my aunt Della's going to die, Lee. I know that. Die like Uncle Frank. Die like my mother died, Lee."

"Why I … I wish I'd met Miss Dawson, Darlene. Knew her. Always wished that."

Darlene pressed her hand along the side stitching of her slacks. "I'm trying to be strong about this, Lee. I am. R-reconcile myself to Aunt Della's death. I … I am, Lee."

Lee looked completely out of it again. "W-what's inevitable, Darlene. Uh, what's inevitable. By the very fact of Aunt Della's will being drawn up today."

"That's right, Lee. Inevitable, Lee. By the very fact of Aunt Della's will today. But … but at least we'll be rid of Royal McCloud and Margaret Ballad. Both—the two of them. Ha. Ha. The two of them. When this is through. Over. At least Aunt Della's death will do that, that much for us. Produce that r-result for us when she dies, Lee—rid us of Margaret Ballad and Royal McCloud. Ha. Ha."

Lee is truly shaken, taken aback by Darlene's remarks. "D-Darlene." He then falls back on his heels. "You … you mean to say you … that you hate them that much? Margaret and Royal? H-hate Margaret and Royal that much, Darlene?"

"Yes, that much, Lee. That damned much, Lee. Ha. Ha. When … when Aunt Della dies it's the last we'll see of them. At the reading of Aunt Della's will. Ever see of them. In Attorney Robinson's office. When the house is turned over to me, Lee. Is mine. Is finally in my possession, Lee. It's the last we'll see, ever see or hear—will have to be around them, in their presence, company, Lee. Margaret Ballad and Royal McCloud again. They will be out of our lives forever, for good. Aunt Della's death. For ... oh ... let me get back upstairs so I can give Aunt Della her sponge bath, baby. Aunt Della must be waiting for me. For me, Lee. Anxiously ... anxiously, Lee. W-wondering where I am ... What I must, I'm up to. By now, Lee. By now."

Darlene stares at Lee as if in a trance and then bolts out the living room.

"Be right there, Aunt Della! I'll ... don't worry, Aunt Della, I ... I'm coming, Aunt Della. I'm coming ... coming to give you your sponge bath, your sponge bath tonight, Aunt Della!"

Lee begins walking toward the front door.

"I just didn't think you hated Margaret and Royal that much, Darlene," Lee mumbled to himself. "No, not as much as that. I hope the house, Aunt Della's house, it—that it's enough, Darlene. Will ... will be enough when the house is finally yours. For you, Darlene."

Margaret sat at the side of the bed; she was tired. The day had been incredibly long. It was a day where you couldn't catch your breath once Attorney Robinson left the house. Before he came to do his business, it's like all she was doing was holding her breath in, massing what she felt was her concept of courage. And maybe it wasn't the right word, she thought, "courage," but she was standing up to something she'd had to face for a long time now, especially since her mother's illness.

At one time it was so hard for her to think she had the right to be her mother's daughter, as if she'd somehow given up her birthright. But not anymore. That had all changed. She felt like a daughter now. She felt like she was inside her mother's heart again. And not because of her mother worrying over her, but because her mother could think of her without worry now that she and Royal were safe in Myles Day City; that she was living a good, clean, decent life; that she was a Christian woman now; that they had washed their sins away.

"But Attorney Robinson came today, and it was as if I were locked away in this room with my thoughts and opinions. It's what I told Royal tonight when he came by. Told him how much I worried. How on edge I felt. How much does all of this, the house, mean to my relationship with Momma after she dies? Will I be bitter if … if …"

Darlene has such unbelievable power, Margaret thought. "There's so much you have to consider, always, be aware of. She's … she's shaped my relationship with Momma over the years. It has defined it. And now the will, the house, Momma telling us we must wait until the final reading of the will in Attorney Robinson's office when that day comes."

She saw the rich arrogance on Darlene's face all day, and she'd felt unchristian enough, for the first time in a long time, to want to slap it off her face. Darlene's face—her rich arrogance, slap it off her face, and it's what she told Royal, confessed to him as if she'd thrown the first stone of sin into pristine waters.

It's how she felt then, and it's how she almost felt now. This "halfwayness," this "inbetweenness" in her feelings. She always had to be careful, cautious— this Christianity in her. She felt she must always turn the other cheek, yes, be courageous, if she were to forgive others as she had too forgiven herself for her sins.

It's what religion had given her to steer her life in a better, more positive direction. It's how she and Royal, mutually, had been able to come as far as they had. He'd brought the power and the beauty of religion to her first, so it seemed to her, as her last resort. When both were so low in Detroit.

"I can't hate her. I won't hate her. She's just so important, so powerful."

And the word was couched there in her vocabulary again: "powerful." Her mother had used it for Royal, and now she was using it for Darlene. But today her mother had the power.

"And Momma used her power today."

Margaret pulled back the comforter and bedspread. She got into bed. She laid her head on the pillow. She closed her eyes. She began to pray. Not for anyone in particular but for things in general.

For the universe, for mankind—for a better world.

*   *   *

Following day.

Della was out her bed and sitting in a chair by the bed.

"While I've got you all to myself, Lee …"

Lee looked around the room. "Yes, just you and me, Aunt Della. No one else."

Della winked mischievously. "I want you to do something for me."

"Ha. I don't like the way you just said that, Aunt Della."

"Oh"—Della looked at the sleeve of her robe— "I got big doings up my sleeve's robe, Lee."

"Y-you do, Aunt Della?"

"Do I. Could scare a scarecrow, but we're talking about Christmas, not Halloween, Thanksgiving, Lee, but Christmas."

"It'll be here soon, Aunt Della."

"Yes, it's on its way, Lee. It-it's why I want you to do a favor, some things for me, Lee. Think you … you could, sweet peach? Do some running around? Uh, up to it, Lee?"

"Aunt Della …," Lee said, expelling a long winding sigh.

"Okay, Lee, okay. I know I'm just blowing steam, off steam, honey, but … oh … oh, Lee …," Della said, clapping her hands joyously.

"Aunt Della, Aunt Della …," Lee said, antsy pants like.

"Got you on pins and needles, don't I, Lee, don't I?"

"Pins and needles, Aunt Della."

"Get my, get my checkbook, Lee. Would you please. It-it's in the bureau chest. First drawer, uh, on your right, Lee. On your right, sweet peach."

Lee jumps out his chair. He gets right over to the bureau chest and opens out the drawer.

"Got it, Lee?"

"Got it, Aunt Della!"

"Can bring, uh, walk over, walk it right over to me, if you would. With it, Lee."

Lee grins.

"With pleasure, Aunt Della."

"Thanks, sweet peach."

Della opens the checkbook. "Have it all planned out, Lee. Ain't gonna have to skip a beat. Not one measure."

Lee grins wider.

Then Della, her hand steady, tears the check out the checkbook's register. "It's all written out, dollars and cents." She looks up at Lee. "Here, honey."

"Now, Aunt Della. W—"

"Called the bank, People's Bank, spoke to Jim Crawford."

"I know him, Aunt—"

"Told him you were coming, Lee. Coming in to cash the check for me."

"Y-you did, Aunt Della?"

"Did it undercover."

"Ha."

"Had to go undercover. Yes … uh, Darlene and Margaret don't know."

Then Della went inside the checkbook a second time and pulled out a short white sheet of paper. "Something else for you, Lee." Della hands the white sheet of paper to Lee.

"A Christmas list, Aunt Della."

"Uh-huh. For my girls and Royal too. Did some catalogue shopping, Lee. What I did. Been going through Delaney Department Store's Christmas catalogue, uh … think you can handle it, sweet peach? Do all right with it?"

"Oh sure, sure, Aunt Della. Sure!"

"Got until tomorrow, but you shouldn't have a problem at Delaney Department Store."

"Not at all, Aunt Della. One bit. Who knows, we might have a pre-Christmas party, Aunt Della."

Then Lee looked into Della's eyes.

"I'm trying, Lee. I'm trying."

"I … I know you are, Aunt Della."

"Want to make it to Christmas and … and the new year too. Beyond. But … but I might have to choose my days, Lee. Come up smart about this whole mess. Situation."

"Uh … uh, yes, Aunt Della."

Cheerily. "And it ain't all I've got planned, Lee!"

"No, no, Aunt Della?"

"Not for one minute!"

"Uh … let me see …"

"No, you won't guess, sweet peach. Too smart for you this time, Lee. See, sitting up in this bedroom, I've got a lot of time to think. Ha. For thinking. A lot of time on my hands."

"Ha."

"A Christmas tree, Lee!"

"Oh, I—"

"You would've never guessed. Usually put it in the living room three days in advance of Christmas, but not this year, Lee. Uh-uh, sweet peach. Called Tom Fletcher out at his place and told him I want the grandest, biggest Christmas tree on the lot this year, Lee.

"You know he supplies us with one each year, so he knows what I want, how wide, how tall—and all you've got to do, Lee, is go out there in the car and get it!"

"I have the rope, same rope in the trunk from last year, Aunt Della, I saved—when I roped the tree to the top of the car roof last year."

"Good and strong, Lee. Good and strong!"

"So … should I get go—"

"Going, you—"

"Lee, I didn't hear you come in the house, Lee," Margaret said, entering the bedroom.

"Oh, hi … hi there, Margaret. Good—"

"I was in the bathroom, running water."

"It's when I must've sneaked down the hallway and into Aunt Della's room on you. Past you, Margaret," Lee teased.

"Guess so."

Margaret and Lee kissed.

"B-but I have to run an errand now," Lee announced proudly. "At the—"

"One of *my* errands," Della said proudly.

"Oh," Margaret said suspiciously. "One of those …?"

"Yes, one of those, Margaret. So Lee can't delay. Tarry, now."

"Oh no, not for a second, Aunt Della. Not—"

"So—"

"You'll see, Margaret. You'll see!"

"You mean you're not going to tell me, Lee? You're—"

"I pay too much for that, Margaret," Della said, reaching out to Margaret with both hands.

"Too … too much, Margaret," Lee said.

"*My spies!*"

"So … uh, see you, Margaret! I'll be back before the night's out though."

"Oh, it's not a two-day, three-day mission then … you're on. Off on? For Momma?"

"No, Aunt Della wants me back before bedtime for this mission, Margaret."

"Now, Lee, don't forget my kiss, sweet peach. Don't forget my kiss!"

It's minutes later when Darlene runs into the room.

"Aunt Della, where do you have Lee rushing off to at this hour?"

"Uh, that's between me and Lee, Darlene. Honey."

"Pardon me, Momma." Margaret walked out the room.

"Oh, uh, it's what he told me, Aunt Della."

"Just following orders, Darlene, to a tee."

Pause.

"How's that dress of yours, for Mrs. Foster coming along?"

"Fine."

"She's demanding."

"I've tamed her. I know how she was with you, Aunt Della …"

"Why … why there were days when I could've wrung that woman's neck. How I re—"

"I'm respectful because of her age, Aunt Della, and I've known her—"

"All your life. Was sewing for her way back—"

"But I let her know I'm the best dressmaker in Myles Day City. That she can't do better than me, and she knows it."

Della looked at Darlene, and she saw a pride in her that some people, she knew, found dangerous; but she knew Darlene needed it like a person needs oxygen.

"All right if I shut my eyes for a bit, a little bit, Darlene? A while, in the chair?"

"Fine, why fine," Darlene said, snapping out of whatever spell she'd been under. "I have a million things to do. Aunt Della."

"I bet you do, honey. All right!"

Darlene kissed Della and then stepped out the room.

Della shut her eyes and then counted to twenty-five and then opened them. "I guess the coast is clear. Everybody's doing something." Della looked around cagily though and called on her ears to give her a shot at hearing a mouse pee on cotton in the attic. "Now for part two of my plan. Operation. Set it in motion. Ha."

The phone was to her right. Della began dialing.

"Royal …"

"Mother Ballad?"

"Hope I'd catch you there, Royal. At home."

"W-what a surprise, Mother Ballad."

"Did you call to—"

"Uh, sorry, honey, didn't call to pray, but … only for you to do me a favor—if you can, you will, that is."

"Oh, thank God. With pleasure, Mother Ballad. With pleasure."

"Just sent Lee off to do one."

"Y-you did?"

"Just a few minutes ago. Keeping everyone busy tonight. Alert."

"So I see, Mother Ballad. Ha. So I see."

"Royal, the devil's in me."

"Ha."

"Can't keep him still!"

"Ha."

"Royal, talking about Lee, my sweet peach, it is for Lee I'm asking this favor from you."

"Yes?"

"Christmas is coming, Royal, and I want to buy something for him. I already know what it is and worked everything out with Delaney Department Store, put it on my credit card there. I have their Christmas catalogue, been through it. Front and back. Saw the most gorgeous watch. Wristwatch for Lee to wear.

"They've wrapped it. Just need you to pick it up for me. W-would you do that for me, honey? Would you?"

"Would I? Why—"

"You can do it tomorrow. No rush."

"Lee's going to love that, Mother Ballad. Just love that."

"It's gonna look good on Lee's wrist. Handsome."

"I bet it will, Mother Ballad."

Pause.

"So how's it going, things going for you, Royal?"

"Great, Mother Ballad."

"And, uh, about that loan, bank loan, you know, what I told you before …"

"I have, Mother Ballad."

Pause.

"Mother Ballad …"

"Yes, honey?"

"One day, don't worry, Margaret and I will be married. Will be man and wife. We won't live like this, not—"

"Now why'd you have to bring that up for, Royal?"

"It's just that sometimes I just want to hear myself say it too, out loud, to someone, Mother Ballad. It … it seems."

"Yes, I know the feeling. Know it all too well. Get like that too. They come along."

"It's the one aspect of this whole conversion situation that hasn't worked out for us, Margaret and me, Mother Ballad."

"And not because of you, Royal, but because of someone else."

"Yes. Yes. And I want to be a father to Marshall, to my son so bad … so bad, Mother Ballad. It seems I'm out trying to help everyone else but—"

"Margaret told me what you're doing. Getting professional help this time, so you just bide your time, honey. God's hand hasn't lost its touch."

"Not at all, Mother Ballad. No, not at all!"

"Now I've done all the mischief I want to for one night, so I'm hanging up."

"The devil's been expunged!"

"Now, Royal, I'm gonna have to look that word up. Up for myself!"

"Lee's going to be pleased."

"Elated."

"Ha."

"Good night."

"Good night, Mother Ballad."

Della hung up the telephone. She loved Lee and Royal so much, she thought. Darlene and Margaret were so lucky to have two good men.

"Oh … they're always thinking of others. When I asked Lee to buy the things for Darlene and Margaret and Royal, not once did Lee act like he was being left out. Didn't see anything like that on his sweet face. He was so happy to just do for them, for me—didn't think about himself, not once."

Della looked back down at the phone.

"And the same with Royal. Nothing was in his voice to say he was thinking of himself, just Lee. My sweet peach. Oh, they're good men. Good men, honest men, just like you, Frank. Carbon copies of you Stand for something. Mean something."

Then Della laughed heartily.

"Could've charged Darlene and Margaret things to my charge card, but I don't want it to run too high with interest fees. They ain't nothing but crooks anyhow. Banks, department stores … ha … uh, just to name a few."

Della was counting her fingers. She still had three fingers left to go.

"Ha …"

CHAPTER 12

December 20.

Della, Darlene, Margaret, and Lee were sitting around the tall, wide Christmas tree in the living room. Lee and Darlene and Margaret had eggnog; Della, a glass of red wine. It was Saturday, early afternoon.

"Uh, by the way, about that tree, Lee, you'd think you chopped it down yourself, sweet peach. With an axe. In the forest."

"Well, Aunt Della, it was the tree on the lot that was better than what Mr. Fletcher, Tom Fletcher, had picked out for you."

"It sure is, Lee. You did it! Have some eye. It's the biggest, grandest tree, Christmas tree this living room's ever had—had standing in it."

"I agree, Momma."

"Ha. Didn't want to embarrass Mr. Fletcher, but he didn't seem to mind."

"Did it cost me, honey?"

"Fifteen, it was fifteen dollars extra, Aunt Della."

"No, Tom Fletcher didn't mind at all. Wasn't embarrassed—not a bit, Lee!"

Darlene didn't appear interested in any of the light chatter but then shifted her body and said, "Uncle Frank, when I saw him bring the Christmas tree into the living room for the first time ... It was so grand. S-so extraordinary."

"You remember, Darlene?"

179

"Always, Aunt Della."

"Yes, your uncle Frank." And then Della turned to Margaret. "Your father knew how to pick a tree. A Christmas tree." Della turned to Lee. "Was like you, Lee."

Lee looked at Della modestly.

"Ain't no harm to brag, Lee. In bragging. Comes from it. Ha." Della sipped more wine from her glass. "Lee …"

"Yes, Aunt Della?"

"Now's the time, sweet peach. Now's the time."

"It … it is, Aunt Della?"

"Uh-huh, Lee."

Lee hopped onto the balls of his feet.

"Yes, it is, Aunt Della!"

"Momma, you sound, might as well be a general, you—"

"I am, Margaret. I am!"

Then Lee saluted Della and Darlene laughed. And off Lee marched with his marching orders to wherever he was going, been commanded to go by Della.

"Lee's on another mission, one of your missions, Momma?"

"One, I'm not, won't fail to complete!" Lee said from the hallway or wherever he was by now. "Just like … ha … the other two I—"

"I thought it was one, Momma?"

"No, two, Margaret. Two. I sent Lee on. You and Darlene will see. Lee, keep marching!"

Lee was out the house. In a jiffy, Lee was back in the house.

"That you, Lee? In the hallway, honey?"

"Uh, yes, Aunt Della. Out the house and back."

"Take your time, Lee. Sweet peach. Catching your breath, Lee." Della sat there on the sofa with Darlene and then gritted her teeth. Della stood. She looked at the Christmas tree. "You did such a wonderful job … the decorations and all, Darlene."

Darlene held Della's hand.

"Another wonderful gift you have, Darlene. Have an eye for just how to arrange things. Make them look right. Just right."

"Well …"

"Don't say it, 'cause I was okay at it. Wasn't much interested in decorating a Christmas tree at anytime. Right, Margaret?"

"Yes, Momma."

"Took me away from my sewing. Even if it was for, meant but for one day." Pause. "Uh, Lee, you tired of standing out there yet? In the hallway?"

"Well, uh, Aunt—"

"A big Christmas tree like this, never looks good, even with all its pretty decorations, without something, some present beneath it. LEE!" Della barked.

"Coming, Aunt Della. Coming!"

And Lee scurried into the living room with a shopping bag in both hands.

"Aunt Della!"

"Momma!"

"Ha!"

"Lee did a little shopping. How about it, Lee?"

"Yes, Aunt Della. Not a, uh, little shopping, but a lot, Aunt Della. A lot!"

"Might as well empty them out. Shake the bags out, sweet peach. Busy yourself, Lee."

Lee pulled one box out after another and arranged them neatly under the tree.

"Did some catalogue shopping. Delaney Department Store's Christmas catalogue. For my children. You, Darlene, Margaret, and Royal, and I didn't forget you, Lee, not you, Lee—my sweet peach. Margaret …"

"Yes, Momma?"

"The left table lamp. The drawer. If you would, Margaret. Honey."

Margaret was over at the table.

"Uh, try to conceal it, Margaret. Uh, hide it in front of you, then behind your back on your way over." Margaret laughed. "Come on over now, Margaret."

Margaret crossed the floor.

"To me." When Margaret got to Della, Della put her hand out. When Margaret handed the gift-wrapped box to Della, Della said, "This is for you, Lee. For … for you, sweet peach."

"For … for me, Aunt Della?"

"What you think, I forgot you, Lee? Scratched you off the Christmas list this year!"

"No, Aunt Della, but—"

"Had Royal in on this caper. Royal. Sent him off to Delaney's. On an errand. Called him. Straight out Delaney's Christmas catalogue. Would you, uh, put it under the tree with the rest of them, Margaret."

When Margaret stepped back from the tree, Della said, "Doesn't that look lovely? Just lovely." Della said it so soft, it's as if she barely made the air around her ripple.

Darlene, Margaret, Lee, and Royal admired the colorfully wrapped Christmas gifts under the tree.

"Did enjoy wrapping them at one time. Now that's something I really did enjoy doing at Christmas time. Was good at. But these department stores, nowadays, do … do a fine job of wrapping. Excellent."

A few minutes had elapsed.

"Think I'll stay downstairs all day today. Eat dinner down here. Climb those stairs … ha … on a full stomach."

"That'll be good, Aunt Della."

"We'll all eat at the kitchen table for a change."

"Then I'll get started, Aunt Della. Preparing dinner."

"Just had lunch. It's—"

"One twenty, Momma."

"So let's eat early tonight, Darlene."

"Five o'clock, Aunt Della?" Darlene said from the hallway.

"Five o'clock, Darlene. Five o'clock it is." Then Della looked at the Christmas gifts beneath the tall tree. "You did a fine job, Lee. A fine, fine job, sweet peach."

"Guess I'm ready to go up, back up." Della got up from the sofa. Darlene assisted her. Della grabbed hold of her walker. "Can get spoiled down here. Spoiled on that sofa. Frank's sofa. Spoiled rotten."

"You deserve it, Aunt Della."

"Seems like I've been down here all day with my family. Well, at least since lunch. Ate that in the room. But my bed must miss me. Might think … ha … I'm not coming back to it." Pause.

"Nope, that's only for when I go to the hospital, St. Bart's, when I have to run off."

Silence.

"Now, now … come, come on, I didn't say anything so bad, awful. Just a fact of life, me and St. Bart. No, no need in trying to hide a kangaroo under a hat. Now … now where … where did I come up with that one? From? Where …?"

Della was at the staircase looking up. She set her walker aside and looked up the staircase.

"And let me get up there, climb up these stairs alone, by myself. Ha. Just stand behind me, Lee. Just in case. Just in case, sweet peach."

Darlene and Margaret stood off to the side of the staircase, and Della's foot landed on the first step of the staircase and then up to the second; and Lee was standing behind her, relaxed, poised, but alert for anything.

"Ha … it feels so good. So good." Della was up to the fifth step. She paused. "How many more to go, Lee?"

"Uh …"

"Seven more, Lee. Twelve in all. Take my word for it, Lee!"

All of them laughed.

"Thought you'd have them all counted out by now, Lee—travel up them enough."

"Do now, Aunt Della," Lee laughed.

"Okay. Let me get started. Get started back up again. Was on a roll. Gathering up steam, momentum, don't know why I stopped. Lord only knows." Della took in a deep breath. "Crank myself back up again. For the long haul this time."

And Della began climbing the stairs, and Margaret stood at the bottom of the staircase and was amazed by what she saw, how Della was climbing the stairs.

And when Della reached the top, she turned to Lee. "I didn't need you after all, sweet peach." She reached up and kissed him.

It's when Darlene and Margaret proceeded up the stairs, Darlene carrying the walker. Della held onto Lee's arm until Darlene put the walker out in front of her, and then Della turned around to it, grasping it. "This old thing's been good to me. It's been a good friend. Good as gold." And like a phalanx, the four proceeded toward Della's room.

When Della got to the side of the bed, she sat down on top it. "Woo …
woooo …" She patted the bed. "Well … I'm back. Was just downstairs—don't
be jealous!"

"Oh, Aunt Della, if I laugh anymore, I think I'll—"

"Die!"

A raw silence.

Della looked at them. "Now why when I say something like that,
everyone … The expression is 'die of laughter.' Been using it all my life. So
why should I stop … Oh, let me lie on my back on this bed. Let me rest my
head. Let—"

"And your sponge bath, Aunt Della. Your sponge bath!"

"Yes, my sponge bath, Darlene. Honey."

Darlene checked her watch. "In … in about, oh, about fifty minutes,
Aunt Della. Fifty minutes."

Della looked over at the clock. "Look forward to it, Darlene. Always look
forward to it, Darlene."

Della eased her head back onto the pillow, and Margaret saw what made
her mother always look beautiful—her hair, that beautiful mass of pepper-
gray hair that framed her face, a perfect portrait for the mind's delicate dance
of memory.

Della stretched her body out on the bed. "Mmm, that's good. Good as
it gets."

"When you sleep, you sleep like a log, don't you, Aunt Della?"

"Good as a log. Yes, good as a log, Lee." Della closed her eyes. "Uh-huh,
uh-huh … Mmmm …" Then she opened them. "But don't think I'm going
to sleep now. Not now. Might stay up all night, after a day like today. Just
might."

"Lee, you have to leave?"

"Guess so, Aunt Della."

"Well, Darlene bathed me. Thanks for hanging around."

"I had Margaret to keep me company, Aunt Della."

"You and Margaret, you two get along so wonderfully."

"From the first day we met. She warned me about—"

"Not smoking in the house!"

"And I didn't heed her warning—"

"Not until I made it plain, Lee. Plain and clear about the rules in my house. Della Ballad's house!"

"Plain and clear, Aunt Della. Plain and clear."

"Made your ears ring, didn't I, Lee? Didn't I, sweet peach? Oh, I don't think we'll never ever forget that day. Stop talking about it over and over, Lee. Uh-uh." Della was off her back.

"You can give me some of that sweet sugar, sweet peach—now." Della reaches up for Lee, her arms holding him behind his neck. "Mmm ... best sugar in the world, Lee. The world, sweet peach." She looks at him with great intent.

"I love you, Lee. Do love you, honey."

"I love you too, Aunt Della. I love you too."

Margaret came into the room.

"Leaving, Lee?"

"What, everyone's trying to get rid of me around here? Ha. Including you, Margaret?"

"Lee, you were kissing Momma."

"Uh ... dead giveaway, huh, Margaret?"

"Yes, positively."

"And ... oh, he kisses good. My sweet peach. Guess I'm all yours now, Margaret."

"Uh, good night, Aunt Della."

"Good night, Lee."

"See you tomorrow."

"Sunday it is, Lee. Sweet peach. Gotta date for tomorrow. Sunday afternoon."

"Good night, Lee."

"Good night, Margaret."

Pause.

"That was such a wonderful surprise this afternoon, Momma."

"Uh, but you mustn't open your gift, Christmas present, until Christmas Day. Those department stores do ... do a good job of wrapping these days—must admit."

"But I'd rather have you wrap it, Momma."

"No"—Della laughed—"I guess nothing still can't top ... match the personal touch. To know somebody took the time to do it."

"Yes."

"That's the key to everything, honey, people finding the time to do for others no matter how big or how small it may seem, might appear at the time. Trying to make somebody happy by giving of yourself. Always giving of yourself. Always your best."

"I'm surprised Royal—"

"Hasn't called me yet? Me too."

"He's probably working on his sermon. Hammering away. Sometimes he gets lost, so lost in them—"

"Can't find his way out, huh? The other end? Ha."

"Ha. No, it's not that bad, Momma. But there are times when I think he's—"

"Lost out in the wilderness with Moses. Needs to lead the Israelites back to Egypt's land!"

"Momma, you are full of spunk today. You really are."

"It … it comes and goes, you know that," Della said reasonably. "Comes and goes."

"But you seemed at full strength today, the way you climbed up the stairs this evening—you … you should've seen yourself, Momma. You were really a sight to b-behold."

"Was I? I … I was? Felt like I was moving pretty good. What I felt like. B-but was I really?"

"Y-you really were, Momma. It really surprised me, caught me completely off guard."

"Wish you'd taken a picture then. Had a video camera or something, Margaret."

"A snapshot—that wouldn't've done any justice, Momma. And a video camera, I don't know if it would've been able to keep up. Not at the speed you were traveling up those stairs."

"Yes, it comes and goes." Della yawned. "Comes and goes, Margaret."

Ring.

"I bet it's—"

Margaret reaches for the phone.

"Royal."

"Hi, Mag. Sorry I'm calling the house so late."

"We … Momma and I were worried about you, Royal."

"Tough sledding. Tough sermon to prepare for tomorrow. It really had me going."

"Momma"—Margaret winked at Della—"had an opinion on what happened. On the subject. Your sermon, Royal."

"Mother Ballad?"

Della has her hand out.

"So here she is. She can't seem to wait to share it with you either."

"Then put Mother Ballad on. By all means. Put Mother Ballad on the phone." Pause.

"Good evening, Royal."

"Why, good evening, Mother Ballad."

"Uh, what I said, Royal, was you must've been lost, lost in that sermon of yours—it's what I said to Margaret before, Royal. Must've been out there with Moses in the wilderness."

"Oh … oh practically. Practically. Ha. It's what it feels like sometimes when you're trying to find the right sermon to preach on for a Sunday morning."

"Oh, it's gonna turn out fine, honey. Like it always does. For you every Sunday morning."

Della and Royal were off the phone.

"Royal said he could see Lee's smile through the phone, the way I described it for him. What happened down in the living room today. But wait until Lee opens his present, Christmas present, on Christmas day."

"Which is?"

"Now, now, what, you think you can sneak one over on me, what, these days, Margaret? Not on your life. Uh-uh. You're gonna have to wait just like Lee is Christmas Day when all of you open your presents and find out."

Margaret smiled. But with that smile was a certain measure of regret, for she hadn't even thought of shopping for her mother for Christmas yet. It hadn't even crossed her mind to do so, or for Royal either, so she was disappointed in herself. It meant her mother was more alert, more on the ball, more with it than her.

But maybe, Margaret thought, she wanted Christmas to get here so badly, too much, too fast, like Thanksgiving had. Christmas, the new year, just to say she had her mother to share on those two festive occasions. Maybe she had blocked out all of the side issues, distractions, that went with Christmas, only focusing on the day, waking up to that day in the house and knowing her mother was there in the house, ready to ring Christmas in with her. It would be her mother's gift to her and God's gift to her mother.

Maybe it was all of that stuff combined generating this feeling.

"Margaret, honey, why so quiet?"

"Oh, sorry, Momma. Sorry."

"Sometimes I wish I could read your thoughts. Get into them."

"That's true for every-everyone, Momma."

"No, there're—sometimes ... sometimes I wish I could, honey. You've always been such a deep thinker. Thoughtful thinker."

"I just make it seem that way, I am, Momma. I, it's just that I have everyone fooled."

"The things that can come out your mind, Margaret. Like gems sometimes. Your father would think so too."

"Daddy, Daddy would, Momma?"

"Oh, he pegged you a genius or something close to it. In that classification by the age ten. You had the grades in school to prove it. The brains. But something more than all of that, Margaret—you thought things through. All angles of it. Since little. Early on."

"I love you, Momma."

"Likewise."

Pause.

"Turning in?"

"Yes."

"Clothes all pressed, done for church?"

"Pressed. Yes. And ready to wear tomorrow."

"Gonna twirl for me, girl?"

"Not on Sunday, Momma," Margaret laughed.

"Now God ain't gonna look—just me."

Long pause.

"Now come here, let me hold you to me. Mmmm ..."

Margaret hugged Della and then kissed her cheek.

"Five more days to go, and you'll see what I bought you, uh, me and Lee, that is."

"And with the help of Delaney's Christmas catalogue."

"That's another thing—used to hate them when they used to come to the house. All those catalogues, national, local. Was on everybody's list. Mail everything to Della Ballad. Must've been what was out there.

"But now they come in handy. Can … ha … shop from home. From bed. In style."

"You finally caught up, Momma."

"Right, Margaret. Right. Caught up with modern times. The modern world. At sixty-eight, Margaret. A modern woman."

"G-good night, Momma."

"Oh, good night, honey."

"I'm going to read through the Bible a little before I turn in. Scripture."

"Good, Margaret."

"Momma—"

"Margaret—"

Both said at the same time.

"You … you go first, Momma."

"No, you—"

"Uh-uh, Momma, you go first."

"Just was gonna say you've been the best daughter. The best daughter a mother could have, Margaret."

"Excluding, you mean ex-excluding Detroit, don't you?"

"I mean excluding nothing. Nothing. I said what I said, Margaret."

"Thank you, Momma."

"And you were going to say …?"

"It-it's not important, Momma, after what you said." Margaret lingered in the bedroom door's frame.

"Good night, Margaret."

"See you in the morning, Momma."

"In the morning, honey. In the morning."

After Margaret left the room, Della shut her eyes and began drawing on the day's activities, keeping them in perfect chronological order, as the day unfolded. Whose smile was biggest when the gifts went under the tree. It had to be Lee's, Della thought. And Royal had told her he'd had it, the watch, that is, put in a box big enough so there would be some trouble, doubt in guessing just what was in it. Good idea, she'd told Royal—excellent idea! When you see a short, slender box, you usually think chain or bracelet or watch; but with the box Royal got, your mind could think of a number of things.

"Yes, from the top of the day till now. Ha. It's been one joyful day. Joyful, joy—"

"Oh, so there you are, Aunt Della."

Playfully, Della rolled her eyes. "Now where else did you expect me to be, Darlene? To find me? But in bed."

Darlene smiled and then looked at Della's walker.

"Can't sneak out the house with that old walker of mine. It won't let me."

"But I ... I wouldn't be surprised if you did, Aunt Della, tried. You've been up to so much mischief today."

Darlene sat on the side of the bed and then, in one clean motion, laid her head on Della's bosom.

"That's right, Darlene. Rest. Rest. You go at it every day for me. Don't you? Work as hard as my pills do for me to keep me going. Hard as Joseph's, Dr. Ives's medicine—"

"I'm not tired, Aunt Della. Just thankful. And now, right now, I just want ..."

"For me to hold you. Hold you, honey. What, something I'm used to doing."

"Mmmm ..."

"Satisfies me so to ... to be able to. Uh-huh. Doesn't it feel good though?"

Della and Darlene closed their eyes. They stayed this way for a while.

"Aunt Della ...," Darlene said, "the water."

"Yes, the water."

"Your two pills."

"Uh-huh."

"Be right back." Darlene dashed out the room and then was back in a flash with the glass of water.

"All set?"

"Been."

The two pills were in Della's hands. She laid them on top her tongue, took the glass of water from Darlene, drank it, and then tossed her head back like it was as limber as a ten-year-old's.

"Aunt Della, you do that so beautifully. And ... and with such grace too."

"Just try to have fun at it, Darlene. Keep the fun in it. From leaving it."

Darlene looked at Della. She knew none of this was fun for her, had never been fun for her.

"That's all it is, honey."

"Can I—"

"Back you go."

Darlene was back with her head on Della's bosom. Silence was back.

"Uh, I can't wait for Christmas, Aunt Della."

"Me either, honey."

"Five more days, Aunt Della."

"What's left, Darlene."

"The first Christmas without Uncle Frank …"

"Hard. Was hard to take. Didn't want to get up, wake that Christmas morning. Wanted to stay in bed. In this bed. I'm lying in now, but … Oh, the dead don't want you to stop living, Darlene. Don't want any of that—to stop. God gives you life, so you've gotta use it. Take it in.

"It's why I got up that morning. Christmas morning like I did. Called on my faith. Used it to give me strength, even though I was full of despair. Didn't think the day would bring any good, d-do me any good, but it did. It was a good Christmas. Wasn't the same without your uncle Frank, but it was a good Christmas."

"Yes, it was, Aunt Della. It was."

"You learn to live out of habit, necessity, the being of something, you might say—like taking those pills over there on that tray. When something bad happens, after a while, and it's gonna take a while. Because life … I … I don't want to sound too preachy tonight too—"

"But, Aunt Della, you are sounding kind of preachy tonight. You are, Aunt Della. Really are."

"Ha. Oh, I thought … I thought I was sounding wise, honey."

"Ha. Aunt Della, you're always wise."

Darlene's head was off Della's bosom.

"Turning in?"

"Yes," Darlene yawned. "Yes, Aunt Della."

"Ain't far behind you."

Darlene stood. "Let me turn off the ceiling—"

"No, keep it on, Darlene."

"But—"

"I want to look up at the ceiling while I do my thinking tonight. The light in the corner ain't good enough. You keep on overnight, Darlene. Ceiling ain't clear."

"Oh, then I'll—"

"And you don't have to come back to the room to turn it off. It's not necessary. You just turn in. Get your rest for tomorrow. Me and the walker can get to the light switch, then back to the bed, okay?"

"But, Aunt Della—"

"You saw how I got up the stairs. Still got the same amount of energy in me. Source. Don't need to call on my reserve tank. Ha." Pause. "Yes, want to keep the light on my thinking. It's been a good day. Yes, a darling of a day."

"The Christmas tree looks spectacular."

"It does. All lit up nice."

Darlene yawns again. "Sorry, Aunt Della."

"Yeah, Darlene, honey, your days are long. Just keeping up with me."

"Aunt Della …"

"Yes, honey?"

"I wish you'd stop saying that. I wish you would, Aunt Della."

"Oh, sorry then, Darlene. Sorry."

"I wouldn't want it any other way."

"Know you wouldn't. Not for a minute would you. Know that, Darlene."

"I love you so, so much."

"I know you do, Darlene. And I love you so, so much."

It was a moment when they just looked at each other.

"My kiss."

Darlene kissed Della.

"That'll last till morning."

"Good night, Aunt Della."

"Uh-huh. Good night, honey."

"And if you forget to turn off the—"

"Oh, I won't forget, Darlene. Won't let sleep come early for me."

"O-okay then. Good night."

"Good night, honey."

Darlene left the bedroom.

Della brushed both hands through her hair and then felt her pillow needed adjusting, so she did that too. She just lay there in the bed looking up at the ceiling, her mind blank, as if savoring this respite.

"Ha. Yes the heat feels good … good in this old room. Doesn't it? That radiator's having a good time. A good time at it. Hissing. Can see the steam shooting up out it from over here. Feels good in this old bed of mine. Does. Just like I've always liked it all … all these years."

Della's yawn is both broad and lazy. "Just feels so good, so warm inside and out. And Lord, Lord, if Royal and me didn't pray tonight. Over the phone. A long time. Long time we prayed together tonight. Made my … I am tired of the pills. Those pills. Those elephant pills. The daily taking of those pills. Of … of—it feels like a deathwatch in this house. All … all these goings … goings on in this house every day.

"And it's done, isn't it? Over with Morgan Robinson a few days back. The house. Did what was best. I know I did. What was in my heart to do. This house." Pause.

"Why did it have to come down to this house? Something material? S-something that you hold onto? It shouldn't be. I love Margaret and Darlene. Why does this old house have to say, make them think I love one more than I love the other. D-do I? But … I do, don't I? I do love one more than the other. I must—what choice do I have? I … I … that was made when Morgan was here. By who got the house—is gonna get the house when I die, wasn't it?

"Oh, Frank! Frank!"

Della's hands fly up to her face. Her body then trembles, and then after a while, it's when her hands come down from her face and she lay there with a high-cheekbone-of-a- smile on her face. She felt the hair that was loose, bordered her face, and her smile lit her skin even more revealingly.

"Oooo … but when Darlene brushes my hair with the brush. Out with the, that hairbrush of mine, it still feels so … But Margaret and Darlene can't stay in the house forever. Taking care of me. Dear, dear Darlene. Margaret too. I want a real bath, a real bath. Soak my body in a tub. In water. Not a … s—but I'm just so weak to do that. Get in a tub and out. In such tight quarters. Can't lift my body in and out. My body just can't do it anymore. Won't let me.

"And that bed pan. Those days when I don't feel like making it to … my bad days, w-when they number up … Lord, I don't want to see another bed pan for as long as I live!"

Della's concentration is on the radiator again, the steam shooting out the radiator, hissing.

"It's at the right time now. Everything's taken care of. My will, it's in order. My heart, it's never gonna get better. Just ain't. No one can repair it. W-wonderful Joseph, no one. The elephant pills, they can't cure my heart. Darlene's tried. Margaret's tried. My family's done its best. N-nobody's to feel regret over any—about anything."

Della's fingers tease the strands of her hair.

"And it was soul-satisfying … soul-satisfying praying the way me and Royal did tonight. Talked to God. The way Royal prayed. I could feel how my soul was opening up. Receiving. It shouldn't be a deathwatch in this house that they're doing for me. And the gifts are bought. Under the tree. Under the Christmas … E-everything waiting for that hour of night, day, including me, me to die. Knowing each day could be my last. My last breath. Each breath I take. Each smell I smell. Aroma. Smile. Word I speak.

"I—but it's done. It's all done. All done with. Morgan has my will and testament in order. Signed, put my signature on it like I, Morgan said to do. Morgan. It's all been authorized, as he said. Officially done. Legally. Legally. Yes, what is my final testament. My last important, significant act on Earth."

Della's fingers stopped teasing the strands of hair. She laid there, stoic.

"All I have to do now, is left for me to do now, is hold them. Hold onto Margaret and Darlene. My two children. It's what I want to do with all my heart and soul before I die. Hold onto my wonderful, two wonderful girls. M-my two beautiful daughters. Hold them to me. Close to me. Tell them I love them and then let them go. Let them go. Let them both go. Be done with it. Everything here on Earth. Done with it. L-like Royal said, God's will … will be done. Will be done … then. Was just how Royal put it for me tonight."

The stoicism left Della's face, and her pretty smile reappeared.

"Yes, Frank, Lee's smile was the biggest, biggest of them all. All right. Ha. But come Christmas Day, he's not gonna be able to guess it's a watch, won't know until he opens the box inside, Frank. Know nothing till he opens that box, Frank.

"Then wait and see how big his smile's gonna be. My sweet peach. Ha. My sweet peach. Ha. Wait and see, Frank. Wait and see."

Darlene's sleep has been patchy, hasn't been consistent. She doesn't know why. Maybe it was the ceiling light in Della's bedroom—had she turned it off? She asked herself what must've been for the fifth, sixth time already.

But now she was determined to do something about it for her own sake, sanity, or at least so she could sleep … But it was more than that, much more than that—it was like something was pulling her, urging her to Della's bedroom now that she was up on her feet, putting her slippers and robe on. There was something about it, as if it could speak, if it had a tongue, it would.

"Let me get to Aunt Della's room. Let me get to Aunt Della's room," Darlene repeated to herself.

She was out her bedroom and into the dark hallway. In her slippers she walked lightly, still feeling that "something" she didn't want to deal with now but, emotionally, her mind was now struggling with.

"The ceiling's light's on," Darlene observed. "Thought it would be. Aunt Della didn't turn it off." Darlene had almost reached the bedroom. "She and her walker. I didn't expect her to. I was right." Pause.

"But that's naughty of you, Aunt Della. Naughty of you. Bad, Aunt Della. Bad." It's when she laughed.

As soon as she got into Della's bedroom, she saw how Della was lying in the bed. Darlene breathed easily now.

"I can see from here you're sleeping well, Aunt Della. Comfortably," Darlene whispered.

"I don't know why I'm up, Aunt Della. But maybe I do know. Okay … I, maybe I don't … I just felt like I should come in here, suddenly, y-your bedroom, Aunt Della. But the light, ceiling light's on, something I knew you wouldn't, and it'll be turned off as soon … But I don't know what it is … But I felt, just felt like coming in here, being with you, into the bedroom to make sure you're sleeping well … all right, Aunt Della. That's all. All, Aunt Della."

Darlene spotted Della's hand atop the comforter while her other hand was beneath the bed sheet.

"Let me fix that. Adjust that for you, Aunt Della," Darlene continued whispering to herself. "Okay, Aunt Della."

And Darlene touched the top of Della's hand.

"Yes, let … Aunt … cold, why is your hand so … as … as cold as … Why is your hand cold as … as cold as i-ice … Aunt Della? Ice, Aunt Della? Ice? Why, Aunt Della? Why? Why?"

Darlene looks into Della's face, and it's as if she's either looked into the face of an angel, in the bright overhead light, or death.

"Aunt Della, Aunt Della, Aunt Della, Aunt Della, Aunt Della …"

It was being whispered crazily to Della by Darlene.

"Aunt Della! Aunt Della! Aunt Della! No, Aunt Della! No, Aunt Della! No! No! Noooo!"

Margaret, she's run into the room, was at the bottom of Della's bed.

"Momma! Momma! Momma!"

Della's body was taken from the house.

It was 2:43 a.m. The ambulance's lights are still set on the house. The ambulance was still parked outside the house. Margaret was in Royal's arms. They were sitting on the couch.

Darlene was in the dining room, her head down on the table. Lee's back was back against the dining room chair; his eyes were closed, his breathing erratic, as if he were wheezing.

Then the ambulance left the house.

Darlene, Margaret, Lee, and Royal barely had the courage to watch the two medics remove Della from her bed and put her bagged body onto the gurney, roll the gurney off to the hallway, down the staircase, out the house, and then lift Della's body onto the ambulance; one medic shut the ambulance's back door.

The four of them barely had the courage to follow all of this and then stand outside on the porch, in the morning's chilly December air.

Margaret was the one who placed the call to St. Bartholomew Hospital for them to come for Della. Darlene was too wiped out, too hysterical, crying over Della's body like she could bring her back to life if she just cried enough, pleaded, maybe, practically dying from it from within.

And Margaret called Royal and then Lee. Both, when they got to the house, had entered it in a panic, having beat St. Bartholomew's medics to the house, stood at the foot of Della's bed with unrestrained emotions as they watched Darlene's body contort, torture itself by pitching itself back and forth incessantly before them what seemed forever.

But St. Bartholomew's medics arrived, and it took all the courage in Darlene and Margaret and Lee and Royal to watch how they performed, what they did to prepare a dead person's body for removal from the house.

Darlene wanted to go off to the hospital, in the ambulance, but collapsed outside on the front porch of the house. She physically collapsed. Then she refused anybody's help, struggling up to her feet on her own.

Margaret knew from the beginning she couldn't go to the hospital, in the ambulance; the legal papers would be signed later in the day. The medic, who knew the family, said it would be okay. Accommodations for the family would be extended to them.

They just stood out on the front porch and then went back into the house. Darlene, for some unbeknownst reason, chose to go into the dining room with Lee following her; and Margaret and Royal into the living room. The ambulance had sat outside the house for a good while before pulling off, sat parked there.

"I'll … I'll call Brother Houston. I'll call Brother Houston. He'll conduct church service for me this morning, Mag."

Margaret's eyes were shut. That portion of her face was swollen. And tears pooled that area of her reddened skin beneath her eyes.

"I … I want to go home, Royal." Pause. "But not now." She kept her head on Royal's shoulder as he continued to hold her.

"Lee. Lee."

Lee opened his eyes. "Y-yes, Darlene."

Darlene lifted her head off the dining room table. "I'm … I'm going upstairs. B-back to my room."

"Y-you're staying the night, Darlene?"

"Yes, I'm staying the night. What did, else did you think, think I'd do? Expect? What?"

"I—"

"Aunt Della! Aunt Della! Aunt Della!" Darlene shrieked.

"Darlene!"

"Get away from me, Lee! Get away from me, Lee! Don't touch me, Lee! Don't touch me, Lee! Don't anyone—"

"Darlene, Darlene, maybe we should—"

"Pray? Pray! Pray, Royal McCloud? Pray!" Darlene said to Royal, Royal having left Margaret, having rushed into the dining room.

"Ha! Ha! Ha! Ha! N-no one, no is to touch me. No one is to touch me. Only Aunt Della ... Aunt Della can touch me. Can touch me. Only Aunt Della can touch me!"

Royal stood there for no more than two, three seconds more and then turned, went back into the living room.

"Ha! Ha! Ha!"

Then Darlene stood. Her legs were wobbly. Lee stood with her.

"Up ... up the stairs," Darlene said at the foot of the staircase, staring up at it. "Aunt ... Aunt Della climbed them today. Aunt ... Aunt Della climbed them today. Y-you saw her, Lee. Aunt Della, Lee. Climb them today. The staircase today. The ... the staircase today."

Lee shook his head; tears were in his eyes.

"If ... if Aunt Della could, I ... I ... I can ... I can too ..."

Darlene began climbing the stairs, and her legs continued to wobble under her weight. Lee watched her. Lee watched Darlene climb those stairs like each step she took stabbed at her feet—the left foot, then the right foot, then the left foot, then the right foot.

Lee just wanted Darlene to reach the top of the stairs; his heart was already burning with so much pain, so much anger and bitterness, and now he was forced to watch this—Darlene, his wife climb the stairs, when all he wanted to do was sit at the dining room table and feel the bluntness, suddenness of death, how, from an afternoon of fun, joy, frivolity, death came, appeared at night, came into the house and took his aunt Della from him.

"Don't come up, Lee," Darlene said from the top of the staircase. "I don't need you. I don't need you, Lee. I'm going to my room. Next to Aunt Della's. Next to my aunt Della's room."

Darlene then disappeared from sight.

"I'm ready to go, Royal. Leave. G-go home."

Pause.

"But ... but first, I want to go upstairs. I ... I won't be long."

Royal shook his head. He stood. He held Margaret. He kissed her lips. He sat back down on the couch.

Margaret, when she got in her room, began crying.

"You're ... you're dead, Momma. You're dead, Momma. You're dead, Momma."

She felt so weak. But she didn't want to stay in the house. She sat on the bed and then laid back. She thought of Royal waiting down in the living room for her but knew there was no problem, him waiting for her as long as it took. She knew that.

She kept dabbing at her eyes with the tissue, knowing that the days ahead, what would be required, would build to a peak—the funeral, the funeral arrangements, and then back to her tears, what she was doing now, hoping she could shut out the world, so she could grieve alone, because she had lost a mother, had kissed her good night, was alive when she'd left her bedroom, who was looking forward to seeing her in her Sunday dress, but more than that, so much more than that.

"I ... I don't want to believe it, Momma. I ... I don't, Momma ..."

Margaret closed her eyes and drifted for a few minutes. When she reopened them, she looked around the room, for she still knew she was in the house, that she hadn't changed out her robe, that if she slept at all, how little or how much, it wouldn't be in the house, in the room down the hall from her mother, in her bed, the bed she now lay on.

Margaret got up. She looked at the dress she'd pressed for church. She felt it. It was a dark-blue dress. It would stay in the house overnight, Margaret thought.

"From the apartment to the hospital, and ... and then I'll come back to get it. Take ... take everything then. All my things. From the house. M-Momma's house."

She was going to try, she thought. She was going to try to be strong, but her mother had just died. Her mother had just died, and she could be whatever she wanted to be now, nothing ... not anything better.

CHAPTER 13

Royal was driving Margaret back to the house.

They'd come from St. Bartholomew Hospital. She'd called the funeral home from the apartment since she'd signed the official release papers, and by this afternoon, Della's body would be released to A. C. Donner Funeral Home. Then she and Royal would go to the funeral home, go over its funeral plan, agreement, fees, and then select Della's casket.

"How are you doing ... holding up, Mag?"

Margaret didn't respond.

"I'm sorry. It's like I had to say something to break the silence in the car."

"It ... it just happened, and ... and now there's so much to do."

"Just happened. Yes ... and it's like you have to put all your ... your ..."

"Grief, Royal? Grief?"

"Yes, grief ... grief, Mag. Put it aside. Brush your grief aside."

"And make sure your loved one, your family member, Momma ..."

"Did I hear it in Mother Ballad's voice, Mag? Am ... am I going to say—"

"Do we have to, Royal? Do we?"

Lightly, Royal's fist struck the steering wheel. "No."

"She's going to let me run everything."

"R-run everything? Who, Mag, who? Darlene?"

"Darlene. Yes, Darlene. She's going to let me run everything. She'll take a backseat. Wait and see. Just wait and see. Of course she will. She'll let me run everything. Be in charge of everything. I'll be in charge, w-wait and see. And ... and then she'll criticize. Criticize. Criticize everything, thing I do. Move I make. Tear everything I do down.

"Wait and see, Royal. Just wait and see."

"L-let's not think of her, Mag. Not—"

"Why not? Why not, Royal? How can't we? She's at the house, isn't she? It's where we're going now, isn't it? The house, to Momma's house."

"Because your energy, energies shouldn't be focused, concentrated, distracted by—"

"Now you're going to tell me how to think? What to think!"

Royal's eyes are off the road and on her.

"Why ... why are you acting ... acting like this? This way? Why are you—"

"Because I hate this day!"

"A day God's made?"

"Don't you ever quit? Give up? Stop?"

"I ..."

Royal puts his eyes back on the road.

Minutes later.

"We're here, Mag."

Margaret opens her eyes.

"At the house."

Royal parked the car in front of the house. Margaret looked at the house and then shut her eyes again.

"I don't want to go in. I don't want to go in the house now. Can ... can you take me back to the apartment, please. Then ... then we'll go to the funeral home." She opened her eyes. "This'll be the last thing I do today. Take my things out the house. Remove them, Royal."

The car started back up.

Lee parked the car in the driveway.

He turned the car's engine off. It was 11:35 a.m. How he'd managed to stay away from the house this long, to get up, not call Darlene—even he had no idea how he did it.

"Aunt Della's dead. Aunt ... Aunt Della's dead."

Maybe it's why he hadn't called Darlene. Maybe it's why, he thought. Maybe he didn't want to talk about it. Think about it—his mind going crazy with it, absolutely nuts with it.

To walk in Aunt Della's house this morning. It was hard enough walking out it this morning, knowing his aunt Della was dead.

The heat in the car was gone. The car was about to turn ice-cold parked there in the driveway; but Lee didn't want to move. It's how it was when he got back to the house this morning, his house. When he inserted the key in the door and walked in his and Darlene's house and he didn't get as far as the living room; he just sat in one of the living room chairs and shut his eyes and fell asleep, didn't bother to move from the chair until he woke up and had to go to the bathroom, which was around 9:25 a.m. "Yes, nine twenty-five."

No, maybe he wasn't giving Darlene her space, he thought, but himself, himself space. Looking out for himself, his feelings, how he was reacting emotionally to his aunt Della's death.

"Sweet peach. Sweet peach. I'm ... I'm your sweet peach, Aunt Della. W-will always be your sweet peach, Aunt Della."

But when I get into Aunt Della's house, put my key in the door, everything will be about Darlene, Darlene's feelings, not mine. "Not mine, mine. Not mine. But D-Darlene's, Darlene's. I- I'm gonna have to prepare myself. I'm gonna. G-gonna."

Lee knew his feelings would be pushed aside, shoved into the background.

"And God knows it has to be that way. It has to ..."

Lee pulled a pack of cigarettes out his overcoat. He needed a smoke, and bad. He lit up.

"Mmm. Mmm. Ha. Not in Aunt Della's house. Not in Aunt Della's house!"

Whatever he said to try to comfort her, he would say—while knowing she wouldn't hear it. Darlene might as well be deaf, and so he couldn't share his horrible grief with her, this beautiful person they both loved, their aunt Della, above, beyond anyone's belief, imagination, for his feelings would be snuffed like the cigarette he'd grind into the ground with the heel of his shoe once outside the car.

Lee took one more puff from the cigarette. He opened the car door, got out, closed the door, and then ground the cigarette into the concrete with his shoe. He looked at the tall old oak tree, where the car was parked at the exact same mark his uncle Frank parked his car from days' past.

"I didn't miss it, Uncle Frank. I … I never miss it, Uncle Frank. W-when I park the car."

Lee turned.

Where was she? He thought. Where was Darlene in the house? Which room? Where? Now he felt dazed, transfixed in fear, in some shocking, ugly, catastrophic event to soon happen to him.

The cigarette had done him little good.

Lee stood at the front door of the house and prayed in his heart that Aunt Della was in the house, in her bedroom, in her bed—that everything was normal. That he and Darlene, the family, were talking about Christmas, preparing, not Aunt Della's funeral. Lee steadied the key in his hand. Maybe another cigarette, he thought, timidly feeling the pack with his hand. No, I don't want to go back into the cold car again, roll down the window three quarters the way down, fan the smoke with my hand, I …

The key twisted in the lock. Lee stepped into the house; there was silence.

He breathed. Of course he expected this. He breathed. This he expected. Of course he expected this. Of course. Of course. Then his aunt Della and Darlene were juxtaposed in his mind—wanting to see Darlene, wanting to see his aunt Della. Both inside the house. Both there.

There.

"Where is she? Where is Darlene?"

"Lee! Lee! Is that you, Lee?"

The voice, her voice came from the kitchen, from out the kitchen, not upstairs like he had imagined, assumed it would, how it would be.

"Yes, Darlene! Yes, yes, Darlene!"

Lee rushed into the kitchen.

"Oh, there you are, Lee. There you are," Darlene said cheerily, brightly.

"Yes. Yes, Darlene. Y-yes," Lee said frozen, like he'd felt inside the car.

"Isn't it a beautiful day? A beautiful day, Lee?"

Lee didn't know what to say, how to react to Darlene.

"I, yes, it—"

"You might as well take off your coat and hat, Lee. And stay. Do that, Lee."

"Yes, sure, sure, D—"

"You are going to stay, aren't you?"

"Y-yes, I … uh—"

"I can smell it from here. I can smell it from here. You've been smoking. Smoking. Smoking in the car."

"Yes, I had to, Darlene, I—"

"But not in here, Lee. Not in here. This house. Aunt Della's house, Lee. Not in my aunt Della's house, Lee."

She was all dressed up, not in a robe or slip or nightgown, but all dressed up. She had lipstick on, a smear of makeup, barely traceable, in a pink blouse, black slacks, crisply pressed, the crease, cut, her black penny loafers shiny.

"No smoking in my aunt Della's house. Sit, I fixed you breakfast, Lee. Breakfast, baby."

"Yes. Yes. I smell it, smelled it as soon as I—"

"I expected you earlier. Much earlier, Lee—"

"I was going to come, but—"

"But—oh, don't worry about it, Lee. Don't worry about it, baby. Hang up your—no, let me take them, let me take them—make myself useful, Lee."

"Thanks, Darlene. Thanks."

He wanted to hug her when she took his hat and coat out his hands. Lee wanted to hug her to him.

"Yes, it's such a beautiful day, Lee."

Darlene was out the kitchen and then back in it.

"Sit, Lee. Sit. I'll heat things up for you."

His mind had gone blank, but now he was back on track.

"Eggs, sausage, hash browns."

"And coffee. Your black coffee, Lee. Don't forget your black coffee, Lee. You mustn't forget your black coffee, Lee."

"I—"

"Just, I just had to get in the kitchen. Get down here this morning. Just had to, Lee. Don't know, don't know why."

Lee took the napkin off the table and then put it back.

"Ha. I knew you were coming this morning …"

"Of course, Darlene. Of course."

"I just didn't know when. When, Lee. Ha. Oh, never mind … never mind, Lee. Never mind."

Pause.

"Just a minute or two more. Just a minute or two more. No more. Just a minute or two more."

"I … I can wait, Darlene. I can wait."

"Just a minute or two more. Just a minute or two more."

"It's all right, Darlene. It's all right."

Darlene turned to Lee.

"I'm going to sit here and watch you. Watch and see. Watch and see, Lee. I'm going to sit here and watch you. Watch and see. Make sure you eat everything. Eat everything off your plate, Lee. Eat everything down. L-like Aunt Della did when … when I first came to the house. When Momma died. After she died. Didn't want to eat. Eat anything when I came to the house, Lee. Just like Aunt Della did, Lee. My aunt Della did. Made sure I ate everything. Ate everything off my plate. Ate it down."

Lee looked up from his bare plate at the table and wanted to say, "Aunt Della's dead, Darlene." Aunt Della's dead, Darlene, but instead, Lee watched Darlene turn and then turn the knobs on the stove higher under the pan, the flames rising, heating things up so the food would be hot for when Darlene served him his breakfast.

Lee's had breakfast. He was watching Darlene wash the dishes—she'd just begun.

"Lee, Lee, you can go into the living room. You don't have to sit there and watch me, baby. Watch me, Lee."

"No, I … yes, the living room. The living room, Darlene. I think I'll go into the living room."

"It's more comfortable there. Uh, in there, Lee. For you. More comfortable, Lee."

Lee got up from the table.

"You sure you don't want—"

Darlene turned to Lee and flashed a smile. "Now, Lee, you know I don't need you, Lee. You know that, baby."

When he got into the hallway, Lee cringed, for he knew why he didn't want to go into the living room in the first place—the memories were still too fresh in him. When he'd just come into the house, he'd gotten but so far, overcome by thought, by responsibility, owing the moment his undivided attention, his whole self, his whole effort, nothing more, nothing less; but now he could concentrate on what was in the living room, what he would have to sit down and look at, confront when he got in there—as if coerced to.

Nervous, deliberate, Lee walked into the living room, touched the Christmas tree, a branch on it. It was the last thing he'd done for his aunt Della. The last big thing, major, significant thing; and he was touching the branch, and suddenly, it was doing him some good, more than the cigarette he'd smoked in the car, so he sat down on the sofa, away from it and just admired it, thought of how pleased his aunt Della was for what he'd done for her and the family when he went to Tom Fletcher's lot for the tree.

"Oh … Aunt Della. Oh … Aunt Della. Ha. Ha."

Ten minutes had expired.

"Ready, Lee?"

"Oh, uh, Darlene. I … I didn't hear you. Come into, the, the living r-room, t-that is."

Silence.

"R-ready?"

"Yes, ready, Lee. To go upstairs, Lee. To go upstairs to Aunt Della's room." Darlene gestured by pointing her thumb up to the living room's ceiling.

"Aunt … Aunt Della's room?"

"Come, Lee. Come." It's when Darlene stuck her hand out for Lee, and Lee, seemingly desperate for what would be human contact, got up out his seat and grabbed Darlene's hand, hard.

"Let's go up, Lee. Up, baby."

And they hadn't gotten far, were at the staircase, when Darlene's hand left Lee's; and Lee knew what Darlene was thinking, the same thing he was thinking, or visualizing, seeing again, Aunt Della climbing those stairs just yesterday for the last time, going up the staircase.

Darlene took the first step up and then began moving swiftly up the stairs. She'd reached the top of the staircase before Lee.

"Come, Lee. Come, baby."

Darlene was halfway down the hallway, and then she was in Della's bedroom.

"Lee, Lee …"

Lee was in the bedroom now, for the first time since—

"Look what I did, Lee! Look what I did!"

Lee thought his heart was going to break into, or fall out his chest and crack into millions of little pieces on top of the rug.

"Aunt Della's bed. Aunt Della's bed. I fixed it. Made it. Made it this morning!"

And Lee couldn't hear anything, nothing at all, filter through either ear.

"Did you hear me, Lee? Did you hear me! Don't stand there, Lee! Don't just stand there and say nothing, Lee! Say nothing at all! I said I fixed, made Aunt Della's bed this … got, got up and made up Aunt Della's bed! The first thing! This morning! This morning when I got up, Lee!"

"It doesn't … it doesn't feel like Sunday today, Mag."

"No, no, it doesn't."

"It hasn't felt like it all day."

They were about two blocks from the house. It was 5:15 p.m.

"So … you're up to this now?"

"I said I was. So I guess I am."

Royal still hadn't been able to thaw Margaret's feelings out, crack them. She was good at the funeral parlor, but as soon as they got back in the car … There was no way he was going to take this personally, in any way let it have a negative effect on him; he was going to tough this thing out. God was making everything possible. He wasn't going to bring up Darlene's name now. He was going to let it stay on ice.

This time when Royal parked the car in front of the house, he knew it was parked permanently—that he and Margaret were going to enter Mother Ballad's house.

"Lee's here. His car's in the driveway."

"Yes, so … so I see."

"I wonder how long he's been here, Mag." Royal might as well have been talking to a wall.

Margaret's head was turned to the right. Royal had no idea what she was thinking.

He'd never quite felt like this before, out of touch with her, distant from her, as if she'd emotionally broken the cord between them, had spiritually abandoned him, moved into her own world and locked him out.

Or was she with her mother right now? Royal asked himself. With Mother Ballad. Where her mother was—her spirit touching Mother Ballad's spirit. No, it didn't feel like Sunday, not at all, only the same day Mother Ballad had died.

They were out the car. Royal held onto Margaret's arm, and then when they got to the doorstep, he drew the house key out and then stepped back. He walked right in the house. Quickly he pivoted to Margaret. "Mag, your coat. I'll hang it up."

"Margaret! Royal!"

Royal pivoted again. Lee ran up to Margaret. They hugged, and briefly, they remained this way until Margaret separated herself from him.

"M-Margaret."

"Lee."

Royal moved to the coat closet. When he swung back around, Margaret was at the staircase.

"I'm going up to my room. For my things." She was solemn. "O-okay, Royal?" she said while walking up the staircase. "Upstairs for my things. Belongings. Out my room."

Royal and Lee watched Margaret until she vanished from view.

Lee and Royal went into the living room.

"I … I don't know about you, Royal …"

Suddenly Lee and Royal were hugging, and neither broke it off, hugging as if this was the miracle of miracles they needed, were looking for to smash open this nightmare both were living in their hearts, in their souls, in their minds.

"Is this real, Royal? Did this happen, Royal?"

"Yes, Lee. Mother Ballad's home, Lee. Gone home with God."

"Oh … sorry, sorry," Lee said while letting go of Royal.

"For what, Lee? For what? I've been wanting to hold onto something all day."

Both sat. When they'd settled, Royal said, "W-where's—"

"In the kitchen, Royal. Fixing, she's fixing dinner for us. D—"

"She is, I mean Darlene's been able to—"

"It-it's been strange around here, Royal. Weird. You have to … to …"

"Lee, Lee, who's in the living room with you, Lee? Who's in the living room with you, Lee? Who came in the house? Just came into the house? I was in, must've been in the pan—"

"It's—"

"Royal McCloud!"

"Good evening, D—"

"Oh, what did you do? Come to pray, Royal McCloud? You came to pray, Royal McCloud? Ha. Ha."

"No, Darlene. No, I didn't."

"So where's Margaret? My cousin? Ha Ha. The other one. I know she's here too. In the house too. Ha Ha. She must be upstairs. Where else? Where else?"

Darlene's in an apron. She undid it. "Dinner can wait. You don't mind, do you, Lee?"

"No, no, uh—"

"Do you, baby?"

"No, not at—"

"It's been a beautiful day, hasn't it, Lee? Hasn't it?"

Lee looked at Royal.

"You've been sitting in here most of the day. In here looking at the Christmas tree, haven't you, Lee?"

Lee looked back at Royal, but Royal didn't look at Lee this time.

"You picked it out, off Tom Fletcher's lot. You did, Lee. You did, Lee. You, Lee. You, baby. And the presents, Christmas presents under the tree. Oh, Lee, oh, Lee … you did that all on your own. All on your own, Lee. By yourself, Lee."

Lee felt trapped, powerless.

"Oh well … oh well …," Darlene said, folding the apron, laying it on top the sofa. "I have better things to do … ha … than stand around here and … and brag about you, Lee Winston. Better things to do, Lee."

Pause.

Darlene shifted her body to her left. "Excuse, pardon me, Lee … Royal."

When Darlene left the room, Lee whispered, "I told you, Royal. See, see, I told you."

Margaret was in her bedroom. She didn't go into her mother's room but had stood outside the room. She saw what, she assumed, Darlene had done. She saw it, and her feelings, she couldn't describe them, just how she felt seeing the bed made, not the way she remembered it just this morning, so many hours earlier ... but made out as if nothing had happened, as if things were normal, but again, she hadn't known what to expect—just how to look at things, feel about things after one day ... the same day your mother's died.

But she was in her bedroom with ambivalent feelings—happy to be in the house, there (just for her clothes), and then the eagerness to leave, to pack the things she had to pack, her things, what she'd brought to the house to stay on, be with her mother during the time of her illness, to be as equal as Darlene, as needed and necessary, to make sure she was included in the process as significantly.

"It'd been going so well, Momma. Between us. We had such a good time every day, Momma. In the house. In ... every day was wonderful with you, Momma."

Looking at her mother's body today, at St. Bart's, before the funeral parlor, A. C. Donner Funeral Home came for her to be transferred over, assigned to them, she'd needed God and Royal, both, simultaneously.

"Momma would be glad her bed's made. That Darlene made it. She kept this big house so neat, so orderly. All the time. Every day of her life."

Margaret sat down on top of the bed; she just felt weak, her stomach, her legs. She'd had orange juice but nothing at all solid. And here it was after five o'clock, and she, her body, was subsisting off ... She got back up, walked over to the closet, looked back at the opened suitcase on the bed and then turned her back into the closet, taking the blouse and slacks off the hangers.

"So you're here. Here. You've come back, Margaret. Back to the house."

Startled but, then again, not, Margaret turned back into the closet, continued doing what she'd been doing. When she had what she wanted, successfully collected them, she went back to the bed and began folding the articles and then placing them in the suitcase, in among the other clothes.

"I was, must've been in the pantry when you and ... When you two came in."

It was her tone of voice, and Margaret felt like screaming.

Darlene was at the foot of the bed, Margaret at the side, the closet to Margaret's right.

"What a beautiful day. What a beautiful day."

It's when Margaret looked at Darlene queerly.

"Do you need help? Oh … I see most of what you came to the house with, Margaret, is packed. Practically packed."

Margaret was angrier.

"I guess you did your part, however useful you thought you could, might be," Darlene said, folding her arms in front of her, walking back over to the foot of the bed. "Ha Ha. Whatever your objectives were. Your intentions for staying in the house were."

There were but three more articles in the closet for Margaret to gather, and now she just wanted to retrieve them, get them off the wire hangers, get them in the suitcase, pack them away, so she and Royal could leave, just leave the house—her mother and father's house.

"Ha. Ha. Ha."

Margaret looked at Darlene. "Why are you laughing? Why, why are you laughing like that?"

"To think, to think—just to think you thought you were, could walk into this house, Aunt Della's house and … and near the end of her life, tail end, you could change things. Change, change … Ha. Ha. Ha."

"Change—"

"It's all right. It's all right, Margaret. I know you went to St. Bartholomew Hospital today. It's all right, Margaret. And to A. C. Donner Funeral Home. It's all right. It's all right. Ha Ha. And you can arrange Aunt Della's funeral. You … you can do all the little things, Margaret. Yes. Yes. All the little things. I'll let you do that. You and Royal Mc … Royal McCloud. Yes, yes, you're good at that. Good at that, Margaret. The little things, Margaret."

Darlene grinned.

"But I'm going to take care of this house. I'm in charge of this house."

"You are?"

"Since the house is mine! Mine anyway!"

"You don't know that, Darlene! You don't know that!"

"It's in the will, Margaret. It's in Aunt Della's will! Ha. Ha. Ha!"

"You don't … I … I didn't come into the house to fight you, Darlene. T-to … my mother's been dead, only been dead … I … I … Not in my mother's house. N-not in—"

"You were never a match for me anyway," Darlene said, rearing back her head, her shoulders, howling again. "You were never a match for me,

Margaret. I could always whip you, Margaret. I could always whip you! Ha. Ha. Ha. Since small!"

Darlene' words paralyzed Margaret.

"Always. Always. I always got the better of you. From the time ... time I came into the house. You were older than me, but I always ... always knew I was stronger than you. My mind, my will ... my personality. Aunt Della and Uncle Frank knew ... knew too, it too—knew who was ... was, had the stronger personality—was, it's why they thought me more important than you. Than you, Margaret. Than you!"

And it's when Margaret thought of her talk with her mother, of their time in the bedroom together when her mother explained herself about Darlene and their relationship, shared her wisdom, the beginning, how the relationship began, how needy Darlene was, came to her seeking love, affection, comfort, trust—seeking it and seeking it and seeking it.

"I ... I just want to pack my clothes and—"

"Leave? Leave? And—"

"I'll be back, Darlene. You can take care of the house, you—but I'll be back. Momma will have to be buried in a dress. A dress of my choosing for her funeral—I choose. And—"

"It doesn't matter, Margaret. Ha. Ha. Yes, do ... do what you have to do. Come back. You can come and go in the house as you wish. Please. For now. The time being. Can, you can use whatever excuse you want, need ... need to use to come into the house. In and out." Pause.

"Yes, you were easy to control. Margaret. It didn't take long. Ha. Ha. You were never a match for me. The older we got, the easier it was. You knew, understood your place in the—"

"I'm finished."

And Margaret, for now, didn't know if she'd said what she'd said to herself, and it'd come out, or for the benefit of Darlene, but it stopped Darlene in her tracks as she looked at Margaret strangely.

"Momma's funeral, the funeral, Momma's funeral will, it will be December 27, December 27 at Clearview Presbyterian Church at ten o'clock. After ... after Christmas. B-before the new year."

Darlene looked at Margaret, shaking her head.

Margaret shut the suitcases.

Darlene walked out the room.

"Pathetic," Darlene said, making her way up the hallway. "You're pathetic, Margaret Ballad. Just pathetic," Darlene said, now out of range of Margaret. "Always been pathetic."

Margaret took the suitcase off the bed. She looked around the room.

"I ... I didn't leave anything, did I? Be-behind?"

It's like she really didn't want to leave the house now. The house meant so much to her, but she turned toward the doorway, and now she was in the hallway, and without stopping, she walked into her mother's room and saw the walker and tray there with its thirteen bottles of pills and listened for the steam that was always hissing, easy to hear; and though sad, she felt cheered, brightened—she felt her mother's presence.

Margret stood there soaking it all in, showing the strength and resolve she'd need for the oncoming days and weeks and that this, what she was doing, was helping her, preparing her for now. Not only her mother's room but the house was being a source of strength for her to draw on.

And she saw her mother in her bed. Della lying there, with all her glorious gray hair, and in her death, as in her life, it looked glorious, lovely, even in the hospital when she and Royal viewed her body, the hair, the hair. "Momma's hair had a life to it. An eternal aura even in death.

"Momma's hair was still alive."

*　　*　　*

"And that was yet another special quality Mother Ballad had. You had to, if you knew her long enough, assign some unique, special ... some ... I called her Mother Ballad as most of you know—Mother Ballad. After knowing her for so long, I had to come up with some way of addressing her that was uniquely different, uniquely mine. Personal. That showed the special love I had for her. The great affection for her.

"So one day, one day ... ha ... I just began calling Della Ballad 'Mother Ballad.' Not Mrs. Ballad, no, not Mrs. Ballad anymore"—Royal smiled from the Clearview Presbyterian's pulpit, delivering Della Ballad's eulogy—"but Mother Ballad."

Pause.

"It made me feel particularly good. And I remember Mother Ballad smiling at me, and then it was as if, as though nothing had happened, had transpired between us. It was remarkable, truly, it was … uh, like I'd been calling, addressing her as Mother Ballad all along. Since the time, beginning of our relationship." Royal began shaking his head as if it were further testimony. Tears were now in his eyes.

"It's how natural and comfortable things came to Mother Ballad. How natural and comfortable Mother Ballad made things feel for a person. And, of course, there were many, many more special qualities about her." Royal looked up from his notes. "Why, why there was one time, I vividly recall, when—"

It was 8:20 p.m.

Royal put the car keys in his pocket. He and Margaret had just come into the house. The first thing she did was go to the bathroom. Before they'd left the house, she'd gone to the bathroom. The ride from the house to the apartment was no more than fifteen to seventeen minutes away. Royal hadn't questioned her motives.

Margaret entered into the apartment's small living room area.

"You're exhausted, I know."

"You can say that again."

"This one was tougher on you than your father's."

"I … I don't think I should, we should compare them. The two funerals."

"Oh, I'm sorry, I'm sorry. What a s-stupid, dumb, insensitive thing to say. For me …"

"In a way though, I guess Momma made it easier. I … I, maybe if Daddy were alive, Momma's funeral would've been …"

"Look, Mag, I have you thinking about something … something you shouldn't be thinking about at all—not now. And I have no idea, clear idea for why I said, just said what I did."

"You'd become so close to Momma."

"Praying with her made me feel just as good. Did just as much good for me as I think it did for her."

"Well … when she got off the phone with you"—Margaret smiled—"it's all Momma would talk about. How the two of you prayed. That she'd prayed with Royal."

"The testimonies at the wake and the things said informally at the house, Mother Ballad was so loved, respected in this Myles Day community, Mag.

It was a wonderful tribute to a wonderful life. I suppose it's all we can ask for when we die, leave this earth with, if not everyone knowing us well enough to love us, at least respect us by our example. How we lived our life. What we gave to others."

"Yes, Royal. Yes, definition. And Momma gave a lot. It … it was incredible."

"Incredible, Mag. Incredible."

Pause.

"Darlene, she's still handling things well. I'm surprised," Royal said, sitting.

"She threw herself on Daddy's casket when he died. At the funeral."

"Yes, I remember you telling me that when you got back to Detroit."

"It … it frightened me."

"But … but we've seen it before. Your emotions, they can take you into strange places, can come out of strange places. But no one should judge. Not a soul."

"It still frightened me at the time, Royal. When it occurred at Daddy's funeral."

"Mag, what's the difference between, when a person feels the Holy Spirit, it's entered them, taken them? What's the difference? When someone's been possessed? When—"

"Darlene, she was the perfect hostess at the house, the repast, when we got back from the cemetery. Wasn't she?"

"Are, was there sarcasm, I heard, just heard in your voice? Was it, Mag? Because—"

"She was, wasn't she?"

"Yes. Yes. Darlene continued to—"

"Do you think she … I … I—"

"What?"

"She's acting like Momma's not dead. Didn't die."

"You know, being in that house, it means everything to her, Mag."

"Are you saying … do you think it's what's keeping her … her—"

"From falling apart? I … I don't know, Mag. I'm not a psychiatrist. But Darlene's in the house, and I think it's where she's always felt most comfortable, in your mother's house."

"She has to know Momma's dead, Royal. Darlene must … must know."

Royal loosened his necktie.

Then Margaret balled her fist. "Why Darlene, Royal? Why Darlene? Why did Darlene find Momma and not me?"

"Mag, you mustn't continue with this, punishing yourself with that question. By going over the same piece of ground day in and day out like you've been doing."

"Why was it that she got up during the night and not me? Why? Not Momma's daughter but ... but Momma's niece? That ... that there wasn't something inside me to wake me. But Darlene. Didn't ... I ... I didn't get out of bed. But she did. I don't know. I ... I just don't know. D-didn't have that connection t-to Momma and ... and—"

"And Darlene did?"

"Yes, Royal. Something got her out of bed and ... and walked her into Momma's bedroom. Something. Told her to go in there. Told her Momma was dead, Royal. Some connection she ... Darlene had to M—"

"Oh, if we only knew, Mag. The answers to all our questions. Mysteries in the universe. It's just that I don't know if it would make things any easier, better for—"

"I wanted to find her, Royal. I told you that, said that to you before. F-find Momma in bed. As morbid as it sounds, I wanted to find Momma if ... if anyone was, at all was to find her. Not Darlene, Royal. D-Darlene.

"Am I sick, Royal? Am ... am I? Am I?"

"No, You're a daughter who loved her mother abundantly. Without—"

"But, God, God chose Darlene, Royal. Why did God choose Darlene to find Momma and not me? Was it because of my past—I'm still not worthy? Am I—"

"And Darlene is?"

"Why not Darlene, Royal?" Margaret insisted. "She didn't do what I did to Momma. Have the past I had with Momma. Darlene never did what I did. Never!"

"God. God. We love God. Are Christians. His children. But he's not the controller of all things. Life has its own—we have to accept things, Mag. Learn to a-accept things in our lives without the influence of God."

"Like next Thursday, Royal? What's going to happen in Attorney Robinson's law office at ten o'clock next ... next Thursday, Royal?"

"And ... and what's that, Mag."

"The reading. The reading. The reading of Momma's will, or haven't you heard about it yet? Gotten … gotten the news? Of it yet?"

"Mag, don't do that. P-please … don't … don't do that."

"Why not? When it's a foregone conclusion. I don't know why, even know why we have to go to the reading Thursday morning. Why … why there should be any bother. R-reason to."

"Mag, d-don't try to speak for your mother. For Mother Ballad."

"I know Momma loved me," Margaret said. "I … I know she loved me."

"Who—why, who could, would doubt or … or question that?"

Margaret looked askance. "B-but did Momma, did she, she …"

There was a long break in conversation.

"I know what you're thinking. What you want to say."

"You do, don't you, Royal? Y-you do, don't you?"

Margaret gets up, crosses the floor, and then kneels in front of Royal. She puts her head in his lap. She looks up at him. "If anyone would know, yes, it would be you."

Royal's hand caresses the side of Margaret's cheek. His head falls back against the couch. "But let's, you and me, Mag, try to learn how to accept things better. Like I said. Starting today, Mag. Right now." Pause. "God is in the universe, owns the universe, yes, of course, but let's learn how to accept things in our life better.

"Darlene found Mother Ballad and so … so that's that—it's over with. Over and done with. Mother Ballad's will, it will be read at ten o'clock Thursday by Attorney Robinson and yes, so … that will be that too, Mag."

"B-but I can't help it, Royal. I can't help it with Darlene. With Darlene at the core of everything in my life." Pause. "Always there, Royal. Without fail!"

Royal sighs. "I don't know how or if this will, any of this will ever work itself out between you and Darlene. And Mother Ballad, I'm sure, had the same concern, f-fear if you will, afflicting her before she died."

"Yes."

"And the house, whoever gets it, it may prove everything to them and, then again, nothing. It may finally free you of Darlene or Darlene of you and, then again, it may not. But whatever's the outcome, Mother Ballad decided should be done with the house, one thing's true: you'll know Mother Ballad's decision was from her heart. That's irrefutable. Something Darlene nor you, in your hearts, can never question, her decision about the house."

"No, it won't be, Royal."

"And, Mag, the heart knows, Mag. The heart always knows. And I've had to search mine regarding the house the past few weeks. It was quite a bit of soul searching, to be honest. I put myself through. But I won't go into detail." Pause. "No. It was when you came by the apartment after Darlene had upset you, and we ate dinner together, r-remember?"

"Y-yes, I do."

"It was after I dropped you off at the house is when I went over to the church to, well … to think. Think things thoroughly through for myself Meditate if … if you will." Royal fidgeted. "And I was looking for thorns in my heart, but found none. And I was looking for self-doubt in my motivations regarding the house, what they could be, but found none. I … ha … was clean. Came up clean, you might say.

"We will be fine, no matter, whatever the outcome may be. The house— you love your mother's house and so do I. There's no shame in that. No crime." Margaret removed her head from Royal's lap. He stood, stretching out his lengthy frame. "Nothing to feel ashamed of, Mag. It's a beautiful old house. A wonderful old house. Charming. Lovely.

"The house you were born in. Raised in. The house where your father and now … now your mother, Mother Ballad, died in while sleeping peacefully in her bed. Where their spirits reside. But with faith comes acceptance. Assurance." Royal helped Margaret to her feet. He took her into his arms.

"And already, Mag, I can feel Mother Ballad's loving spirit at work inside me. What is Mother Ballad's lovely legacy to us at work. Already, Mag. Her spirit."

Margaret hugged Royal.

"And another thing …"

Margaret looked up at him.

"I … I … I want to make Mother Ballad my guardian angel."

"Guardian—"

"If you don't mind, that is."

"No, of course not, I don't," Margaret laughed.

"See, Mag. I think it'd be nice to have one. And Mother Ballad, she … she would be perfect. The perfect choice for me."

"Momma, a guardian angel. Ha."

"Mother Ballad's going to be great. Just great at it too. Wait and see."

"Suppose I—"

"Uh-uh. Not a chance. I beat you to it. Was my idea first. So don't get any ideas."

They didn't move. Margaret didn't feel as tired now, all the planning, all the people turning out for her mother's wake, and then the funeral, the ride to the cemetery where her mother's casket was buried next to her father's, the Janice Akin Cemetery, plot, both had chosen, and then the drive back to the house, church folk (Clearview and Hands of Christ) helping out, and now with this peaceful time with Royal as if there *was* a balm from Gilead.

"It takes a few months though for them—"

"Guardian angels?"

"Yes. Ha. Guardian angels. Uh, for them to get going. To spring into action though. Uh, hit their stride. Reach the top of their game, Mag."

"It does, does it?" Margaret said with a pronounced question mark on her forehead.

"Uh, yes, sure, Mag. They, uh, have to get acclimated first. In, uh, heaven first."

"And then, then what happens when all that's done? Is worked out?"

"Done—oh, you'll see, Mag. You'll see, all right. In a few, a matter of months. Five, six months tops. You'll see."

"Come on, Royal. Let's go to bed. I think you've been up on your feet much too long today."

"Yes, just give Mother Ballad a little time," Royal said while Margaret dragged him by the arm. "Time to get acclimated. To settle in, down. That's all. Ha. That's all … Mag."

*   *   *

Furiously the snow had been blistering the sky for the past two hours. The sky was a white canvas. For Myles Day City, this was serious stuff. It was forecast, by the weather service, as a major storm in the making; and a major storm in Myles Day meant something extraordinary. The weather service predicted the snow accumulation would run anywhere between thirty-nine to forty-two inches. And as always, Myles Day City would be able to dig itself from under the piles of snow, but it would still cripple many normal city activities or knock out power lines or close roadways—in other words, stamp its own nasty brand of chaos on top the city.

Royal was driving back to the apartment. Tomorrow would be the reading of Mother Ballad's will in Attorney Robinson's office. It was on his mind. On and off his mind, to be more accurate, for most of the day. He watched the windshield wipers as they swiped at the snow, kicking the snow off the windshield. The flakes were big and chunky and heavy; driving through the snow was like the car was under assault, something any Myles Day City citizen was accustomed to, knew from winter to winter, year to year.

"The house … Marshall. Marshall."

Christmas had come and gone; now it would be the new year in a few days. He and Margaret didn't go by the house. They asked Lee if he would drop the presents by the apartment. They'd almost forgotten about them, what Mother Ballad had ordered out of Delaney Department Store's Christmas catalogue.

Margaret's gift from her mother was a beautiful winter-green dress, modern looking, stunning in detail.

When he saw his present, the size of it, his immediate thought was a Bible, but it wasn't. It was a dictionary. A big fat pretty juicy-looking dictionary that made his old one look like a supermodel on a Slim Fast diet. Instantly, he found a special place for it in the apartment, partially because the dictionary was so special and partially because of the dictionary's significance and, of course, sentimental value. Christmas day, he and Margaret spent in the apartment. Christmas Eve, there was church service at Hands of Christ Church.

How was their first Christmas without Mother Ballad for them? It was most difficult. Christmas dinner was tasty, but Margaret kept mostly to herself. He let her; he gave her space.

But to be honest, he was having his own problems. He'd thought of Marshall too much on Christmas Day. Death, someone dying, always repurposes your thoughts, and exposes just how short life is, that death can come, strike at anytime, anywhere, and yet even knowing he was still young, there certainly are no guarantees and he wanted to see his son, to be included in his life any way he could, knowing that he would be a good father, a dependable father on whatever level Eve would grant him (by whatever circumstance) to function on.

Today he'd called down to Detroit. He'd called from the job. The hall's pay phone. He talked to Earl Simmons, the private investigator Ronny Bowers had recommended, and Earl Simmons had come up with nothing, absolutely nothing regarding Eve.

And, therefore, nothing had changed. Earl said he'd keep trying but said he was beginning to run out of possibilities. For there was no material way to trace Eve—credit card, bank account, et cetera—and no one down in Detroit who knew Eve McCloud was talking. She had a circle of friends, but they weren't talking if, presumably, they knew anything of Eve's current whereabouts. Earl said he couldn't offer them money (so that was out the question), pay for information (something he knew Royal couldn't afford), and he said sometimes when you do, you can get sent off on a wild-goose chase. You're the one "holding the bag at the end of the day," so you just chalk it up as a "bad source," informant, someone you wouldn't do business with again.

Royal felt so frustrated, so rudderless. He was praying. Praying. He just wanted to be a father to his son. He felt so responsible to him, for him. He'd brought him into the world and felt it awful the condition he was born under, how Marshall had to start his life. He could beat himself up all day over this, but it wouldn't change anything for him or Marshall. It's why he had to find him. It's why this was so important to him.

"I'm not going to bother Margaret with any of this when I get in the apartment. There's no need to concern her with this for now. Today's disappointment. I'll wait. Just keep waiting. Maybe Earl'll get lucky. Our luck will change."

But what if Eve still didn't want anything to do with him? Royal thought. Then what? If Earl Simmons found her, then what? Then what would his strategy be—if he had one? If there was such a thing as a strategy.

The snow was still steady, heavy, blanketing Myles Day City's gentle landscape a fairytale white. It was just beginning its work, involved, silent—but oh so powerful in its quiet, simple drive.

As soon as Royal got into the apartment, he smelled food.

"Mmm …"

He'd decided in the car he was going to be in good spirits. The best of spirits.

"Royal! Royal!" Margaret charged at him. He hadn't taken off his coat and ski cap yet, but already Margaret was hugging the cold coat and him.

"Mag, Mag, what's—"

"Attorney Robinson called. Attorney Robinson called. W-with the storm coming, there … there'll be no reading of Momma's will tomorrow. T-tomorrow in his office!"

"There … there won't?"

"No."

Margaret let go of Royal. She walked back into the kitchen; her body sagged.

What could produce such panic? Royal thought. He hung his coat. Royal took his time. Darlene's name would come up again, in full flower, full bloom, would flourish, be alive and vibrant and abundant, and all-consuming—he was sure of it. *I wonder what Darlene's doing right now, right now, how she's taking the unexpected news?*

When he got into the kitchen, Margaret's hands were supporting her head, her elbows propped up on the table; she was gazing out into space, her eyes, a stony, hard-baked stare.

He loved her so much, so much. She was running into obstacles, hordes of them, and maybe now her faith was sustaining her. In no way had it deserted her, but she wasn't calling on it, summoning it, letting it serve her for a better good.

"What's wrong, Mag. Tell me, what's really wrong, going on?'

"I can't do it, Royal. I just can't do it. I can't go to the reading next Thursday at ten o'clock. It-it's back to ten o'clock next Thursday. Attorney Robinson said if … if it was all right. I … I said it would. Darlene, Darlene already agreed to it. He'd already called her first. Yes, I … I said it … it would be all right. Next Thursday at ten o'clock. The reading.

"But I can't do it. I can't do it. Darlene can have the house, Royal. She … she, I—Darlene can have the house. I don't want it. I don't want it!"

She stared at Royal. Royal didn't budge.

"It's snowing." Margaret stood. She looked out the window. "Ha. Ha. Ha. H-how mean. How cruel all of this is becoming. How mean. Cruel. All of this is playing itself out to be. Ha. Ha. It's snowing. Snowing." She walked back to the kitchen table. "I don't care anymore, Royal. I don't care any …

suppose … suppose it snows next Thursday too. S-suppose, just suppose, Royal? Suppose!" Margaret's looking wildly at Royal.

Royal walked over to the kitchen table. He was about to sit but, instead, walked over to the same window Margaret had been at. "It's snowing today. I don't know about next Thursday. That I, no one knows about."

"I'm … I'm not going to get the house, Royal. I'm not going to get it. There … there's every sign, indication. I … I don't mind. I don't care. I don't, I don't, I don't, Royal. Momma, Momma made the right decision. I … I won't be angry, bitter, upset, mad at Momma. No, no, not at my mother, Royal. N-not at all."

"It's just snowing, Mag. There're no signs. It always snows in December, around this time in December in Myles Day City. How many times has it happened? Been before? And it's just, it just so happens that it's before the reading of Mother Ballad's will, and Attorney Robinson, knowing the forecast, anticipating tomorrow's accumulations, put everyone on, you and Darlene on notice by cancelling tomorrow's reading, doing what was best. It's all—"

"Can't he say something!?"

Royal hadn't expected that comment; he didn't know how to deal with that kind of comment, outburst—what to say.

She stood.

"You're hungry?"

"Yes."

Now Royal was at the table.

"With school not starting up again until the new year, I like getting home early," Royal said, ending the silence between them.

"I like it too, Royal."

"It's not, I mean it's not a grind, but we all need a break. A break from our usual routine now and then."

The gravy for the meatloaf was bubbling in the sauce pan. Margaret reduced the flame.

"You know, Mag, I love you."

She turned to him.

"I love you, young lady."

"Ha. Young? How long ago was—"

"Well … ha … you'd better be, because I'm not old."

Margaret laughed with Royal.

"Thank God for a sense of humor. That our hearts can shine through when we let them. When we give them a chance to."

"I ... I just want to be able to breathe again, Royal," Margaret said, switching off the stove. "When it's, all this is over. Momma's will is read. I'll be able to breathe again, Royal."

"Breathe, Mag. Breathe. Don't stop breathing. Ever stop breathing. Keep breathing in God's air. Good air." Pause. "I think too much too, Mag. You're not the only one. I have to keep breathing too."

"Is ... is my faith being tested, Royal?" Margaret said, holding the pot of mashed potatoes firmly in her hand.

"Yes."

"I'm ... I'm so emotional."

"Uh, you're human. How's that. Ascribing that to yourself. You are still a member of the human race. Human species. You haven't reached divinity. But your faith is your foundation."

"But if Darlene gets the house, it won't bother me."

"But it will."

"Yes. Yes, it—"

"It might break your heart, Mag, but you mustn't let it break your soul. Your spirit. That's what could be dangerous, at stake, be negative about Thursday's reading."

"Because it'll mean ... mean ..."

"We can't say it, can we, Mag? Out loud, can we? The very essence of it. Between ourselves. B-because we both know what it'll mean. Because of Detroit, me being a pimp. You my prostitute. We'll know its meaning, symbolically to us. What Mother Ballad couldn't quite overcome. Quite rid her heart of."

"Yes, Royal."

"That mountain she could never quite scale. Get over."

"I put there for her."

"With my help."

Royal stood.

"I'm going to wash my hands."

"When you come back, your food'll be on the table."

"Piping hot."

Royal went to the bathroom just off the kitchen.

"Oh, uh, by the way, Mag, the heater in the car's sputtering. It's on the frizz. I'm afraid. About on its way out."

"Oh, it is?"

"Uh-huh. We're going to need a new car by next winter, I think."

"We are?"

"Secondhand though. I'll look for a good deal on some local car lots around here. My eyelids almost froze into icicles on the way in."

"Ha."

"They did, Mag. I'm telling you, they practically did!"

CHAPTER 14

The weather service was right: the snowstorm dumped forty-three inches (just an inch off the mark) of fresh snow on Myles Day City. And after a few days, the snow was plowed and pushed off main-road arteries, and things in Myles Day City got pretty much back to normal.

But now, after seven days, things *were* back to normal. It was a new year, a few days beyond the new year. There was snow on the ground but no snow falling out the sky. It was just a cold January day. The kind of day to make your teeth chatter, especially if they were out on a windowsill in a glass of water.

Lee didn't have to be told what time it was. He came out the kitchen. When he looked up the staircase, Darlene was at the top. She stood there. She was dressed beautifully, tastefully, with an imperial look on her face.

"Today, Lee. Today. After this morning, this will all be mine. Mine, Lee. Mine," Darlene said, her eyes glinting, looking from side to side and then focused back to the front of her.

"This house, Lee. This house!"

"I'll get the—"

"The red one, Lee. The red one. The one I just made, created for, just for this occasion. Today, Lee. Bright. Cheerful. Colorful. Full of life. Joy. Oh, Lee. Oh, Lee …," Darlene said, flying down the staircase.

"How I've waited for this day, Lee. How. How."

"I know you have, Darlene," Lee said, holding onto Darlene's cardinal red coat.

"The storm just postponed it. It's all. Just postponed the inevitable, Lee. But didn't change anything. Not for Margaret Ballad. Ha. No, not Margaret Ballad. The will, Attorney Robinson has it in his office, Lee. It's the same document, the same exact one Aunt Della signed. Aunt ... Aunt Della's signature's on. Aunt Della's signature is in cement, in stone ... on.

"Let her suffer. Let her suffer another week. It's what I said. What I said after I hung up the phone. After Attorney Robinson called last ... last Thursday, Lee. Ha. When the date was changed, Lee. Ha."

Pause.

"Another—oh, oh, thank you, Lee. Thank you, baby."

Lee had slipped the coat over Darlene's shoulders.

"Oh, the bitch! The bitch!"

"Darlene, Darlene, we-we're in Aunt Della's house. W-we're about to go to the reading. To Aunt—"

"My hat, Lee. My hat. The red hat, baby. The one I made. Get it for me. Get if for—"

"Oh, sorry, I ... I—"

"I got up that morning. I found Aunt Della. Aunt Della. I found Aunt Della. Not Margaret. Not her. Not her daughter. But me. Me. Me, Lee."

"Yes, I know, I know. I ... I, you keep—"

"Thanks. Thanks." Darlene placed the cardinal red hat on her head.

"How do I look, Lee? How do I look, baby?"

"Oh ... oh beautiful, Darlene. B-beautiful."

"Thank you, Lee. Thank you, baby."

"I love the coat you, that you made t—"

"What do we say at Clearview Presbyterian every Sunday, Lee?"

"Uh ... uh ..."

"Pastor Holmes has us ... Now he's a real minister. A real minister, Lee. Not like Royal McCloud. Not like, you know what I call him now, Lee, Royal McCloud now..."

"Yes. Yes, I—"

"Ha. Ha. Ha. The ... oh ... ha ... the 'basement minister.' Basement minister. That's what. That's what. Oh ... oh, uh ... This is the day that God made. This is the day that God made, Lee!"

"I, yes, it's what minister, Pastor Holmes, we say every Sunday at—"

"And don't you look handsome, Lee Winston. Ha. Don't you look handsome now in … in your pretty blue suit. Oh, oh yes, you do, Lee Winston. Yes, you do. L-like you did at Aunt Della's funeral. Aunt Della's—you looked handsome then too, Lee.

"But it was black then. Your suit black, not … Oh, let me help you with your coat—"

"Thanks, Darlene. T—"

"There. There. Oh … oh, Royal McCloud had no business being there, at Aunt Della's funeral, family … oh, I was so … And delivering the eulogy. Delivering Aunt Della's eulogy. Only … only someone like Margaret, someone like her would … but you did, Lee. You did.

"You belonged at Aunt Della's funeral. You did, Lee. And he'll be there t-today, Royal McCloud, Lee. This morning in Attorney Robinson's office. At the reading. You'll see. Sitting up there … How I loathe him, Lee. How I loathe him. Somewhere where, someone like Royal McCloud does, doesn't belong, him or Margaret Ballad. Him or—"

"Don't say that, Darlene," Lee said with great angst. "Don't say that. Why, why you shouldn't say that a-about Margaret, Darlene."

"Ha. Ha. Ha. You'll see, Lee. You'll see. I found her. I found Aunt Della. Instinct, nothing else. Nothing else. More. More. It … it was my spiritual connection with Aunt Della. My spiritual connection with Aunt Della. You'll see, Lee. You'll see, Lee."

For Della had forgotten all about the light in the bedroom that night. How Della said she would turn it off, but Darlene had not really expected her to. How it had pressed on her mind, the light. She'd blocked it out of her version of what happened that night. It'd been forgotten, dropped from her memory.

"Not her! Not her! Oh, you'll see, Lee. You'll see, Lee. All … all right. You'll see. If there are any doubts as to why, Lee. You'll see. Aunt Della didn't want Margaret Ballad to find her that night. It … it was Aunt Della's last … last d-deed. Her last deed against her dau—"

"You shouldn't say things like that. T-things you know nothing a-about. You shouldn't. You shouldn't, Darlene. You—"

"But I do. I do, Lee. See? See? Ha." She began flitting around Lee. "I know you … you look handsome this morning, Lee Winston. In you pretty blue suit. And … and I know—"

"Stop this, Darlene. Stop—you've got to stop this kind of behavior, this … this—"

Darlene took her forefinger, and it began sliding sensuously down the length of Lee's narrow face. "Don't you want to know what else I know, Lee? Don't you, baby? Don't you …?"

Lee wished he had a cigarette in his hand, that he was smoking one right now. Darlene hadn't left the house since their aunt Della's death. She hadn't come back home to their house. He was there; she'd been here. He didn't try forcing her back; he knew it would be hopeless, absolutely hopeless to try.

"What are you thinking, Lee? What are you … It's all cleaned like … like I told you, the house. Cleaned from top to bottom, Lee. In … in preparation of today. Dusted and … and Aunt Della's clothes, Lee, nobody wants to do anything about … with … with, about Aunt Della's clothes yet, Lee. B-but I'll have to do some—"

"It can wait, Darlene," Lee said forcibly. "All of that can wait now. For—"

"Another day? But today can't wait, Lee. Today can't wait. Even … even with all the sadness of the past few weeks surrounding us, me having to stay in Aunt Della's house every day to make sure everything's okay, all right, as … as Aunt Della would want me to, Lee. Today can't wait.

"For today has come. Around, Lee. No one could put it off, delay it any longer. Certainly not a, some silly little snow … What time is it, I—"

"Eight, eight fifty-five, Darlene. Eight—"

"Oh, how she must feel today, Margaret Ballad. Tormented. Tortured. Tormented by knowing, knowing, Lee, what Aunt Della's done, has done to her, with the house. B-but I'll see her face at the reading today. See it-its reaction when the will's read by Attorney Robinson. In his office. The official announcement's made.

"I'll see her face for myself. It-it's all I've been waiting for, Lee. For this moment to come. A-arrive. Today, Lee. Ha. Margaret Ballad. Ha. Oh, I … I knew, Lee. H-how did I know to get up to, that my aunt Della would … she needed me, Lee? Me? How, Lee? How? I … just knew, Lee, Lee. How did I … I … Like the house, Lee. Like this house today. I know, Lee. It belongs to me my, my aunt Della's house. I … I hate you, Margaret Ballad. I hate you. God I hate you!

"Lee, Lee, hurry. We must hurry. We mustn't be late. We mustn't be late for the reading. Not for the reading of Aunt Della's will."

Darlene smiles delightfully.

"Aunt … Aunt Della's last deed, Lee. Ha. My aunt Della's last deed!"

"Now you can really see what I'm talking about, can't you, Mag?"

"Yes, I can, Royal."

"Your feet by now …"

"I can't feel them. They're numb."

"Mine either."

"We have money, Royal."

"But some of it's going toward Marshall right now. Eve and Marshall. I'm glad I told you. That I finally got it off my chest. That things haven't gone well in Detroit. With the investigation. That there've been roadblocks. I just didn't want to burden you with any more, any more things for you to have to worry about."

"I know." Pause.

"You, you look good."

"Thanks."

"What about me?"

"Oh, y-you do too, Royal. You—"

"You know I was fishing for a compliment. Even though you do look—"

"Old … it's an old dress I'm wearing. Have on today."

"I know. But you make it look new."

Margaret looked at Royal sternly but playfully. "Royal, just what are you up to?"

"Nothing, nothing, absolutely—"

"And put your hands back on the steering wheel before the car spins out!"

"What do you know about a spinout?"

"Daddy had one … one time after a heavy snowfall. He was explaining something to Momma, became excited, yes, was … his hands went up … up in the air, off the steering wheel, and his foot hit the accelerator too hard, and—"

"Spinout!"

"Yes, spinout!"

"That's a sure recipe for one. Guaranteed."

"We laughed so."

Royal looked at Margaret. "W-was Darlene in the car?"

"Yes."

"She—Darlene laughed too?"

"Yes."

"You remember, Mag."

Margaret nodded her head.

"Relax, Mag. Just relax."

And this annoyed Margaret, what Royal just said. It sounded, even with the brevity of words, Margaret thought, as if she were being lectured to. She didn't like it. She was relaxed, she thought. The week had done her some good. The postponement. She felt under control. More herself. She felt she would hold up well today. In Attorney Robinson's office.

"You heard me, Mag?"

"Yes. I'm fine. I'm completely relaxed. I'll do fine today."

"Good."

Yes, it does annoy me, Margaret thought. *But maybe I'd do the same, act the same if I were Royal and he me. It's more than likely, probably, what I'd say too.*

A lot of snow was outside, at the base of the five-floored building. Attorney Robinson's law office was on the third floor. Royal wheeled the car into the building's driveway. He looked at his watch.

"We're early, Mag. Now relax, Mag. Relax."

Yes, she wished he'd stop saying that. God, how she wished that!

Royal pushed the bathroom door open. He smelled …

"Lee!"

"Royal!"

"Hi, Lee. Hi."

"Oh, Royal, Royal—its' so good to see you, Royal."

They hugged. Lee stepped back from Royal. "I … I needed a smoke."

"Margaret and I saw your car in the lot. Behind the building."

"She's inside. Inside the office. Did—"

"No, Margaret's outside Attorney Robinson's office."

"Oh, I thought they were, Margaret and Darlene …"

"No."

Lee took another drag on the cigarette. He was about to extinguish it.

"No, now don't do that on my account, Lee. I just came in to use the bathroom."

"It's what I told Darlene, what I was doing," Lee said, watching Royal move over to the wall urinal. "She-she's going to smell the smoke on … in my suit, but I had to … I had to take a smoke, Royal. I—my hands were shaking. S-still are."

Royal was washing his hands. Lee had finished his cigarette.

Royal was in a black suit complimented by a white shirt and a short black tie. He was wiping his hands with a paper towel. When he turned, Lee asked innocently, "Are we suppose to be enemies, Royal? Today? In opposite camps?"

Royal laughed. "No, I don't think so, Lee."

"I don't like what's about to happen today, Royal."

"Me either, Lee," Royal said, his face already showing the strain of the day.

"The … the family's already divided. What's going to happen today in the next half hour or so will divide it even more. Split, break it further apart."

Royal agreed.

"And I love you and Margaret, Royal. I love you two."

"Oh, thanks. Thanks for saying that, Lee. Because you know how much Margaret loves you. And our relationship, we've always had such great respect and love for each other."

"B-but Aunt Della had to do what she had to do."

"She, Mother Ballad couldn't split the house into half, down the middle."

"No."

Pause.

"I know I just said the obvious, Lee, I—"

"It-it's hard not … not to, Royal, under these circumstances."

Pause.

"You know, Lee, if I was ministering to a family who was caught in this crossfire, I would say let's pray."

Lee smiled.

"But since I'm so intimate with the facts, the situation—I just hope no one comes out of this scarred by the events, what's to unfold today, Lee. It's my hope."

Lee had gone in the office to join Darlene. Margaret and Royal were standing outside Attorney Robinson's office. Before Royal had gone off to the bathroom, Margaret held onto his overcoat. Once he got back, Royal relieved her of it. In fact, he was holding her coat and his.

Upon greeting each other, Lee and Margaret kissed outside Robinson's office. It's when Margaret smelled the fresh smoke in the pores of Lee's skin, the same smoke in the fibers of Royal's suit when he stood but a foot or two from her.

Attorney Robinson knew she and Royal were outside the office. He said he'd come out for them.

She and Royal were saturated in silence; she was glad about that. She didn't want to hear anything or say anything more. She didn't want to think about God or her mother. She just wanted to stand outside Attorney Robinson's office, stand there like she could carry a big mountain on her back and let Royal see it in her eyes if he was to be the only witness to the feat, for today wasn't going to destroy her, she'd promised herself a thousand times by now. Darlene getting the house. It wouldn't destroy her. Darlene wouldn't walk away with a victory. She wouldn't let her rip her soul out.

Attorney Robinson's door opened.

"Margaret," Attorney Robinson said, "Rev. McCloud, we're ready for the reading of the will to commence."

It was to be the first time she was to see her today! It was to be the first time to see her today!

"Thank you."

Attorney Robinson waited for Margaret, keeping the door open for her.

When Margaret entered the office, she and Darlene's eyes clashed, and what she saw was this twisted look in Darlene's eyes. She did not look away from the hate spewing from them, and Royal and Attorney Robinson looked at the two of them looking at each other too.

"Your seat, if you'd like, Margaret, is to the right of my desk."

She's in red, Margaret thought. She' in red. Darlene's in red. *Why's she in red?* She didn't know what to think. What symbolism was at play, was going on. Up to now, she'd canceled Darlene out, but not now; she was in the room with her and felt her domination, hectoring. She wanted to reach for Royal's hand but knew she mustn't.

Attorney Robinson sat behind the desk.

"I must say, I was disappointed that last week's reading of your mother's will, Margaret, your aunt's will, Mrs. Winston, was postponed. Since everything was, Mrs. Ballad's assets are so clearly, explicitly designated—what parties should receive what from the estate. It will be a simple, uncomplicated procedure but, because of its legal domain, must be handled in an official venue."

Lee sat behind Darlene. Royal sat behind Margaret. Their status overtly defined by how the chairs in the office were selectively arranged.

Robinson went into his bottom drawer. When his hand stopped, and then reappeared, he had, what appeared, a legal folder. He pressed the intercom's button.

"Uh, Ms. Rose, you may come into the office. We're about ready to proceed with the official reading of the will."

Shortly, an older woman, Attorney Robinson's paralegal secretary, Vanita Rose, entered the room. Vanita Rose was short, gray haired, and a bit overweight. Her chair was to the right of Attorney Robinson. She was holding onto a yellow pad and a plain colored pen.

"Ms. Rose will record the official minutes. That at 10:06 a.m., the will and testament for Margaret Ballad, deceased, was read by Attorney Morgan Robinson, to Miss Margaret Ballad, the daughter of the deceased, and Mrs. Darlene Winston, the niece of the deceased, the two named beneficiaries decided in the final will and testament of Della Ballad as receiving the only extant material assets of her estate, as Della Ballad declared on November 22 of the year—"

Margaret wasn't hearing anything. Her mind was numb. What she wanted to do, really do, was shut her eyes and go into a deep sleep—a tranquil sleep.

"And all legal papers by Mrs. Ballad were legally notarized and, therefore, deemed official documents of the court and, therefore, this state."

I wish he'd shut up! Just shut up! Why do I have to hear that? Listen to that? All of that! I don't care. I don't care. He's trying to make a game out of this. He's trying to make himself look, seem, appear important. *Too damned important. Well he's not. And he has to be paid out of Aunt Della's estate for this? Look at her. Look at Margaret. No, I don't want to look at her. Something so pathetic. So putrid. If she sat there in that chair and shriveled up and died ... Oh ... ha ... That would be a sight, wouldn't it? Wouldn't it? Margaret Ballad. Margaret Ballad shriveling up in a chair ... And he's right behind her. Right behind her. I heard Robinson say Rev. McCloud. Some ... She's going to need him. All his prayers. Every single one of them. All right.*

"Is everything clear, Margaret, Mrs. Winston?"

"Yes, it is. Quite clear."

"And you, Margaret?"

"I ... I ..."

"Margaret, Margaret, Attorney Robinson wants to know if—"

"Yes, Royal. Oh, I'm sorry, A-Attorney Robinson."

So weak! So weak! So damned weak!

"Everything's clear, isn't it, Margaret? This will and testament was drawn in good faith, under no mental duress, but it—"

"Yes. Yes. Yes."

"Mag, you are okay, all—"

"Ms. Rose, because Ms. Rose could bring you a glass of water before we go on. Proceed with the reading, Margaret. Ms. Rose, would you kindly get Miss—"

"No. No. I ... I, please, please read the will. My mother's will. Please, you must, I in ... there must be no more delay ... delays. None whatsoever, Attorney Robinson."

"Yes, of course, Margaret."

"I agree with Margaret. There must not be any more delays," Darlene said, looking sharply into Robinson's eyes. "It's the will. It's why we've gathered here. For the will. The will."

Robinson opened the folder. He pulled out the papers. He looked closely at the top sheet.

"So you would want me to, for me to eliminate the legal jargon for the record?"

"Yes," Margaret said.

"I agree," Darlene said.

"Ms. Rose, you will please enter them into the record verbatim, at the conclusion of the reading."

"Yes, Attorney Robinson."

"Thank you." Pause. "Yes, uh … so the first item of business is Della Ballad's insurance policy. Her personal insurance policy, which is valued, currently, at $72,320." Robinson looked at Margaret. "The full value of your mother's personal life insurance policy, Della Ballad's insurance policy, is bequeathed to you, Ms. Ballad. Mrs. Ballad's daughter, Margaret Ballad."

Margaret is shaking her head. She looks over her shoulder at Royal, who's smiling back at her.

None of this seemed to bother Darlene, not any of it, not in the least.

Attorney Robinson cleared his throat. "And now for the second order of business. All of Mrs. Ballad's savings, personal savings." Robinson looked at Darlene. "Two accounts, savings accounts of $27,628 at People's Saving Bank and a personal certificate of deposit, CD, of $32, 952 deposited with the same acting fiduciary, has been bequeathed to Mrs. Darlene Winston, Mrs. Ballad's niece, for a total of $60, 580."

"Thank you, Aunt Della! Thank you!" Lee blurted out.

Darlene sat in the chair unmoved, emotionless, seemingly in no way surprised by her aunt's generous action.

"And now for the property at 38 Eckert Street, Della Ballad's house." Pause. "Uh, my, may I, at this time, moment, please, uh, interject my personal, own personal feelings, recollections and reflections in regard to this matter, I, if … if I may."

Margaret nodded her head.

"I don't see where, that you should bother, have to b—"

"Mrs. Winston, I don't normally do this during a reading, the reading of someone's will, uh, do … do I, Ms. Rose?"

"No. Certainly not, Attorney Robinson. It's most unusual, Attorney Robinson."

"B-but … could I … I offer, just offer a few, all of you a few sobering … the imagery of an agonized woman. A torn woman. A woman who had, I'm sure, made up her mind before, well, before I arrived to the house at two o'clock that afternoon, who, ultimately, the house would be bequeathed to. It's just that I was so taken by her agony, the overt pain Mrs. Ballad seemed in. W-was visibly demonstrating to me." Pause.

"The flexing of her hand, tension in her hand before signing the … In fact, in fact, Mrs. Ballad leaned, eased her head back on her pillow what seemed, for me, at the time, in-inexorably in relation to time, for relief.

"It certainly created a strong mental picture. Im-impression. My mind has yet forgotten."

Darlene's eyes looked darkly into Robinson's.

"But ... but, uh, she, Mrs. Ballad signed the document I gave her, and so Mrs. Della Ballad, being of sound mind and under no mental or physical duress, assigned the house, bequeathing the house at 38 Eckert Street to Ms. Margaret Ballad. Mrs. Ballad's—"

"No! No! No! No!"

"Water! Water! Water, Ms. Rose! Water! Water! Mrs. Winston's fainted! She's fainted!"

"Darlene! Darlene! Darlene!"

Darlene was on the floor. She'd toppled out her chair. Lee was down on his knees, at her side, attending to her. Ms. Rose dropped her pen and pad and rushed out the office for, presumably, a glass of water. Margaret sat in shock in the chair.

"Give her room to breathe! Give her room to breathe!" Royal yelled.

"Mrs. Winston! Mrs. Winston!" Attorney Robinson was looking grimly at her. "I wasn't prepared for this. I wasn't prepared for this. Not this. Not this!"

Darlene had been revived. She was groggy. Margaret and Royal were still in Attorney Robinson's office. Both sat across from Darlene. Darlene and Lee were seated on the couch. Lee was holding Darlene. Everyone was waiting for her senses to clear, hoping that they would. Attorney Robinson said they could take their time. His next appointment in the office was not until 1:00 p.m.; it was 10:38 a.m. Attorney Robinson was no longer in the office. He was in another section of the building. The law firm was a partnership—Robinson & Franklin Attorneys-at-Law.

"Why are you staring at me? Why the hell are all of you staring at me like that!"

Darlene tried standing, only her legs weakened under her. "Oh, Lee. Oh, Lee." She grabbed Lee. Then she stared back at Margaret and Royal. "I ... I don't need your pity! I don't need your pity! I have Lee! I have Lee! M-my husband! Don't I, baby? Don't I, Lee! Don't I, Lee!"

"Yes, yes, Darlene. Y-yes."

"The house. Aunt, Aunt Della's house. It's true, Lee. It ... it's true, isn't it? Isn't it? My ... my aunt Della's house!" Darlene clutched Lee, the lapels of his suit.

"It ... I fainted? I ..." Darlene tried standing again but couldn't. "Gloat. Gloat. Go ahead and gloat, Margaret Ballad! Gloat! Gloat! Gloat!"

"We want you to be all right, Darlene. F-feel bet—"

"Shut up! Shut up! Shut up, Royal McCloud! Shut up!"

"I'm as shocked as you are, D—"

"Leave me alone, Margaret Ballad. Leave, tell them, Lee! Tell them to leave, Lee!"

"Maybe, Margaret, Royal, you'd better, it'd be better ..."

"Yes. Yes, Lee," Royal said. "Of ... of course. By all means."

Then Darlene turned from Lee, flinging herself to the other side of the couch, burying her fist in its soft leather; and she began beating it badly, badly beating it with both fists.

Margaret walked out Attorney Robinson's office.

"Lee, would you?" Royal whispered, motioning to him.

Lee stood.

"Lee," Royal said when Lee got to him, "this has been devastating. Devastating. I know Margaret and I ... I suppose you heard us whispering over here while—"

"Yes."

"Yes."

Pause.

"We're in no rush. I mean, about the house."

Both looked at Darlene, her position not having changed. They, the two continued to whisper.

"The transition period into the house. We know Darlene's there, living in the house. I mean, it's all right. All right, Lee. Darlene can leave the house when she likes. Whenever she likes. See fits to—like I said, there's no rush. Absolutely none. All Margaret wants to do is for you to call her when Darlene does ... does decide to leave the house. Since Darlene—"

"Won't ... she, Darlene won't. Yes. Yes, I, there'll be no problem. I'll see to it, Royal. I'll take care of it. I'll call Margaret as soon as Darlene—"

"We're sorry, Lee."

"There's no need to be, Royal. To feel that way, Royal. You to," Lee said, shaking Royal's hand. "Aunt Della, she was more than generous to us, Royal. I don't care about the house. I only care about Darlene. My wife, Royal."

"Let me get out there to Margaret. She's waiting for me."

"Thanks."

"Sure, Lee. Sure."

Royal left the office.

"Take me home, Lee. Take me home," Darlene murmured.

"Yes, Darlene. Yes."

"T-to Aunt Della's house, Lee. T-to my aunt Della's house, Lee."

He was in front of Darlene. The key felt cold in his hand before he inserted it into the lock. It's like he could hear everything—even if the door felt too heavy. But Lee didn't want to look behind him, only he knew he would have to do that as soon as he unlocked the house's front door.

In the car, she might as well have been dead, he'd thought. Her arteries might as well have been clogged. He had to hold her on the way out Attorney Robinson's office, the building, to the car, support her; getting her into the car as if she'd turned old overnight, decrepit, her body arthritic, full of aches and sores, riddled by pain; closing the car door, him getting into the car, silence breeding silence seconds at a time, multiplying, fighting for space, greedy, assertive, wanting more of it.

He just did his duty, that which he must do.

At the stoplights along the way, the trip back to his aunt Della's house, he kept his eyes pinned straight ahead, forward, or looked at the dashboard or a few times at the steering wheel, sometimes looking there but maintaining a strictness, a purpose, an awareness, knowing the house loomed ahead, that Darlene would have to face it, her heart already beaten by today's events, the idea of something she assertively assumed was hers but now Margaret's, was snatched from her. It's how he, at the time, maintained his sense of balance, the sanity he was trying not to lose in this whole matter.

The key felt like ice. Lee inserted the key into the lock, and he opened the door. He stepped aside for her.

"Darlene, we're ... we're ..."

Darlene walked into the house.

"It's Aunt Della's house. It's Aunt Della's house," Darlene said chirpily. "It's my aunt Della's house."

And Lee looked at her, and what he saw was the Darlene Winston who walked out the house at 8:55 a.m. this morning.

"I'm home, Aunt Della! I'm home! Darlene, Aunt Della! Darlene!"

Darlene' body had sprung back to life; she walked like before, each step springy and alive.

"Ha. My coat, Lee. My coat. Take my coat, Lee."

"Yes, your, your—"

"Oh, I feel good. Oh, do I feel good. Thanks. Thanks, Lee. Thanks, baby."

Lee stood there with Darlene's coat, holding it.

"Now ...," Darlene looked at him brazenly. "Why are you standing there like that, Lee. My coat can't hang itself!"

"No ... no, I. No, it can't, Darlene. It ... it ..."

"We're back. We're back. We're back, Lee!"

Lee hung the coat in the closet, and then he felt a sharp pain in his lower back. He didn't want to turn around; he'd rather look at the coats in the closet, hanging there—his aunt Della's coats.

"Are you hungry, Lee? Are you? Oh, I'm not hungry. I'm not going to fix anything."

Lee took off his coat, hanging it. He turned back around, and he saw Darlene looking at the house as if it were the first time she'd seen it, as if it were inciting her senses more and more, look by look. He felt that pain in his lower back again, as if it were there to stay, had cut open a deep wide vein there and settled.

She was looking around and twirling herself in her dress; her red hat was still on top her head, cardinal red, the hat she'd made for today's reading of the will.

"I ... I want to sit on the couch. The couch. Uncle Frank's couch. Here on Uncle Frank's couch, Lee!"

Lee shut his eyes. He wasn't going to run from room to room with her. In the house. He wasn't going to run from room to room with her, be a part of her madness. He heard her, from the hallway, as she sat, as she let out, emitted another shrill laugh; and he kept his eyes shut, hammering in his head that she was his wife. He loved her, he loved her, she needed him more than ever now. More than ever now.

"Lee. Come in here, Lee. Come in here, Lee. The living room, Lee."

Pause.

"Yes, Darlene, I ... I ..."

"What happened today, Lee? What happened today? Tell me, tell me what happened today?"

"I ... I—"

"It wasn't Aunt Della's fault. It wasn't Aunt Della's fault, Lee."

Lee was alert now, intrigued.

"It ... it, you ... you mean—"

"Royal McCloud! Royal McCloud!"

"Royal?"

"Don't you see, Lee? See? Get it? Get it? You can't be that stupid. That dumb!"

"What do you mean, Darlene? What do—"

"I thought about it. I thought about it. Thought it through. That ... that's all ... all ..."

"And ... and ..."

"What do you think I was doing in the car? In my mind, Lee. In my mind?"

Lee wrung his hands out in front of him.

"What do you think ... think, Lee? What?"

Lee was shaking his head. "I ... I—"

"I thought it through, Lee. All through. Thoroughly, figured it—it was Royal McCloud. Rev. Royal McCloud!"

"How did ... did you f-figure—"

"How? How! Oh, Lee, Lee, do you believe in the devil?"

"B-believe in the devil, the devil, d—"

"He's Royal McCloud. He's Royal McCloud. Rev. Royal McCloud. The devil!"

The silence in the living room was like the silence in the car now, multiplying, contagious.

"Ha. Ha. Ha." Darlene finally shrieked. "Ha. Ha. Ha."

Darlene's eyes shut, and she held onto herself and began rocking herself rhythmically, frighteningly. Her eyes afire, both shimmering anew.

"Praying with Aunt Della. Praying with Aunt Della. On the phone. On the telephone. Praying with Aunt Della. All the time. All the time. That's what did it. That's what did it. W-what was he saying in those prayers, Lee? What was he saying in those prayers? What was he telling Aunt Della? What Lee? H-how does the devil pray, Lee! How does the devil pray!? Tell me how. Tell me how. What does he say, Lee? What does the devil—"

"You, I don't know, Darlene. I don't—"

"It was never between me, between me and Margaret Ballad. It was never between me and Margaret Ballad. How could it be? Aunt Della, Aunt Della had the devil in her ear, Lee. On the phone. When he prayed with her. Nightly. Nightly. Royal McCloud. Royal McCloud. When he prayed with her. W-when he came into the house. Tricks. Tricks. The devil's full of tricks. Full of them. Ha. A con artist. A pimp. Royal McCloud. Royal McCloud, a—"

"Darlene, Darlene, I have to go to the—"

"Sit, Lee. Sit. I'm not finished. I'm not through!"

"No, Darlene, I'm going to the bathroom. The bathroom!"

"Oh ... oh ...," Darlene was startled.

Lee felt his heart racing, searing through him. He hurried out the room.

Lee was in the bathroom. He stood behind the bathroom door and had his hand against the door, his arm outstretched, stiff, as if blocking the door from behind, making sure no one got in. But he needed a smoke, a cigarette— but he was in his aunt Della's house. And he didn't have to use the bathroom. And it was going to be a long day and night, and he needed a cigarette badly, for the last time he had one was in the bathroom with Royal at Robinson & Franklin's—the first time he had some order of peace today.

And he felt like crying. Crying. Crying because he missed his aunt Della. Crying because of how today had turned out for Darlene. Crying because Darlene hadn't really cried yet. He hadn't seen her cry from her soul yet. Grieve. Grieve. Grieve from inside out in a normal, natural way.

Lee shut the bathroom door. He didn't want to go back into the living room but must. The conversation with Darlene wasn't through, finished, over—she'd said there was more, more for them to discuss, continue with, talk about.

"Lee ..."

Lee moved forward. He looked up. Darlene was at the top of the staircase.

"I'm going to my room."

"D-do you need—"

Lee's foot was on the staircase's bottom step.

"Don't come up."

"Then I'll—"

"Go home, Lee. Go home."

"Go home!"

"I don't need you. Go home."

"But I was going to stay with you tonight. In the house with you. I thought—"

"Go get your coat and hat out the closet and go home. No one's staying in this house with me tonight. No one. I don't know who, why ... why you thought, what made you think that. Get your coat and hat out the closet, Lee. And leave. Go home. Go home, Lee. You may come for me in the morning."

"The morning? B-but what ... what time, Darlene? What time in the morning? Do ... do you want me to—"

"It doesn't matter. It doesn't matter. I'll be gone before Margaret Ballad gets here. I know that much. For ... that much."

"B-but Margaret said—"

"Who cares what Margaret Ballad said! Who cares. Who the hell cares!"

"She's giving you time," Lee said anyway. "Time to make the transition, Darlene. A ... a transition. Giving you a transition period. Y-you don't have to leave in the morning. Margaret's willing to meet you halfway."

Darlene turned.

"I'll be here. I'll be here in the morning, D-Darlene. I'll be here in the morning."

Lee was out the house. He looked back at it. "It belongs to Margaret. Aunt Della was ... was so generous with us. So good to us today. Kind. The money—Aunt Della's savings. I just wish ..."

He shook his head. He realized the symbolism of the house. He got in the car and looked in the rearview mirror and knew the car wasn't going to move out the driveway for a while. He struck the match and lit the cigarette and felt the pain leave his lower back after one strong puff, and he puffed again and again, trying to feel better, get rid of everything that was ailing him.

"The water's ready, Mag."

"Oh, it is?" Margaret was lying on top the bed; Royal had just come into the bedroom.

"Thanks." Margaret was in a slip. She came off the bed and removed her slip.

Royal, it was as if his eyes were feasting on her in her panties and bra.

"Mag, you still have some figure. Shape."

Margaret smiled timidly.

"The—was it the wrong thing to say?"

"No, no, not at all, Royal. A woman always loves a compliment, especially one my age."

"I, oh, I didn't know that," Royal said coyly.

"I'm just going to … When I get in the tub, I'm going to sit in it and just let the water wash over me. S- soothe me."

"It's warm."

"Good. So don't look for me anytime … anytime soon, Royal."

"Stay in the tub as long as you want, Mag. Don't worry a—"

"I hope she's all right."

"Darlene, Mag?"

"I hope she's all right."

"She's the first person I'll, I'm going to pray for tonight."

"Me too, Royal. Me too."

"Her spirit's been crushed by today's events."

"I'll just wait for Lee's call. There's no rush or hurry, Royal."

"I hope Lee was able to … to convey that to Darlene, Mag. Your sincerity."

The tub of water was warm and soothing to Margaret. Her body needed the warm water as well as her mind, for it was serving an extraordinary purpose. She'd laughed at how paradise can be reached by such a mundane effort.

"When will I recover from the shock? Momma. Momma. When will I recover from the shock I felt in Attorney Robinson's office to-today when he said … when … Oh, Momma. Momma."

She wouldn't be able to articulate or describe the feeling, not now, probably not ever. But she didn't feel as though she'd won anything over Darlene. Darlene might feel she'd won something over her, Margaret thought, but she never tried to win anything over her. What she'd won was what she and Royal had kept most secret between them, something they still hadn't yet openly discussed—had not dared to, was still taboo, in a way. But it wasn't something she'd won over Darlene, something she could gloat over. It's not the secret she'd held in her heart, the true gift her mother gave her today, not the house, not something tangible but an intangible source that she still could not acknowledge, that would all but sink in her and weigh in her heavy and feel so good as for her never to fully appreciate but would forever be indebted to her mother for fulfilling.

"Thank you, Momma. Thank you. Oh … thank you, Momma."

Margaret splashed the water on her face. She did it twice and then shut her eyes again.

"Darlene. Darlene." Margaret opened her eyes. "I do love Darlene, but why? Why?"

She never made Darlene her rival, but Darlene had made her hers. Darlene created the rift between them, drove the separation between them. But why did she still love Darlene? And after today she suddenly realized she did. Was it because, in part because her mother loved Darlene so therefore … She had been so wonderful to her mother, so sacred—was that it? So she loved Darlene as if through her mother's eyes?

It felt weird, strange, abstract. But before Darlene had lost her aunt Nettie, she loved her aunt Nettie like Darlene loved her mother. And she and Darlene had gotten along, played together, loved each other; but no one had ever talked about that, those times, the years before Darlene moved into the house. She'd not even discussed it with Royal, the good part, the healthy part, for their relationship had been poisonous for so long—when no one would ever forecast, predict what would happen to them, would go wrong between them in the future. Not anyone who saw was privy to how they played, how they loved one another then, back in those days.

"Am I playing the … no, I'm not a saint. Not in the least am I playing the saint, trying to rise above the situation so, therefore, rise above Darlene. No, not in the least."

She knew Darlene was in her mother's house, crushed right now as Royal had said.

"She's devastated. I wonder how I would've felt had it been me today. But … but I had already imagined my scenario," Margaret said edgily. "I'd imagined every detail of it. Step by step. Emotion by emotion. What it would've been like a thousand, a hundred thousand times."

She'd be lying in the bed, not in the tub. She'd be under her blanket shivering, trying to keep her body warm, not soothing it in the tub like now. She wouldn't know when she would've gotten around to this, lying in the tub in the warm water, if the house had been bequeathed to Darlene. The house's deed was in Darlene's name, not hers.

CHAPTER 15

If there was ever a time he wanted to smoke a cigarette, puff on one, maybe it was now.

But now he felt like a coward, someone who couldn't, didn't want to stand up to the duty that now lay before him. Turn from it, away from it, and run like a yellow streak ran up his back. If he could go in the back of the house and bury himself in the snow, he would, but instead, he kicked the snow off the sidewalk that the snowmobile in the garage had banked.

I've got to go into the house. I've got to go into the house, that's all. That's all! Lee said.

What had he imagined last night? What had run through his head last night? All the things that kept him awake, jamming together, wanting to call Darlene and then not. Not knowing how sincere her feelings were, genuine, real. And now he looked at the house, his aunt Della's house as if it would collapse in on him, the walls crumble the moment he put the key in the lock and turned it, the house would fall down on him, his aunt Della's house, his aunt Della's house.

"No, I'm not gonna smoke. Smoke a cigarette before I go in. No. No, why should I? Why should I?"

He felt for the pack of cigarettes in his overcoat pocket, pressed them with his fingertips, heard the cellophane wrapper crinkle under the strain of his fingertips, and then he wanted to get out of the cold, for it was cold today.

He wanted to get out the cold, hear the steam hiss in his aunt Della's room, if he could, from the radiator; that might make him feel better, Lee thought. It's what might do it for him.

"That … that old cast-iron radiator in … in Aunt Della's room."

Lee moved like he was cold, his bones brittle as old chalk, like he was seeking heat. The door unlocked. Lee looked straight ahead as though he were prepared for anything Darlene might offer him.

She was alone in the house last night (nothing new), but now it was for the last time. Now it was Margaret's house. Now Darlene knew she wouldn't step back into her aunt's house even if it were on fire, and if she did, it would be for her aunt Della and uncle Frank why she'd save the house, not for Margaret, Lee thought.

"She's on the second floor. Darlene's on the second floor."

Lee stopped at the staircase, looked up, and then began climbing up them, taking one step at a time, measuring them. "What's in store for me? What's in store for me?"

Darlene's door was shut, but Lee could see his aunt Della's room door was open. Lee's breathing was labored and then it sped up fast, as if his heart would be the first thing to explode, to tell Darlene he was now inside the house. He was there for her.

He was at Darlene's bedroom door. He raised his arm, for he was about to knock on the door, say something, let Darlene know he was—

"I'm in Aunt Della's room, Lee. My aunt Della's room, Lee."

Her voice sounded. He couldn't describe it. He couldn't describe it any— maybe childlike, maybe.

"Ha. It's where I am, Lee. It's where I am."

It felt as if he'd stumbled, the first step he took forward; but he wasn't sure, not at all sure.

Childlike. Childlike.

"In Aunt Della's room."

Pause.

"Lee."

"Darlene."

"Good morning, Lee."

"G-good morning, D-Darlene."

She was sitting in a chair by Della's bed, the one Della would sit in when she was out the bed. She wore what she wore yesterday, what she wore to the reading, to Attorney Robinson's office, the same exact outfit, what she'd worn.

"You came, Lee …"

"Of course, Darlene. Of …," Lee didn't know how to react, what to say, and then he looked to his right and saw the two suitcases there.

"I was hoping you'd come."

"But I said, we—"

"I'm all packed, ready to go."

But she sat there in the chair.

"Yes, yes, I see, Darlene. You're packed, ready to go. Ready to go, Darlene."

Lee's knees bent; he reached for the two suitcases.

"Oh, not yet, Lee. Not yet. Baby."

Lee hesitated, looking back at Darlene.

"Not yet."

Lee heard the steam hissing from the radiator as his knees straightened.

"Have you eaten, Lee, h—"

"No, I—"

"Neither have I."

Pause.

"I think I'll … well … well I'll skip lunch too. What about you, Lee? What about you?"

"Uh … yes, Darlene. Uh, yes, It's probably what I'll—"

"I don't have to eat. It's not im—"

"But you have to eat, Darlene. It is im—"

"Maybe dinner. Dinner. Tonight. Lee, baby. I'll fix us, the two of us a nice dinner. Pot roast. Pot roast. What about pot roast, Lee? Pot roast, Lee?"

"Yes, pot roast. That … that'll be fine, Darlene. Pot roast."

"It'll take a little time to cook in the oven, to do, but … by then we'll be starved. Starved, Lee. Starved to death."

Lee said nothing.

Darlene stood as if she were going to say something, gesturing animatedly, and then sat back down in the chair. Her body arched forward in the chair.

"G-guess where I slept last night, Lee? Guess?"

Her voice sounded so delicate, fragile, practically ready to splinter like candy.

Lee didn't want to guess.

"Where ... where, Darlene?"

"Why don't you look at me, Lee? Why aren't you looking at me when I speak, talking to you, Lee?"

"I ... I—"

"That's better. Lee. That's much better, baby."

"Sorry, Darlene, I—"

"Here, silly. Here. In Aunt Della's room."

"Not in Aunt Della's—"

Darlene shot to her feet, furious. "Not in Aunt Della's bed! Not in Aunt Della's bed!"

"No, I mean, I'm sorry! I'm sorry! I said—"

"Not in Aunt Della's bed!"

Suddenly Lee wanted to slap her, knock her out of her insanity, this thing that had ripped into her.

"I slept on the floor, Lee. On top—"

"The floor?"

"It wasn't cold. I took the blanket off my bed. I slept on the floor. It wasn't cold, Lee, on the floor, on the floor—not at all. At all."

"Oh ... oh ..."

"Aunt Della's bed." Darlene touched it. "Aunt ... Aunt Della's bed ..."

Lee wanted to leave, get out the house. This was too much. This was too much to take.

"I ... I saw her last night, Lee. I saw Aunt Della last night, did I tell you? Did I tell you that, Lee? Did I tell you that? Of course not. Of course not. Of course I didn't, Lee. It's the first time I've seen you all day. All day. You just got here.

"Aunt Della, Lee. Aunt Della, baby. Aunt Della. My aunt Della. Ha. She ... she still loves me, Lee. Aunt Della still loves me. She told me so, Lee. Last night. Last night. She told me so. Aunt Della told me so, Lee. Ha. She still loves me—Aunt Della. M-more than ever, she said, Lee. More than ever, she said. Than she did before. Ever did before—it's what she ... Aunt Della told me. Lee. It's what Aunt Della told me."

Lee's knees bent.

"W-where are you t-taking my suitcases to, Lee? Off to?"

Lee looked back at Darlene. "To the car, Darlene. Out to the car."

"But—"

"I'll be right back, Darlene. I'll be right back to take you home in the car."

"Home. Home. Yes, home. Home, Lee. Our home."

"I'll be right back, Darlene. I won't be long."

"Oh … I know you won't, Lee. I know you won't. You're so good, Lee. So good."

"Thanks, Darlene. Thanks."

Lee was out then back in the house.

"I'm back, Darlene."

Darlene stood up from the chair. Lee walked to her.

"I brought—"

"Yes, my red coat and hat. My new red coat and hat."

"Let me help you, Darlene."

Darlene put her hat on, but Lee helped with her coat.

"You look pretty, Darlene."

"Like yesterday, Lee? When we went to the reading? Aunt Della's reading?"

"Yes."

"And you looked so handsome, Lee, in … in your blue suit, Lee. S-so handsome too, Lee. At the reading, Lee. At Aunt Della's reading. Did I tell you that yesterday, Lee? Did I, did I?"

"Thanks, Darlene. Thanks."

Darlene looked around the bedroom.

"So we're ready, Lee? We're ready?" Darlene said.

"Yes, I think so."

"I … to leave Aunt Della's house? M-my aunt Della's house, Lee?"

"Yes. Yes, Darlene. Uh … yes, w-we are."

"Take my hand, Lee. Please take my hand. Please, Lee."

"It's right here, Darlene. My hand's right here."

Lee put his hand into Darlene's. They began walking out the bedroom.

"Thank you, Lee. Thank you."

Pause.

"D-do you hear the steam, Lee? The steam?"

"Uh, yes. Yes. The steam."

"Hissing."

"Yes."

"Aunt Della loved to listen to the steam. The steam, Lee. From the radiator, Lee. From the radiator, baby. Hiss."

"Yes, I know, Darlene."

They were in the car, about to pull out the driveway.

Lee looks over at Darlene. He wants to ask her if she's all right but knows there is too much distance between their worlds, how their realities worked right now.

"It's such a nice day. Like yesterday, Lee. Was."

Lee looked into the rearview mirror while backing the car out the driveway.

"A typical Myles Day winter. Cold. But it's why, what they make warm houses in Myles Day City for, Lee."

Lee loved her.

"Lee, why aren't you looking at, in the mirror, Lee? The rearview mirror, baby?"

Lee looked into the rearview mirror while he backed the car out the driveway. The car was at the tip of the driveway.

"Good-bye, Aunt Della. Good-bye, Aunt Della."

Darlene began waving her hand at the house.

Lee bit his lower lip, for he wanted to wave at the house too, along with Darlene.

Lee picked up the kitchen phone. He dialed.

"Hello, Margaret."

"Lee ... h-hello, Lee."

"Well, it's done, Margaret. We're out the house."

"Oh, Lee. Oh—"

"I didn't mean to say it like that. Like ... how ... how it must've sounded, just sounded to you, Margaret. C-came off."

"I know you didn't, Lee. There's no need to, for you to explain any—"

"What's happening, Margaret? What's happening? I mean what's really happening!"

Margaret didn't answer.

"Oh ... oh, I'm trying, Margaret. I'm trying. I'm ... I'm really trying. But sometimes. Sometimes. Oh ... oh ..."

And then no more words came from Lee.

"Lee, where is she? Darlene?"

Lee was choking back tears.

"Upstairs. Upstairs, Margaret. In the bedroom. L-lying down."

It was 12:22 p.m.

"She's a child, Margaret. Darlene's a child now. A ... a wounded child. R-reduced to a child."

"N-not like before, Lee? Not like—"

"B-before?"

"When Aunt Nettie died."

"I didn't know Darlene then, Margaret. I—"

"Of course you didn't, Lee. Of course you didn't—but I did."

"She'd lost Mrs. Dawson."

"Aunt Nettie. Her mother. The love of her life. Another perfect mother. My mother, Aunt Nettie ... another perfect mother."

"I ... I don't know what to expect next, Margaret. From Darlene. I just don't, Margaret."

"How, what, what happened to—"

"It's just beginning then, Margaret?" Fear was in Lee's voice.

"Pray, Lee."

"I can't. I can't right now, Margaret."

Margaret felt like Royal. She didn't know why, but she felt like him.

"But you must, Lee. You must pray."

"I ... I do pray, Margaret. I do. But ... but I don't know, Margaret. I don't."

"Do it now, Lee. Let's do it now. T-together."

"Now ... now? Over the phone, Margaret?"

"Yes. Let me help you, Lee. May I help you? W-with this?"

"Help ... cer-certainly, Margaret. Help me? Cer—yes, Margaret. Help me. Help me."

"God who art in heaven ... want to repeat that, Lee, after me, Lee?"

"God ... God who art in heaven ..."

"Hallowed be thy name, in giving me the strength on this day—"

"Hal-hallowed be thy name in g-giving me the ... oh, Margaret, Margaret, I can't. I can't!"

"But you can. You can, Lee."

"I can't, Margaret. All I can do is think about, about Darlene right now, not about—"

"Yourself?"

"Yes, yes, myself."

"Lee, Lee—oh, how I love you, Lee."

"From the first day, first day I walked into Aunt Della's house, Margaret?"

"Now you had to give me a little time, more time with it than that, Lee."

"Ha. I … I guess so, Margaret."

"But I did tell, warn you about smoking in—"

"Aunt Della's house."

"Which I ignored. I was so nervous at the time. I wanted the date to go well. I was so infatuated with Darlene."

"Don't worry, Lee. Darlene felt the same about you."

"She did, Margaret? Darlene did?"

"I saw how she was flitting around the house that day. Behaving, Lee. The excitement in her. I haven't forgotten. It's like yesterday."

"It is. It is."

"That's what, it's what makes life what it is, Lee."

"What, how, Margaret?"

"Things seem only yesterday, but they're not."

"No."

"Big events. Important things in our lives, Lee."

"Dating Darlene. Getting married. Buying the house."

"Event by event by event."

"Time—"

"Flies."

"Ha."

Pause.

"I'm going to look out for myself, Margaret."

Pause.

"Did you hear me, Margaret?"

"Yes, Lee. Ha. I believe you, Lee."

"I've learned how, Margaret. I know how strong I am."

Margaret smiled.

"So when do you and Royal think you'll be moving into the house?"

"We haven't discussed it, Lee. Hasn't come up in conversation between us."

"Of course, you don't have to worry about anyone doing anything to the house, breaking into it, vandalizing it, if it's not occupied—not in that neighborhood."

"Not at all."

"Ha."

"What, Lee?"

"I have to get off the phone. I have to cook."

"Ha."

"A pot roast. At the house, Darlene had said …" Lee fell silent.

Then.

"I love you, Margaret."

"Thanks, Lee. Thanks."

"I … I mean it from the bottom of my heart."

Lee was off the phone.

"You're going to eat, Darlene. I'm going to make sure of it. E-even if you said you aren't going to eat again. Ever again when, once we got back to the house, when you … you ran upstairs to the bedroom, Darlene. I undressed you, Darlene. You didn't sleep well on the floor last night … comfortably, Darlene. I got you in bed. Our bed."

Lee walked over to the pot roast out on the kitchen counter.

"Margaret's right," he said, pausing, "times does fly. We say it all the time, but do you know what, it … it really does. It's true."

Lee whistled.

"I just have to tenderize this thing, that's all. Let me see, uh, what temperature do I have to cook it at and how long again?" Lee pulled out the drawer, and then out came the fat cookbook next.

"Hmm. Pot roast. Pot … There. Uh, there." Pause. "Now hmmm … let's see, it says cook it at 350 degrees for—"

The phone rang.

Margaret was expecting the call. For most of the past hour, she'd expected the call from Royal.

"Hi, Mag. How's it going?"

"Just awful."

They weren't going to waste any time.

"Darlene?"

"Yes, Darlene."

"Is she still in the house?"

"No … she's left it."

"When?"

"This morning. Lee called this afternoon."

"Did he tell you—"

"Only that she's resting. Nothing more, Royal. I … I didn't ask how it went when he got to the house. I didn't feel it my place or appropriate to ask. Lee doesn't have to share everything with me—or do I need to know."

Pause.

"This is so upsetting. This is upsetting me so much. I'm worried for her."

"Me too."

"I really am."

"Me too, Mag."

"I told Lee. This is like when she lost Aunt Nettie. So similar. Close."

"What did he say?"

"It was after he told me Darlene was … was being childlike, Royal."

"That's a dangerous sign—very."

Long pause.

"Children, children don't accept things. Accept reality. The reality of something."

"I … I never—I hadn't thought of that, Royal. I—you're right."

"It's either they're too young to know, or they shut out, block out reality, totally."

"It's what Darlene's doing."

"I wish I could've talked to Lee. We could've prayed together."

"I … I tried."

"You did?"

"Yes." Pause. "I wish it'd been you, maybe … we got but so far."

"Then Lee wasn't ready."

"We ventured off into something else. Onto something else."

"Did it help any?"

"It seemed to."

"It's all that matters."

"He has a strong sense of himself—who he is, Royal. Even, when at times, you might, it might be easy to perceive differently."

"He's much stronger than anyone thinks. Gives him credit for, Mag."

"It's not going to be easy though."

"The human heart … God only knows. God only knows, Mag."

Margaret's thoughts clung to those words.

"What makes it ache and cry and laugh and … it's always there. Always. The first organ to stop working when we die, unless we'd keep on living, Mag. The blood, the … And it's actually in your chest. Located in our chest. We've all seen it. Know what it looks like, I mean, they do heart transplants, Mag.

"It's old news in the medical profession. A heart. This heart of ours. And Darlene's …"

"There's such demand for her sewing, Royal. She has so many customers, people who depend on her, Royal."

"You'd think, hope … but who knows, Mag. What will sustain Darlene now, in the upcoming days, months. Yesterday was the reality of Mother Ballad's will, the bequeathing of the house to you. And already it feels like it happened weeks ago"

"Royal."

"Oh, right, Bill. Be right back."

"I heard him, Royal."

"My supervisor. He said a couple of minutes. I guess they're up by now."

"See you tonight."

"What's on the menu?"

"Food."

"Oh. Ha. Couldn't resist, huh?"

"See you."

"Okay."

Margaret looked at the phone still in her hand, and then she kissed it after Royal hung up.

"That's for you, Royal. For you. No one but you."

CHAPTER 16

Margaret and Royal had walked every square inch of the floorboards of the house from top to bottom, and they'd been outside the house too, troubleshooting. You'd think they were realtors or home buyers, not owners. But Royal, who had a Mr. Fixit mentality and a keen eye, would see things Margaret wouldn't. He had pointed out minor things on the tour, things that were easily fixable, repairable, things that he could do with a simple tool kit.

They began the tour in the living room and now were back in the living room. They'd come full circle.

"Mag, it's either that this house was built for three hundred years without a problem, or Mother Ballad and your father ... It's unbelievable the condition of this house. How it's been maintained over the years. Why, I even looked for termite damage in the basement, but"—Royal shook his head in disbelief—"it was clean. Ha. Clean as a whistle. To no avail."

"You were like a silent partner, Royal. The whole time."

"I only spoke when I had to."

"And that wasn't much."

"Not by my standards. Just pointed my finger like a beagle points his tail. Said what I had to say and then moved on." Pause.

"But this house is remarkable. A testament to whomever built it. That time and age."

Margaret sat. Royal kept standing. This was a Saturday, the third day since the reading of the will.

"Mag," Royal said with a troubled look, "I don't know if it's the right time to bring this up, but … but …"

"What, Royal?"

"If I could make this work, but I can't, so what's the use in continuing to pursue it."

Margaret looked perplexed.

"It's Marshall. It's not working, Mag. This whole private investigation thing—we can't seem to crack it. Get a lead on Eve. Or … or Marshall. So I—"

"You're going to give up, Royal?"

"Why not? It's not getting anywhere, the investigation. And it's becoming ex—"

"Expensive?"

"Yes. Expensive."

"But we have money. We have money now that—"

"And don't say Mother Ballad's insurance policy, Mag. Because Mother Ballad didn't leave you that money so I could find Eve and Marshall with … So … so don't mention your inheritance money to me. Don't."

"Why can't—"

"Because it should come out of my pocket. It's my responsibility. It's been mine for a number of years now. A lot of years now—in fact."

"But you're giving up, Royal. Quitting. That's not like you."

"I'm just being realistic, that's all, Mag. Really—maybe now's not the time. The right time to find Marshall," Royal said, shrugging his shoulders.

"Y-you believe that, really believe that, Royal?"

"You know, just because I think it is, doesn't mean it is."

Royal sat in a chair and turned his body halfway away from Margaret.

He's fighting this, his own personal battle, Margaret said to herself. *His own private war, and all I can do is let him*, she thought. *Let him do it his way.*

Royal turned to her. "Sorry, sorry, I was just thinking. I didn't mean to be rude, Mag. But give me time on this. I'll be okay. All right. With God's guidance, Mag. I'll call Earl Simmons when we get back to the house. I don't think it'll be any surprise to him."

They were in the car, driving back to the house. The car's heater was doing its thing: being unpredictable but, by the same token, predictable, sputtering and then rising to the occasion like some diabolical, sinister plot underfoot.

"May I say something?" Margaret said, gently tugging Royal's arm. "We're getting a new car, Royal, and that's final!"

"We are?"

"Yes!"

"But," Royal cautioned her, "still as we planned, a good secondhand car, and I can find one easily. E—not a new one. New off the lot. Uh-uh. We're not millionaires. And we're not going to start acting like—"

"It's my money."

"And you're still going to act responsibly with it. Our plan was to buy a secondhand car, and Mother Ballad's inheritance isn't going to change that either. Not one bit."

"You're so stubborn."

"Mag," Royal said, taking Margaret's hand, "I don't even want to think about that seventy thousand dollars. Even want to think Mother Ballad's money's come into our lives."

"I'm not afraid of it."

"Who … who said I'm afraid of it? By ignoring it, it doesn't mean I'm afraid of it."

"I stand by what I said, just said," Margaret said, looking out the car's passenger side window.

"You can feel the way you want, but I … I—"

"You're not that anymore, Royal. Someone who wore fancy, expensive clothes, who bought fancy cars. You're not—"

"Mag, stop. Right there. Okay!?""

"Just because you refuse to use Momma's money to find Marshall and Eve doesn't mean we can't use it to move the church out of Mr. Tolletson's basement and on to Bayer Street."

"Bayer Street!?"

"Yes. Yes. Yes, Royal, onto—"

"How'd that come up? How'd that—what's … what has gotten into you, Mag? Tell me, what!"

"Nothing. I'm just being practical and—"

"And … and foolish."

"W-won't you let someone do something for you, Royal? W-won't you!"

"Someone, someone—how about God? God. God's all I need. He is the giver. The provider. God. He's done everything for me. I thought ... thought it's how you felt too, Mag. It's"—his eyes are glaring at Margaret—"but I guess not. I was wrong about you."

Margaret was furious with him, by what he'd just said, practically accusing her of—but she wasn't going to fight him back. *For I have nothing to prove to God or Royal!*

The car's heater was sputtering again and then came on full blast, averaging about six to seven minutes between each action, one too long, the other too short. And Margaret and Royal sat in silence in the car like a wall of ice, the car almost at the apartment, only a few cold minutes removed.

Royal, when he parked the car, got out in a jiffy, quick enough so he could open the car door for Margaret. When Margaret got out the car, he closed the car door and, as quickly, was on the driver's side of the car. Margaret was caught off guard.

"Uh, I'm not coming in, Mag. The apartment."

"Y-you're—"

"I need time to myself. To think. Meditate. You hit me with some hard blows. I can't think in the apartment, and I don't want to continue, for us to continue like ... like we're mad at each other—when we're not."

Margaret wouldn't argue.

"These, these are soul-searching questions I have to put to myself. That's all. All." Royal pulled down on the front bill of his hat. "I won't be long."

Margaret angled herself toward the apartment. The car engine started up.

Royal was in Hands of Christ Church.

He'd driven in the car to this little church in the basement. Hands of Christ Church. He'd been there for a number of hours now. He'd gone down on his knees, prayed and prayed and meditated and even fell asleep in a chair until he awoke, gathered himself by exercising, by limbering his neck muscles after feeling a small creak in his neck. But all of this had been of little consequence. Right now, this very moment, he didn't know how to feel. Glorious or ordinary. If he'd been touched by the Holy Spirit or if it'd dodged him. He didn't know if he'd been delivered to heaven's gate or dumped off by the side of the curb.

Only, he hadn't lost his sense of humor. It was guarding him like a saint. For he laughed at himself as much as he contemplated life. He had walked through his life in these hours down in the basement as he and Margaret had walked through the old house today. And it was Margaret he was thinking of now, for he had been in the church, in this space, for a long time. And he'd told Margaret that he wouldn't be long, but he had been, by estimates, over three hours. But he would tell her where he'd been, and then the rest would be clear to her anyway since she would know why it was in the church where he must tie all his thoughts, opinions together, the spiritual power that was in him, in his Father's house.

"Oh, I'm being tested. Tested today. Mightily, God."

Royal was sitting in the chair, not on the makeshift platform. He wasn't standing behind the pulpit or the Bible on top the pulpit. He was simply sitting down looking up.

"I do want out of this basement. Every time I step in here now, I want out." Pause.

"I ... I do want to feel as if I'm—no, no not me, but the church, God, the church is making progress. Is moving forward. I do want to feel that kind of momentum, impetus, push, of surging forward in my ministry. I am the spiritual leader of the church—I must present a vision. I must give it direction. Guide it. Sustain it overtime." Pause.

"And I've yet to do it on a—"

Royal paused for a second time, for he'd heard something in the basement.

"Who ... Mag! Mag!"

Margaret stopped walking and then began again.

"Mag ..."

They were in each other's arms what seemed in one seamless motion.

"Sit. Sit. Sit with me," Royal said, holding onto Margaret's hand.

"How'd you get here?"

"By cab."

"I had to come ... come here, Mag. To Hands of Christ. I had to think. Think here. Nowhere but here. In God's house. I ... ha ... even if it's a basement."

"You've been struggling."

"You don't feel cold."

"The taxi's heater was working."

"Oh. Ha."

Margaret kissed Royal's cheek.

"Yes, I'm struggling. Vacillating. Vacillating, Mag, more than anything else."

"I've been thinking too."

"Of course, of course," Royal said, patting her hand.

"Will you listen to me this time, Royal?"

Royal was about to say something but stopped.

"Will you?"

"Yes," Royal said, subdued. "It is your mother's, Mother Ballad's inheritance we're talking about."

"And Momma would want us to use it. If she didn't have me and Darlene, she would've left all her possessions, Royal, either to the church, her church, Clearview, or a charity. If Momma didn't have heirs, me and Darlene to consider." Margaret rubbed Royal's hand.

"You wouldn't disagree so far, would you?" she asked, turning to Royal.

"Uh-uh. No."

"And, Royal, we never meant to stay here long anyway. Here in Mr. Tolletson's basement. We took what we could get—and felt thankful, fortunate at the time for it."

"I still am, Mag."

"And if this church is to grow, it must grow physically. From the inside out. At … at least it might give the appearance, the tangible evidence that it's growing physically from the inside out in order to attract more people to it. To want to come to join."

Royal shook his head.

"Agreed. Agreed. So true. So true. What you're saying is so true, Mag."

"Because even if we want more parishioners to worship here, we can't accommodate them. We can't fit them in these tiny quarters."

"No, no way, Mag. No way!"

"Ha!"

"Don't stop. Don't stop!"

"Peyton Management Company and … and—"

"Turn that Bayer Street property—"

"Into—"

"A church. A church, Royal!"

Royal leaped out the chair and leaped up onto the platform.

"Preach, Sister Margaret! Preach!"

"A three-year lease! A three-year lease—what you wanted all along, Royal! What you wanted all along!"

"Preach, Sister Margaret, preach!"

"I have no more to say!"

"Mag, you don't?"

After pausing playfully and looking at each other with open suspicion, they broke out laughing.

"Ha. Ha."

"It'll be like putting new paint on the church. Hands of Christ. Like we've turned the corner, and there's a new stretch of road ahead that we have to cover."

"Preach, Rev. McCloud! Preach!"

"Heading for a finish line that God never quite lets you see or reach. One you can only imagine is there. But your feet keep moving … moving faster and faster toward a finish line … Oh, I'll never stop loving God, Mag. Never, Mag. Never!"

*　　*　　*

Three weeks later.

Everything appeared back to normal. Margaret was back at work, back at her bookkeeping job for International Retailers Inc. And Royal was back at school. It was a new year. The house was still unoccupied. Royal took it upon himself to check the house every day, inside and out, thoroughly. Even though it was in a safe part of Myles Day, there were always teenagers bent on mischief. Margaret would go to the house but only to clean it. And as for Marshall McCloud, Royal had officially dropped his search for him and Eve with Earl Simmons.

"Mag, it's like a magnet. A magnet—I'm so drawn to it."

Margaret was in bed, Royal in his pajamas and staring at the object atop his highboy like it indeed was a magnet and his eyes had metal in them.

"I …"—Royal looked back at Margaret—"you really surprised me with this one. Caught me off guard."

Margaret laughed. "I thought you needed a little surprise."

"I just can't keep my eyes off it."

"But you have to come to bed some time, Royal," Margaret joked.

"That's right. I can stare at it from our bed too."

"Yes."

"Even when the lights are off? I'll still know where it is, won't I? It's not going to move, is it?" Royal laughed. "In the dark? Is it, Mag?"

"No, it'll be there all night. It's not going to move."

"Thought not."

What the object of Royal's attention was a certified check written out for twenty-four thousand dollars and made payable to Peyton Management Company for the leasing of the Bay Street building property (store front) for a total of three years. The check was written out when Margaret got in from work. She couldn't wait, not after Royal told her, over the phone, that everything had been worked out between Hands of Christ Church and Peyton Management for the leasing of the space. The papers had been signed, et cetera, and all Peyton needed from him was a certified bank check, the one on top the highboy, the one Royal was currently staring at with such rapture his eyes might burn a hole through the thin paper.

"I can shake someone's hand at the bank tomorrow, then hand them a check and then … and then go about the business of building a church. Hands of Christ Church from the ground floor up."

Margaret lay her head back on the pillow to rest her eyes. Suddenly, she felt Royal in bed with her. He kissed her shoulder. She turned to him and her arm rested on top his hip. He kissed her shoulder a second time. She felt romantic, in the mood for him, their sex life always sensual, exciting. Margaret kissed his neck, her lips tracing his smooth skin. She felt Royal react, his hand slide down the outside of her leg, and her body felt more than warm blood rushing through it. He reached for her, bringing her more into him, her heart, her mind, kissing the divineness, the sweet, kind person she was. Kissing the temple of her soul, Royal, a pyramid rising second by second beneath the sheet; Margaret, spreading her legs open for him to enter her wetness.

They lay together in bed. Both awake but with their eyes closed. Margaret's head was on Royal's shoulder. They were going to get up to wash themselves but not yet.

Royal was thinking, had been thinking all day. It was something that had been building, and for him, maybe it'd reached its terminus. The only thing at the back of his mind was the timing. Was now the right time to ask Margaret the question that had built to this point? Sex tonight never felt so good. It felt inspirational. It felt—

"Mag …"

Margaret's head shifted on Royal's shoulder. "Yes …"

"Mag, when are we going to move into the house? Your mother's house?"

"M-Momma's house?"

"Yes, Mother Ballad's house, Margaret. The house."

Her hand darted up to her mouth. "I … I …"

"We've just gone about establishing a, setting a routine. Me going by the house every day. You cleaning the house when needed. But we haven't discussed—"

"When we're going to move into the house."

Royal pressed Margaret's hand.

"I … I don't know why we haven't, Royal."

"Neither do I, Mag. I … I have no idea."

"What's going on in my head? In … in there—here," Mag said, pointing to her head and then thumping it. "My silly little mind anyway?"

"Don't say that, Mag."

Pause.

"I do want to move in. But I haven't done anything to this point. But why, Royal?"

"There's no time, fixed timetable, I—"

"But you're asking me something I, by now, should've asked myself … By now."

"And you haven't?"

"No … not until just now, Royal. This minute."

"To be honest, it's something I've been thinking about the past week or so. I wanted the timing to be right. In no way, uh, not in any way imperfect."

"It isn't, wasn't, Royal. It wasn't."

Royal rolled out the bed. Margaret took his hand.

"Coming?"

"Oh yes."

Royal walked over to the highboy.

"The check's still here, Mag."

Margaret laughed.

"No one stole it, came into the bedroom to steal it while—"

"We made love."

Slowly Margaret rolled out of bed.

"We're marching, Mag. We're marching. For higher ground. Straight for the kingdom!"

*　　*　　*

The following day.

Margaret was outside Della's bedroom. Of course by now she'd been in it many, many times since Della's death, but today she felt her breath hollow out inside her. It just unexpectedly collapsed in her chest, and she'd felt it when it did.

This morning, she told Royal not to bother to check on the house, that after work she would. And she had, checked the house inside and out, and now this was the last room she would check as if it had to be checked—her mother's room—as if some deadly disaster lurked within its walls.

Today, the anticipation of taxiing to the house had bothered her. There was agony in her; it was just there in the pit of her stomach and didn't want to leave. But it was there, big like a rock. It's not the first she'd acknowledged it. She'd acknowledged it all right; she didn't want to be bothered by it. But that was impossible. Something that was totally, sufficiently undoable.

Margaret entered her mother's room. Without hesitating, she sat down on the bed. She was still in her overcoat. She was just outside the house. It felt like now, after sitting down, that she'd been wandering all day—no matter whatever distraction came along with the day.

"Momma, what am I to do?"

For Margaret knew why that big rock was lodged in her stomach. A big rock. A big rock you can't miss. You can see it in your mind, what it was made of, from—that you can't miss. And what she was suffering, she had to deal with, for Royal, last night, had made it as plain as day. It was not some needle in the haystack, but it was the big rock it was. It's why she had to come by the house today, visit the house, get a feel for the house again. It's the house that set her life right again, and it would be the house that would eventually rid her of the rock in the pit of her stomach, smash it, leave it in ruin, but, paradoxically, bring real peace and solace to her almost a month after her mother's death.

Darlene, Darlene, Margaret thought. She hadn't spoken to Lee since they last talked over the phone. The day Lee let her know Darlene had left the house.

"How is she doing? How is Darlene doing, Momma? You know. You know, Momma."

For it truly worried Margaret about how Darlene was doing, her mental state. Her health. Yes, she loved Darlene. *She really loved Darlene.* She could forgive her. It was in her heart to do so. It was there. It'd always been there. Darlene could be a good cousin, a good friend, Margaret thought. She had many more good qualities, attributes, than she had bad ones. So many. And she didn't feel as if she were being charitable or Christian-like or naïve for that matter. She was just being honest. As honest about Darlene as was possible.

But it was the house, the house was still at the heart of everything, her happiness, her future.

"This house is still directing my thoughts. Making me consider things I-I've never had to consider—I thought I would never have to consider. Momma and Daddy. The house."

Margaret lay back on the bed in her overcoat.

And while she lay this way, on the bed this way, she remembered why she wanted the house in the first place. The only reason why she wanted her mother to bequeath the house to her and not Darlene. The sole, solitary reason why.

"Oh, Momma, Momma, thank you, Momma. Thank you!" Margaret said this while coming off her back, her smile flashing, the problem solved. The rock that was in her stomach feeling like a pebble she merely had to brush aside, clear away, talk to Royal, get his take on the matter, and then act on it—call Lee and see if he could talk to Darlene so she and Royal could come by the house, so she could meet with Darlene, for there was something she had to tell Darlene. *It's urgent, Lee, one of the most important things I will ever do in my life, Lee. But I must see Darlene. Tell Darlene that I must see her, Lee!*

Margaret locked up the house. She would take the bus home. She'd walked half of the block and looked back at the tall standing house, the one Royal said must have been built for three hundred years of living in; it was built on that kind of rugged foundation.

Margaret opened her pocketbook to retrieve her change purse. She sniffed January's air. She hadn't gotten a cold all winter, she thought. She laughed, for that was usual by now, typically, during winter, she would've had three colds by now. Today, right now, it was the best she'd felt in a long, long time.

She really breathed in the January air this time. To her it felt delightful, practically sinful.

∗   ∗   ∗

"Lee, oh, it's ... it's so nice talking to you too."

"I miss you, Margaret. You and Royal."

Margaret shut her eyes.

"I ... I thought—was beginning to think I'd never talk to you again. But when Mr. Baker gave me ... I got your message, Margaret. It was all I could do. I ... I got goose bumps."

Margaret's eyes opened.

"You did ... did, Lee?"

"Big ones, Margaret. Big ones. Big red ones. I don't think I could've hid them if I tried."

Lee was at his job but after hours. He was calling from inside Mr. Baker's print shop. He'd planned it this way.

"Lee ..."

"You're going to tell me why you called, Margaret? Why you called? You're going to—"

"Yes. Yes, I am."

Long pause.

"Lee, I have to see Darlene."

"Darlene? Darlene! See ... see Darlene!"

"I have to meet with her."

"Darlene!"

"I didn't mean to shock you. Should I give you time, Lee? T—"

"Yes. Yes, Margaret. Oh God, yes, yes."

"I … I guess, s-suppose you never ex—suspected this."

"This? No, not this, Margaret. Oh, oh no, not this."

"Why did you think I called?"

"I was thinking … I really wasn't thinking, Margaret. As to why … why … I was just glad, I guess, I could, would be able to talk to you, speak to you after all this time. I …" Pause. "And then I thought, when I did think … think, Margaret, m-maybe, I don't know. You have …

"You're such a good person, Margaret. Maybe you wanted to find out how … how Darlene's doing. How—"

"No, I just want to see her, Lee. See her. T-talk to her. It's urgent. It is."

"Urgent, Margaret? Ur—now I really don't un-understand, Margaret. Any of—"

"It will be one of the most important things … I must see Darlene. You must tell Darlene, Lee. Y- you must tell her I must see her."

There was no response from Lee; he was just breathing hard into the phone.

"Then, the—it-it's almost like you're asking the impossible, the impossible then, Margaret."

"I know," Margaret said. "I know, know it is, Lee. But in my heart, if nothing else, I … I think Darlene will be curious. If … if nothing else then … then curious as to why it's so urgent on my part. If … if nothing else, Lee. It's what I'm count—"

"Royal, does Royal know about this?"

"Yes."

"Yes. Yes. It … it was dumb, s-stupid of me to ask, Margaret. Knowing the kind of relationship you and Royal have. I w-wasn't thinking. B-because I don't know how to make this work. Bring … bring up, even bring up your name or Royal's either to Darlene." Pause.

"She hates both of you. The two of you, you and Royal so much, Margaret. S-so much. You know that. You know that."

"I know, Lee. I know."

"Do you really know, Margaret? Really know?"

Margaret remained mum.

"It was bad before, but now … oh … well … oh well, like you said, you didn't call for that. Any of that. Not for … How … how do I do it, Margaret? How … how … Tell me how—"

"At the house. At the house."

"Do I … I just come out and say it, Margaret? To Darlene? Darlene? Just come out and say it. Tell her that Margaret said she wants to see you. Come to the house, Darlene. Our house. Margaret and Royal. Margaret and Royal. Our house with Royal."

Pause.

"You know she doesn't … doesn't talk about the house. Aunt Della's house, Margaret. Darlene doesn't talk about the house."

Margaret looks up at the ceiling.

"Not since the day we left the house. It-it's been strange. Strange. Real strange. Not one day. Not—"

"So you'll—"

"Do it—yes. Yes. I'll do it when I get home. Tonight. I don't know how. Don't ask me, but I'll do it." Pause. "Can I call you this time tomorrow evening, Margaret? I mean, I don't want to leave you in suspense all day, tomorrow, on your job, but—"

"As long as you call, Lee."

"Oh, good. Good."

"I love you, Lee."

"I love you, Margaret."

"You take care of yourself now."

"You … say hello to Royal for me."

"Will do. Will do. Oh, Lee, and if Darlene agrees, it has to be on a Saturday. Otherwise, it's bad for us. R-Royal and me. A Saturday evening, Lee."

"Oh, okay, okay, Margaret."

"And then that'll give me time to … oh … Oh well …"

"I'd better get going. Darlene, Darlene's expecting me. S-she really doesn't like for me to get home late, to be off, off schedule these days. E-especially these days."

"Good night."

"Good night."

CHAPTER 17

Eight days later. Late Saturday afternoon.

The morning (from the time Margaret awakened this morning), it'd felt long, monotonous, like she was marking time a second at a time. Royal had handed her good news; he was always handing her good news about what was going on at the church at its new location, the Bayer Street location. Normally, on a Saturday, she'd be with him. Today, there were volunteer painters, something Royal liked doing, paint. They wanted to spruce up the church walls with a new coat of paint. Royal said five others, besides himself, showed up. After he told her what'd happened, it's as if he purposefully found something in the apartment to do in order to give her privacy, something she was holding onto today, tightly, fiercely.

There was a serenity in her, but it wasn't able to offset her tension, the first time she would see Darlene since the reading of her mother's will, her collapsing on the floor, seeing her on Attorney Robinson's couch anguished, out of sorts, as if she were fighting for her life—every second counting. The mental image of Darlene in Attorney Robinson's office haunted her last night; it was difficult for her to sleep. Then it was difficult for her to wake when she finally fell asleep, when she, this morning, thought of what lay ahead for her.

"Mag. Mag, are you ready?"

"Oh yes, yes, I am, Royal."

Royal had peeked into the bedroom.

"I'll get your coat."

"Thanks."

Margaret stood. She walked over to the dresser's mirror.

"Do … do I look all right? D-do I look all right?"

She studied her hair, her lipstick. She wanted to make sure, certain she looked all right, her appearance, physical appearance, self.

How is Darlene going to look? How is Darlene going to look? Margaret asked herself.

"Mag …"

"Oh yes. Yes." Margaret stepped away from the mirror. Royal was assisting her with her coat; he had his coat on. Margaret turned to the bed. "My bag, Royal." It was an oversized leather bag on the bed, and next to it was a plain white envelope. "And the envelope."

Margaret picked the envelope up off the bed and put it in the leather bag.

"I'm ready, Royal. Don't worry about me. I'm okay."

Royal was surprised, for he hadn't asked for this kind of detailed information. They hadn't been talking at all, the whole time; he was about to say something, but nothing came out.

"Yes. Yes. I'm okay."

Royal looked to his left, for he had to steer the car left onto Fall Street. He'd had his own thoughts today, with the paint brush in his hand, putting new, fresh paint on the church walls (several coats). This new big store front, open space to worship in, what now felt like home, that he'd entered heaven. He never felt he could be so happy, so rewarded by God's love. But when he looked at the fresh coat of paint, suddenly he—

"What does she look like?"

"Darlene?"

"Darlene."

He'd thought that too. He knew he wouldn't see her in Myles Day City. That their paths would not cross. Royal knew that. Not Darlene. Not Darlene Winston. That was out, out the question. Their paths never crossed in Myles Day. This was nothing new. This was old hat. This typified their relationship.

He never ran into Darlene Winston in Myles Day City, not by accident, not by some misguided fate—no, that'd never happen.

"I ... I just want to see her, Royal. Darlene. Isn't that odd? Isn't that a strange thing to say?"

Margaret didn't turn to Royal. She looked straight ahead, out the car's windshield.

"Is ... is that the house? Lee and Darlene's house?"

"Yes, yes, I believe it is, Mag." Pause.

"It's a nice house."

"Yes, pleasant."

Then Royal looked over at Margaret and saw her hand grab at the bag's strap on her lap. He thought of the envelope inside the leather bag.

"The heat's so good in this car, Royal. Feels so good."

Suddenly Royal wanted this day over with. How he wanted this day over with.

Royal rang the doorbell. He had his arm around Margaret's waist. The door opened.

"Lee."

"M-Margaret."

"Lee."

"Royal."

Pause.

"C-come in, Margaret ... R-Royal. Come in."

There was this pain in Lee's face, something that made him look older, his eyes a dead giveaway; you could see the last month in them better than if you counted the expired days.

"Let ... let me hug you, Margaret. Let ... let me hug you. Please. Please."

"Oh ... oh yes, Lee. Oh yes."

"And ... and Royal ..."

Lee and Royal hugged.

"Y-your coats. Y-your coats."

Margaret and Royal removed their coats. Lee hung them up. They were inside the tiny vestibule. Lee was in a suit. He was wearing a tie. After Lee hung the coats in her closet, the three stood in front of each other. It had a caution in it, a wariness that seemed built on the foundation of fear of the unknown—certainly nothing more.

"D-Darlene wants to meet us in the kitchen, she said. D-Darlene ..."

Darlene, Margaret thought, *in control. In control. Always in control. Whatever made me think it would change. Could ... would be any different? What?*

They were in the kitchen, and there was no conversation passing between them.

"You're ... you're welcome to sit. At the kitchen table. You ... you and Margaret, Royal."

Royal looked at Margaret. "Margaret and I, we'd rather, uh, would prefer to stand. To stand, Lee, thank you."

"D-Darlene did hear us. She is expecting us, is—"

"All ... all Darlene wanted me, wished for me to do, asked, was ... was for me to answer the door when you got here, Margaret, you and Royal. That's, and, uh, bring, es-escort you into the kitchen. She said she would be down, come down into the kitchen as ... as soon as the doorbell rang—uh, rang."

Control. Control.

"The church, Royal ... the church. It's on Bayer Street. Over on 20 Bayer Street now."

"Yes, it's on Bayer Street all right. It's on ... on Bayer Street, all right!"

"I was happy when I found out. F-found out, Royal. A-about the church. Heard about it."

"Just came from there. Uh, had a paint brush in my hand t—"

"M-maybe Darlene didn't hear the doorbell, Lee. When it rang. When—"

"No, no ... uh, but, uh, she did, not at all, Margaret. Not at all. Darlene did. She would. I left our—the bedroom door open. Uh, for her, Margaret. It's at, right at the top of the staircase, stairs—our, our bedroom."

It was many seconds later when the three, Royal, Margaret, and Lee, heard Darlene. It was her slippers on the floor. It's what they heard. It's what they heard so distinctly, finely.

Darlene wasn't lifting her feet off the floor. You could hear her slippers drag across the floor, sliding across it as if scraping it as she approached the kitchen. Margaret looked at Royal, and he the same. They stood inside the kitchen, not near the entranceway where they could see Darlene before

Darlene got into the kitchen. But Lee was standing where he could see Darlene, and he was looking at her, and if he looked older at the front door when Margaret and Royal entered the house, he looked older now. And his eyes, you could see the deep pain in them each time Darlene scraped her feet over the hallway's floor.

"D-Darlene …"

Margaret and Royal could hear Darlene, her tacit tenacity not to answer Lee back. Margaret braced herself.

Margaret knew it was Darlene, her cousin, but the days had rolled forward without her, for she too looked older, worn, gaunt. She was in a powder-blue bathrobe. Then when her head finally lifted, she looked at Margaret. And it's when this look of hers—the crippled, defeated look—disappeared, was replaced, abruptly, by what seemed an implacable defiance.

Darlene walked past Lee, Margaret, and Royal.

Her hair, which was combed, looked as defiant and wild of spirit as she now looked. Her eyes looked down at the kitchen chair. She waited. It's when Lee ran over to her, pulling the chair out for her. She didn't bother to look up at Lee but, instead, sat as if wounded by her own haughtiness, superiority.

There was quiet, Darlene maintaining her grandeur, the center of attention. She ran her finger across the kitchen table and then back again. After the third time doing this, her eyes looked up at Margaret to look her full in the face.

"And … and so you won, Margaret Ballad. You won," Darlene said as if she were picking open an old wound, like the reading in Attorney Robinson's office had happened just yesterday, not a month ago.

Margaret approached the kitchen table.

"No, no one won, Darlene. That day. It's not what Momma planned, for someone to—"

"So you've come to gloat. Is that it, that it? Finally … finally you've come to gloat—you and Royal McCloud. You and Royal McCloud. Is that it? To—"

"No, we—"

"Come to my house to gloat. Ha. For … for I know it's what I would've done to you if … First I … I told Lee he should've hung up the phone, hung up the phone on you when you called—at … at such a suggestion. Making such a damned suggestion." Darlene looked arrogantly at Margaret and then at Royal and then back at Margaret. "Ha. Ha. Ha. Come over here? By here? To my house? To do what? What? Ha. Ha. Ha. W—

"But … but then I caught on. Y-yes, Margaret, Margaret Ballad. Then I caught on, and fast. You couldn't leave me alone. Couldn't leave … let me lick my wounds. No, not you, Margaret Ballad. Not you, Margaret Ballad. Aunt … Aunt Della knew this side of you and Royal McCloud too … too— this e-evil side of you and Royal McCloud, yet … yet she still … Oh, what a mistake Aunt Della made. What a damned mistake Aunt Della made. My aunt Della made. T-to give you the house. Will it to you. The house. The damned house!"

Darlene's body trembled, but then Darlene sucked in her breath.

"But it was you, Royal McCloud. It was you. You! You!" She pointed her finger at Royal, and Royal could feel her finger's power.

"P-praying to Aunt Della. Praying to Aunt Della … yes … yes, praying to my aunt Della like the devil, Royal McCloud. Like the devil! The devil you are! Have … have always been!"

Royal was shocked.

"Oh … the words, the words you must've used, Royal McCloud. Formed, came out your mouth. The persuasion. The … the poison you must've put in those prayers, Aunt Della, my aunt Della heard. Heard, the … Day after day after day … Oh, oh, if I could've slapped that smile off your face at the reading. If … Oh, if I could've, Margaret B—if I—"

"But you fainted, Darlene. You—"

"Shut up, Lee! Shut up! You—just, just shut up, Lee!"

Then Darlene's finger worked the table again; her fingernails were raking the table's hard wood.

Margaret opened the leather bag she'd brought into the house.

"So now … now you've come to my house. My house to a … a house you and Royal McCloud have never stepped foot in. In-invited to. B-barred from, forbidden to come, come into. My house. My house. Ha. Ha. Ha. My … Lee, Lee, come over here, Lee. Come over here, Lee. Stand by me, Lee. Beside me, Lee. Lee. Lee." Darlene reached out her hand. Lee grabbed it.

"I need you, Lee. I … I need you, Lee. Oh, oh, how I need you, baby. Aunt … Aunt Della loves me. Aunt … Aunt Della loves me, Lee. Aunt Della loves me, Lee …"

Margaret pulled the white envelope out the bag. The envelope was in her hand. Darlene looked at the envelope and then up at Margaret as her gaze widened. Margaret looked at Royal.

"W-what are you holding ... holding in your hand, M-Margaret Ballad? Your hand?" Darlene yanked her hand out Lee's; Margaret looked at Royal again.

"It's the deed to the house, Darlene. To Momma's house."

"Aunt ... Aunt Della's deed? Aunt ... Aunt Della's deed, M-Margaret? T-to the house? T-to my aunt Della's house?"

"And it's your, Darlene. Yours. The deed's yours."

"D-Darlene's, Margaret? Darlene's!"

"Yes, Lee. Yours and Darlene's." Then Margaret put the deed down on top the kitchen table, and Darlene stared at it with disbelief, confusion, and continuing shock.

"Mr. Robinson worked everything out for us, the legal details, aspect, but there's still more that has to be done," Royal said. "Before there can be legal transfer of the title, full ownership of the property, the house can be turned over to you and Lee. Things such as registration of the—"

Lee looks up from the table. "But why, Margaret? Why?"

Royal went over to Margaret; she took his hand.

"Because, Lee. You see, I always knew my mother loved me unconditionally. I knew that about Momma. A mother's unconditional love for her child. But what I didn't know was if Momma trusted me. That was the one thing I didn't know since Royal and I returned to Myles Day City. From Detroit. That meant everything to me, Lee. Everything. And so now I know by what Momma did, Lee."

Pause.

"We, Royal and I don't want the house. We have no need for it. Not now, Lee. Not since Momma's will was drawn."

"Lee, uh, we're ... we're leaving."

"Oh ... oh then ... then let me get your coats and show you to the—"

"You don't have to get our coats, see us to the door, Lee," Royal said. "It's all right."

"Sure, sure, Royal." Lee went to Margaret and kissed her cheek. Next, he shook Royal's hand.

"Good night, Lee."

"Good night, Margaret."

"Night, Lee."

"Uh, yes, uh, g-good night, Royal."

Hand in hand, Margaret and Royal walked out the kitchen.

Lee turned to Darlene and saw she was still staring at the deed. Then she finally picked the deed up and looked at it and held it in her hands as if to express if she didn't, the deed might disappear.

And while this was taking place, it's as if Lee was not there, present in the kitchen with her.

Lee looked on a little longer but then left the kitchen. When he got back into the kitchen, only seconds later, he saw the same scene being played out. Lee was holding onto his coat.

"Darlene, I-I'm going out on the back porch. Yard. I … I need a smoke. D-Darlene."

Darlene's hands continued to clutch the deed, and her eyes continued to stare intensely at it, and her ears didn't seem to hear anything Lee had said.

"Bad, Darlene. I … I need a, me, me a smoke b-bad, D-Darlene …" Lee opened the back door of the house. "Bad … bad, Darlene." Then Lee closed the kitchen door behind him.

Margaret came out the bathroom. Royal got up and followed her. When he got into the bedroom, Margaret looked back to him.

"You don't have to follow me like a shepherd following his sheep. Stand over me. I'm tired. I'm going to bed."

"So today's event really hasn't—"

"I don't want any analysis. To analyze it. Or … or pray on it. I just want to go to bed. I'm tired. Tired."

"You said once you'd made the decision, made up your mind to turn the house over to Darlene, that your pain was gone, Mag. You felt it leave … leave your body. It's—"

"I don't know what I said. I … I don't know what I said now!"

She was deflated. Sluggishly she sat down on the bed and then pulled her legs up on top the bed and lay in a fetal position.

"Did you see her? Did you see Darlene, Royal?"

"But didn't you expect it, Mag? As much? I mean—"

"We pray for people."

"You're not testing our faith again, are you? Our beliefs?"

"We pray for them—"

"Because we love them. It's that simple. It's no more simple or complicated, complex than that. Because we love them. Darlene's not our enemy. She's her own enemy. If there are any enemies to look for. No matter what she says to me or about—"

Margaret lifts her head. "Are you saying that for your own protection, Royal? To protect your ego? Protect it?"

Royal's hands are in front of him. He clasps them. "When I let you stand in judgment of me, it's when I'll leave. I'll walk out of this place. Out of here."

Royal turns to leave the room.

"Don't go! Don't go, Royal! Don't go!"

She was sobbing. He went to her.

"Mag. Mag."

He was holding her.

"I ... I do love Darlene. No matter how much she hates me. No matter how much she hates me, Royal. No matter!"

"I know. I know, Mag. I know."

"I don't want to see her like that, Royal. H-how she looked today."

"But ... but maybe this will help her. Maybe Mother Ballad's house, turning the deed over to her—"

"It's what she wanted."

"Yes."

"All along."

"All along. All along, Mag."

"And ... and I've provided her with it. I've provided her with it, haven't I, Royal?"

"Yes. Yes, you have, Mag."

Royal stopped rocking her. His head's back against the headboard. He's still holding her to him though.

"I want Darlene to have it, but ... but I didn't want it, Royal. I never wanted the house, Royal."

"It's too big. For the two of us, at least."

"I think I would've sold it. I ... I think so," Margaret said, clearing her tears. "It is too big."

"I just pray Darlene finds some peace of mind. The house gives her that. That much."

Pause.

"Only, you know, Mag, once you gave it up, Darlene, the deed to the house, you gave up the house for good."

"Yes, I—"

"She won't let you back in the house. Step foot back into your mother and father's house again. Y-you forfeited that right today."

Margaret agreed.

"You gave up a lot today."

"But it was worse the other way. It was worse owning it. Having it. Far, far worse."

"We'll buy our own house one day."

"I'd like that."

"So are you going to turn in for the night?"

"Yes. I am tired. I ... I was being genuine before."

They kissed.

"I'm going back into the kitchen and do my schoolwork, and then—"

"Prepare tomorrow's sermon."

"Ha. Right, Mag. Right. Same old routine. Saturday night for Rev. Royal McCloud."

"Ha."

CHAPTER 18

"Oh, Lee. Lee. Hurry, Lee. Hurry!"

"Darlene, you look so pretty!"

"Don't I, Lee? Don't I!"

Darlene twirled around at the top of the staircase.

"Yes, yes, I feel so pretty. So pretty, baby."

She was coming down the short inclined staircase.

"And here's your coat, Princess Darlene."

"Thank you, Lee. Thank you, baby."

Lee smiled and then helped Darlene with her coat.

"Oh ... I can't wait, Lee. I can't wait to put my key in the door. The lock of the door, Lee. Insert the key in ... Oh, Lee. Lee. I'm so excited, Lee."

"Ha."

"I would've had you drive me to the house last night. Spent the night there but ... but ..."

"The shock. Shock of what happened, D—"

"Took time to wear off, exhausted me. It exhausted me, Lee. I could barely move, get up from the kitchen table. I was physically exhausted, Lee." Pause. "Y-you must've been too. It's why you stayed, were out on the back porch for so long."

"I didn't know, uh, you noticed, Darlene. No-noticed. Were aware of—"

"I was, Lee. I was. But you were there when I needed you. I finally got on my feet. Helped me to bed. Up to … Let's go, Lee! Let's g-get there, to Aunt Della's house as fast, quickly as we can!"

"Right this way!" Lee said, rushing to the door, opening it. "Right this way, Princess Darlene."

Darlene, playing along with Lee, was spirited out the door.

They were in the car. From time to time, Lee would glance over at Darlene. Each time he did, he felt the same after seeing the glow on Darlene's cheeks. Each time. He had gone through another chapter with her, this woman, this complicated woman who he knew Darlene was. But he'd made it through another chapter, he thought. And now it was the beginning of a new one for them.

"Guess … ha … I'm back to shoveling two residences again, Darlene. There's going to be another snow, big snow—"

"Two residences? Two properties, Lee?"

"Uh, yes, sure, Darlene, yes—ours and—"

"We're selling our house as fast as possible. We can. As quickly as possible, that little house of ours."

"Oh … yes, I … I wasn't thinking. I wasn't … I was just talking about the immediate future. S-since the storm will be here—"

"You, oh, you made it sound like something permanent. Permanent, Lee."

"Oh, sorry. Sorry, Darlene. I didn't mean to. Sorry."

"Something of a permanent nature."

"Uh, no, oh … sorry, Darlene. Not at all. I-I didn't mean to, uh, give you that impress—"

"Snow. Snow. I hate snow. If it wasn't for Aunt Della, my clients, the house, I'd move to a warm climate. California or … or say Florida. Out of Myles Day City. That's for sure. For … Oh, oh, Lee, Lee—the house, there it is, Lee! There it is! The house! The house, Lee!"

And Lee looked at the house and then at Darlene, and it's as if Darlene were looking at the house for the first time in her life. It's how her eyes fixated and radiated, for Darlene's eyes were two sapphires, two gems. And for Lee, he'd rather see this than the other, he thought, than the Darlene of the past month who couldn't cry but would rant and rave lustily instead and then fall silent, her slight body bottling anger for what seemed for its own protection, survival.

"Oh … when I step in there, the … the house, Lee, I'm not going to tell you what I'm going to say. What … what will come out my mouth. What I … I have planned, Lee."

"Y-you aren't, Darlene?"

"Ha. Not now, Lee. It-it's a secret. A big secret."

Lee pulled the car into the driveway. When he braked the car, Darlene said, "Let me close my eyes, Lee. Close, j-just close my eyes."

Lee smiled.

"It … it feels so satisfying. So satisfying."

Lee pulled down on the brim of his hat and patted the scarf against his neck.

"You take your time. You take your time, Darlene. Okay?"

"F-for someone who was in such a rush before, I … I …," Darlene said, her voice fading.

But then she opened her eyes and took the manila envelope off her lap. She opened it.

"The deed. The deed. Should I take the deed into the house, Lee? Now, Lee?"

Lee was baffled. "Uh … you, uh, you do what you want, Darlene. With it. Yes, you may do what you want, wish to, uh, with it, Darlene. Af-after all, it is your deed. The house is yours, Darlene. It is your house. It b-belongs to you."

Darlene shut her eyes, but this time Lee didn't see her clutch the envelope at first as if it would disappear from out her hand if she didn't, and then as if she couldn't believe it was hers, the deed to the house was really hers.

"Let's go, Lee!"

"Right, right, that's—"

"Why are we sitting here?" Darlene laughed. "In the car for? In the first place!"

"I—"

"You will open the door for me, won't you, baby?"

"Oh, gladly, Darlene. Ha. Gladly!"

Lee scooted over to the car's passenger side. He opened the car door. "You may step out now, Princess Darlene."

"Oh, you're so much fun today, Lee. Not like you've been the past month. I noticed. Noticed, Lee. Over the past month … so gloomy. So serious, Lee. Baby," Darlene said, her hand brushing Lee's cheek. "I saw it, Lee. I saw it."

"Uh, right, Darlene. Right."

"And now to the front door we go. Of the house we go, Lee." Darlene stuck out her hand. "Will you lead me, Lee? Will you, Lee? Will you?"

Lee took her hand.

At the front door of the house, in Lee's eagerness to continue to please Darlene, he got the house key out his front pocket.

"No, no, Lee. Not you. I'm the one. Only one to … I'm going to use my key. My key, Lee, to open the door. Open my aunt Della's house back up with … with my key."

Lee stepped aside.

"Oh … I feel so warm inside, Lee. S-so warm right now. In-invigorated."

"Yes, I can see it, Darlene."

Darlene patted her left cheek.

"I …"

And she looked at the tall deep-brown-stained oak door.

"Ha. You should see how you're looking at the door, Darlene. You should see yourself."

"I … I should, Lee? I … I should?"

"Yes, you—"

And then the house key aimed for the lock in the door, and Darlene inserted the key in the lock and flung open the door, and she ran inside and waved the deed in the air and said, "I'm home, Aunt Della! I'm home!"

Darlene and Lee had been in every room but their aunt Della's. Both Darlene and Lee passed by the room, of course, but when Darlene passed it by, Lee followed suit since he was following her step for step.

Both were back on the second floor. Darlene turned back to Lee.

"Where haven't we been in the house, Lee? Tell me? Tell me? What room haven't we been in, in the house, Lee?"

"Now, Darlene …"

"Tell me, Lee. Tell me. Don't spoil the fun, Lee. Don't spoil the fun for me, Lee."

"Oh … right, Darlene. Right."

Lee smiled; Darlene smiled back.

"Aunt Della's room, Darlene. Aunt Della's room."

"Oh … Lee, you're so smart. So smart, Lee."

It's when Darlene took hold of Lee's hand and drew him to her. She kissed Lee's cheek.

"You're so smart, baby."

Then abruptly, she turned, and it's when she ran off.

"Aunt Della! Aunt Della, oh, Aunt Della!" Darlene said, running into the bedroom.

Lee walked into the bedroom and saw Darlene touching everything, physically touching everything with her hands.

"Margaret, Margaret didn't take anything, Lee. From the house, Lee. From the house. Margaret didn't take anything, Lee. Nothing, not a thing, Lee!"

And that was it, Lee thought. *That was it.* When they walked the house, he'd never seen Darlene's eyes more alert, unilaterally purposeful, her body taut, but loosening each time—now that he knew, at those particular times, it was indicating approval.

"Nothing's been removed, Lee. Taken. Of Aunt Della's, Lee. Of Aunt Della's."

But hearing Darlene say this again disgusted Lee more, for if he could take his head and stick it in a hole in the ground, he would. It's how ugly and shrill and obnoxious Darlene's words were to him.

"I … I didn't know what to expect when I walked in here, Lee. What to expect …"

Darlene sat in the chair next to the bed.

"From Margaret, Lee."

Lee took his eyes off Darlene. For a long time there was silence.

Lee turned back around, and he saw Darlene sitting in the chair, her head back, her eyes shut; a delightful smile framed her face. She's lost in some world, Lee thought. Darlene's lost in some world by herself. He was getting the urge for a cigarette. The urge was building in him by the second. Some days he just wished he could fight the urge back and win. Actually beat the damned thing. The damned habit, be victorious.

"Oh … Lee." Darlene's eyes opened. "Oh baby …"

Lee suddenly felt lost.

"We'll eat here … Do you want to eat here tonight, Lee?"

"Dinner, Darlene?"

"Yes, baby."

"Oh yes, uh … uh … that would be fine, Darlene. All right by me, Darlene. By all means."

"I can't wait to cook on Aunt Della's stove, Lee. Again. It seems so long, doesn't it, Lee? Long ago. Doesn't it?"

"Yes, in a way, Darlene. In a way it does."

Darlene stood.

"And, Lee … Lee …," Darlene said, rushing over to him, taking his hand. "I … I want to spend the night here, Lee. Is it all right if I spend the night here, Lee?"

"S-spend—"

"It's all right, isn't it, Lee? Is all right, isn't it?"

"Uh … I don't see, uh, can't see why not, Darlene."

"Oh, thank you, Lee. Thank you."

"But your—"

"Would you get them, Lee. Drive back. Get them for, from the house for me … My nightgown and toiletries and—"

"Of course, Darlene. Of course."

Darlene looks into his eyes. "You're so good to me, Lee. You're so good to me. Don't think I don't know that, Lee. Don't think I don't know that."

Lee was at a loss for words again. And then Darlene kissed him on his lips. *I really love you, Darlene*, he said to himself.

*   *   *

Three weeks later. A Saturday morning.

It wasn't a moving van but a rental van parked in front of 38 Eckert Street. Lee had parked the vehicle there. It'd just gotten there. Lee was in the house but then back out to the van. The van's back door was open; Lee was carrying boxes into the house. There were a number of boxes Lee had loaded in the van. The next and final items would be the clothes, his and Darlene's clothes. Darlene would go back to their old house with him. Their labor was equally shared. Darlene, of course, couldn't carry the big boxes, only the lighter ones (and Lee had bought a hand truck for the bigger boxes). It was just him and Darlene; they didn't need anyone else's help. All the boxes were marked by a red magic marker, as to what went where—in what room.

Lee was back inside the house. Darlene was stepping lively.

"Oh, Lee, that box isn't too heavy, is it? For you?"

"Not at all, Darlene. Ha. Not at all. Don't you worry about me. Me any. Uh, it's marked for the bedroom. Our bedroom. So I'll scoot, just scoot right up there with it."

Lee paused for a second. Darlene looked so good in her slacks, he thought. Her shape, figure.

"Lee. I know what you're thinking, Lee."

"Uh, caught me, huh, Darlene?"

"Ha. Now you go ahead and do what you have to do, Lee Winston. And take your mind, your thoughts off me."

"Do I have to, Darlene?"

"Oh, Lee, Lee, we're going to have so much fun in this house. In my aunt Della's house, baby!"

"Yes, uh, come to think of it, this box *is* getting heavy, Darlene!"

Lee and Darlene had made a second trip to the house in the van. In three weeks' time, they'd sold practically all their furniture. It was beautiful furniture to be sure—consistent with Darlene's exceptional taste. Their house was up for sale. It'd been on the market for two days. Their realtor, Ed Kelly, told them it would be snatched off the market *in no time flat*. They weren't asking for anything more than what was the house's current market value. They'd set a price, and it was fixed. It was not to be negotiated up or down, it's what Ed Kelly was told.

All the furniture in the house was sold; all of it but the bedroom furniture. That would stay in the house until the house was sold. They decided they still wanted to maintain a presence in the house, that Lee would still spend nights there, off and on, until the new owner moved in. Darlene's bed in her aunt Della's house could accommodate both she and Lee easily. Lee and Darlene would be sleeping in it for the first time tonight. Her bed in the bedroom.

They'd eaten and bathed, and Darlene was in bed in her sheer nightgown and Lee in his pajamas.

"Lee, can you believe this day?"

"No, Darlene. No. Not at all."

"I couldn't've dreamed it up any better, Lee. For myself."

"Me either. I must admit, Darlene. I thought I might miss our house the first night, but so far, tonight—"

"It's Aunt Della. Aunt Della. We're in Aunt Della and Uncle Frank's house."

"Has to be. W-what it is. That we're in Aunt Della and Uncle Frank's house. It's why I'm not even thinking about the, our ... our house, Darlene."

"Where, it's where we belong, Lee. Where we should've been all along. All along, Lee. "

"Ha."

"What, Lee? What?"

"Thought I was in good shape, but those boxes ..."

"Make a muscle, Lee."

"A muscle, D—"

"Go ahead. Go ahead, baby."

"Uh, you mean like this, Darlene? Like—"

"Oh ... Lee, Lee ..."

"Even when I was skinny, a scrawny teenager, when we first met," Lee said, the light on his smooth brown skin, "I had a muscle. I don't know why. Could make a muscle. A good one. Do you remember, Darlene?"

"Now, Lee ..."

"I know I'm fishing for a compliment, Darlene, but—"

"Lee, baby ..."

Then Darlene hopped out the bed.

"I'm going to turn off the lights, Lee. O-okay, L-Lee?"

The way Darlene said it totally excited Lee.

"Uh, sure, sure, Darlene. Sure. Fine by me. I'm ... I'm ready to turn in. Call it a night. Q-quits."

Darlene turned off the ceiling light.

"Darlene, let me turn the nightstand's lamp on so you can—"

"Now, Lee ... I can reach from here to the bed all right. Without a light. Any light. A light in the room, baby. I've done it so many times before. Without the light. Any light."

"Right, Darlene. Why, right."

Then Lee saw the outline of Darlene's body, and as she drew nearer the bed, she said, "I saw how you looked at me in my slacks today, Lee. When you had the, that heavy box in your hands. Maybe I should wear slacks more often."

"I … I couldn't keep my eyes off you, D-Darlene. I admit it, admit it, Darlene. I … I couldn't—"

"It seemed that way, Lee. It seemed that way—what it looked like to me, Lee. From where I was standing, Lee."

She was in bed; Lee could feel her next to him.

"Darlene—"

"It's our first night here, Lee. Our first night here."

"Yes, D—"

"I saw how you looked, Lee. At me. I saw …"

"B-because I—"

"I was turning you on, Lee."

"Yes, you were—"

"I still turn you on, Lee? Do I? Do I, Lee?"

Lee felt Darlene's skin warm.

"Yes, oh yes, Darlene, you still—"

"Then why don't you …"

"I … I can, Darlene? I … I—"

"I'm here, Lee. I'm here, baby." Pause. "Do you want me, Lee? Want me?"

"Yes, I—"

Darlene rolled over on top of Lee. She straddled him. She touched his chest.

"Do you, Lee? Do you?"

"Oh yes, I—"

Darlene slipped the nightgown over the top of her head.

"Do … do you, Lee …?"

*   *   *

The next evening.

"I'm going to miss you tonight, Lee."

"I don't have to—"

"Now, Lee, the bed's at the house. We left it there for a reason, Lee."

Lee frowned. "Uh, yes, I—"

It's when Lee brought Darlene to her.

"Lee—"

"After last night, Darlene …"

"Oh, that's why you're so—"

"Last night was so—"

"Now, Lee, we're in Aunt Della's house."

Lee looked at Darlene. "Ha. It didn't seem to matter to you last night, Darlene."

Darlene pecked Lee's cheek. "Now that's all you get from me tonight, Lee Winston. All."

"Ha."

"Now you call when you get to the house. Let me know you got there safe."

"Will do, Darlene. Will do."

"Oh, I'm so happy, Lee. I'm so happy. So happy here, Lee."

"Me too, Darlene. Me too."

"Now you go." Darlene opened the door. "Go."

"One more kiss, Darlene?"

Darlene shook her head and then smiled teasingly. "Oh … all right. All right, baby."

Lee kissed Darlene full on the lips.

"Now go, Lee. Unless I might not let you …"

"Y-you mean that, Darlene? You—"

"Ha. Ha."

Darlene shut the house's front door.

"Oh … the house is mine again. I'm alone again!"

Darlene went into the kitchen. She had to wash the dinner dishes. She put her apron back on. She walked over to the kitchen sink and then stopped.

"Margaret. Margaret. Margaret Ballad—why … why did I just think of Margaret, Margaret Ballad? Margaret Ballad for?"

She hadn't thought of Margaret in such a long time, since the last snow in Myles Day City, Darlene thought, even though a storm, the weather service said, was heading their way.

"Why? Why?"

It snapped her mood. It just snapped her mood, so now Darlene was reaching for the bottle of dish detergent differently, as if her hand had been stricken. Darlene ran the tap water. She poured the liquid detergent out the bottle and watched the water fill the sink. And as she watches the suds and bubbles build, for the first time, she feels alone in the house; for the first time she's occupied the house.

"I—what's come over me? What's come over me?"

Darlene picks up the dishcloth, and it feels heavy, particularly heavy to her. She drops the dishcloth down into the water. She looks at the small stack of dishes and suddenly doesn't feel in the mood for washing them. Then she looks back down at the water in the sink, and then her mind is white, plain, so her body falls backward, her hands are wet, having been in the sudsy water, and she begins wiping them again and again into the dry apron. Her hands keep repeating this torrid, rapid pace until they are dry. She looks at them and wants to smile, wants to—but doesn't. She doesn't have the energy for that—to do that—make a smile.

The chair, the kitchen chair—Darlene needed it. It's what she was focusing on now, her eyes, mind, getting over to the chair. Making it over to the chair. The kitchen chair at the kitchen table. But no, no, she wanted to go upstairs. She wanted to go upstairs in the worse sort, kind of way, upstairs to her aunt Della's room, to be in her aunt Della's room.

"I … I have to be with my, my aunt Della. Aunt Della. W-with Aunt Della."

She was thinking about the stairs, the staircase, how she was going to make it up the staircase, for whatever had bit her, whatever poison had gotten into her veins, poisoned her arteries. It'd come without warning, this thing that was slowing her down, debilitating her, making her, for now, doubt herself.

She wanted to take off her apron, from around her waist, but didn't feel that she could. She actually couldn't see how she was going to do it, how she was going to be able to perform that task, untie the apron from around her waist.

"I have to get upstairs. Upstairs to Aunt Della's room. Aunt Della's room …"

She'd made it up the staircase; Darlene didn't know how. She wasn't going to look back to see how. She just staggered forward, the next step and the next, so unsteady, so distrustful of her next step that she felt each step like old sores now were in her ankles. It's how discomfiting it was—it'd been. She felt wrapped up in some unclear, unrelenting, abnormal thing, something she had no idea of; and it was when she'd thought of Margaret, Margaret Ballad, when she'd felt this momentum, push, illicit something, stagger her, make her veins feel as if they'd been poisoned and everything had become too heavy for her to bear, lift, even the dishcloth in the kitchen, that phenomenon; and now she was breaking out in a sweat as if the poison had warmed in her and it was pouring out her skin and out the top of her head, seeping out through her hair, and her hair couldn't clear it, absorb it, or breathe it out, not any of it—her hair was clearly, distinguishably matted down with it, thickly coated in it.

And when she got into the room, her aunt Della's room, she was hoping it would bring her relief, some relief, some comfort; but it didn't. It failed, totally failed, her aunt Della's room.

Now a temperature boiled in her, surely boiled in her, that poison in her, powerful poison, and when Darlene touched her forehead, felt the sweat once again … But this time letting her hand stay there, rest there; it was as if it were the hot radiator in the room she'd touched. Her skin was hissing, making steam, and so now she was frightened, really frightened, scared—fenced in by her fear.

Darlene felt desperate, her mind breaking down, and if she thought the name again, *Margaret, Margaret Ballad,* a new kind of poison would enter her, something more evil, malevolent than before; but this time it would be without limit, well beyond her small means, efforts to suppress it, think to make it stop in its tracks—just stop there.

Darlene looked at the phone as though willing it to ring by the sheer terror and panic in her, that operated in her mind, the direction of fear in her heart, not knowing how to blunt this thing, soften it, this loneliness, this despair in her that was maybe hiding in her all along like a great joker but just now, today, was exposed, had reared its head, had been shut away in her like some blinded monster, deceitful, but all too real, not imagined, but flaming her stomach, her insides, burning through much of her.

She could scream.

Ring! Ring! Ring!

"Lee!"

"Darlene!"

"Oh, oh, Lee!"

"Darlene, what's … what's—"

Darlene's shaking. "Wrong? Wrong, n-nothing's wrong, Lee. Nothing. Nothing's—"

"But you … you, how you just—"

"I was startled, I—"

"Startled? S-startled, Darlene? Where are you? Are you now?"

"In … in the kitchen, Lee. In the kitchen. Baby. In …" Her voice had slowed. "I … I put my head down on the kitchen table. On, down on the kitchen table, Lee."

"You were tired? Tired, Darlene? You didn't look—"

"Just for a second, instant, Lee. For a—but I don't know what came over me, Lee.

"I—" Darlene's eyes flashed—"but maybe it was last night. Last night, Lee."

"L-last night, D—"

"What we did last night, and it now, just now caught up with me this … now, now, Lee."

"Ha …," Lee laughed. "Maybe so, Darlene. Could be. A delayed reaction. We really did go at it. We—"

"And when I heard the phone—I didn't know how many times, if, it might've rung, and I didn't want to miss—"

"You know I wouldn't hang up, Darlene. I'd wait."

"Oh, no, no, not you, Lee. Hang up? Oh, oh no, Lee, no, not you, baby."

"Only if I thought you were in the bathroom. Had gone to the bathroom would I. Hang up. Then I'd call you—"

"Right back. B-but I didn't want to take the chance. A chance. Since … since I said, I didn't know how many times … and I didn't want to miss your call." Pause.

"Tired, huh?"

"Yes, Lee."

"Yes, it was some night, last night. Some—"

"And now I'm up on my feet, and I can get, do the dishes now. Wash them."

"No, if you're tired, Darlene. You can let the dishes—"

"Wait? Wait, Lee?"

"Sure."

"No. No. You know me better than that. I put my apron on as ... as soon as I came into the kitchen. As soon as you left."

"Oh, by the way, Darlene, I'm going to drop by the house before I go to work. I forgot the cancelled check Mr. Kelly wants to look at, even though he says there's no rush. I thought I'd drop it by his office during lunch. Drive over there."

"Y-yes, Lee, the sooner the better, Lee."

"So I'll do that, just—"

"Are you used to the For Sale sign in the yard, Lee, of the house, Lee, yet?"

"It still, well ... thought we'd live in this house much longer than—"

"Well, have to go, Lee. The dishes are staring at me, baby. Waiting."

"Ha."

Darlene was shaking again.

"Now you turn in early now if you're tired, Darlene."

"I—"

"Promise, Darlene?"

"Promise, Lee. Promise."

"Lee ... Lee ..."

"Yes, yes, Darlene?"

Darlene was shaking badly.

"It ... it was just our house. Mr. Kelly saying it'll be off the market, sold in no time, Lee."

"Oh."

"And, oh, don't worry about me. You gave me a second ... second wind. My head's been cleared. I'm going to do Mrs. Arthur's dress tonight. Start on it. Surprise her, Lee."

"I bet you will, Darlene."

"The design I have in mind. The pattern, Lee. Oh ..."

"Ha."

"Good night."

"Good night, Darlene. See you in the morning. First thing."

Darlene waited for Lee to hang up the phone, and when he did, it's when she slammed the phone down.

"Oh, what now? What now!"

It was worse now, more intense than what it'd been before. This thing, this craziness she was feeling, that was controlling her. She hadn't thought of Margaret, she thought, Margaret Ballad. Not once. Not once. Not once! And now she looked at the bed, and she thought of something she'd never do, never think to do, but did now. She did now.

"It ... it would be sacrilege to ... to ..."

But she had to be saved. Darlene felt she had to be saved, and it's when she put her head on Della's bed, had bent over her body and put her head down on Della's bed as if it were the ground and she was listening for sounds from it like heartbeats drumming, a human heart.

"Oh, Aunt Della. Aunt Della."

And now Darlene's body slid onto Della's bed, on top the pretty-looking comforter, and her head rested on top the pillow at the top of the bed.

"Why am I so lonely, Aunt Della? Why am I so lonely, and ... But I'm in your house, Aunt Della. And I'm happy, Aunt Della. But I'm happy, aren't I? Aren't I, Aunt Della? Aren't I?"

Darlene's eyes are shut.

Her life was so full, always, but now felt empty. She'd brag, say she was the best seamstress, dressmaker—whatever title she'd give herself—in Myles Day City once her aunt Della retired from sewing. There was no doubt in her mind, whatsoever. But it didn't seem important to say now—*I am the best dressmaker in Myles Day City*—to make the boast. It wasn't enough to sustain her, to carry her through the day, to assert the feeling the day was hers, that she, Darlene Winston, owned it. For now she didn't feel that way. She'd lost something, some chink in her armor and didn't know what it was.

"Aunt Della. My whole life was Aunt Della. It was you, Aunt Della, and then ... then ... I didn't know it. I love Lee, Lee, but you're the only family ... family, Aunt Della. It's family, Aunt Della—you're only family I had before you died."

When Darlene opened her eyes, she was on top Della's bed, but she couldn't get up. She couldn't get up, she was too tired physically. She was too tired. Drained. And her mind felt as tired as her body. It felt as drained, as exhausted, so she couldn't move. Her body and mind felt locked in inertia. She could barely move her eyes, she thought—but not her limbs. And if she had to get up to go to the bathroom, she didn't know what might happen. She was an invalid. She was an invalid.

What would she do if she had to go to the bathroom? Darlene thought on top the bed. *What? What? What!*

*   *   *

Lee felt good about himself. Why shouldn't he? he thought. He and Darlene were hitting it off great now. The house, it looked like it would be sold any day now, Mr. Kelly told him. He was just checking the credit background on this one person whom he was certain was going to be the lucky buyer, as he'd put it. But it wasn't just that. He and Darlene, yes, they were really having fun, a great time at it. Packing their belongings together, her helping him, going back and forth between the houses in the van (okay, it was just that one time, but who cares, Lee thought). And their sex the other night in the house was as good as it gets, as good as he could remember in all their years of marriage. And he thought Darlene, in the house, Aunt Della's house, the first time they had sex, initially, would be timid, modest, like what she was yesterday when he brought the subject up about the previous night, when she cautioned them they were in *Aunt Della's house.*

Lee laughed aloud. He was in the car, on the way to the house.

No, he didn't expect Darlene to be as wild as she was the first night they had sex in Aunt Della's house, not initially, not right away (to have the orgasms she had); but she was, she most definitely was. The house, then, was a good thing. He was disgusted by everything when it happened, shocked by Margaret and Royal's sudden actions, for he knew he mustn't forget Royal, but disgusted by Darlene, the greed in her eyes that Saturday evening; he had to get out the house, go out to the back porch and practically smoke his brains out, cigarette after cigarette until he undid his emotions, unknot them enough so that he could look at Darlene again, get back in the kitchen with her, be her husband, remember those days when …

"Oh well. I bet Darlene's made me breakfast. No doubt about it. Darlene's preparing breakfast for me. It's why I've given myself time. Some extra time before I go to the shop this morning. Hash browns sound good. Awfully good for the appetite I have this morning."

When Lee opened the house's front door, he sniffed the air. He was disappointed.

"D-Darlene hasn't cooked any … I …"

Then he brightened, for Darlene said, Lee thought, she was tired last night, and then said she wasn't, and maybe she got carried away with Mrs. Arthur's dress and worked late into the morning, something she'd often do.

Maybe it might be better, he thought, if he tiptoed through the house. After all, it was 7:05 a.m. (he had to be at work at 8:30 a.m.). He laughed to himself. He was quiet enough, a thin-framed but tall person like himself— how much noise could his body make anyway, possibly make? Lee laughed.

With the quietude of the kitchen and no food smells emanating from it, Lee looked up to the staircase. He made his entry onto the staircase, moving stealthily, up it, light-footedly. He looked down the hallway. He wasn't going to awaken Darlene if she was sleeping; he was just going to get the cancelled check he'd come for (it regarded credit too) for Ed Kelly (he knew where it was) and exit the house without waking Darlene and then, later, call her from the job.

Lee walked into their bedroom.

"D-Darlene. D-Darlene's not here. D-Darlene's not here."

Now this turn of events threw him off stride, out of balance.

"Maybe she's in the bathroom."

But how could she be? The door was open, and I didn't hear ... when I just came down the ...

This was really unexpected, Lee thought. Really. And now the house felt so still, so quiet. It was 7:05 a.m., 7:06 a.m. in the morning, but the house felt as dead as a doornail, like there was no energy in it, was sapped of it.

Lee looked over at Darlene's sewing machine and saw the cover was on it. What does that mean? What does that mean? Nothing, nothing. Nothing. Nothing at all. And now for the first time, suddenly, he felt scared, frightened, as if he'd come into the house, stumbled upon something, fell into something bad, awful. It just exasperated him like that, the thought, the—

"Aunt Della's room. Aunt Della's room. Darlene has to be ... But what ... what—"

Lee ran right away.

When he got into Della's room, he stopped, abruptly. He was relieved, but—

"What are you, why are you lying on Aunt Della's bed, Darlene?" he whispered to himself. "Why—in, in your clothes, Darlene? Clothes you had on from yester—"

He went over to the bed. He had to disturb her. Awaken her. He had to. She was lying on Aunt Della's bed. For him, Lee, it felt sacrilegious—objectionable.

He just lay his hand gently atop her forehead and whispered, "Darlene, Darlene. Darlene, wake up. Wake up, Darlene. You … you're on Aunt Della's—"

"Lee! Lee!"

Her eyes had snapped open. She grabbed Lee, and she began crying, crying as hard, bitterly as Lee had ever seen anyone in his life cry; and he held Darlene, just held onto her as strongly as he could and thought, *Darlene's grieving. Finally grieving for Aunt Della.*

Lee had gone off to the bathroom. He was back in the bedroom.

"T-thank you, Lee. Thank you."

Lee handed Darlene the wet washcloth. He was holding a towel. Darlene was washing her tears from her face. Lee handed her the towel.

"Thank you, Lee. Thank you."

Darlene did the same with the towel, wiped her face clean with it. And then, suddenly, startled, she said, "I'm on Aunt Della's bed. I'm on Aunt Della's bed!"

And she tried to move, but Lee could see she was weak, unable to.

"I have to get off Aunt Della's bed, Lee. I—"

"Let me help you, Darlene."

Helping her, Lee held Darlene around the waist with one arm and then moved Darlene over to the chair by the bed. She sat.

"Are … are you comfortable?"

"Yes. Yes, Lee. Yes, I am."

Lee stood looking at her with his arms crossed. Her eyes were a bloody red. It was from the crying, the likes of which Lee had never seen before, never seen crying like that, as raw or primal as that—something he'd never forget.

"D-do you feel better, Darlene?"

"Yes."

"Are you sure?"

"Yes."

He looked into her eyes, and she didn't appear in any way embarrassed or ashamed by what had happened. He was sure he saw that much in Darlene's light-brown eyes.

"Lee ..."

Darlene handed the towel back to him.

"I'll—"

"No, I'll take them back to—"

"No, Darlene, you sit here. Relax. Let your—"

"I want to brush my hair, Lee."

"But you don't—"

"And my teeth. Brush my teeth. I feel better. I can make it to the bathroom and back. I want to brush my hair. Brush my teeth," Darlene said, repeating herself. She pushed herself up from the chair. She wobbled briefly.

"No, Darlene. No. I insist. I—"

"Let me try, Lee. L-let me try."

Lee shook his head.

"Please. Please. I want to go to the bathroom and brush my hair. Brush my teeth."

Darlene reached for the towel. Lee handed it to her. She smiled at him when he did. He smiled back. She walked past him, and he did feel, now, as if Darlene could make it to the bathroom and back to the bedroom on her own—without his help.

He was sitting in the chair when Darlene got back. He hopped out the chair. He didn't know what he'd been thinking while she was away in the bathroom.

"Y-you look better, Darlene."

"I ... I feel better, Lee. I do, baby."

He didn't know what that meant, relatively speaking, what to make of it. He took Darlene's hand, and she sat back down in the chair as he stood and looked at her and saw some faint sign of her old self spring back.

Darlene looked up at him, and her eyes were blood red, only, Lee didn't notice them now. It's like they'd become a part of a permanent landscape, for it was a different look he saw on Darlene's face, and it wasn't his imagination, nothing of the kind—it was Darlene's face, what he saw.

"I ... I don't know how I got in here last night, Lee." Darlene repositioned her shoulders. "I don't know, Lee. I ... I just remember being down in the kitchen, washing the, I ... yes, I was about to wash the dishes, Lee, the dishes,

Lee, when I felt … it was horrible, horrible. Just horrible, the pain I felt. It was horrible. J-just horrible." Pause. "And … and then you woke me, Lee. Your phone call. I heard your voice. And then you woke me, Lee. The phone. I'm … I'm repeating, beginning to—"

"But now you're all right? All right, Darlene? Feel … feel better. R-right?"

"Yes. Uh, yes, fine, Lee. Fine, baby."

Darlene's body hardened.

"It's … it's the first time I've cried, really cried since Aunt Della's death. Not at its sudden impact, when I found Aunt Della, emotionally, but … but since … Isn't it, Lee? Isn't it?"

"Yes. Uh, yes. Yes, it is, Darlene. First time."

"I really cried."

"Today."

"Today, Lee."

"I, it was something … I was wondering when you were really going to cry, Darlene. Grieve."

"You were? I … I didn't know that, Lee."

"I did, Darlene."

"Everybody but me, Lee. But me, Lee."

Lee nodded his head.

"I … I don't know why," Darlene said disgustedly. "I don't, Lee."

Lee wasn't going to act like an amateur psychologist. He didn't know everything there was to know about grieving, something so personal. He had no theory, no smart, quick answer, no axiom—he was just glad Darlene had acknowledged what he knew all along.

"Today, this morning I cried, Lee. I cried, Lee. Actually—finally cried."

Darlene's head dropped, and then it was raised.

"But … but that's not all, Lee. When I went into the bathroom, had I thought about it last night, last—I don't know. But … but it was in me. It was in me, Lee. Inside me, and I don't know how it … not unless it's what I was thinking about last night, what must've driven me, drove me up here last night, Lee. B-because I was thinking of family. Family, Lee."

"Y-you and me, Darlene? You and—"

"Yes, yes. B-but more, but more than that, Lee. More than that …"

"Aunt Della, Uncle Frank?"

"Yes. Yes. I love you, Lee."

"Thanks, Darlene. Thanks. I … I always love to hear you say you love me—but I … I know what you're saying, Darlene. What … what you're talking about. Getting at, Darlene."

"We go so far back, Lee. Don't we, Lee?"

"Yes, Darlene. We do."

"You know everything. Practically everything. It-it's what's so good about us, Lee, our relationship, baby."

"I know your hurts. Your pains. What makes you happy. What makes you sad."

"Then you understand what I mean when I say 'family'—yes, of course you do, Lee. Wasn't I just listening? Wasn't I, to my own words? To myself. What I just said? Aunt Della, Uncle Frank and … and Margaret too."

"M-Margaret? Margaret, D-Darlene?"

"Yes, yes, Lee, Margaret, Margaret too. Don't you see, Lee? Don't you see?"

No, I don't see, Lee thought. *No, I don't, Darlene. No, I don't! Not in a million years do I! You're not going to hurt Margaret again! You're not. I won't let you!*

"Y-you see, I want to see Margaret, Lee. See, I—"

"No! No! No, Darlene! No!"

"But—"

"Listen to me. Listen to me, Darlene. This time. This time. You've done enough to hurt Margaret. You've done enough … enough to hurt her in your lifetime!"

"I … I have, haven't I? Haven't I?" Darlene said softly, reasonably.

"You have, Darlene. You, you … yes you have."

"In my lifetime."

"You have the house, Darlene. What else do you want? Want to have? Want!"

"I'm not happy. I … I thought I'd be happy, Lee, but—"

"The world doesn't revolve around you, Darlene. Stop or … or go, or … or … I know I've been guilty as anybody, as … as everyone else. Aunt … Aunt Della, Uncle Frank, but the world doesn't revolve around you. You just can't destroy people, continue to destroy Margaret and Royal and—I won't let you. I won't let you do it, Darlene. Not under any circumstance stand,

stand by and let you do it this time, Darlene. I'm putting my foot down this time, Darlene!"

"I deserve that. I know. I deserve all those words. W-what you said, just said, Lee."

"I'm … I'm sorry, Darlene. But I had to tell … tell …"

"The truth. You had to, Lee. I forced you to."

Pause.

"But it doesn't change anything for me or … or for Margaret either, because we are family, Lee. We are family. The Ballads and the Dawsons. We were raised in this house. The same house. Here, Lee. Here. By … by the same people, two people, Lee: Uncle Frank and Aunt Della. The two people we love, Lee. It doesn't change anything."

Lee paused, for he was about to say something, counter Darlene, but either he didn't want to or couldn't. He couldn't string together words that would do anything. He looked at his watch (the beautiful watch his aunt Della bought him for Christmas; every day he kissed it reverently and thanked her). Then he looked at Darlene. *She needs me. Darlene does need me*, he thought.

Lee walked over to the phone, picked it up, and began dialing it.

"Oh, good morning, Mr. Baker. Yes, sir. Uh, sorry for the short notice, and I know it's Monday morning, not … not a good … But a family emergency arose, uh, just came up. Family, and I won't be into work today. Yes, thank you for your concern. But, oh yes, I'll be in tomorrow. Sorry. Sorry. Yes, thank you so much, Mr. Baker. See you tomorrow, sir. Yes. Yes."

Lee took Darlene's hand.

"I'm going to fix you breakfast since I'm going to be around the house all day."

Darlene, again, struggled to her feet.

"I … I want to take a bath, Lee."

"You do what you want. Wish, Darlene."

Pause.

"Just let me know when you're out the bathroom, so you can come down for breakfast."

"When, last night, when you said you were coming by the house for the check for Mr. Kelley, I was going to—"

"Have breakfast waiting for me this morning. On the kitchen table. When I came in."

"Yes, Lee."

Lee was holding on tightly to Darlene.

"It's what I was thinking in the car, on the way over."

"You know me, Lee."

"Ha. We know each other, Darlene."

Margaret was rushing for the phone. It was ringing. She was already irritated by her job. She had a team of eight bookkeepers she currently supervised; she'd gotten a promotion, and International Retailers was switching over its computer system, a total overhaul, and there were manuals in both her hands, and here she was rushing to the phone while just getting in the apartment from work, and she could kick the teeth out the phone if it had teeth to kick.

"Hello!"

"Oh, uh ... sorry, sorry, Margaret, I—"

"Lee!"

"Yes, uh, it's me. It's me, all right, Margaret. Me, Lee."

"Oh, sorry, sorry, Lee. I didn't mean to yell at you when I answered the phone."

"A bad day? Day at work?"

"Yes. Yes, you can say that again," Margaret said, hunting for somewhere where she could lay down her newly acquired manuals. The telephone's extension cord let her extend it as far as the kitchen table.

Next to Royal's school books was where the manuals wound up.

"I ... I didn't go to work today, Margaret. To the print shop. I've been home with Darlene. All day. From, since, uh, uh, early this morning."

"Darlene ... she, Darlene's all right, all ... is-isn't she, Lee?"

"I ... I don't know. I don't know, Margaret."

Margaret's hand covered her mouth. "What's wrong, Lee? Wrong with Darlene?"

"Margaret, please, please don't get angry with me, don't, please, don't—"

"Lee, I just explained, told you it was the job. I shouldn't've answered the phone like that. I never have, but I was so annoyed, frustrated by—"

"Darlene wants to see you, Margaret."

Margaret pulled the phone off her ear and stared at it and then put it back to her ear.

"S-see me? D-did you just say, did I just hear you say D-Darlene wants to see me!"

"I … I don't understand it either, Margaret. All day … B-but she wants to see you, Margaret."

"And … and I'm supposed to do what? Say what!"

"I don't know. I don't … I have no idea. B-but this morning I was, I … I put, I guess I put my foot down, tried to Margaret. At least. She's hurt you enough, Margaret. Darlene's hurt you enough. Royal too. But of course, mostly you, Margaret.

"I told her the world doesn't revolve—w-we've all catered to her, me, Aunt Della, Uncle Frank … her mother dying, Mrs. Dawson, and her father running off. She's always felt lost, abandoned, I … I don't know, Margaret. I … what do I know."

"No, Lee. No. This will never work. Tell Darlene no, I—see her? No, Lee. Right now Darlene's the last person I want to see. The—"

"S-she's been dragging all day. All day long, Margaret. All around the house. I … I've never seen her like this. So … so determined. All day. All day—"

"What about the house?" Margaret said sarcastically. "Her precious house?"

"I … I said what I said, Margaret. I meant what I said."

"No, I won't see her. Not under any circumstances. Not under—"

"It's—this morning when I came into the house, I didn't stay in the house last night, but our house—it's … it's up for sale you … B-but when I came into the house on … on my way to the shop, she was upstairs on … on Aunt Della's bed. D—"

"Momma's bed? Momma's—but why! Why would she lie, be on Momma's bed!"

"S-she didn't know why. Answer me why. She … she couldn't remember, Margaret, remember how she got upstairs, to lie on Aunt Della's bed. I … I woke her. I … then she cried, Margaret. Darlene finally cried … cried since Aunt Della died. I mean she … I've … I've never seen anything—it was hysterical. Hysterical. I—"

"But that's Darlene, Lee. The actor. There's always drama, great drama. Theatrics. Hysteria—"

"No, I know real from fake ... fake. I do, Margaret. I do."

Margaret shut her eyes, and her hand was at her mouth again, blocking it.

"There's something going on, Margaret. With Darlene, Margaret. I mean it. I really mean it. And I don't know what, but there is. I couldn't go to work. I had to call in to the shop. Be with Darlene. I knew she really needed me."

Margaret wished there was a chair by the phone she could sit in. It's what she wished, for she didn't care to move, walk over to the kitchen table. If she was going to slump, she wanted to slump there, at the phone.

"I wanted to help her all day. I wanted to help her ... But she knows what time you get in from work. I was in the kitchen, and she came from upstairs, from her room, where she's been all day since I fixed her breakfast."

"So she's eaten."

"She skipped lunch."

So what? Margaret said to herself. *So what, Lee!*

"I had to talk ... talk her into eating dinner."

"Lee, can't you see? Can't you see that I don't care? I-if she wants to see me, tell her, have her call me!"

"You ... you don't mean that, Margaret. I know you—"

"I do, Lee! I—"

"She won't call you, Margaret. You can't expect Darlene to call you. I'm the only one to call you. Who can do that. The two of us know t-that much, Margaret."

Margaret clenched her fist.

"You're right, Lee. Yes, you're right. Of course you're right."

"Margaret, I wanted, was hoping she'd drop it too. Hoping all day long too, Margaret. But Darlene came down in the kitchen. She's been in her robe since this morning, when she took her bath and said you'd be home. From work. And if I would call you and ask you—"

"If ... if I'd meet her."

"Yes. Then she turned and went back upstairs. So I—"

"Called."

"Yes."

"Yes ... yes ... yes ... yes ..."

"Yes, yes what, Margaret? Yes, yes w—"

"I'll meet Darlene. I'll meet Darlene. I'll meet her, Lee. I'll meet her!"

"At ... at the house, Margaret? At the house?"

"Yes! Yes!"

"At the—"

"Don't say it again, Lee. P-please don't say it again. For ... for I am as ... But ... but it must be with Royal."

"But Darlene wants—"

"It must be with Royal. I don't care what Darlene wants. I walk into my mother and father's house with Royal, or I don't walk in there at all. It's the condition, terms I'm setting, Lee, and Darlene can either take it or leave it, Lee. I don't care. I don't care, Lee."

"Can ... can you wait then, Margaret? Or do you want me to call back? P-prefer I call you back? I'll ... I'll have to go up to Darlene's room. Up to—"

"I'll wait, Lee. I'll wait. Stay on the phone and wait."

"Thank you, Margaret. Thank you. I'll go to the room. Up to the room then."

And it was the first time Margaret felt annoyed with Lee. *Go then! Go!* She wished he was gone! How she wished Lee was gone!

"Please ... please don't hang up, Margaret. Please don't hang up."

Then Margaret could hear Lee hurry off like some animal scampering in the woods, and it felt like her brain would, was going to split open. And now wasn't the time to cry. Now was the time for her to ... But Darlene. Darlene was back in her life. She was letting Darlene back into her life.

And she could hear Lee again, coming down the staircase, carrying himself, his feet fast, moving like a gazelle's in her mother and father's house.

"Margaret ..."—Lee was huffing, puffing—"I'm ... I'm back, Margaret." Lee was huffing, puffing. "Darlene said yes, Margaret. Yes, as long ... as long as you come. As long as you come Royal ... Royal can come too, Margaret. It, it doesn't matter to—"

"Then—"

"B-but not tomorrow, but would it be all right, Thursday. Thursday evening? Eight o'clock Thursday evening, Darlene said."

There she was again, Margaret thought, setting the agenda, the parameters, calling the shots, controlling everything.

"Why not to—"

"I don't know. I don't—"

"If it's so important, that important she see me, why not—"

"Let's not fight her, Margaret."

"Oh no, no, Lee, we must not, mustn't do that. We never want to do that, Lee. Not Darlene. Not Darlene Winston, Lee."

Lee was mum.

"Good night, Lee."

"Margaret, I don't know what this is about, any of this is about, but thank you. Thank ... thank you, Margaret."

"Royal will think this a good idea. I don't—and Royal won't convince me differently. Not at all. I ... I just want it over with, Lee. Like so many things I've ... I've been involved in over the years with Darlene. In ... in our relationship." Pause.

"Good night, Lee."

"Good night, Margaret."

Pause.

"Oh, Margaret, say hello to Royal. Give him m-my best regards."

Royal was pumping gas. The tank was full. Royal looked up at the sky. He felt more like a preacher turned weatherman.

"Hmm ... I wonder what God's up to now."

Yes, it was going to snow. What Myles Day City citizen didn't know that? Royal thought. Not unless they were new to Myles Day, just arrived to its shores and didn't know about the city in November, December, January, February, and March. But if they moved to Myles Day City, they'd better know, because its winters, of course, did not suffer fools lightly.

He'd just come from church after leaving Haverford University. He just liked looking at the church. He didn't have to go in, step in it, even though he did tonight; but he just enjoyed looking at the store-front church, to see how far he'd come and to know it would progress, that there was some kind of linear line, continuum he was a part of. Just being above ground, out in the open, one might say, not in a basement, had done wonders for not only him but the parishioners of Hands of Christ Church too.

Royal was cleaning the car's windshield with the gas station's wooden pole with the rubber wiper at its tip end. That's it, Royal thought, they were always in God's house, but the new church was so clean, so bright. Every day of the week—in his heart—he thanked Mother Ballad. And even though new membership hadn't grown by leaps and bounds, exponentially since occupying the new spot, there'd been seven new church members and more people in attendance to join the regulars for worship, and so that was a positive sign. And those new faces were beginning to worship, pretty much, on a regular basis.

The windshield was spotless.

"It takes time. It takes time. I want it to take time," Royal said, putting the wiper back in the bucket of water. "I don't want to be an overnight hit, wonder," he laughed. "Overnight sensation. Not doing God's work."

Royal was in the new secondhand car he and Margaret just recently bought. He started the engine and pulled the car out the gas station. He felt the heat in the car. He had so much to thank Mother Ballad for, he thought. So much. His toes felt toasty, actually toasty, roasting inside his shoes.

"Come on, snow, I'm ready. New tires too. God and I are on a … uh, let's not get carried away here. Was, uh, I was about to say a 'roll'? I wasn't, no, I … I was too, wasn't I?" Pause.

"Oh well, I feel we are. Most definitely." Royal laughed more. "Thank the Lord!"

Royal was rocked by the news. It hit him as hard as it'd hit Margaret when first hearing it.

"Let … let me sit. Let me sit … sit down, Mag. I … this is too much for me. It's …" Royal sat on the bed.

Margaret was on top the bed, in her work clothes. He'd expected dinner on the table when he walked into the apartment, but when there was none, he walked into the bedroom, and it's when Margaret angled herself to him and told him the news, and he was rocked back solidly on his heels.

It'd happened just now. Just seconds ago.

"And you said? And you said … what? What?"

"Yes, Royal. Yes."

"Y-you said what!" Royal said, looking at Margaret with astonishment.

"Yes."

"You mean y-you want to see Darlene? Meet with Darlene? At the house? At your mother's, Mother ... Mother Ballad's house?"

"Yes."

"I ..." Royal held his head in his hands. "No one expected this."

"No one."

"Not this."

Pause.

"I ... I do pray for both of you," Royal said. "I do pray for reconcilement based on what, I don't know. I don't know, Mag. Based on, maybe, I guess, some common, mutual ground you might find. Realize you have Mother Ballad, Mr. Ballad, Mrs. Dawson being the nucleus. The core. But Darlene, she has the—"

"House. The house now."

"Uh, yes, oh yes, Mag. Darlene has the house. The prize you might—"

"What does Darlene want now?" Margaret said weakly. "My soul?"

"No, she won't get that! Not your soul! And God, God who I know is in heaven, is in heaven, Mag—she's not going to get that! Darlene's not going to get your soul!"

"Y-you'll go with me, won't you, Royal? Won't you?'

"I'll be right there."

Pause.

"How dangerous is she, Mag? J-just how dangerous is she still? Darlene? The-these days?"

"It's what scares me, Royal. Really scares me. And I don't want to fight in Momma's house. Daddy and Momma's house. I've always avoided it at all costs."

"But you might have to take a stand. You might have to fight her. Fight Darlene for the final time. T-to end this thing between you two. Once and for all, Mag."

"I don't want to. I still don't want to."

"But you might have to, Mag. There might not be any other choice open to you."

"Yes."

"You know I ... I've always tried to be charitable when it came to Darlene. But she's been Darlene Winston at every turn. Step along the way. And I—if there was to be reconcilement, I thought she would come to you, Mag, not you go to her. The reverse. That it would be some sign from her of concession, contriteness, her willingness to … to … well yield ground in some civil, uh, symbolic way—sense.

"But you going to your mother's house, it seems she wants, is holding onto her power. Her arrogance, aggressive nature is still intact. Yes, she's holding onto her power. All right."

"But Lee, the way Lee described her. Her to me, Royal."

"How was that, Mag?"

"She seems to be down, Royal. Despondent. Depressed. She seems—"

"God help me. I want to believe it's true. Her feelings, emotions are genuine. I don't want to violate my faith-base, because it is being drawn into question. That … that people can change. Look, j-just look at you and me. Look at, it's what our whole lives are founded, based … based on now."

"But we wanted to change."

"Did … yes, we did … my train of, Mag, I lost my, that quick … I lost my train of … No, I … it's you, Mag. It's you …"

Margaret's face puzzled.

"Yes, it's you. It's always been you. Now I got it back. I got … Darlene feeds off you. Darlene … it's as pleasant, nice—delicate as I can put it. State it. Darlene's—should I say evil. It's in the world. So much out in the world. I speak, preach of evil forces in church every Sunday, from the pulpit, Mag, the forces of good and evil.

"And evil forces feed off good things, Mag. Things which are counter, counterintuitive to its nature. Things that—"

"Why did I agree, Royal? Why did I agree … give in? Give in to Darlene!"

"In your heart … In my heart I want what you want, Mag. But it's not always possible, attainable. It's the revelation, the gospel, the bad news—that you can't always change another person's heart no matter how many prayers you pray or sermons you preach … No matter."

"It feels like the house again."

"It does."

"Eight … eight o'clock Thursday night, Royal."

"It's a good comparison, the house, I mean as far as the anxiety level, Mag. Goes." Royal's rugged handsome face suddenly brightened. "But it was your mother's will we were dealing with then, Mag. Mother Ballad's decision. A decision based on, what we knew was based on goodness and hope, no matter the outcome. But not this, Mag."

"No, not this, Royal."

"This is different. Much, much different."

Pause.

"Mag … you … you must be hungry."

"Yes."

"Let me cook. Cook something for us."

"Go ahead, Royal. Go ahead. I won't stop you."

Royal walked across the floor and then looked back at her.

"She wants your soul this time, Mag. Thursday night."

"But she won't get it."

"Not on your life." Pause. "But, oh, she'll try, Mag. Oh, how Darlene is going to try."

CHAPTER 19

Thursday. February 7.

Margaret was in the backseat of the taxicab. She was on her way to meet Darlene at the house. She was alone in the taxicab, in its backseat. This is how Margaret wanted it: to be alone, by herself, in the taxicab. This felt right to her, sitting in the backseat of the taxicab by herself. She was glad she'd decided to do it this way. She knew how she had, why she had, but she had to believe that some higher power had guided her decision.

She didn't need Royal at the moment. She wanted to feel independent of him. If he'd driven her to the house in the car, there might've been complete silence between them or words laying track over the same emotional network.

I've had enough, she thought. *Royal and I have talked about today enough, until I'm blue in the face and he's blue in the face.* This was the wrong time for this meeting with Darlene anyway. With her job's new demands, this was the wrong time for this meeting. If there ever was a basket case, she was it. All day, between the job's demands, the new computer system to be implemented, and this bigger demand.

Royal would meet her outside the house. It'd been worked out. The only human contact she wanted was with the taxicab driver; and he was as quiet as a clam. On TV, especially movies depicting big cities, cab drivers were talkative entities; but here in Myles Day City, they only talked when talked to, and she wasn't talking to the cab driver, no way! Margaret laughed.

See, if I were in the car with Royal, I ... who am I trying to fool? Why am I ...

I'm glad Mag wanted it this way. We've run out of words. What can I say. The trip to the house would've been brutal. Simply brutal on us, I think. She thought of it, not me. Never would I have thought of it, not in a million years. Thank God though. Thank God. I'm going to need all my strength. All of it after tonight, I think. Lee and I won't be a part of this anyway. In-included in this. We won't take part. Not anywhere near. There's no reason for us to. We'll just be there to pick up the pieces. After the wreck, the wreckage, I'm afraid ... afraid to say.

I don't want to think this way. I don't want to ... But it's how we'll serve them. Our women. The women we love. It's the only reason why we should be there. In the house. In the first place—for the aftermath.

Oh God, how I would like for things to be different tonight. Go differently for them. To have, for me to have such confidence in Margaret and Darlene.

"Lee, Lee, at least I'll get to see Lee. My buddy Lee."

It was eight o'clock.

Margaret and Royal were standing on the house's doorstep.

Royal, it was like he had heartburn. He rang the doorbell.

Angrily, Margaret thought, *Royal has to ring the doorbell for me to go into my mother and father's house.*

"Lee!"

"Royal!"

Pause.

"Margaret!"

"Lee."

"Come in. Come in!"

And as would be expected, they looked at each other as if they hadn't seen one another for all the time, the many days and weeks they actually hadn't.

"Margaret, oh, Margaret, you look wonderful. Wonder ... uh, you too, Royal. You too."

Margaret and Lee hugged.

"Let me take your coats."

Before Royal handed his coat to Lee, they hugged, and the tension was there. They both felt it. Lee compared what he'd felt in Royal's body to what he'd just felt in Margaret's.

Lee was in the coat closet, and as soon he turned, Margaret said, "Where is she, Lee? Darlene?"

"Up, uh, upstairs, Margaret. Upstairs in Aunt Della's room. She's waiting for you. Seems like she's been waiting all day," Lee said ominously.

Margaret straightened herself. "I've been waiting all day too."

"We all have," Royal said.

Margaret turned and looked up the steep staircase. Royal went up to her. He kissed her. Margaret began walking up the staircase as Royal and Lee watched. When she got up on the second landing, it's when she felt her breath leave her.

"Lee, you … you look wonderful, too."

"Uh, thanks, Royal. Thanks. Do … do you want, would you like something to drink, or—"

"No. No, it's all right. Maybe later. All I want to do is talk to you. Right now. Catch up on things. How things are going with you."

"Just fine. J-just fine."

Midway in the hallway, Margaret hesitated.

"Margaret, is that you?"

"Yes. Yes, it is. It's me, Darlene."

Again, silence ensued.

Margaret proceeded forward. She stopped again and then took another breath.

"I'm in Aunt—"

"I know where you are, Darlene."

Was this how it was going to be between them? Margaret thought. Was this how it was going to be? The exchanges? The obvious obviously heightened, heightened to absurdity, pointless contrivance? Is it? Is it!

When they looked at each other, it felt strange on both their parts.

Darlene was sitting in the chair by Della's bed. She stood. Right away Margaret saw Darlene was in slacks; she wasn't in a dress. When was the last time she saw Darlene in slacks? she thought. *I can't remember.* And she didn't look bad or despondent or depressed as if she'd been dragging herself around the house, not the way Lee had described, made her out to be only two days past. She looked like Darlene—except for the dark-blue slacks.

"Thanks for coming, Margaret. For meeting me here at the house. Thank you."

Margaret noticed Darlene looked calm, rational.

Margaret nodded her head.

Then Darlene sat back down in the chair. Margaret crossed over to the window and looked out. She stood there with her back to Darlene.

"Royal ... Royal's downstairs? He came with you?"

"Yes," Margaret said, turning abruptly to Darlene. "It's what I wanted."

"What I agreed on."

Margaret turned her head back to the window.

"I must talk to him too."

For a second time, abruptly, Margaret's head turned to Darlene. "About what?"

"There're things we must discuss. All of us must discuss, Margaret."

"Says who? Says who? You, Darlene?"

"I—"

"I only came because I wanted to get you, finally get you out my system. Once and for all. Get you—"

"B-but that's not what I want, Margaret. That's not what—"

"Why would you? Yes, why would you, Darlene? Royal ... Royal figured you out, evil people like you. Evil people like you feed off people like me. Evil—"

"I know. I know."

Margaret stood there tensely.

"Then you do know. You do know!"

Darlene looked away from Margaret.

"Ha. Don't I know. Don't I?"

"You—"

"We relish it? People like me. Evil people. A person like me relishes it."

"And it's going to end today. Tonight. Now. Because I'm going to stop it. Put an end to it, Darlene. Starting now. Tonight. I'm not going to be a part of your ... your evil game anymore. Yes, yes, it's why I'm here. Royal and I are here. We—"

"R-remember when I walked into this house after my mother, Aunt Nettie died, Margaret?"

Margaret looked at Darlene vaguely.

"Do … do you? I do. I do. When you walked into the room, it's what I thought of," Darlene said, standing. "H-how it must've looked."

And now Margaret felt that strangeness, the awkwardness she had just felt; it's what she saw some twenty odd years ago, but it was Darlene then, entering her mother and father's bedroom.

"Aunt Della, you and Aunt Della were in the room, here in the room. And I had one of my suitcases with me."

"Yes, you did. Y-you insisted you'd carry it upstairs to your room—"

"But I came in this room first. And you and Aunt Della were in the room. Uncle Frank was downstairs. Downstairs doing something as … ha … as usual. He would do."

Margaret couldn't laugh with her. She just couldn't laugh with her. She couldn't bear to laugh with her. What was there to laugh about with her!

"My … my feelings were so mixed. So mixed up. I had a house but lost it—but loved you and Aunt Della and Uncle Frank so much. So much, Margaret. But I still had mixed feelings. W-was ambivalent. My f-feelings. Then. Then."

"I'm going to sit, Darlene. It's what I'm g-going to do, sit … sit down."

Darlene waited for Margaret.

Margaret sat in a chair against the wall, near the radiator.

"I loved you, did you know that, Margaret?"

"Yes."

"When I came to this house. I loved you in the beginning. Before I lived here, we, I looked forward to being with you so much. Living here. Aunt Della and Momma were real sisters. I mean real sisters."

"You don't have to tell me that, Darlene. They, Momma and Aunt Nettie, were inseparable," Margaret said twisting herself in the chair.

"Inseparable. They were. They were. Inseparable, Margaret. Inseparable."

If Darlene said that word "inseparable" one more time, Margaret felt as if she could strangle her. Literally strangle her.

"Something we were, because of Momma and Aunt Della—inseparable. We had that kind of relationship too. When we were small."

Pause.

"I loved you, until I began to compete against you."

Margaret hadn't anticipated this kind of honesty from Darlene. But then again, she thought, Darlene was always honest, forthright; she'd never hidden her feelings toward her, about her, but this had some kind of positivity to it, some kind of confession shaping it.

"What, are you confessing to me, Darlene? Making some … some kind of confession?"

Darlene crossed her leg.

"Do you ever think of me, Margaret?"

"I … I, why should I—I wouldn't give you the satisfaction of knowing, of knowing, even if I did. If I did or not."

"You do, don't you? Don't you? Because I know I think of you. I think of you all the time."

She was taking the lead, initiative, and Margaret didn't know why. *Why?* She thought. *What kind of evil, pernicious game are you playing now, Darlene? With me? How have you plotted this one out? Wired this thing? To what end? To what consequence, proportion? How deep was going to be the wound? This time? This time, Darlene?*

"You do, Margaret. Think of—"

"You have the house."

"Oh yes, the house. The house," Darlene said matter-of-factly. "I knew I'd get the house."

"So did I."

"But I never thought I'd get it through you, but when I did …"

"What? What?"

"What …?"

"Don't, please don't make this any harder, any more difficult than what it is, this already is. Me meeting with you. Here. Having me come upstairs into Momma's room, bedroom and—"

"I thought it was going to make me happy. The house. That's all. That's all, Margaret. All … all I'm saying. The house."

Margaret leaned forward in the chair. "And it, and what, it hasn't?"

"No."

"Oh … because now … now I can see what you're up to, Darlene. You've won everything, and so … so now that there's nothing more to win, you think you can beat, try beating me up again," Margaret said, charging to her feet. "Well, no thanks. No thanks!"

Margaret was turning to leave the room.

"Margaret, Margaret, you're the only family I have. And ... and I'm the only family you ... you have."

Margaret stopped short.

"You're my family, Margaret. You're my family, Margaret."

Margaret held her hands up to her face, and she turned, and she saw a mix of anguish and sincerity on Darlene's face—a mix of pain and hope.

"You ... you are family. W-we are family, aren't we? After all, after all, are ... aren't we? Aren't we?"

Margaret nodded her head.

"Happy. Happy. I haven't been happy either. Not since Momma died. Deep down inside ... inside—I ... I've had my moments too. I ... no, no, I'm not going to make myself so vulnerable in front of you. Share them. T-trade my emotions with you. Mine, mine with yours. No, no ... in front of you—I ... I refuse to. I refuse to, Darlene!"

"I don't care, Margaret. I don't care what you think," Darlene said, fighting back tears. "I love you. I love you. There's something to love in me. There's—Lee loves me. Aunt, Aunt Della loved me. Uncle, Uncle Frank. There's some good in me. I'm loyal, I'm—"

"I don't want to find out, Darlene. I just want to—"

"Please, Margaret! Please, Margaret! Please!"

Darlene ran to Margaret and fell down on the floor at her feet.

"Please! Please!"

"Get up, Darlene! Get up, Darlene! Get up! Please get up!"

"No! No!"

Darlene looked up to Margaret.

"Get up ..."

"I can't, Margaret. I ... I can't ..."

Margaret felt the tears run down her face, and she looked up at the ceiling and then down at Darlene.

"Then ... then I'll help you up, Darlene. I'll help you up."

Margaret reached down, and she took Darlene's hand and then helped her up to her feet. With her arm around Darlene's waist, Margaret helped Darlene over to her chair. When Darlene sat, she let loose with a torrent of tears. Margaret handed her tissues out the box, tissues still left there from the tissue box Della drew her tissues from.

"Oh … oh … I'm … I'm so embarrassed, Margaret. I'm … I'm so embarrassed."

"You needn't be. You needn't be, Darlene."

"I … I feel so weak. My …"

"You charged me. Charged at me."

"Used up the last energy I …" Darlene began crying again. "I've … I've been so hateful. So hateful toward you, Margaret. I know my sins. I … I …"

"Here …"

Margaret handed Darlene another tissue.

"Y-yes, thank you. Thank you."

Margaret walked back over to the chair and then sat. Darlene kept dabbing at her eyes with the tissue.

"I want you back in my life. B-back in my life." Darlene stood. "As a cousin. As a cousin—b-but mostly as a friend, Margaret."

"Momma said you were needy. She said Daddy said, he first called it hungry, hungry for love, then, that you starved for it."

"I don't know. I don't know … may-maybe I never really learned how to love. N-not unless I controlled people. I don't know, Margaret. I … I just don't know."

"I do love you, Darlene. In what way, why, how, I haven't been able to figure that out either. It's a, still a mystery to me. But as you said, we did have a time. Momma knew it. Daddy and Aunt Nettie—well they knew of it too. Saw it. Saw it when they were alive. But not Royal or—"

"Lee."

"No. They didn't know those times. We had. I haven't shared them with Royal."

"Nor … nor I with Lee, Margaret," Darlene said, her eyes bloodshot.

"They didn't know the fun we had together. The dolls. The trips in Daddy's car. The trips we'd take. To the amusement parks in Myles Day. The fairs in Myles Day. D-during the summer."

"No. No. R-riding in the backseat of Uncle Frank's car. Holding hands. Pretending we were sisters, not cousins, Margaret, but sisters. Al-always sisters. Always pretending."

"After all, we were the only children in the family. The two families. No brothers or sisters. It … it was just the two of us. We just had each other."

"It's what it is now, Margaret. It's what it is now—just you and me."

"Yes."

"You've been the better sister. The better cousin. The better friend. I … I was as responsible for Detroit as anyone."

"Detroit …"

"I drove you from this house. Out of this house."

"You didn't create Royal."

"No."

"I was the one who brought Royal into my life."

"And … and look what he's done for you, Margaret."

"Yes. But now it's coequal. It's balanced now. It's no longer lopsided."

"What did he think about … about our meeting?"

"He prays for you. Ha," Margaret laughed nervously. "R-Royal prays for everyone. Everybody. But he expects me to come down those stairs outside, in the hallway—how can, shall I put it, Darlene …?"

Darlene stood.

"I feel better."

"So do I."

"I want to go downstairs, Margaret. If … if it's all right with you."

"Yes, yes, we can do that, Darlene."

Royal was in midsentence, when he stopped, altogether stopped. Lee looked back over his shoulder. Then they just looked at each other, neither blinking, making the effort to blink, but preparing themselves.

Margaret and Darlene walked into the living room hand in hand. The tears were still there, in their eyes, lingering and evident.

"Would you stand, Royal …"

"S-stand?"

Margaret gestured to him that he should stand.

"Stand. Stand, yes … stand, Darlene."

Darlene looked at Margaret and then let go of her hand. She walked over to Royal and then kissed his cheek.

"Please forgive me, Royal. Please forgive me for the past, what I've done, what I—"

"Why, why if you want to kiss the other cheek, you may. You may, Darlene. Go right ahead. Straight ahead!"

"No, one cheek is enough, Royal. I might get jealous!"

Lee, Royal, and Darlene laughed.

"Oh, Darlene! Darlene!" Lee said, hugging Darlene to him.

"Mag ..."

Royal and Margaret hugged.

"I ... I just don't know. I just don't know. I ... I didn't expect this. Not this!"

"We're going to try, aren't we, Darlene? Aren't we?"

"Yes, Margaret."

Margaret walked over to Darlene and took her hand again. "We want to try so badly. So badly."

"How did it happen, Mag? How in the world—how did it happen?"

"I don't know, Royal. It just did."

"Amazing," Royal said, shaking his head. "By the grace of God. By the grace of God. Amazing."

"You said common ground, and ..."

"It's, it's nine forty. Now nine forty. In one hour and forty minutes, a miracle happened. Took place in the world. Well at least in Miles Day City. At 38 Eckert Street."

"Yes."

"There's still a lot of work ahead for the two of you."

"Darlene and I know that, Royal."

"For me, forgiving her, our relationship ... it was easy. I love her as a human being, as one Christian to another. Yes, as a person. But you want more."

"I need more."

"Both of you do."

Pause.

"C-can you love Darlene, Mag?"

"I do love her, Royal," Margaret said point-blank.

"Oh happy day!"

"I sensed it was going to be different for us the moment I walked in the room. There was something ... I didn't want to acknowledge it. I tried resisting it—f-fighting it. I was guarded. After all, I was dealing with Darlene. But …"

"And it all happened in Mother Ballad's bedroom."

"Momma's bedroom. Yes, Royal."

"Yes, Mag. Your mother's bedroom."

Warily, Margaret was looking at Royal. Royal looked back at her, winked, and hummed another spiritual, not on the order of "Oh Happy Day" but something less lively, upbeat, but lyrical, soulful. The pitch was square center, dead-on. Royal really had a good sense of pitch and rhythm.

"Darlene, your throat's still dry?"

"Yes, Lee."

They hadn't left the living room.

"I'll get you some water."

When Lee got back in the living room with the glass of water, he handed it to Darlene.

"Darlene, you look beautiful."

"Thanks, Lee."

Darlene wasn't sitting on her uncle Frank's sofa but next to Lee, on the larger one. Lee didn't know if it was done consciously or unconsciously by her; right now, it didn't matter—he didn't care.

"Mmm … that's better."

"Everything's better. Everything," Lee said in a much broader context.

"I couldn't tell you, Lee. I'm sorry," Darlene said, taking his hand. "I'd never done anything like this before. Ask for someone's forgiveness—not even you, with you, Lee. E-even after all these years of marriage. I was so scared, baby. About everything, Lee."

Lee squeezed her hand.

"When you said family the other—"

"I meant it, Lee. I wanted Margaret back in my life. And I couldn't see how I could change. But now I know I can. I-I just have to prove it t-to myself. And to everyone else, Lee."

Lee squeezed her hand again, but he was still jumpy, on edge. They sat there as Darlene drank more water out the glass. Lee hoped Darlene didn't feel the tautness extant in his hand.

"Darlene, I … I need a smoke, Darlene."

Darlene looked at him.

"You … I, uh, you don't mind do, do you, Darlene?"

"No, no not at all, Lee."

"Okay then." Lee stood. I'll—"

"Lee, you don't have to go outside, why don't you smoke in the house. Here in the house."

"In the house?"

Darlene paused as if she couldn't quite believe what she'd just said herself.

"Yes, in—"

"Your house?"

"Our house, Lee. Our—"

"Aunt … Aunt Della's house?"

"Yes, Lee, Aunt Della's house, I—"

"Let's not move too fast on this, Darlene. Let … I'll get my coat. Hat. Go out in the back. Backyard. I … I don't, I couldn't do that. Smoke in Aunt Della's house. Uh-uh, not that, Darlene."

When Lee came back into the house, Darlene was in the kitchen. Lee began taking off his jacket.

"Ha. I feel better, a whole lot better, D—"

"I'm going to call Margaret, Lee."

"Mar—"

"You … do you think it's all right?"

Lee froze up.

"I—"

"They, she and Royal should be home by now."

Lee removed his coat.

"You, I don't think you should rush things, Darlene. Move too fast, Darlene."

"Am I, Lee? Am I?"

"It's what it seems, sounds like you're doing. Darlene. T-to me."

"But I have an idea, Lee. Something I want to ask you first, consult with you about first. And then discuss it with Margaret."

"Uh, that's fine, Darlene. Fine with me. But it can't, uh, can't wait? Wait until, say tomorrow? Call Margaret tomorrow, Darlene?"

"Oh yes, you're right, right, Lee. You're right. Of course you're right."

"Uh, I'm gonna hang up my coat, o-okay, Darlene?"

"Oh … right, Lee. Right, baby."

Lee had hung his coat. Only by now he was questioning himself, big time. *What am I doing, trying to change her? The woman I love? Take the passion, life, energy out of her, the enthusiasm out her now that it seems so positive, focused in a positive way? I don't need to be in on everything. Kingpin. I don't need that—never have. I want Darlene to be who she is, who she's always been, not some wimp, but Darlene, Darlene, Darlene Winston!*

"Darlene …"

"Yes, Lee?"

Now Lee was in the kitchen.

"They should definitely be home by now, uh, by now, Royal and Margaret. In the apartment. It's been a little while. Yes, a little while now." Lee glanced at his watch.

"Go, go and call her, and whatever you want to do, it's okay with me. Always been … always will be. I'm just going to run upstairs. Now I have to use the bathroom. And you know I prefer the one upstairs. Never could figure out why. Why I—"

"Oh, Lee."

"Ha."

Ring.

"Margaret."

"D-Darlene?"

"S-sorry, but I had to call, Margaret."

"Oh."

Royal was at the kitchen table. Margaret frowned at him and then shrugged her shoulders as if to say she didn't know what Darlene wanted either.

"I, now I feel stupid that I called."

"No, don't feel that. That way, Darlene."

"Lee, Lee said I might be rushing things."

"Between you and me?"

"Yes."

Pause.

"Trying to make up for lost time."

"We both know we can't do that, Darlene."

"Yes, of course, Margaret. Of course, of course not."

Pause.

"It's just … just that I was hit by this, struck—can you come by … by again tomorrow evening? The house, Margaret?"

"The … Darlene, I'm under a tremendous amount of pressure on the job now. I'm a supervisor now, uh, these days. I have people under me, and we're switching over to a new accounting system. Computer based, and … I'm sorry, to answer your question. No, Darlene. I have manuals that I have to—"

"I understand, Margaret. I … I understand …"

"But what … what about Saturday? I mean it's just one day away, D—"

"Saturday … Saturday would be fine. Just fine, Margaret."

"In the afternoon."

"Twelve … twelve o'clock?"

"Twelve o'clock it is."

"Twelve it is. See you then, Margaret."

"O-okay, Darlene."

Margaret hung up the phone.

"I—"

"I heard you, Mag. Twelve o'clock Saturday." Royal frowned. "I hope Darlene's not rushing things. Between you two."

"It's what Lee said."

"Oh."

"Did Darlene say—"

"You know, I didn't even ask her why she wants me by the house Saturday."

"Maybe Darlene should slow down a bit."

"If we're going to have a really honest, open relationship, I have to accept Darlene for who she is. What she is."

"W-warts and all, Mag. Ha."

"On all levels, Royal."

CHAPTER 20

Saturday. One fifteen.

Margaret and Darlene had had lunch. Darlene had surprised her. They were seated at the kitchen table. They were the only ones in the house.

"Full, Margaret?"

"Full, Darlene."

"Food and talk."

Margaret laughed at Darlene's remark. "Yes, both."

Then Darlene began clearing the kitchen table. When she'd finished, she stood in front of Margaret.

"Are you ready, Margaret?"

It sounded like an invitation to a great adventure to Margaret. One she was more than open for.

"Of course, Darlene. Of—"

"Up to Aunt Della's room we must go!"

"Right!"

When they got into Della's room, Darlene's energy flagged somewhat. Margaret saw it too.

"Margaret …"

"Yes."

They were in the middle of the room.

"How do I say this … I thought I never would. I really thought I never would," Darlene said in a rather faraway voice. "I was going to turn this room, Aunt Della's room into a monument. A shrine for Aunt Della, and I know now she wouldn't want me to ... to do that."

"Not Momma, Darlene."

"Not at all, Margaret."

Darlene looked around the room, and so Margaret followed her lead, and what they were looking at was old but beautiful furniture, beautiful by its own standards, by its sheen, finish, patina—beautiful by its provenance and how it'd been maintained over the years.

"Margaret, I want to move our bedroom set in here, Lee and my bedroom set in Aunt Della and Uncle Frank's room."

"That'd be fine, Darlene. Just fine."

"It ... it would, Margaret? It would?"

"If Royal and I moved in, I'm sure we would've done the same. Just the same."

"But the furniture ..."

"Do you want to sell—"

"Lee and I, no, not an outright sell, for the public, a public sale, Margaret, but—"

"Ha. It has to be an antique store. And there're plenty of them in Myles Day City. Plenty."

"We have a buyer, Margaret. For the house."

"Oh, good."

"And the original plan was to move our bedroom furniture set from the house to my room, but now ... No, it would've been awful, terrible if I'd turned this room into a shrine, monument for Aunt Della. Terrible, Margaret. J-just terrible. I know that now."

Darlene smiled at Margaret.

"That's a big, big load off my mind."

"Momma's too!"

"Ha. Oh, Margaret!"

They were at the front door of the house saying good-bye.

"The next lunch is on me, Darlene. At my place."

"Okay."

"Now back to my manuals. I have a stack of them sitting on the kitchen table."

The taxicab driver got out the taxi. He opened the door for Margaret.

"Be right there," Margaret said from the front porch.

Darlene and Margaret kissed.

"Don't let the job drive you crazy, Margaret. Nuts."

"It's certainly trying to."

"But you won't let it."

Margaret hurried for the taxi.

"You know me well, Darlene. You know me well."

∗   ∗   ∗

Two months later. April.

"Oh, Mother Ballad! Oh, Mother Ballad! You're at work, Mother Ballad! You're at work in the universe. In the heavens, Mother Ballad! Oh, I knew you would be! I knew you would be, Mother Ballad! Never had any doubt! Had every confidence you would be!"

Royal was in the kitchen, jumping up and down, doing an Irish jig, doing the boogaloo, doing a tango, fandango, reggae, tap dance, Watusi—just making a complete, plain fool of himself. He was so happy, joyous, overwhelmed.

"Mag! Mag! Get home from the hairdresser, Mag! What's taking June so long to do your hair today! What? Oh, come on now, come on now, walk in here as gorgeous as the sunset, the sun melting the last vestiges of snow in Myles Day City.

"Come on, Mag. Come on, Mag. Before I start going crazy in here. Nuts. Insane in here from … from …"

And Royal started *getting down* again with the Irish jig, boogaloo, and all the other assorted dances but added the funky chicken, flapping his arms. Then he thought, what about a James Brown split? But there wasn't enough room in the kitchen for that, so he settled for the Russian dance, where you hold your arms out in front of your chest and squat and kick out in front of you with both legs, one at a time—that one really looked "nutsky" (maybe if he had a bottle of vodka, Smirnoff's in both hands, it might've looked a whole lot better, more Russian, authentic).

She wasn't even through the front door, and Royal was dancing with Margaret.

"Royal! Royal!"

"Just dance, Mag! Dance! Dance!"

"W-what's gotten—"

"Try to keep up. Try keeping up with me!"

They were spinning through the small apartment without bumping into anything. When they got to the kitchen, Royal undid Margaret. She looked at him with astonishment, giving him a long take.

"H-how long, many months did I tell you Mother Ballad would"—Royal was catching his breath—"it would take ... take Mother Ballad to really go to work? Uh, in heaven, Mag? In heaven, uh, that is?"

"Uh, six, let me see—about, you said, estimated about six—"

"Well, she's beaten the odds, and by a lot. A good margin. I knew she would. Mag. Mother Ballad—"

"If anybody would, Momma—"

"Sit."

"Why?"

"Oh, sit down, Mag—and stop giving me a hard time."

"No. Why should I, you just had me dancing around the apartment like—"

"Mag, I ..."

Margaret was standing by a pulled-out chair. Royal pushed her, from the top of her shoulders, down into the chair.

"Royal!"

"Well, you wouldn't listen. So I had no other choice. Just say the devil made me do it."

"The devil?" Pause.

"You had your miracle, your miracle a short while back, and now I have mine."

"Which is?"

"I ... I heard from Eve today!"

"Eve, Royal!?"

"I ... I get goose bumps just saying it. Just—when I say it, Mag. G-goose bumps. Really. Really."

"E-Eve, Royal? Eve?"

"Yes, Eve. I ... I get goose bumps. God is good, Mag. God is infinitely good. Just let me say it again. God is good! Yes, he is!"

"All the months you were looking for her."

"And then I dropped the whole thing. The whole investigation. But she knew about it, Mag. Eve knew about it—word got back to her from Detroit. Whoever it was knew where she was staying, passed it on to her."

"Where? Where?"

"Of all places, Akron, Ohio."

"How did she get—"

"I didn't ask. Bother to ask. "I ... she's engaged. Engaged to be married."

"Engaged? But she's still—"

"Eve wants a divorce. So ... so you know what that means, means for us, Mag," Royal said, his face radiating. "We can get married, Mag. Not live, continue to live in sin."

"I never felt we were living in sin. That way."

"Well, I have. Have. I wouldn't be true to my Christian principles, doctrines, if I didn't."

Royal walked the small piece of floor; Margaret knew what he was going to say next.

"My son. My son. Marshall's doing well, Eve said. He's doing all right, Mag."

Margaret was relieved.

"He's a ... get this, the man Eve's engaged to, is going to marry, he's an insurance agent. Has his own insurance company in Akron. She says he's a straight arrow."

"Does he know about her—"

"Yes. Her past, Mag."

"She was always honest, in her own way."

"Yes, it's one good thing I can say about her."

"Did she say what she'd been doing all this time, Royal? With her life?"

"Mag, I didn't ask. I didn't want to complicate anything."

"Do you think she's found—"

"Christ?"

"Yes."

"I don't know. She just said her life's been turned around. She, Eve knows how we were able to turn our lives around. Everyone doesn't have to find Christ, Mag, to be saved. Put God in their lives. Even though he's there and they don't even know it. He's invisible to them.

"No, I didn't ask. She's happy. Says she's happy, and this man, his name is Harry Watkins by the way, loves her and Marshall, and that's more than good enough for me.

"Of course, Royal."

"He's the one who encouraged her to call me."

"She would eventually, if they are to get—"

"She could've served me with papers. She just said that Harry Watkins thought ... thought it best she get in touch with me. Talk to me. She call."

"Sounds like a nice man."

"He does."

Pause.

"So there's where it stands."

"Stands?"

"Yes, she's to call me back."

"Oh."

"She didn't offer her telephone number to me, so I did ... didn't ask for it. P-press the issue. She said she'd get back in touch with me, and soon. Eve said Marshall still knows who his father is. His 'real' father is—it's how she put it."

"When you put your life on the right track ..."

"Good things happen."

Margaret agreed.

"It's why I was dancing so—scared you half to death, didn't I, Mag?"

"I'm glad you realize that—now."

"And June, as usual, did—your hair looks spectacular, magnificent, Mag."

Margaret smiled and styled. "Why thank you, Royal."

Royal opened the refrigerator door and pulled out a bottle of vegetable juice. He unscrewed the bottle's top and then took a long swig from it.

"I can't wait for Eve's phone call, Mag. It ... it can't come soon enough."

CHAPTER 21

Three days later. At the house. A Saturday afternoon.

"The bank check for the sale of the house came in the mail yesterday, so we had to have a party. A celebration!" Darlene said, handing the plate of cake to Royal and then Lee (Margaret already had her plate of cake). "I had to get you guys over here today. Even though I know how busy you—"

"We're gonna put it in the bank Monday morning. First thing. As soon as the bank's doors open!"

"Me, Lee, me, Lee—not you!"

"Ha. Can I trust you with it, Darlene? That sum of money?"

"Ha."

"Mmm ... homemade cake, Darlene. Nothing like it."

"Homemade, Royal," Darlene laughed.

"Love me some homemade cake. Uh, double-layered homemade chocolate cake, that is!"

"Me too, Royal. Especially the way Darlene bakes it!" Lee said.

They were in the living room. Darlene and Lee were sitting on Frank Ballad's sofa. Royal and Margaret were over on the other one.

Royal looked at Lee; he looked jittery.

"Lee ..."

"Know what you're about to ask, Royal. Need a smoke. A cigarette."

They laughed.

"Pray for me, Royal!"

They laughed even more.

"So I guess I'll be heading for the back, out back for—"

"I told Lee he could smoke in the house."

Lee was standing.

"Can you believe that? Can you?"

"Why not?" Margaret said. "Why not, Lee?"

"In Aunt Della's house, Margaret. In ... in Aunt Della's house?"

Lee's body was shaking.

"Like I said, why not? Daddy would've. Daddy always said—remember, Darlene—if he smoked, he would smoke in his own house. Never mind what Momma might say. She wouldn't chase him out his own house if he wanted to smoke. Wouldn't make up such a silly rule."

"Uncle Frank did? Uh ..."

"Yes, I ... I remember him saying that. It too, Margaret."

"I ... I mean, you do, Darlene?" Then he looked at Darlene questioningly. "Aren't, you aren't making this up? J-just making this up? The two of you? You and Margaret?"

Margaret and Darlene shook their heads in unison.

"You know Daddy, Lee."

"Yes, baby, you know Uncle Frank."

"Well, then, if you don't mind, if any of you don't mind, that is," Lee said, sitting back down on his uncle Frank's sofa. "I think I'll smoke right here." Lee pulled out his pack of cigarettes and then his lighter. "In my own house."

"Let me light it for you, Lee!"

"Sure thing, Darlene!"

They'd been talking up a storm when, suddenly, Darlene popped up off the sofa.

"What's wrong, Darlene?" Margaret said, startled.

"She's got a surprise for you, Margaret!"

"Lee!"

"Oh, that's right. I wasn't supposed to tell you, Margaret."

"Be right back!"

"What is it, Lee?" Margaret whispered from across the room.

"Now, Mag, Lee's in enough trouble as it is."

"Right, Royal. Ha. Right. Don't want me to smoke two cigarettes in a row around you, now—"

"No, Lee, one was quite enough."

"Shut your eyes, Margaret!"

"What's behind your back, D—"

"Mag, come on. Follow instructions."

"Oh, all right."

"In fact, put your hands over them. Your eyes."

"But, Royal, Darlene said—"

"Mag ..."

"There. Done!"

"Here, Margaret. Here," Darlene said, handing Margaret the gift-wrapped box.

Margaret opened the box, paused, and then removed the lid.

"A dress!"

"I made it for you."

Margaret stood, and she let the beautiful navy-blue dress fall out in front of her.

"A perfect fit."

"Perfect, Mag. Perfect."

"Oh, thank you, Darlene," Margaret said, hugging her.

"What made you ..."

"I just wanted to do it, Margaret. That's all."

"A bank check after a house sale can make you do a lot of things, Margaret."

"Amen, Lee. *Amen!*"

"And speaking of amen's, Royal, I'm getting a little tired of hearing the same dusted-off sermon every Sunday morning from Pastor Holmes. Being preached from his pulpit."

"Me too. He is becoming boring, Royal," Lee said.

"Well, we can hit a snag, Darlene, Lee. Redemption. Salvation. Good. Evil. These are main themes all ministers have to—"

"So we, Lee and I, were thinking about a change of scenery, venue this Sunday. Of coming to Hands of Christ Church tomorrow morning."

"Hands of Christ Church, Darlene! Did—"

"Yes, it's what Darlene said, Royal. Hands of Christ Church!"

"You're welcome. More than welcome to come!"

They were holding hands at the front door.

"Come on, come on, you two. Say good-bye."

"Looks like they could stand there all day, till next winter. The next snowstorm that blows into Myles Day, Royal!" Lee said.

"I have a sermon to prepare for tomorrow. Come on, Mag. Come on."

"Call you when I get back to the house, Darlene. So I can tell you how pretty I look in my new dress."

Royal was holding onto the dress box; Margaret had given it to him.

"You're going to look gorgeous. Just gorgeous in it, Margaret!"

"Thanks, Lee."

"Come on, Mag. Come on, before I drag you out of here. Caveman style."

"Love you, Margaret."

"Love you, Darlene."

"Lee, we'll pretend we didn't hear that."

"Hard not to, Royal. But it-it's starting to get real soapy."

"Very, Lee."

Royal was holding Margaret's hand, and Darlene was holding Lee's.

When the car pulled from the curb, Royal honked the horn. Darlene and Lee waved.

Margaret and Royal had been on the road for a few minutes.

"Royal, where are we going? Home is—"

"I want to show you something, Mag."

"Not another surprise?"

"Why not."

"Two in one day? The dress is s-so lovely."

"Gorgeous, gorgeous like you."

"I could kiss you."

"Do."

"But you might run the car off the road."

"The car insurance, it's up to date."

About fifteen minutes later.

Royal parked the car.

"Look at that lot on the corner. Over there. Smack dab on the corner, Mag."

Margaret looked at the huge raw lot on Lawn Street. The lot had been there for a long time. It was probably the city's, city owned, Margaret thought.

And then Margaret, after a while, began putting two and two together.

"A church, Royal! A church! You're thinking about a church! A church being built there! Aren't you? Aren't you!"

"One day, one day, yes, Mag, yes, we're going to build a church on this corner. You're right, Mag. From the ground floor up."

"Yes, Royal."

"Hands of Christ Church, Mag."

"Hands of Christ Church."

Then the car began pulling away from the vacant lot on the corner of Lawn Street.

"There's just so much going on now. In our lives, Royal," Margaret said, holding onto the box.

"Yes, there is, Mag. Yes ... and think, just think, in three days, in three days time, I'll see Marshall. My son. Will fly out to Akron, Ohio, to see him. Be with him for three days. Yes, there is, Mag. There is."

"I wish I could be there with you ... I mean, I know why I can't, Royal."

"This meeting, it's our time, Mag, together. This must be between just the two of us. Marshall and me. Father and son. Don't worry, you'll see him again. There's been every indication from Eve he'll come visit us in Myles Day after school's let out in June."

"And the divorce."

"It's next."

"Eve's already taken action. Filed legal papers with the state of Michigan."

Margaret took a glance out the car window. Spring indeed was in the air. In fact, the car window was three quarters the way down. Myles Day City springs were as mild as Myles Day City's winters were cold.

"Mag, can I get that kiss now?"

She kissed Royal's cheek.

"See, I didn't run the car off the road."

"No, you didn't. Not even close." Margaret smiled, holding on tightly to Darlene's gift.

"And if I did, it'd be a sunset I'd run it off onto. A sunset. Not the side of the road."

"How romantic, Royal."

"It's spring, Mag. Spring. I have an excuse for talking this way. Silly. Not making any kind of sense, whatsoever—out of anything."

"Just get me home."

"So you can try on your new dress."

"Yes."

"And you can call Darlene."

"Yes, Royal. Call Darlene."

"So you two can chat away, Mag."

"Just the two of us, Royal."

Pause.

"And I'm going to look pretty in it too."

"What, uh—"

"The dress, Royal," Margaret said. "The dress. Darlene's navy-blue dress. What else."

Royal smiled.

The End